Puzzles

Book One

A Detective Love Story

Russell F. Moran

Puzzles

Coddington Press

Copyright © 2019 by Russell F. Moran

www.morancom.com

Printed in the United States of America

ISBN - 978-1-7338872-1-2

This book is a work of fiction. The characters, names, incidents, dialogue, and plot are the products of the author's imagination or are used fictitiously. Any resemblance to actual persons or events is purely coincidental.

Covers and text design by LuAnn T. Palazzo
www.TheDesignDiva.net

DEDICATION

This book is dedicated to the men and women of the nation's police forces.

ACKNOWLEDGEMENTS

As always, I thank my wife, Lynda, for her attentive reading, rereading, and editing of my many drafts, and for laughing at my jokes. Lynda is to me as Bobbie is to Bob. I also thank my friend and editor, John White, for his keen editorial eye. I thank LuAnn T. Palazzo for her expert interior and cover designs. I also thank Dennis Ciano, retired NYPD homicide detective, for his expert advice. And I especially thank my readers, many of whom are a constant source of inspiration and encouragement for me.

AUTHOR'S NOTE

Puzzles Book 1 is the first book of *The Puzzles Series,* the adventures of detectives Bob and Bobbie. Bob and Bobbie are two of my favorite characters, and I think of them as old friends. As I wrote this book, we took a lot of adventures together. I hope you will see them that way too.

You will find a **Cast of Characters** after the last chapter of the book. It can be frustrating to come across a character on page 150, that you first met on page 20, especially if you've put the book down for a few days. I've seen this done in Russian literature, and I happily add a cast of characters to *Puzzles* as well as my other novels.

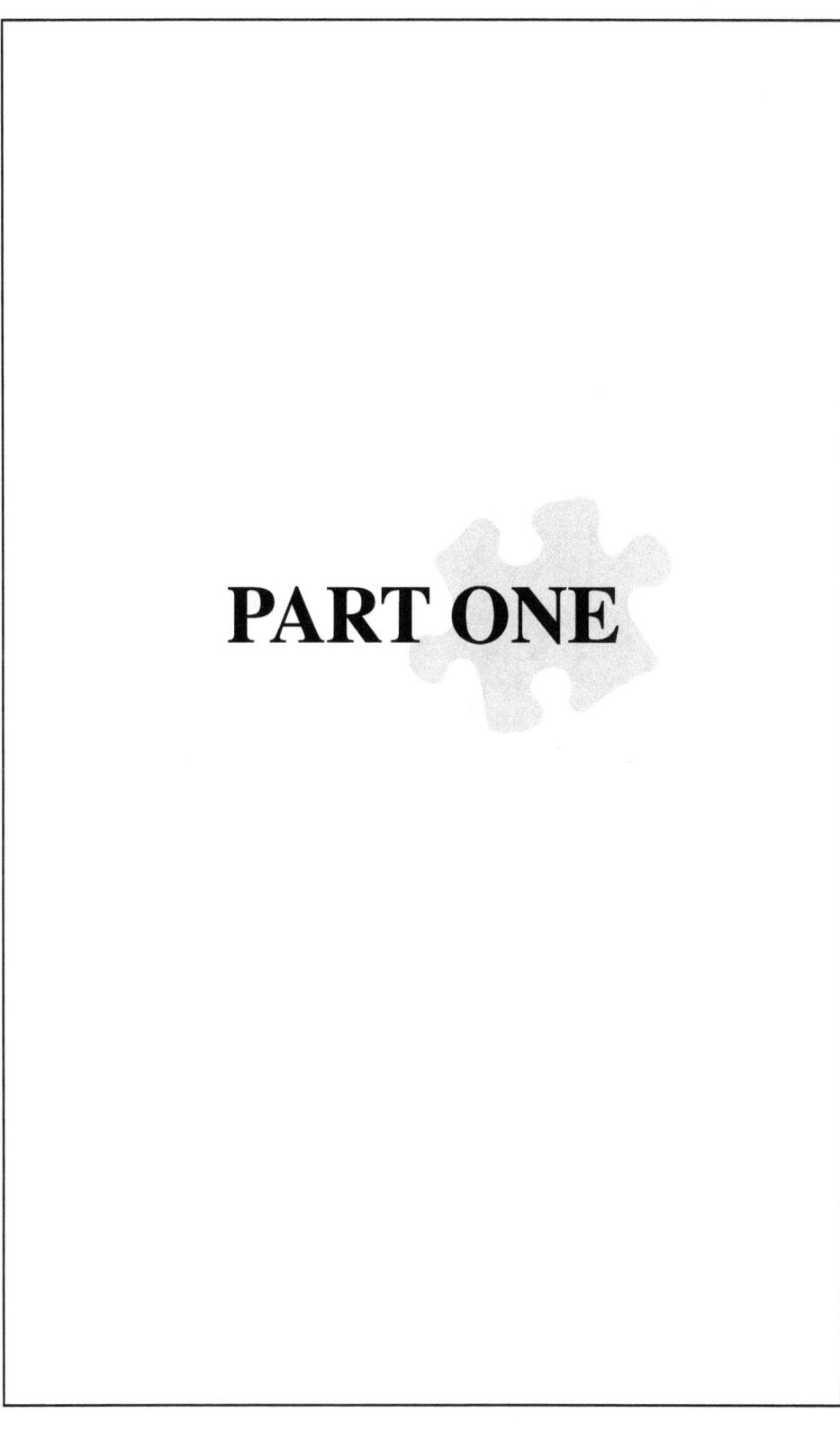

PART ONE

CHAPTER 1

Bobbie Nelson

Knowing how you *should* feel doesn't always line up with how you *do* feel.

I should feel excited. I should feel elated maybe. I should even feel flattered.

So why do I feel terrible?

I got a call from a famous man, none other than Ralph Norquist, the Commissioner of the New York Police Department. Not only does he want to have lunch with me, but he's flying out to Chicago just for that purpose. That's what he said, anyway. Maybe he's got a dozen other things to do out here and told me that his visit would be about me only. I've learned that sometimes important people can be full of shit.

The NYPD is going through a massive scandal involving cops taking bribes. Hundreds have been arrested, both uniformed cops and detectives. The various police unions tried to jump in to protect their members, but the New York City mayor decided to take on the unions and, in the first time in anybody's memory, has begun recruiting people from other states despite the union contracts. He basically said, "Screw the contracts, I've got a city to run." So, given what I've read in the newspapers, why am I processing this? Why am I going crazy questioning myself? The important thing is that he wants to meet me for lunch, no matter whatever else he needs to do in Chicago. But as soon as I have that thought, doubt creeps in. I think I use self-doubt as a defense against disappointment. When I applied to the University of Chicago Law School, my mindset was that of a person who hoped to win the lottery after buying one ticket, all the while knowing that it wouldn't happen. Why did I feel that way? I had excellent grades as an undergraduate at Yale, and scored high on the Law School Admission Test (LSAT), so why was I gripped by doubt? Because I was playing defense, as I often do. My doubt would insulate me from the pain of not getting in.

I must admit I'm a damn good detective. *The Chicago Tribune* wrote an article about me in *Trib Magazine*. The author of the article called me a "real-life Sherlock Holmes." Even though Sherlock Holmes was a fictional character, I was flattered as hell to have that said about me. I do have a way of cracking cases that most people thought were uncrackable. My mom told me I'm like a snapping turtle. Once I chomp down on something I never let go. There's one thing about which I have no doubt—I love my work.

Oh yeah, I was admitted to the University of Chicago Law School in the first round—on a full academic scholarship.

With a degree from such a prestigious school, I could have looked forward to a lucrative career as a lawyer, but instead I opted to be a cop. Did self-doubt have anything to do with that decision? Of course, but sometimes self-doubt can work in your favor. I found something I love to do. I solve puzzles.

The commissioner and I planned to have lunch at the River Roast restaurant on North LaSalle Street overlooking the Chicago River. The place advertises itself as a new American spin on British food, served in an upscale restaurant. I remember interrogating a suspect at this restaurant two years ago. The guy had no idea I was a detective, of course. I'm quite skilled at concealing my identity. If you're undercover, *stay* undercover. Cops have certain habits they need to ditch when they're in plain clothes. For example, cops tend to walk with their hands away from their bodies to avoid scratching their elbows on their sidearms. Cops also sit with their backs to a wall in a restaurant so they can see what's going on. We also tend to scrutinize people's faces. Criminals are aware of these tendencies, and you need to be careful to keep your cover on tight. The suspect at the River Roast thought I was the buyer of a carload of stolen new furniture he was trying to fence. He's still in prison and will be for 10 more years. When my work results in somebody being locked up I seldom gloat, but I was delighted to see that guy sentenced. He was such a slime I couldn't wash my hands enough after I collared him.

It was a mild sunny day in May, so the commissioner and I sat at an outside table right on the Chicago River. Ever since I've lived in Chicago, I've discovered that looking at the gentle, meandering river calms me down, which was a good thing because I was nervous as hell. Ralph, as he insisted I call him, told me he'd heard and read about my detective skills. Ralph is a tall man at 6'2," impeccably dressed, with deep brown eyes. He's a good-looking man with black hair streaked with hints of gray. I read that he's 61 years old, is married and has one son in college. He had a way of looking at me I found intimidating. But that's okay, I'm easily intimidated, especially around powerful people.

A colleague of mine, Mike Toner, a Chicago detective and old friend of Ralph's, told him about me.

"Mike tells me you're the best detective he's ever worked with, and he's been around for a while. So, I Googled your name and wow, the world of journalism seems fascinated with your work, not to mention your good looks. That big *Johnston* multiple murder case seemed like it was a closed file until you took over. The reporter who wrote the article in the *Chicago Tribune* was blown away by your scientific approach to your job. A five-year-old case involving seven dead bodies, and you opened it up and nailed the perps by reworking the forensic evidence."

Can you please get to the fucking point and ease my self-doubt? Of course, I didn't say that, but I wanted to. I guess I should have felt like hot stuff being interviewed by the famous Ralph Norquist. There's a lot of talk that the president may nominate him as attorney general. I chose to ignore his comment about my "good looks." Why do powerful guys think it's necessary to flirt when they want to make a point?

I'm a bit skilled at interpreting non-verbal language clues, and Norquist seemed to want to do some heavy persuading. He kept leaning so far forward (a sure sign of someone wanting to connect) that I thought his face would fall into his soup. Obviously, he wants to make me an offer of some sort. Or maybe he's writing a book and just wants to use me for background. Self-doubt to the rescue. But my gut and his facial signals told me he wanted to make me a job offer.

"Bobbie, I'm sure you've heard about the problems the NYPD is going through, the biggest corruption scandal on record. Not only have we found hundreds of crooked cops, but the unions themselves are also corrupt to the core. That's why, on direct orders from the mayor and the city council, I've begun recruiting cops, especially detectives, from other police departments. You've got one hell of a background, Bobbie. You're a cop but you graduated from one of the best law schools in the country, the University of Chicago. In a way you remind me of that Jamie character on *Blue Bloods,* my favorite show. In the show, young Jamie graduated from Harvard Law School but chose to follow the family tradition and become a cop. But you're different. First, obviously you're a woman, a very pretty one at that, (*there he goes again*) and second, you're a senior detective not a uniformed officer. And you're only 35 years old."

Flattery will get you nowhere.

Bullshit. Flattery goes a long way, as he seemed to know intuitively.

"Bobbie, I want you to come and work for the NYPD, the best police department in the country, or at least it was until this goddam scandal hit. I offer you a job as a Detective First Grade. My research tells me that you make $80,000 with the Chicago Police Department. One of our detectives at your level earned $160,000 last year including overtime. An old friend of mine (this guy seemed to have a lot of 'old friends') is the publisher of the *New York Daily News*. He wants you, the famous Bobbie Nelson, to write a weekly column on police matters. I know you love to write, having read a few of your articles in the Chicago PD newsletter. For that part-time job with the *Daily News* you will be paid $45,000 a year. So, you can make over $200,000 a year, including the writing gig. With your background you can probably knock out an article every week in two hours. I know that you're single, having divorced two years ago, and have little family in the Chicago area. Hell, you grew up in New York City, so you won't have a lot of adjusting to do. Bobbie, with your brains and skills you deserve the limelight of the best police department in the country. It will do wonders for your career. I don't doubt that someday you may occupy my chair as commissioner (This guy was in *hyper-flattery* mode). Please accept my offer to at least come to New York and check us out in more detail. No pressure. You can make your final decision after you visit us in New York."

Holy shit. He was offering me a prestigious job where I'd earn over $120,000 more than I made in Chicago, including overtime and that column in the *Daily News*. And he's right, I grew up in New York City, in the Whitestone section of Queens. I had good friends in Chicago, but no family, and I wasn't dating anybody. I'd already made up my mind, having put my normal self-doubt on hold. But I decided I would take him up on his polite offer to visit the NYPD first before giving my formal acceptance. I had a lot of accumulated leave time, so I planned to take a couple of days off the following week, as he requested.

As soon as lunch was over, I called Janice Patton, my good friend. I do my best thinking when I have somebody to bounce ideas off, and Janice always fits the bill. We arranged to have dinner at The Nile of Hyde Park, a restaurant close by both of our apartments near the university. Janice is a math professor at the University of Chicago.

I was sipping a martini when Janice walked in. She looked at me wide-eyed, a sure sign that she was dying to hear what I had hinted at. I told her all about my lunch with Norquist and the offer he made.

"Bobbie, you've got to be fucking kidding me," Janice said in her usual dainty manner. "Why didn't you just accept the offer and start to pack your stuff?"

"Norquist seemed to want to be polite and move slowly. But I think he really wants me to take the job."

"*Of course,* he wants you to take the job. You're the best detective in the friggin country, and he's offering you the highlight of your career. I'm in New York a few times a year to visit my folks, so we'll still get to pal around. You go, girl. Take that wonderful job."

"I'm due in New York next Tuesday. I'll let you know how it goes."

CHAPTER 2

Bobbie

The following Tuesday, I caught an early flight from O'Hare due to arrive at JFK at 9:05. My stomach was in a familiar condition, a goddam knot. I considered outlining a book I've thought about writing called *Self-Doubt for Dummies*, but instead absent-mindedly leafed through the inflight magazine.

A car awaited me at JFK, making me feel like serious hot stuff. It was a big black SUV, of course. What would government agencies do without big black SUVs? A simple patrol car would save a lot on gas, but nobody asked me. My self-doubt loves to cram my brain with a lot of extraneous bullshit to keep my mind off the present. I arrived at One Police Plaza (affectionately known as "One PP") at 11:15, after spending an insane amount of time in traffic, something that New York and Chicago have in common. One PP is a building of 13 floors and looks like a box with windows. Beautiful is not a word that pops to mind when first seeing the place. The architectural style is known as *Brutalist*, and it's easy to see why. A couple of uniforms greeted me at the entrance, a man and a woman. They were both polite and friendly, and spoke with that charming old New York (*New Yawk*) accent. New York City cops are famous for their manner of speaking. I wondered if I'd lose my charming Midwest

7

accent and *tawk like dis*.

We took the elevator to the 13th floor where Commissioner Norquist's office is located. Although our meeting wasn't scheduled for another 20 minutes, Ralph's assistant escorted me right in, easing my self-doubt. The office was huge, as I had expected. It reminded me of Commissioner Reagan's (Tom Selleck's) office in *Blue Bloods*. Norquist had told me that's his favorite show, and I wondered if he ordered his office decorated accordingly.

"Good morning, Commissioner," I said. Although he insisted I call him by his first name when we had lunch in Chicago, I thought it was appropriate to address him formally in his office. He seemed to agree and didn't correct me. He motioned for me to sit as his assistant walked in.

"Mayor Paxton is here, Mr. Commissioner," his assistant said.

Holy shit! The mayor of New York City has been invited to our meeting? Arnold Paxton is a tall, handsome, black man, known for his direct talk and gentlemanly manner. I hoped he didn't notice that I was freaking out.

"I won't keep you folks," Paxton said. "I just wanted to stop by and say hello to the famous Detective Nelson. It's an honor to meet you, Detective. I do hope that you will accept Commissioner Norquist's offer to join the ranks of New York City's finest. God knows, we can use talent like yours."

"The honor's all mine, sir."

I almost said, "where do I sign?" but managed to keep my cool. Wow, I think these guys really want me here.

"I must run to another meeting, but I just wanted to greet Detective Nelson. I hope you will soon join us."

"Walter Simpson is here, sir," the commissioner's assistant said.

"Bobbie, I want you to meet Walter Simpson, a damn fine real estate broker. He works a lot with the NYPD. He's got some good rental deals on apartments not far from here. You may want to buy a condo or co-op rather than rent, but that's up to you, of course."

Simpson handed me a folder with about 10 pages in it, and said he'd be in touch. I couldn't believe that Norquist had arranged for a real estate guy to help me find a place to live. I almost expected somebody to say that my bath was drawn.

Norquist then took me on a personal tour of One PP, showing me the most important offices. The place was huge, much bigger than police headquarters in Chicago. We walked into the IT department where Norquist introduced me to Tim Shackleford, the head of the department. He carried the title of detective lieutenant, but his job was computers, period.

"Knowing your expertise in designing computer algorithms, Bobbie, you will be working closely with Tim on your cases."

I noticed that he said I "will be working" with Shackleford, as if I had accepted the job already. I certainly would have if only he had put a friggin piece of paper in my hands to sign.

We returned to Norquist's office.

"Okay, I accept the job, Commissioner." I figured it was time to stop the pre-hiring foreplay.

"That's great, Bobbie. When do you think you can join us?"

"I estimate it will take me a month to tie up my affairs with the Chicago PD. I think that's the minimum notice I should give them."

"Knowing your dedication to duty, Bobbie, I fully expected you to say that. Let my assistant know if your timing needs to change. Welcome aboard, Detective." He reached out and shook my hand.

"Before you leave, do you have any questions for me?"

"Do you know who I'll be working with as a partner, sir?"

"That's still under evaluation, Bobbie. I'm extremely careful about assigning partners. It can be a critical part of the job, as you know. I'll notify you in advance of your joining us. I'm pretty sure I know who it will be, and you'll find out soon enough. Have a good flight back to Chicago."

I was excited as hell. I was impressed that Norquist said he's careful about assigning partners, and I couldn't agree more with his diligence. Frank Jackson, my detective partner in Chicago, is a terrific guy to work with, although he's getting up there in years and will retire soon. Yes, having a partner can be great.

Or it can suck.

CHAPTER 3

Bob Lawton

Two Weeks later

G reat, just fucking great. The commissioner just told me who my new partner will be after Steve Rimland retires in two weeks. None other than the media darling of Chicago, the famous and amazing Detective Bobbie Nelson. If I've seen her face on TV once I've seen it a thousand times, not that she has a bad face to look at. Why do I feel like I'm about to become a prop in a costume drama? *The Chicago Tribune* called her "a real-life Sherlock Holmes." I wondered what they'd call me.

I spent a couple of hours reading about Bobbie Nelson after I Googled her name. I only spent two hours, but I could have spent more. Dear Lord, she's like the Oprah Winfrey of detectives. Newspaper articles, magazine articles, TV interviews. Holy shit, this lady's name and face gets around. Seems like she has her own YouTube channel.

After I finished reading, I clicked on the TV to catch the latest news. And who was on being interviewed by CBS? Yes, the incredible Bobbie Nelson. She was being questioned about a huge murder case she just solved in Chicago.

Am I being an asshole? Probably. I'm often quite good at that.

I try my best to put on a placid face before a camera, and in front of people in general. Stiff upper lip and all that. Truth is, I'm feeling anything but placid. I'm feeling like a guy who will soon become the assistant to the Great Detective Nelson. With all her notoriety, I have the sinking feeling that she just may be an insufferable obnoxious bitch. And I'll be her boy-Friday.

I've been on the NYPD for 15 years, and I think I've done a good job. I must have, otherwise I wouldn't be partnered with the Great Madam Nelson.

Like many a cop, I was divorced a few years back. I read that Bobbie Nelson was divorced too, a couple of years ago. I wish I could get in touch with her ex to see what I'm about to get into. She's my age, 35, which means we'll be working together a long time—if I can take it that long.

Shit, if I jump to conclusions like this on the cases I work, I may as well hang up my shield. Have I mentioned that sometimes I'm an asshole?

Commissioner Norquist gave me Bobbie Nelson's private email address, with her permission. He suggested that I drop her a line and "make nice," as he put it. He knows I can be a jerk at times, hence the "make nice."

Okay, so here goes my first contact with Detective Queen Nelson.

"Hello Bobbie,

"I hope you don't mind my calling you Bobbie, but let's face it, we'll be working together closely. I've read quite a bit about you, and I must say that I'm quite impressed (yes, 'make nice'). ~~I hope you'll mention me when you're being interviewed on TV.~~" No, scratch that. What a dumb-ass thing to say. Time to wrap it up.

"I look forward to meeting you in a couple of weeks.

"Your partner, Bob Lawton"

Something tells me I'm going to get a wiseass reply, if she ever does get around to answering me.

At least she's good-looking, judging from the zillion photos of her in the papers as well as the YouTube scenes of her many TV appearances. Good-looking? Hell, she's flat-out gorgeous. This will be an interesting working relationship.

I looked at my inbox. Wow, it's only been five minutes and she answered me already.

CHAPTER 4

Bobbie

Hello, Bob,

"Thank you so much for your kind email. I have also read quite a bit about you, and I am extremely impressed. Being assigned to work with a partner can be a stressful thing as I'm sure you know, but I think Commissioner Norquist handled this in a professional way. He even picked two people with alliterative names—Bob and Bobbie.

"I look forward to working with a real pro like you. See you in a couple of weeks,

"Your partner, Bobbie Nelson."

So, my new partner and I have met—through email, the normal way of meeting these days. I really don't know much about this guy, but I'll soon begin a ton of research on him, as I do with all new matters. I'll make a few phone calls (incognito, of course) and find out more about this man. His email to me was polite but he seemed to avoid any real communication. I hope this guy's not a jerk.

I Googled his name and saw a book on Amazon authored by a

Robert Lawton. I looked it up, and there was a book entitled, *An Army of Blue – Stories of New York City Cops*. The author's biography noted that Robert Lawton is 35 years old, the same age as me, and has been with the NYPD for 15 years. Yes, my new partner was the author. The book, which is a reality-based novel, boasts 1,235 five-star reviews, and the stats show that it's a best seller. Impressive. I bought the book and downloaded it to my Kindle.

So, he's my age, divorced like me, and has been on the force for 15 years. From what I've read about him, he's a solid professional, not to mention a best-selling author. With his impressive background, I hope he isn't a pompous idiot. I tentatively look forward to working with him—I hope.

Also, he's cute as hell.

CHAPTER 5

Bob

I sat at my desk at 8:15, going over a file the commissioner just handed to me. Holy shit, a mass murder. This will be an interesting day.

My new partner, Saint Bobbie Nelson, is due to arrive shortly. I really need to cut this crap out. In her emails she seemed to be a nice person. I can at least reciprocate by not being an asshole, as difficult as that may be. At 8:35 Bobbie walked in. Oh my God, she's gorgeous. Her shimmering blond hair was cut in a fashionable bob. She has Caribbean blue eyes and wore a well-fitted business suit that draped her stunning body like skin on a peach. She's tall, about 5'11" I'd guess. Okay fool, time to act—and think—like a professional.

She reached out to shake my hand, flashing a beautiful smile that caused my heart to miss a beat.

"It's a pleasure to finally meet you, Bob. And just think, we don't have to hit *send* to communicate."

Not a hysterically funny joke, but definitely an indication of a sense of humor. A good sign.

"I read your book, *An Army of Blue*, last night in one sitting. I loved it and couldn't put it down. You are one hell of a writer. I gave it a five-star review, of which you already have hundreds."

If she thinks I'll be positively disposed toward her for praising my book, she's absolutely right. I thanked her profusely, of course. I don't dislike her nearly as much as I did five minutes ago.

When you work closely with someone, especially in a partnership, politeness counts. It's difficult to get your job done if you don't like the person you're working with. So far, Detective Nelson seems to be courteous and polite. So far.

"I bumped into the commissioner on the way to our office (*Our* office? I guess so). He said he just gave you a huge file that he wants us to start working right away."

"Yeah, Bobbie, it's big. A mass murder. Let's go through the file on our way to the scene. It's on William Street. We should get there in about five minutes."

We climbed into the car and I drove, which was good because I was inclined to just sit and stare at her beautiful face. She is one good-looking lady. Okay, bozo, time to pay attention.

"Bobbie, this case is about a big shooting at the Manhattan Mosque on William Street. It looks like a mess."

When we arrived at the scene, we clipped our shields to our jackets and ducked under the yellow police crime scene tape. What we saw hit us like a bat. It was chaotic.

"Oh my God," Bobbie said to the captain in charge of the crime scene, "do you have a body count?"

"This is fucking unbelievable, Detective. We have 85 bodies, and there's no evidence of any explosion. This was all done with guns. Our forensic people from CSU (Crime Scene Unit) have just started to sort this out, but they think there were a lot of shooters. The relative orderliness of the bodies tells us that the bullets were fired in a short period of time. As far as we can tell—but we still have a lot of bodies to examine—every one of the shooters got away. We've been watching this place for years."

"Captain, do you have a preliminary opinion as to what happened here?" Bobbie asked.

"I avoid jumping to conclusions, Detective, but I think this happened fast, over just a few minutes. It may be terror-related."

At first, I felt a bit put off the way Bobbie seemed to take charge. At first. But she was asking all the right questions and sure as hell seemed to know what she was doing. I'm not easily impressed, but I *was* impressed. Also, she was polite when she asked questions, often touching my arm as if to let me know I was in on the deal. Another good sign.

We walked past a group of uniformed NYPD cops. Normally, no police commander would ever dream of entering a mosque without permission, crime scene or not, but this was different. The imam in charge called the NYPD and *requested* that we come.

Typically, the initial responders to a crime scene are uniformed officers, the people who respond to the 911 call. I've always made it a point to be respectful and courteous when talking to the responding officers. They can make your work as a detective a lot easier. Your most important job when reporting to a crime scene is to take a deep breath, calm down, and don't let adrenaline-induced excitement cloud your thinking.

"Holy shit," I said, a bit too loudly, ignoring my self-reminder to calm down.

"Is that your professional opinion, Detective Bob?" She *does* have a sense of humor.

"Yes, it is, wise-guy. Knowing you, Bobbie, you probably have this figured out already. So, give me your take on what happened here."

"This mosque has been on the NYPD radar for years, as the captain-in-charge just told us," Bobbie said. "I just Googled the place on my phone. According to an article it's a gathering place of extremists and radical activities, including speeches and planning meetings. It's a Sunni mosque, and not very popular with the Shiites."

Wow, she does research on the fly while inspecting a crime scene. Impressive.

Ever since 9/11, every law enforcement officer in the country found it important to keep abreast of radical Islamic culture. I knew, as did my new partner, that the Sunni Muslims had no love for the Shiites, and vice versa. But the most important job, at this point, is not to jump to conclusions.

"Let's review a bit of history, Bobbie. Maybe it will help us to understand what happened here. The Sunni branch of Islam believes that the first four caliphs after the Prophet Mohammed were the true successors. The Shiites believe that only the heirs of the fourth caliph, named Ali, are the legitimate heirs. So that clears it all up, no?"

"No, Bob, I've been studying this stuff for years, just as you have, and I simply don't get it. Are we telling ourselves that this carnage has something to do with a succession dispute from the seventh century?"

"I don't get it either, Bobbie. But let's not get ahead of ourselves. We can't conclude that this shoot-out was pulled off by Shiites. At this point, we just don't know. Let's look at what we've got in front of us."

"Bob, I read that you were an officer in the Marines. Give me your gut feeling when we walked in here."

I was impressed that she had researched my background. I was also impressed by her shapely little ass.

"My gut tells me this was a military operation. It was a carefully planned action, *not* a wild shoot-out."

"On that point, Bob, here's what we know right now. First, look at the position of the bodies. They were lined up in neat rows on their knees, obviously at prayer, when the shooters opened fire. The CSU people will report their findings later, but from the position of the bodies and the blood spatter marks, it appears that the shooters were lined up, maybe evenly spaced across the back of the room."

Wow, this cop knows what she's doing.

"Type of weapons used?" I asked.

"From the shell casings it looks like at least one M16 was used, or an AR-15, the civilian version. We'll know more when the CSU people are done."

"Bobbie, how the hell can a group of guys just walk in with a bunch of guns and start blasting?"

"Well, we've found pieces of duct tape on the bottom of that long bench at the back of the room, Bob. I think the shooters walked in looking like worshippers, reached under the bench to get the weapons and started firing. Of course, that would indicate inside help, someone who taped the guns to the bench."

"Any reports of gunfire from any people in the neighborhood?" I asked a nearby cop.

"Yeah, quite a few people called 911. There would have been a lot more, but the shooting occurred around sunrise, the time of the

Morning Prayer or *Fajr* — around 6:30 a.m."

"How long till the first police car arrived?"

"Bob," she said, politely interjecting, "you know as well as I do that cops are notorious story tellers when it comes to reporting response time. At least they are in Chicago, and I doubt that New York is much different. But we're just a few blocks from One Police Plaza, so for the time being I'll accept what I've heard — which is two minutes." Interesting observation. This lady knows her shit.

"These guys got out of town fast, Bobbie. They must have had a getaway car waiting for them."

"With fully automatic machine guns in the hands of people who know how to use them, they could have done their deed in a half minute or less."

"How many survivors, officer?" I asked one of the CSU people.

"Only six, if you can believe that. One guy wasn't even wounded. He was lucky enough to be behind a pillar when the shooting started. He was probably busy hiding for his life. Three are in critical condition, but two have wounds that I've been told aren't life-threatening."

"The CSU people can do more here than we can at this point," Bobbie said. "Hey, Bob, gray isn't a very becoming color on your face."

"I don't know how you can take the stench, Bobbie. I need some fresh air. Care to join me?"

"Sure. Over the years I've learned to get used to something like this, but 85 bodies in one room is a bit much even for me."

She cautiously sprayed a squirt of disinfectant on her wrist, being careful not to contaminate the crime scene. She raised the bottle to her nose and took a deep breath, and then handed the bottle to me. "Here, this helps." This lady has been around the block a few times.

A TV reporter and a cameraman walked over to us.

"Mind if I ask a couple of questions, Detectives?"

"You can ask Detective Lawton, here," Bobbie said. "I'm needed inside."

Holy shit. What just happened? Bobbie gave up a chance for her pretty face to appear on the evening news and she handed it off to me. This wild crime scene we're working isn't the only shock I've had today.

Bobbie and I spent the next two hours walking the scene and jotting notes. As the senior detective, I was the officer in charge, but I listened carefully to everything my talented new partner said. She *really* knows her stuff.

After we investigated as far as we could, Bobbie and I got back into the car to return to One PP. We needed to wait for the results from the CSU people before we could go any further.

As I looked at her, Bobbie calmly reviewed what we had learned so far, citing detail by detail from memory. So, this is the person who I expected to be an obnoxious bitch, a scene stealing princess who lorded it all over people. But no. The person I saw was a total professional the way she worked that crime scene, the best I had ever seen. And when she ducked the TV camera, that nailed it for me. I hope she doesn't think I'm staring at her, but I am. It's hard not to. It was good I was driving, otherwise I wouldn't have taken my eyes off her gorgeous face.

Maybe I'm not the total asshole I can sometimes be. Maybe. But one thing is becoming clear;

I think I'm okay with my new partner. So far. I think.

CHAPTER 6

Bobbie Nelson

Talk about an interesting first day on the job. That Manhattan Mosque attack has my head spinning. In all my years, I've never seen such carnage. Bob and I will review the preliminary CSU findings, which are due later this morning.

I'm glad we have a major case to work on. I was nervous as hell to meet my new partner, something that can always be stressful. But I'm no longer apprehensive. I've done an enormous amount of research on him, so much that I feel like I've known him for years, and what I found impressed me. The guy is a real pro, and a hell of a fine writer. Men can often be defensive when a woman shows them something they hadn't thought of before. But that wasn't Bob. He seemed to want to learn from me, which I'm happy about, and listened intently to everything I said. Not to be egotistical, but I know I'm a terrific detective. And I found that working the crime scene with Bob got my brain into full gear. Bouncing thoughts and ideas off one another worked beautifully, as it's supposed to with partners.

I just wish he wasn't so goddam handsome. He's six-three, has light sandy brown hair, a great build, and heavenly hazel-colored eyes. I find thinking about him distracting. Where was I? Oh, right, the Manhattan Mosque attack.

Bob walked in and did a little pitter-patter on his desk with his hands, which I found adorable. *Adorable?* What the hell am I thinking? I haven't known the guy for 24 hours and already I'm starting to collect cute mannerisms that I like. He took off his suit jacket and hung it on the back of his chair. My goodness, does he have a great build. He has a slim waist, accentuated by his broad shoulders. He must work out regularly. He wore a lightly starched white shirt, which cast his ruddy complexion in a nice glow. Like many detective partners, our desks face each to make for easy conversation. It also made for a wonderful view of his marvelous eyes. I've got to cut this shit out now, *right now.* I wasn't hired to flirt with a handsome hunk, handsome as he may be. Yesterday we got off to a good professional working relationship. I want to keep it that way. Since my divorce two years ago my life has been celibate. I didn't plan it that way, and it's not as if guys don't make a play for me. But I wanted to bury myself in my job to help drown my memories of my ex. He started out as a great guy, until he started drinking, and then he never stopped. Then came the beatings. I'm fairly athletic, which is good, because I found myself physically defending myself quite often.

So, I haven't had sex in two years. I was looking at Bob as I had that thought. Why is my face so flushed? I must be coming down with something.

Two officers with the CSU walked into our office, each carrying a bulky briefcase. The briefcases were loaded with charts of calculations of the trajectories of bullets and spatter marks. The actual canvassing was done by dozens of CSU people, some borrowed from other commands.

"Bobbie, are you thinking what I'm thinking?"

Yeah, let's get naked and play around. *Stop this crap right now.*

"You're wondering why we're going to concentrate on blood spatter data and bullet trajectories when our job is to find out who did this."

"Exactly. I think we should be going door to door for two square blocks to see if anybody knows something."

"I hear you, Bob, but I've found out countless times that pouring over forensic data often results in a clue. What could the clue be? I have no idea, I just work the file and let the clue hit me in the face."

"Bobbie, you're *good*."

And wouldn't I love to show you just how good I am. *Stop*.

"Okay, let's work through the documents one by one and see if anything hits us," I said. "I'll bet you a dinner that we find something."

I thought it was totally cool the way I worked in that dinner idea.

After two hours we both shouted, "What?"

Until we hit that page, all the bullets were identified as having come from an M16 rifle. But the body of one of the victims showed he was killed by a Colt 45 revolver, and that it's quite an old vintage, based on the firing pin marks on the spent shells, probably going back to the nineteenth century.

"Didn't I read that the pistol Wyatt Earp used was a 45 revolver and that it was stolen from the Museum of the City of New York recently?" Bob said.

"You're right, babe, I mean Bob (I really need to watch my friendly mouth). It's a flimsy lead but it *is* a lead. We need to track down the ammunition that Earp used and see if it matches the bullet in question." When I accidentally called him *babe*, I noticed that he smiled and winked at me. I took a deep breath. Why am I perspiring?

Bob looked at his watch. "It's 5:45. Have we earned a dinner?"

"We certainly have, but it will be Dutch treat because we both noticed the clue."

We decided on the Brooklyn Chop House on Nassau Street, a short walk from One PP. Bob recommended it.

CHAPTER 7

Bob

This is nuts, this is totally fucking nuts. Bobbie and I haven't known each other for more than two days and here we are flirting and having dinner. Well, maybe it wasn't a bad idea to bet a dinner over finding a lead, but I have the distinct impression that Bobbie just wanted to go on a date. Like I didn't? Hell, a few days ago I was prepared to hate this woman, but now I'm just enjoying being with her. She is brilliant, no doubt about that, but she doesn't rub it in my face at all. I'm really getting to feel comfortable with this woman, my new partner. Maybe *too* comfortable.

I think of myself as a professional and I like to do things by the books. Having an affair with your new partner is definitely *not* in the books, but that's what I want. This is wrong. I've got to stop this shit, and so does Bobbie. Hell, she even called me babe rather than Bob. And it isn't just sex that I want. I find myself really attracted to this lady — *really*.

I suggested the Brooklyn Chop House because it's not dark and candle-lit, but kind of open and airy. I figured a romantic place would send the wrong signal. That would be a bad idea. Right?

I asked for a table in the back because I knew we'd be talking about our big case and I wanted privacy. When the waiter showed us to the table at the back of the room, Bobbie touched my arm and said softly, "Wow, this is really nice." So much for working the case.

"We should talk, babe, I mean Bob."

"About the Manhattan Mosque case?"

"Yeah, that too, but mainly about us, our new partnership. I guess you were concerned, as I was, about how we'd get along as partners. Well, I'm no longer concerned. I think we're going to work out great. People tell me I'm a good detective because I notice things. Well, yes, I do notice things. I'm embarrassed as hell to say this, but I notice that I'm comfortable with you as a partner, *extremely* comfortable. Ayn Rand once said that you can avoid reality, but you can't avoid the consequences of avoiding reality. And the simple reality is that I'm happy with my new partner. How's my detective work so far, Bob?"

I hope I don't embarrass myself by passing out on the floor. She's being as straightforward as I could have ever have imagined, but there was something kind of nice about it. Looking at her beautiful face was also kind of nice.

"I agree, Bobbie. We *are* good partners. I know that I'm sure as hell comfortable with you. But, hey, we're detectives assigned to work together. Are we being professional?"

"No, we're not being professional. But we're also human beings. I did a ton of research on you before coming to New York, and what I read I liked. I even phoned a bunch of cops and told them that I was a reporter for a made-up newspaper called the *Downtown Gazette* and I was writing an article about Detective Bob Lawton. I often use a fake reporter scam to get information. They couldn't have been more open and praised you to the hilt. So, I know you, Bob. I feel like I've known you for years, not somebody who I just met recently. When I met you in person, I liked it all the more. When we were assigned as partners after I did my research, I felt like we're old pals."

"But we were partnered only two weeks ago," I said.

"I'm a detective, remember. I asked around and found that you were my *likely* partner. And when I heard that your current partner was due to retire, I took that as a major clue. If you weren't assigned as my partner, I would have requested it—based on my professional evaluation, of course. I'm being entirely too forward, aren't I?"

"Yes, you are—and I kind of like it. Tell me more about yourself, stuff that I didn't read in newspaper and magazine articles."

"Well, as you know I divorced two years ago. I was married to a wife-beating drunk. It started out as a good marriage, but then it turned to shit. I avoided men for two years after that experience. But, and I'm going to embarrass myself again, that was until I met you. I'm definitely not avoiding *you*."

I don't know where this is all going, but I think I like the direction.

CHAPTER 8

Bobbie

Thank goodness we got our shit together last night after our lovely dinner. Our sweet nothings were leading toward a premature overnighter, but we both dug into whatever adulthood we could muster and went our separate ways. My life is involved in sorting through a lot of gruesome mayhem. Often, when examining the bodies of a family that had been murdered, I would often have one thought — life's too short. I don't doubt that Bob has a similar attitude toward life. That's probably why we indulged in our adolescent flirty nonsense last night. Bullshit, it wasn't adolescent nonsense. I like this guy. I really like him. I enjoy working with him, I respect his professionalism, and I just enjoy being with him. What's wrong with that? As a detective, I think I'm a pretty good judge of character. My gut feeling, coupled with the huge amount of research I did on him, tells me that Bob is a man of real character, nothing like the scumbag I married a few years ago. And also, he's gorgeous — insanely gorgeous. We're both pros and we know what we're doing. We both understand, as we discussed last night, that a romantic entanglement can interfere with our work. But is it really an *entanglement*, or just two people who are attracted to each other, two people who also work together? This is complicated.

Bullshit—It's not complicated. Life's too short.

I sat in our office, knowing that Bob was due to arrive in a few minutes. I was gripped by a gnawing fear. I was afraid that Bob would walk in and announce that our evening together was a big mistake, and the adult in him told him to knock off the nonsense. I was worried that *Bob the Adult* would show up.

At 8:05, Bob walked in. He did that cute little pitter-patter on his side of the desk. Then he walked over to my side of the desk, all the while looking at me with those goddam beautiful eyes. He reached out and stroked my face, giving me a wink.

I let go of a breath that I had been holding. *Bob the Adult* was nowhere to be seen.

He sat down and reached for the phone.

Maybe he's calling to reserve us a hotel room! *Stop this crap right now.*

"I'm going to call my favorite informant. Do you know what I mean?"

"Sure," I said. "In Chicago I had a few favorite informants, low-level crooks whose asses I'd look out for in exchange for some inside information. I always think of them technically as CIs or Confidential Informants. I'm gonna guess that you want to track down the theft of that Wyatt Earp pistol that we're speculating may have been used at the Manhattan Mosque."

He laughed. "I guess I shouldn't be surprised that you're right on top of me."

I wish I *was* on top of you, or you on top of me. Of course, I didn't say that. *Okay, stop.*

"Hey Franco, Bob Lawton here. Haya doin buddy? My partner

and I would like to stop by and ask you a few questions. Okay by you?"

Bob was being a smooth pro, talking to his confidential informant like he was an old friend. I was beginning to be impressed by my new partner. I was also impressed that he's so damn adorable.

"Franco's pawn shop is a few blocks from here. It's a nice day so we can walk and get some exercise."

As we walked down Beekman Street, I looked at Bob.

"Hey, Bob, do you notice something?"

"Notice what?"

"We're holding hands."

"Whoops," he said as he released my hand. "Bad idea."

"Well, the idea isn't bad, but the setting is."

We walked into Franco's Pawn Shop and were greeted warmly by Franco. Bob introduced me.

"I heard about your new partner, Bob. She's quite an accomplished detective from what people tell me. And she's a lot better looking than your last partner."

"Okay, wise guy, no flirting with my partner. Can we go into the back room so we can talk?"

Franco told his clerk to man the counter and we walked into his back office.

"Franco, I'm sure you heard about that Wyatt Earp pistol being stolen from the Museum of the City of New York. We're wondering if you can help us with any information you may have."

"Matter of fact, I do. A couple of days ago an Arab-looking guy tried to sell it to me. I had already heard about the gun being stolen from the museum and I realized it was too hot for me to handle. So, after the guy left, your law-abiding pawn broker reported it to the desk officer at Police Plaza. I guess the word hasn't gotten to you yet."

"Would you be able to identify the man from a photo?" I asked.

"Not only that, but I have a photograph of the guy right here. I'm very careful when I deal with creepy customers."

He reached into his desk drawer and pulled out a photo, handing it to Bob, who gave it to me.

"Here's another shot taken from behind, showing you about how tall the guy was."

"Oh my God," I said, "it's got a date and time stamp on the back." I held the photo out to Bob, pointing to the date and time. It was a few hours after the Manhattan Mosque shooting.

"Hey, old Franco knows what he's doing. Anything I can do to help the police department, I'm at your service."

I was sure Bob often looked the other way in exchange for Franco's helpfulness.

"Did the man speak with an accent, Franco?" I asked.

"Yes, a very heavy Arab accent. The guy said, 'How about you buy these?' That's all he said."

"Have you ever seen the guy before?" Bob asked.

"Yes, I've seen him around the neighborhood but never in my shop. Hey, I just thought of something. I did buy some bullets from the gun. I paid $20 for six bullets."

Oh my God, this man is a gift from heaven.

Bob reached into his pocket and pulled out a twenty-dollar bill.

"Here, let me give you a receipt."

"Don't worry about it, Franco."

"Bob? Chain of custody?"

"Oh shit, you're right, Bobbie. Yes, Franco, please give me a receipt and note the date and time of purchase and a brief description of the guy you bought them from. Put those in one bag, and the bullets in another. I can attach it to the photos. Franco, thank you so much, my friend. If anybody hassles you about anything, you have my number."

As we walked back to Police Plaza, Bob seemed upset.

"Hey, something wrong?"

"I cannot believe I almost overlooked the chain of custody. Thank God my sharp partner covered me. I can learn a few tricks from you."

And wouldn't I love to teach you a few tricks. *Stop!*

CHAPTER 9

Bob

When Bobbie and I got back to One PP we immediately ordered the bag of bullets and the photos to be delivered to the forensics lab, along with the receipt showing chain of custody—thanks to Bobbie. We'd find out soon enough if they're gold or just a waste of twenty bucks.

That afternoon we received the information we hoped for. The bullets did, indeed, match the ones found at the crime scene. But we still didn't have the stolen antique Colt 45.

We posted a couple of surveillance cops at Franco's Pawn Shop, with orders to arrest the mysterious Arab gun seller should he appear. They would identify him from the photos that Franco took. Franco had said he often saw him in the neighborhood.

A week went by, then two. Bobbie and I were in our office going over evidence for the zillionth time. My God, I thought, we've been partners for almost a month. And I was enjoying it—every blessed minute of it. This lady was starting to hit me—hard. Hard in a nice way. My phone rang.

"Detective Lawton, it's Officer Benedetto. We've got your guy!"

"Thanks, Tony. We'll be right there."

We went to the precinct where the man was in custody, which was right nearby.

"This is either a breakthrough or a dead end," Bobbie said. I could tell she was excited from her eyes. She looks especially sexy when she's excited.

We walked into the interrogation room of the precinct. Officer Benedetto stood next to the prisoner, who was handcuffed to the table. After Bobbie and I sat, Benedetto left the room and posted himself outside.

"Please tell us your name." I said.

"Muhammed Ursuri," he said with a heavy Arabic accent.

"And your address?"

"23 Willow Place," Muhammed said.

I jotted the address down on a piece of scrap paper and handed it to Benedetto in the hallway.

"Call this into the commissioner's office. He's expecting it."

Bobbie, no surprise, had already prepared a search warrant and gave it to Norquist. All it needed was the name and address. Have I mentioned that my new partner knows her stuff? Warrants would normally take a few hours, but Norquist pulled rank and hustled them through. Norquist likes to work fast. On direct orders from the commissioner, the warrant was executed by two uniforms and a detective at the same time as we continued our interrogation.

"Mr. Ursuri," Bobbie said after she read him his Miranda rights, "did there come a time when you attempted to sell an antique Colt 45 to Franco's Pawn Shop on Beekman Street?"

"Yes, I did."

"And Mr. Franco did not buy the pistol from you, is that correct?"

"Yes, that is correct."

"And do you still have the pistol in your possession?"

Ursuri looked uncomfortable, like he wished he had asked for a lawyer when he was read his rights. I didn't remind him of his right to a lawyer because Bobbie had already Mirandized him. Fuck him. Bobbie continued her expert interrogation.

"I repeat my question: Do you still have possession of the pistol?"

"Yes."

"And where did you obtain that pistol?"

"I don't know."

I was about to say, "What the fuck do you mean you don't know?" when Bobbie continued her calm, intelligent line of questions. I was learning a lot from this woman, this gorgeous woman.

"Have you ever been to the Museum of the City of New York?"

"Yes,"

"When was the last time you were there?"

"About a month ago."

"You are aware, are you not, that the pistol in question was stolen from the museum a month ago?"

"Yes."

"Did you steal the pistol from the museum?"

"I meant to bring it back. I just borrowed it to show to a friend."

"What is your friend's name?"

"Mustaffa Cururi."

"Where does Mr. Cururi live?"

"On Sidney Place on the corner of Joralemon Street. It's right near my apartment."

"And could you please describe his physical appearance."

"Excuse me," I said. I walked into the hallway and called the commissioner's office. His assistant picked up.

"Betty, we need to collar a guy on Sidney Place on the corner of Joralemon Street. He's a suspect in the Manhattan Mosque shooting. His name is Mustaffa Cururi." I gave her the guy's physical description.

"Consider it done, Bob. You two are keeping us busy."

Bobbie continued. "Mr. Usuri, did there come a time when your friend Mustaffa Cururi returned the weapon in question to you?"

"Yes, but then he took it back. He still has the gun."

"Had the weapon been fired?"

"I don't know. The gun had been cleaned."

Bobbie continued her skillful interrogation of our suspect, asking new questions and repeating others she already asked. By my count, our suspect is facing at least three class B felonies. I didn't jump in but let Bobbie do the questioning. My partner is one cool customer. We were about 45 minutes into the questioning when my phone rang. I took it in the hallway.

"Bob, it's Dennis Macklin. I'm at the apartment of that suspect you wanted us to arrest, Mustaffa Cururi. He's dead. Bullet to the back of the head. From the advanced *rigor mortis* signs, it seems like he was killed about 12 hours ago. The medical examiner is on the way and he'll narrow down the time of death. We're searching for the gun now."

Holy shit, this case is getting more interesting by the minute. I reentered the interrogation room. I leaned over to whisper to Bobbie about the death of Cururi. She had a slight hint of perfume on her earlobe. My God she smelled great. When I told her about the murder, she stared at me wide- eyed — with those dreamy blue eyes.

Another half hour went by when my phone rang. I walked into the hallway. It was Officer Phil Macklin, the guy in charge of executing the search warrant on Usuri's apartment.

"We got the gun, Bob. We're still searching the place for other evidence. See you later at One PP."

I was happy as hell. We had a key piece of evidence. But mainly I was happy that I had another excuse to whisper into Bobbie's wonderful-smelling ear. I did. She smiled and kissed me on the cheek. She kissed me! It was only Bobbie, me, and Usuri in the room. The one-way mirror could give people in the hall a view, which was the only thing that stopped me from wrapping my arms around her and planting a big wet one on her lips. The Manhattan Mosque matter isn't the only case I'm working on.

"We've gone as far as we can for today, Bob. I suggest that we return the suspect to the lockup after we read him his rights again, and then go to the apartment where Cururi was assassinated."

She "suggests?" Bobbie is so friggin polite and solicitous of my feelings. Have I mentioned that I like my new partner — *a lot.*

CHAPTER 10

Bobbie

After the hours of interrogation of Muhammed Usuri, Bob and I decided to go to the apartment where Mustaffa Cururi was killed. The most critical evidence had already been found— the antique Colt 45. Officer Melissa Tompkins was in charge of the CSU group on the scene. Detective Lieutenant Jack Abramowitz was the detective in charge. He's an old friend of Bob's.

"Anything you can tell us, Jack?" Bob said.

"This was a cleanly executed hit, Bob. No struggle, just a bullet to the back of the head. But we're gathering a ton of stuff, including radical literature, most of which is in Arabic. Our translator is going to have a lot of translating to do."

"There isn't much for you folks to do here," Melissa the CSU honcho said." *Except get in our way*, I'm sure she wanted to say, although she politely did not. I'm often hesitant to let CSU people take over a crime scene, and usually supervise it myself, as Jack Abramowitz was doing. But Bob said he knew these people well and that they're real pros. That was good enough for me. Bob knows what he's doing and is smart as hell. Also, he's impossibly gorgeous, which has nothing to do with his knowledge of the CSU people, but it just popped into my mind. It often does.

Bob and I returned to our office at One PP.

"This has been one hell of a day, honey, but I think we got a lot accomplished," I said.

"Honey? You called me honey. I think that's wonderful."

"I called you that because that's how I'm starting to think of you — my honey. Oh my God, I'm getting carried away with myself, aren't I?"

"Know what I need, Bobbie?"

"No, what?"

"A hug, accompanied by a kiss, followed by a nice dinner."

I walked up to him and wrapped my arms around his handsome neck and we kissed — a long, wet, wonderful kiss. I noticed that his hands found their way to my butt, which I've caught him staring at often. I also noticed a strong movement below my waist. Maybe we should skip dinner. No, no, let's do this right.

Bob chose the River Café on Water Street. He didn't want us to be known as a fixture at The Brooklyn Chop House. Besides that, he said, The River Café is more romantic. That was more than fine by me. It was only 5:30, so we would have an early dinner. As we walked out of the office, I grabbed my overnight bag with a change of clothing. I learned a long time ago that a detective's time is often controlled by circumstances, and you never knew when you'd have to crash overnight at a hotel near a crime scene after working 20 straight hours. An overnight bag is also useful for other unforeseen situations like, well, you know.

We walked into the River Café and were warmly greeted by the *maître d*, who obviously knew Bob well. He showed us to a cozy table in the back. I immediately noticed the candles on the table.

"Hey, Bob, that guy greeted you like you were his brother. You seem to be pretty popular in this place."

"I handled a case involving this restaurant a few years ago. A waiter was murdered by a patron."

"Didn't like the service?" Bob cracked up. "No, wise guy, it was a hit. Seems that the waiter ran afoul of some mob people and they decided to take him out. I poured on the steam and wrapped up the case in two weeks, arresting the killer, who's doing 25 to life. Luis has been a big fan of mine ever since."

"He's not your only big fan," I said as I winked at him. Holy shit, I've really got to knock off this crap. Or do I? Why?

He stroked my face and winked back.

"So, Bob, we've been working together for a whole month, and it's been quite a month, not to mention today. I feel like we're going in the right direction."

"Bobbie, I gotta tell you, today was our best day together. You absolutely amazed me the way you interrogated our suspect. Your legal training showed through. I love working with a partner I can look up to, and that's definitely you."

"Thanks, Bob. You have no idea how happy that makes me. And I look up to you too. I'd say we're good partners."

"I'm glad to say that you look more relaxed than I've seen you in weeks, Bobbie. Are you always like this when you get a big lead on a case?"

"Sure, I love big leads, like our finding that Colt 45, but it's more than that. I've decided to stop my mental gymnastics of trying to think of you as just a fellow employee of the NYPD. And yes, it was mental gymnastics, which is a euphemism for bullshit. I've decided to let my feelings about you go where they want to go. As I said, after my research and reading your book I feel like I've known you for years, even though it's only been a month. And therefore, I've come to a conclusion."

"Want to share your conclusion with me, Detective?"

"I love you, Bob. I'm wild, crazy in love with you."

Bob just stared at me with those amazing eyes of his. I was scared out of my mind that he'd find what I said to be too forward. Maybe I *was* too forward to tell him I loved him, but shit, it's the truth. I drop dead friggin love this guy. He pulled his chair next to mine, put his arm around my shoulder and kissed me, a long, sweet kiss. I wasn't scared anymore. That kiss wasn't just a kiss; it was meant to communicate something, something wonderful.

"I agree, baby, enough of the bullshit. As you said, let's let our feelings go where they want to. I love you, Bobbie. My God, do I ever. Just like you, I played mental gymnastics with my head, telling myself that you were a professional colleague and nothing more. That was total bullshit, as you observed. Hey, today we worked together like the team we are. And our feelings for each other didn't interfere one bit. I think our feelings even helped us get the job done. We're a team, baby, a very close team."

"Hey, let's have a light bite to eat and get on with the evening."

"You mean like go to my place, Bobbie? It's right nearby."

"That's the best idea you've had all day, Detective. I was even farsighted enough to bring an overnight bag with me."

"I noticed," he said with a cute wicked glimmer in his eyes.

After our light dinner—we weren't really interested in food—we went to Bob's apartment, a few blocks away. I felt wonderful. Bob and I told each other we're in love. And we were about to show it.

"This place is beautiful, Bob. I should have guessed that you're a man of exquisite taste. I love your masculine leather furniture. It even smells nice."

"It has two bedrooms, not that that's important, and two full bathrooms. I even have a small gym. You can work out and keep that beautiful body of yours in shape. How about a kiss?"

We took off our guns and lay them on the dining room table. Then we wrapped our arms around each other and made out like a couple of teenagers.

Bob said he needed a shower. I was worried that he'd crack a dumb joke about "conserving water." Things are moving fast, but sometimes it's a good idea to slow down *just a little*—and take separate showers. We walked into the den in our robes. Bob made us a couple of martinis. Then we kissed again. I don't think I'll ever get enough of kissing Bob. He reached down and put his hands under the shoulders of my robe. In one gentle movement, he dropped my robe to the floor. I reached out and dropped his. Since I first laid eyes on him, I realized that Bob was ridiculously handsome. What I didn't fully appreciate, until that moment, was that he had a crazy hot physique, a body I never want to let go of. We made out again, this time naked. Bob held my hand and gently walked me to the bedroom, and then to the bed. We began the most wonderful night of love I could ever imagine.

I'm glad we made this step. Yes, we're pros, but we're also in love, something we both agreed would only help our work, never get in the way of it. And no, I'm not bullshitting myself. Oh my God, I love this man.

CHAPTER 11

Bob

I just spent the most amazing night of my life. Bobbie and I are in love, and we both know it's real. A month ago, I was prepared to hate her. Now I love her, and she loves me, and we both shared our feelings with each other. And then we began the most wonderful sex of my life. I can't remember feeling so great, and I can't count how many times we made love last night. There's something about Bobbie that does wonders for my stamina.

To keep up appearances, at least for the near future, we agreed that Bobbie would walk alone to our favorite diner and I would join her a few minutes later.

Breakfast in a busy diner isn't exactly romantic, but that's exactly how we both felt. We sat in a booth, which provided some sort of privacy. We avoided holding hands across the table, although we wanted to. A steady stream of fellow cops walked by our booth saying hello.

Bobbie leaned closer.

"Last night my life changed, Bob, and I'm not exaggerating. I feel liberated, now that we've told each other how we really feel.

I'm so friggin in love with you I can't believe it. I respected you as a detective, but last night I couldn't get over how sweet a lover you are. Have I mentioned that I love you?"

"People will start to talk, Bobbie. So, what? The Governor of New York lives with a woman he's not married to and nobody makes a peep. Last night was a total game changer. I went from liking my partner to admitting to myself that I'm in love with her. And, because we're the pros we are, our detective work will be all the better. Hey, we should go. We've got a lot of work to do."

We walked to One PP, being careful not to hold hands, which wasn't easy.

CHAPTER 12

Bobbie

When Bob and I walked into our office we saw a memo on the desk saying the commissioner wanted to see us.

"You don't think…" I said.

"Of course, not. Do you think the NYPD has my apartment bugged? He probably wants an update on the Manhattan Mosque matter."

We walked into Norquist's office. He sat there with his usual poker face, then smiled to greet us. Ever since he flew to Chicago to interview me and offer me this job, I've taken to liking this guy. He's a straight shooter and a good boss. Also, because he hired me for this position, I got to meet Bob. *My* Bob. The man I love. The man who loves me.

"I'm not given to exaggeration," Norquist said, "but let me just say that you two are amazing. Bob, you've been one of my best detectives for years, and partnering you up with Wonder Woman over here has made you all the better. I pat myself on the back for that idea. Within a short time, you two blew open that Manhattan Mosque case and put it on the road to a solution. I hope I'm not going to disappoint you, but I'm taking you off the case. I just got off the phone with the Justice Department and the FBI. Because the case is politically sensitive, they want it to be a strictly federal matter. I agreed that the both of you would serve as consultants when they have questions, which they will.

"I have a new case for you to work on, an incredibly important case. Take a deep breath because I'm about to shock you. It hasn't hit the news yet, but Mayor Paxton and his wife have apparently been kidnapped. Yes, you heard me—fucking kidnapped. Whatever else is on your desks, put it aside. This is the only matter I want you to work on. This will be a joint investigation between the NYPD and the FBI, but I want you two to do the heavy lifting. The Paxtons were last seen at Gracie Mansion. The three of us will go there now."

Oh my God. The Mayor and his wife, kidnapped? Obviously, the Police Commissioner needs to be on the scene with a case as dramatic as this, but I wish he wouldn't join us. I've found that working alone with Bob is the best way to get things done. After last night I realized that Bob and I get a lot of things done. Big things. Exciting things. Wonderful things. Okay, time to focus.

Bob and I walked down the hall to the parking lot to hop a car for Gracie Mansion.

"I cannot believe this, Bob. The Mayor of New York City has been kidnapped, along with his wife. Have you ever worked a kidnapping before?"

"Over the years I've worked on three when I was assigned to the major case unit that handles kidnappings. How about you, Bobbie?"

"You're ahead of me. I've only worked one."

"Yeah, but you probably solved it in one day."

"Well, it took me *two* days."

"Gimme a kiss, Wonder Woman. Hey, it's going to be a long day. How about my place after we're done?"

"People are going to start to talk, Bob."

"Fuck 'em."

"No—fuck *me*."

"I fully intend to. Later, baby."

The three of us piled into the commissioner's car—a big black SUV of course. Norquist sat in the first row of bench seats and Bob and I sat behind him. The drive to Gracie Mansion would take at least a half hour. Norquist took a file out of his bag and began to go over his notes with us, sitting sideways so he could see us. Both Bob and I had our notebooks poised. If you take away a detective's notebook, you may as well tie her hands behind her back.

The weather forecast called for rain, which sucked. Nothing is more efficient than rain for washing away evidence.

"Here's what we know, which isn't a lot," Norquist said. "They were last seen at 11 p.m. last night as they headed upstairs to their bedroom. Six detectives from the Intelligence Division are at Gracie Mansion at all times, basically as bodyguards for the city's First Family. But here's the kicker—two of them are missing."

"Holy shit," Bob and I both yelled.

"Yeah, holy shit. My reaction as well. We have a file on all personnel, of course, but I ordered Internal Affairs to update the records on those two. I'm not telling you two what you don't already know, but obviously those missing cops will be the focus of your investigation."

Our car pulled up to Gracie Mansion. Even though I grew up in New York City, I decided to educate myself on everything I could when I was offered this job. I read all about Gracie Mansion recently. The place is the official residence of the Mayor of New York City. It's located uptown in Carl Schurz Park on 88th Street and East End Avenue in the Yorkville section of Manhattan. It overlooks the East River. The place was built in 1799 by a wealthy tobacco merchant named Archibald Gracie. The real name of the building is the Archibald Gracie Mansion, but everybody calls it Gracie Mansion. It became the mayor's official residence during World War II when Fiorello LaGuardia moved in. The place is pretty, not a huge imposing structure, but pretty. And now it's a crime scene.

When we pulled up to the mansion, I noticed the parking lot was crowded with vans from every major network. Obviously, the press got wind of the kidnapping. As we got out of the car, we were surrounded by reporters with microphones and cameras. Bob and I discreetly drifted into the background to give Norquist space. This was definitely a police commissioner show. One guy apparently recognized me from my TV appearances and walked over to us.

"Detective Nelson, you have worked on major cases when you were in Chicago. Can you tell us what happened?"

"My partner and I were assigned this case just this morning, and we're about to start our investigation."

"But can't you tell us what happened?"

"We haven't completed our investigation." Besides that, no way in hell would I talk to a reporter about an open case.

Dipshit.

The commissioner, Bob, and I walked through the front door. We slipped on our latex gloves as we always do when entering a crime scene.

"I'm going to leave this in your good hands," Norquist said to us as he put his gloves into his pocket. "I'll be outside answering stupid questions for a while and then I'll head back to headquarters. That guy over there in the brown suit is Detective Williams, the last person who saw the mayor and his wife. I guess you will want to interview him. See you later."

"Detective Williams, I'm Detective Nelson and this is my partner, Detective Bob Lawton. Please call us Bob and Bobbie."

"My pleasure, and welcome to the NYPD, Bobbie. My name is Jack. I haven't had the opportunity to meet you before. Great to have somebody of your caliber, not to mention your good looks, with us." I had the distinct impression that this jerk was flirting with me. *Buzz off. There's only one man in the world I want to flirt with.* We walked into a small room off the main hallway, carefully avoiding the crime scene tape.

"Bob and I need to ask you a few questions, Jack. Please begin by telling us what you saw or heard and the time that you recall."

He looked at his notepad.

"At exactly 11 p.m.—I always make a note of the time when the Paxtons retire for the evening—I saw them walking up the main stairway. They both turned to me and said, 'good night.' That's about it."

"Were any detectives on the second floor at that time?"

"No, all six of us were on the first floor. On orders from the mayor, we always respect their privacy in their living quarters."

"I notice a lot of windows on the second floor," Bob said. "Have they been checked for any signs of forced entry?"

"Yes, all the windows were checked as soon as we realized the Paxtons were missing. Also, all the windows have alarm devices."

"Were the devices checked?"

"Yes."

"At what time did you realize the Paxtons were missing?" I asked.

"At 7:30 a.m. They're pretty much creatures of habit, and they always come down no later than 7:30, sometimes earlier, but never later."

"And what did you do then?"

"I buzzed the intercom in their bedroom. I got no response, so I waited five minutes and buzzed again. Hey, I figured they may be getting dressed. No sense being a pain in the ass. Still no response. Detective Parker and I then climbed the stairs at 7:36. When we got to the top I repeatedly shouted, 'Mr. Mayor.' I have a pretty loud voice, so I realized there was a problem. We drew our weapons and went room to room. And here's the shocker. Their bed was neatly made. It didn't appear to have been slept in. A maid is assigned to make their bed for them, just like in a hotel. The bed was perfectly neat, just as if a maid had done it up."

"Were any articles of clothing strewn about?" Bob asked.

"No, none. The room didn't look as if it was occupied at all. I can show it to you now, exactly as I found it just this morning."

"I understand from the commissioner that two of your colleagues are missing," I said. "When did you realize that?"

"When we realized the Paxtons were missing, I called all of the detectives on their listening devices and told them to assemble in the kitchen. Detectives Simone and Fitzgerald didn't show. That was at 7:40 a.m."

"Who had the night watch last night?" Bob asked. "In other words, whose job was it to be awake and guarding the Paxtons?"

"Simone and Fitzgerald, the two guys who are missing."

"Are the night watch schedules done at random or are they prepared in advance like in the military?" Bob asked.

"The schedule is prepared a week in advance. Everyone knows when he or she will be on night watch duty."

"Who prepares the schedules?" I asked

"I do."

"Please tell us how you prepare the schedules, Jack."

"This is where it gets random. I have six cards with the name of each detective. I shuffle them and make the assignments. That's right out of the Gracie Mansion Procedures Manual. Hey, wait, hold on. I just remembered something. A few weeks ago, Simone asked to be assigned the night watch with Fitzgerald. He said they like to read the same books and talk about them. I told him flat no, that it was against regulations. But, randomly, a few weeks later Simone and Fitzgerald appeared on the same night watch."

Bob and I looked at each other. I've noticed over the past few weeks that Bob and I can communicate without saying anything.

"Well, I think we've all come to the same conclusion, the unavoidable conclusion," I said. "Simone and Fitzgerald are dirty. They're the perpetrators. Jack, can you tell us more about Simone and Fitzgerald?"

"I knew Simone well, or I thought I did. I recall that recently he'd been having some serious financial problems. Something about an investment gone bad. I constantly heard him on the phone wrestling with creditors. I was about to relieve him of his Gracie Mansion duties after checking with the commissioner. I didn't know Fitzgerald well, because he only started working here two months ago. All I know is that he was a big Yankees fan."

"Is he a gambler?" Bob asked.

"Yeah, now that you mention it. He often asked me if I wanted to place a bet on a Yankees game."

"Let's take a short break while I call legal," Bob said. The NYPD legal department is in charge of getting search warrants from a court, and Bob was right on target. We need search warrants for the Simone and Fitzgerald houses. I listened as Bob gave the legal department guy enough probable cause to choke a python, all based on the facts we heard from Detective Williams. Bob also told the guy to put out an APB (all points bulletin) for the whereabouts of Detectives Simone and Fitzgerald.

I have a great partner—not to mention a great lover.

CHAPTER 13

Bob

Bobbie and I spent the rest of the day interviewing everybody at Gracie Mansion. We didn't learn much beyond what Detective Williams told us. Sometimes things become clear fast. We know we have the bad guys, Detectives Simone and Fitzgerald, the guys on night watch at the mansion, the guys who disappeared, along with the mayor and his wife.

So, the Simone and Fitzgerald houses are being searched, and an APB is out for the two of them. Sometimes a case, no matter how important, reaches a point where you need to take a deep breath and wait. The important thing is to be available and on call. That's why I bought an apartment near One PP, so I could jump into action immediately. That's why I want Bobbie to move in with me, although I haven't sprung the idea on her yet. If I had any lingering doubt about working as a detective with someone I was in love with, today dispelled that doubt. Bobbie and I flat out got the job done.

We walked into our office at 7:45 p.m. As soon as I closed the door, I wrapped my arms around her, and she did the same for me.

"Hey, we need some rest. Let's go to my place."

"I thought you said we need some rest. Last night at your place we didn't get much rest, did we?"

"Well, exercise and rest often go together. Got your overnight bag?"

"Of course, I do."

"Then let's go to my place and, well, you know."

"I know what?" She was playing games with my head.

"Let's screw our brains out, that's what."

"You always have excellent ideas, Detective Lawton."

We walked to my apartment, doing a good job of not holding hands. We walked in at 8:15.

"Hey, let's take off our guns, get naked, and take a shower," Bobbie said. "You know, when I moved to New York, I expected excitement, but I never expected anything as exciting as you, handsome."

After we showered and made love, we lay there, our arms around each other, spent and happy.

"You know I can help you pack, honey."

"Pack? Pack what? Where are we going?"

"I think you should move in here, baby, for the good of the department."

"How romantic. You want me to move in with you for the good of the NYPD?"

"I'm only partially joking. Hey, we're just three blocks from One PP. Sometimes, and you know this too well, we detectives need to put in long hours. Being able to run back here, take a quick nap and freshen up helps relieve the stress of our job. And I'll be with the woman I love."

"Bob, how do you think this will go over in the commissioner's office? I mean two detective partners shacking up? I think Norquist will hate this idea."

"Hey, honey, this is a legal two-family apartment with two separate entrances. We won't be shacking up. You'll be my tenant."

"Just what I always wanted, to screw my landlord," she said, laughing.

"No, I'm serious. Hell, there are even two addresses. Apartment 212 A and 212 B. You will list B as your new residence. How long do you have to go on your lease on that little place you live in?"

"I wasn't sure if I'd like it there, so I took it on a month-to-month lease. Hey, honey, I'm starting to like this idea. Truth be told, I think I *love* this idea."

CHAPTER 14

Bobbie

I walked to the diner and Bob would join me in a few minutes. I guess this will become our standard routine to placate prying eyes from One PP. It was okay with me, kind of fun actually. Hey, we're detectives. Nothing wrong with a little cloak and dagger. Bob and I had moved through the BIG ISSUE—our relationship. To others, we're detective partners. But to us, we're two people in love with each other. To me, that's what really matters.

It was early, 6:45 a.m., because we had a lot of work to do on the big case, the Paxton kidnapping. We had our brief time off last night, a wonderful night—*another* wonderful night. I love Bob's idea of my moving in with him. He's right. Besides doing wonders for our relationship it will definitely make our jobs more manageable. I had never thought about the idea of walking to work but Bob got it right, as usual. It will make my life less stressful. And sometimes we can take an extended lunch and, well, why not? We plan to move my stuff in a week, but I had already moved in with a few essentials. Certainly, my head had already moved in. I secured us a booth by the window. We definitely will not be holding hands this morning, much as we want to. Bob walked in about five minutes later. My God is he handsome. We agreed that we wouldn't talk about the Paxton case in public. Too sensitive. No problem, we're only two minutes from One PP.

We walked into our office at 7:20.

"Okay, let's review what we know, honey," I said. We had given up on the idea of addressing ourselves formally when we're alone. Honey, sweetheart, or baby works fine with us. Hell, he *is* my honey. If somebody hears us, get over it.

"Well, here's what we know about Simone and Fitzgerald," Bob said. "They're both single, having divorced a couple of years ago. From the search of their apartments, we know that both of them are having financial problems, especially Simone. After his divorce he was living paycheck to paycheck, and the settlement required him to shoulder his wife's huge mortgage payment. I'm surprised Internal Affairs hadn't dumped these guys long ago. But one thing has me stumped. If this was a kidnapping for ransom, where the hell is the ransom demand, and more important than that, where will the money come from? The Paxton's have no kids, so who will pay the ransom, the City of New York?"

Bob's phone rang.

"I'll put you on speaker, sir."

"It's the commissioner," he whispered.

"Well, folks, the shit just hit the fan. The APB that Bob put out has gotten results, but not the outcome we were hoping for. Both Simone and Fitzgerald have been murdered. And we have no idea where the mayor and his wife are. I think it's safe to assume that whoever killed the detectives is the same person or people who planned the kidnapping. It's been at least 24 hours and we have yet to see a ransom demand. I want you two BBs to brainstorm like all hell and try to get us somewhere."

Norquist has taken recently to referring to Bob and me as the "BBs." Kind of dumb, if you ask me, but I'm not the commissioner. In a way it's sort of cute. Bob and Bobbie, the *BBs*.

"Okay, Bob. Let's review the simple rules of brainstorming," I said. "First, nothing's off the table. If one of us says something really stupid, we don't process it but move on the next idea. "I'll set a timer on my phone for 10 minutes and then we'll review what we've come up with."

"Bobbie, shouldn't we come up with a question we want to focus us? Like what person or group would want to harm the Paxtons?"

"Great point, honey. Okay you go first."

"The mayor is a black man. Maybe there's a racist component."

"Excellent," I said.

"Hey, no voting, just take down the idea. Your turn."

"They're an interracial couple. Some people hate that. I'll call this Racist 2. You go"

"He's a Democrat, so maybe it's a Republican," Bob said.

"Do you really think a Republican would do something like this?" I said.

"No voting!"

"Whoops, sorry. My turn," I said.

"He wants to end rent control. A hot issue. You go."

"A ransom. Somebody wants a lot of money and they figure New York City will cough it up," Bob said.

"Revenge. Maybe Paxton did something to hurt someone and that person wants revenge." I said. "Your turn."

"Jealousy. Paxton's been accused of dallying with a few women. So maybe it's a jealous husband or boyfriend," Bob said.

"Excitement," I said. "Somebody was looking for a thrill."

"Okay, time's up." I said. "What's your major thought, Bob?"

"I think it's a ransom kidnapping, and that we'll hear a demand shortly. The other stuff requires action on the part of the mayor, such as rent control. No way could that possibly be considered a legally enforceable contract. No, I think it's for money. What do you think, Bobbie?"

"I'm not sure. Where the hell is the ransom demand?"

"Something tells me we'll see it soon."

I hope Bob's right. One of the frustrating things you encounter as a detective is when you're up against something over which you have no control. We have no idea who is behind the kidnapping, and the people who executed it are dead. Our mayor and his wife are somewhere out there and there isn't a goddam thing we can do.

But something tells me that this case isn't as obvious as it seems. Over the years I've learned *never* to look at a case as obvious.

CHAPTER 15

Bob

A nother day without a ransom demand and I'm feeling negative. When Bobbie and I brainstormed, a couple of ideas we tossed out involved possible revenge or retribution, having nothing to do with money. I'm having the sinking feeling that maybe the Paxtons have been killed, a horrible feeling.

Bobbie was upstairs in the commissioner's office giving him an update, not that she has a lot to update him on. My phone rang.

"Detective Lawton, may I help you."

"Be prepared to take down an address," said a heavily disguised voice.

"21-25 147th Street, Whitestone," said the voice.

"And to whom do I have the pleasure of speaking?"

"None of your business. I have one word for you. *Paxtons*. Good day, Detective."

There was no identification on my caller ID. I called the commissioner's office.

"Sir, I just got what may be an anonymous tip. A heavily disguised voice gave me an address in Whitestone, Queens. All he said was 'Paxtons.' I need a couple of plain-clothed officers to go with Bobbie and me."

"Bobbie's on her way to your office now. I'll have the officers waiting for you in the parking lot."

Bobbie walked in.

"Saddle up, honey, we're taking a road trip." I told her about the "tip" I just received.

"The fact that he called you tells us that the guy knows something about NYPD inner workings," Bobbie said. "Where is the location?"

"21-25 147th Street in Whitestone, Queens."

"Wow, I grew up two blocks from there. Whitestone has such charming street names."

"We're going with a couple of plain clothes. We don't know if there may be shooting, but I want you to stay in the car until we get the all-clear."

"Hey, honey, I've been a cop for 15 years. Don't worry about me; I know how to handle a gun. You've seen me on the shooting range. We should bring our Kevlar vests just in case."

Forty minutes later we drove down 147th street. Our car was a red Camaro, not readily identifiable as an unmarked patrol car. The house was the second from the corner, so we drove onto the side street and walked to the back across the neighbor's lawn. Officers from the nearby precinct were already there. We had our guns drawn but kept them at our sides. I'm tall enough to see through the first-floor window so I peeked in. Nothing. According to good tactical procedure, we then walked to the front door and rang the bell. This may be good procedure, but it's also a scary procedure. After five attempts we got no answer. Bob Curtin, one of the cops with us, is built like a linebacker. He lowered his huge shoulder and broke the door open.

"Police," he shouted.

We heard a groan from upstairs. Not really a groan, more like a muffled yell.

"You two stay here," Curtin said to us. He was once a member of the ESU or Emergency Service Unit, the NYPD's equivalent of a SWAT team (Special Weapons and Tactics). Curtin is one of the combat-ready cops on the force. He and Bill Mason, his partner, walked slowly up the stairs. Within two minutes he shouted "Clear" from the top of the stairs. "Come on up, Detectives."

As we walked into a large room on the second floor, Curtin and Mason were undoing the bindings around Mayor Paxton and his wife Nancy. "I need to use the bathroom" they both said. We would soon learn that they had been left tied up for four hours.

When they came out of the bathrooms, the mayor said, "Are you guys ever a sight for sore eyes. A pleasure to meet you again, Bobbie. Last time I saw you was when I welcomed you to New York in Ralph Norquist's office."

"And it's great to see you again, Mr. Mayor. I just thank God that you and Mrs. Paxton are okay."

A patrol car that had tailed us pulled up, along with three other units. The cops from the patrol cars began to establish a crime scene. Bobbie opened the refrigerator with her latex-gloved hands and retrieved a couple of bottle water for the Mayor and Nancy. She handed them gloves so as not to disturb any possible fingerprints.

The Paxtons are best described as a "handsome couple." Arnold Paxton is a tall black man at six-four, slim and good-looking. Nancy

Paxton is a stunning woman, about 50, with wavy light brown hair, blue eyes, and a great smile.

"Mr. Mayor," I said, "we can get you and Mrs. Paxton back to Gracie Mansion now, if you wish. My partner and I can ask you questions in the car. But it would be better if we questioned you here on the scene in case you need to bring anything to our attention."

"Yes, we'll stay right here for the time being, not that I like this place." Mayor Paxton was once a cop himself, so he knew the drill with crime scene investigations.

The four of us walked into the dining room and sat around the table. Bobbie turned on the recorder.

"Mr. Mayor, can you tell us how you were abducted from Gracie Mansion?" Bobbie said.

"It happened at one in the morning. I'm sure you know that Detectives Simone and Fitzgerald kidnapped us."

"Sir, we noticed that your bed didn't seem to have been slept in," I said.

"That's because the bastards handcuffed us, put tape on our mouths and led us into a guest room," Nancy Paxton said. "They kept us at gunpoint until the people downstairs were asleep."

"I don't know if you're aware of this, sir, but Detectives Simone and Fitzgerald have been murdered," Bobbie said.

The Mayor and Nancy stared at us, wide-eyed.

"Oh my God," Paxton said. "I guess that explains why there was a different cast of characters here. There were three of them. For some reason I can't figure out, they suddenly left four hours ago. There was a phone call and one of the men mumbled something and they just left."

"Can you describe them?" I asked.

"We can't give a description of their faces because the men wore masks. When they spoke to each other they referred to one another by number, not by name. Obviously, they wanted to keep their identities hidden."

"Can you tell us what they sounded like? Did they speak with accents?" Bobbie said.

"This may be crazy, but two of the men sounded like cops. Heavy New York accents. The other guy spoke with a distinct Middle Eastern accent."

We all knew that a better identification might come from examining the forensic evidence, one of the more monotonous tasks in law enforcement. Once the CSU people are done processing the scene for prints and DNA, the analysts will try to match them to known criminals and suspects. Unlike on TV cop dramas where the hero saves the day by shooting the bad guys just after the last commercial, most crimes are solved by the tedious process of photo, fingerprint, and DNA analysis. Fingerprint analysis used to be a slow process, with the results sometimes showing up long after a criminal had been convicted based on other evidence. But, since 1999, with advances in computer technology, fingerprint analysis took off like a rocket. Using the Integrated Automated Fingerprint Identification System (IAFIS) prints can be compared to a vast database of fingerprints in seconds. IAFIS is available 24/7. Investigators can learn the identity of a suspect the same night he committed a crime. But unless you have a print to analyze, the IAFIS isn't worth shit.

As of now, we had nothing, which is normal at this stage of an investigation.

After two hours we had exhausted our questions, and the Paxtons got into a car to take them to Gracie Mansion.

Bobbie and I got into the back of the squad car to return to One PP. Today we had a driver. I started to review what we knew about the Paxton kidnapping case, when Bobbie put her index finger over her lips, indicating that I should shut up. She leaned over and whispered in my ear.

"Remember what Paxton said. The kidnappers sounded like cops. I think we better wait till we get to our office to talk."

We just stared at each other. She's right, I realized. This case was weird from the start, but it's just gotten a lot weirder.

CHAPTER 16

Bobbie

When Bob and I walked into our office, the intercom went off. It was the commissioner's office calling us for a meeting. When we walked in, Norquist did something I'd never seen him do before. He locked the door. He didn't smile when he greeted us. Actually, he didn't even greet us; he just motioned to the chairs in front of his desk.

"Give me one word or phrase that you think summarizes the Paxton kidnapping matter," he said. "Bobbie?"

"Inside job." I said.

"Bob?"

"I agree with Bobbie. This job was pulled off by cops. We already know that the two actual kidnappers were cops, Simone and Fitzgerald. Although the men who held the Paxtons in Queens kept their identities hidden, the mayor said they sounded like cops with heavy New York accents. But one of the men had an Arabic accent. Mr. Commissioner, Bobbie and I agree: The Paxton kidnapping was an NYPD operation, although we're not sure what that Arab accent was all about."

"Bobbie, remember when you and I first met in Chicago? Why don't you review for Bob and me what we discussed at that time?"

"Well, sir, you told me that the NYPD was in the middle of a huge scandal," I said. "I was familiar with the issue because it was the talk of the Chicago PD at the time. I was shocked when you offered me the job because I was a detective from another state."

"And the reason I offered you the job was because Mayor Paxton tore up the union rule book and decided to rebuild the department from the ground up. He sent me on a national recruiting tour, something unheard of in a big city police department. He ordered me to find the best detectives I could, people like you, Bobbie Nelson. That was about as popular with the unions as cancer, and just as difficult to treat. Yes, I agree with you two, it looks like it was an inside job, and that's why I need to resign."

"Nonsense," I yelled, embarrassing myself. "You're an excellent commissioner and you know it. I don't doubt for a minute that your resignation is one of the objectives of whoever is in on this. Commissioner, turn Bob and me loose on this. Why not assign us to Internal Affairs for the balance of this investigation? We'll find those bastards, and you know we will. You know how Bob and I work together. Have you ever seen a better team than us?"

"No, I've never seen a better team than you two. And I also notice that you hold hands a lot," he said as he winked. (Holy shit, I thought Bob and I were being careful.) "I believe you two are becoming what's known as 'an item,' and that's fine by me. Okay, I accept your challenge to postpone on my resignation. I'll give you folks a month. If the Paxton case isn't close to being solved by then, I'm stepping down—for the good of the department."

Before we ended the meeting, I figured now was a good time to put something on the table.

"I'm going to be moving closer to One PP, Commissioner. I'll be renting an apartment in Bob's condo three blocks from here."

Norquist laughed. "That's a great idea, Bobbie. I think my observation that you two are becoming *an item* is accurate." Oh yes, Bob and I are an item. My God are we ever. Of course, I didn't say that.

CHAPTER 17

Bob

obbie's recommendation to the commissioner that we be assigned to Internal Affairs was a good one, and, thank God, it caused Norquist to hold back on his resignation. He's a damn fine commissioner and now it will be our job to help keep him in *his* job.

Internal Affairs is best described as "a police force policing itself." And from every indication of the Paxton kidnapping case, we can see that the NYPD needs a lot of internal policing. Working in Internal Affairs can be stressful as hell. You know that you may need to arrest a cop who you've become friends with. But Bobbie and I agreed that this case looks like an inside job, and the commissioner agrees.

Tim Franken is the Deputy Commissioner of Internal Affairs, and an old friend of mine. He's a former detective and a good one, as I know, having worked many a case with him.

Our office was moved to the third floor, next to Franken's. That afternoon, we met with him in his office.

"I'm delighted to have the BBs working for me," Tim said, using the moniker that Norquist picked out for Bobbie and me. I told him that Bobbie and I would be moving in together. I wanted to make sure that he didn't have a problem with that.

"Problem? You two are an *internal affair*," he said, cracking up at his own dumb joke. Tim always did have a good sense of humor, something needed for a stressful job like his.

"Bobbie, Bob, you two are the best detectives on the force, and I think it's great that you'll be working for Internal Affairs. I intend to destroy those fucking scumbags who kidnapped the First Family." Tim has a reputation for colorful language.

"The commissioner already told me that you two plan to move Bobbie's things this afternoon, so I won't detain you. I'd offer to assign somebody to help you, but we're pretty stern about keeping a distance between the force and personal matters."

"No problem, Tim. Bobbie here is neat as a pin and we already have her stuff packed into boxes. We're going to pick up a van and go there now."

"A van?"

"Yes, a rented van, not a police vehicle."

"Good. At Internal Affairs we're strict about not spitting on the sidewalk and shit like that. See you guys later."

Bobbie and I picked up our rental van at a local U-Haul. I was nervous as hell. Why? Because I'm on asshole alert, that's why. By asshole alert I mean that I'm worried that I may revert to sabotaging myself as I've done so many times in the past. Whenever I had a good thing going, I would often turn into a complete jerk, and it always involved relationships with people. It began with my father when I was a teenager, and for the life of me I can't remember what it was all about, other than I would avoid talking to him for weeks on end. I finally patched that up, thank God. Dad is a great guy, not deserving of the shitty way I treated him. Then there's the subject of my first wife, Dolores. She was a terrific lady; pretty, smart, and good natured. Bob the Asshole reporting for duty. For some reason I can't figure out, I began to ignore her when she spoke to me. Why did I do that? I have no idea, other than it somehow made me feel powerful, like I was in charge, not her. That lasted almost a year when we both agreed to a divorce. I bumped into her a few months ago at a convenience store. Our split had been cordial, so we exchanged pleasantries. *Cordial*? What began as love had become cordial? Assholes also have their own manner of speech. She walked up to me with a look that said, "Why did you do this?" Good question. Why did I do it? We chatted for a couple of minutes, then moved on.

Which brings me to Bobbie, and why I'm so nervous. Nervous? I'm scared shitless. I'm scared that I'll blow it as I've blown so many other relationships. I'm insanely in love with my beautiful partner, hence my fear. I feel calm with her, warm around her, and happy. Yes, happy. Fertile ground for Bob the Asshole to work his magic. Don't let me blow this one, please God, *not this one*.

We pulled up to Bobbie's building.

CHAPTER 18

Bobbie

Bob and I pulled up to my building at 4 p.m. I'm about to move in with the man I love. So, I should be happy, no? My good old self-doubt was rearing its goddam ugly head. What if our love affair is just that—an affair. What if our dizzy love-making won't withstand the rigors of domesticity? He says he loves me, but does he? I keep myself in pretty good shape, I must admit, and I'm not hard to look at. What if his "love" is nothing more than "lust" for my hot body? We spend all our time together as professional partners, then more time together as lovers. Will this wear off? Will our relationship devolve into a simple working partnership? My self-doubt shield was trying to protect me from disappointment, from unhappiness. Why the fuck do I do this to myself? Why can't I just let my happiness flow to where it wants to go? Why do I need to beat myself up when I should be consumed with joy? Good question.

"My God, you're so neat," Bob said when we walked into my apartment. He looked at the boxes arranged against the wall in order of size. "This place looks like one of your case files, perfectly organized."

I put my self-doubt on hold as I walked up to him, put my arms around his neck, and kissed him. As we stepped back I said, "Hey, don't go anywhere, I want another kiss." I was starting to feel the way I always do around Bob—wonderful. My God, I love this guy. But my goddam self-doubt continued to gnaw at my stomach.

My apartment was furnished, so we didn't have a lot of heavy lifting, just boxes full of clothing and years of keepsakes and mementos. We had two hand trucks, so our move was surprisingly easy. Bob, always the gentleman, insisted that he do most of the lifting. No problem with me. He's big and strong and has a lot of stamina. My God, does he have a lot of stamina—*a lot*.

We pulled up to Bob's building at 5:10 and loaded up the hand trucks. Fortunately, the building had an elevator. The move-in was just as easy as the move-out from my place. We piled the boxes into the large den, and figured we'd do the emptying later. Where the heck is Bob?

"Hey, honey, where are you?"

"I'm in the kitchen, baby. Come here."

I walked into the kitchen and saw Bob kneeling on the floor.

"Planning something kinky?" I said, laughing.

"No, I'm planning something much more long-range."

He reached out, gently grabbed my left hand, and slipped a beautiful diamond ring on my finger.

"Marry me, Detective. Make me the happiest cop on the force."

I knelt and wrapped my arms around him.

"The answer is yes, baby. Oh my God, the answer is *yes, yes, yes*."

"So now we'll be partners forever, Bobbie."

My self-doubt vanished. Bob and I are getting married. I felt so happy I thought I'd faint.

CHAPTER 19

Bob

Because we both love neatness, we decided to take off a half-day to finish unpacking Bobbie's stuff. After working the morning at One PP, Bobbie and I walked to our (yes, *our*) apartment at 1 p.m.

Bobbie walked up to me as I had just picked up a box. Bobbie, my *fiancée*.

"This note was on the side of your computer, honey. It says *DBT*. What the heck does it mean?"

"It's an acronym for an old Navajo phrase," I lied. "It means, 'I love you.'"

What it really means, to me anyway, is "Don't blow this." I memorized it and repeat it to myself constantly. *Bob the Asshole, you've just been fired.*

"That's so cool, baby. I love the word."

"It's the truest thing I've ever said. Believe it."

We spent the next couple of hours unpacking Bobbie's stuff.

Although she had already moved a few boxes here in the past few weeks, I felt great to think that now Bobbie lives here and will be with me full time. We agreed that we'd spend the rest of the evening planning our wedding. God how I loved the sound of that, *our wedding*.

"Hey, honey, what should we do to celebrate our engagement?" I said.

"I'm thinking of an old Navajo word—*SOBO*."

"Sounds nice, Bobbie, what does it mean?"

"Screw our brains out."

We helped each other out of our clothes, walked into the shower, and did just that. *Don't blow this,* I reminded myself.

CHAPTER 20

Bobbie

After our wonderful love-making, Bob and I put on our robes and walked into the kitchen for some soft vanilla yogurt, our favorite post-sex indulgence. Time to start planning our wedding. Yes, *our wedding*. My self-doubt tried to assert itself, but I ignored it as best I could.

I called my parents in Florida. I thought my ear would fall off they both screamed so loud. I had told them all about Bob in emails, along with photographs, and I know they're dying to meet him.

"Bobbie, I think you should keep your maiden name, Nelson. I'd love for you to be known as Mrs. Lawton, but let's face it, you're nationally famous as Detective Nelson and I don't think that should change."

"I think Bobbie Lawton has a nice ring to it, honey. We'll talk about it."

"When should we get married?" Bob asked.

I was about to say, tomorrow, but I wanted Bob to go first. I hoped he didn't want a date far into the future. Self-doubt loves delays.

"How about next month, Bobbie. I think the only issue is giving our folks enough time to plan. It's getting kind of late, so we can work it out with them tomorrow."

Next month!

I leaned over, and kissed him. "That's a great idea, honey, no sense putting off that wonderful day."

"When should we tell the commissioner?" Bob asked, and then added, "There's nothing against regs for cops to be married to each other—just like on *Blue Bloods*."

"We should let Norquist know tomorrow. Something tells me he'll be happy for us."

"I assume we'll get married at St. Mark's," Bob said, referring to the church we always attend when not on assignment. "That nice guy, Father Rick Sampson, the pastor, will be happy to join us in marriage."

"Agreed, Bob. How about the wedding reception?"

"I'm thinking about Cipriani's on 42nd Street, a beautiful place."

"Yes, beautiful, but expensive as hell. We can't expect our folks to foot the bill. Do you have a stash somewhere, honey?"

"Oh, I never mentioned it to you, but now that we're engaged there's something you should know. Ever heard the name Neville Turner?"

"Isn't he that software genius who sold his company to Google?"

"Yes, he was my uncle. He passed on three years ago. He left me a nice inheritance, so you'll be happy to know your fiancé has a few bucks. He left me 15 million. After the divorce settlement with my former wife, I still have 10 million—I mean *we* have 10 million."

"And you're still a cop?"

"Hey, just like you, I love my work. What the hell would I do, sit around and watch TV? Now that I have somebody to share it with, I think we should buy ourselves a nice beach house in the Hamptons so we can get away every now and then."

"No wonder you could afford this beautiful condo."

"I don't just own the condo but the whole building, all eight units."

So, my fiancé is handsome, sexy—and rich. My self-doubt is definitely on hold.

CHAPTER 21

Bob

We walked to the diner to have breakfast—*Together*—*Holding hands*. We even held hands across the table in our booth. I noticed Bobbie place her left hand against her face, so passersby could see her engagement ring. Our fellow cops will need to get used to it.

Then we went right to Commissioner Norquist's office and broke the news.

"So, I was obviously right about you two being an item," the commissioner said. "You were both polite to ask for my permission, but it isn't mine to give because there's no regulation against it. You *do* have my blessing. A lot of police marriages don't work out, but I'm not worried about you two. I think you have a rare relationship, and something tells me that your marriage will actually help your work here. When is the wedding?"

"Saturday, October 12," I said. "Your invitation will soon be in the mail, but please accept this as a formal invitation for you and Marlene."

"I graciously accept. Hey, don't forget to invite Mayor Paxton and his wife. They're quite fond of you two."

So, we've made our big announcement to the boss.

Don't blow this, I repeated to myself. That's becoming a mantra, one that I like because I have every intention of obeying it.

Norquist's intercom sounded. "Deputy Commissioner Franken just called, sir. He requests that the BBs go to his office when they're done with your meeting."

The BBs. I'm kind of getting to like that. Bobbie and Bob, the BBs. And soon to be Mr. and Mrs. BB.

We walked into Tim Franken's office.

"This shit's getting weirder by the minute," he said. "Two more cops, both detectives, have gone missing. Neither showed up for work yesterday or today, and neither one responds to messages. Their names are Bradley Jones and Michael Livingston. Their service records are clean, which doesn't surprise me. The people involved in this have been careful to keep their actions hidden. We do know they may be involved with the kidnapping, because they were both assigned to Gracie Mansion duty recently. Okay, I suggest you hit the road. Here are the addresses. A search warrant for each of their houses will be ready in a few minutes. I suggest you visit each of their homes to talk to the detective who will execute the warrants."

Time to change the subject. "There's something we have to tell you, Tim. Bobbie and I are getting married."

"My God, that's wonderful. You two can make it work. I hope you'll be staying on with the department."

"Yes, we're definitely staying with the NYPD, partners in every sense of the word."

When he said the words, "You two can make it work," he was

mouthing basically the same thing Commissioner Norquist said. Police marriages often do not work.

Bullshit. *Don't blow this.*

We pulled up to a house on Ocean Parkway in Brooklyn, the house that belongs to Detective Bradley. Three detectives and two uniforms were already there. I immediately noticed crime scene tape. Crime scene?

"What have we got, Jack," I said to Detective Muller, the man in charge of the search warrant.

"A picture is worth a thousand words, Bob. Come have a look. Hi Bobbie."

I've noticed Jack Muller ogling Bobbie on several occasions. Get used to it, I told myself. She's a traffic-stopper, so it's normal for men to stare at her.

Muller showed us into the living room. The floor was covered with blood, and I mean covered. He handed us hair covering, which is basically a shower cap, as we put on our latex gloves and booties.

"CSU is on the way," Muller said. "Meanwhile, watch where you step, not that I need to say that to you two."

"I don't see many spatter signs," Bobbie said. "It seems that this may have been caused by a knife up-close. Also, I don't smell any gunpowder. Judging from the quantity of blood, I think this may have been more than one person. The CSU people should be able to tell us soon when they run blood tests. Bob, look at that, the imprint of a torso in the blood. It seems as if the guy was stabbed while he was kneeling facing that way and then fell forward. And notice the footprints. They're only surface indentations, obviously made on top of a carpet or blanket of some sort, which was then probably used to wrap the body and carry it outside. Whoever did this butchering was very careful to conceal evidence."

I was taking notes, which I always do at a crime scene. But my notes were of Bobbie's observations. Every time she opens her mouth at a crime scene, I'm amazed at the things she notices. Have I mentioned that my partner knows her stuff?

"Look at this, Bobbie," I said, happy that I could contribute something. "Bone fragments. It seems like somebody was hacked to death."

"Does anybody know when this happened?" I asked of nobody in particular.

"I'm guessing at least three hours ago judging from the large number of flies," Bobbie said.

Flies? Yes, flies. Detectives spend a huge amount of time working blood evidence, and flies are part of the deal. Blood creates patterns, which can often lead to solving a case. There are three basic types of bloodstains, passive, projected, and transferred. Passive stains are created by a wound that drips blood, obeying the laws of gravity. When a drop hits an object, like a floor, it creates what we call spatter. When it hits, the blood drop often changes into smaller droplets, called secondary spatter.

Projected bloodstains are those caused by something other than gravity, such as squirting from a severed artery, the centrifugal force of a flailing body member, or something else that pushes the blood away from a body, such as a blow from an object like a stick or a bat.

Transferred bloodstains are caused when a bloody object touches something, like a bloody hand against a wall.

"Bob, are you familiar with the formula for finding the angle of impact of blood?" Bobbie asked.

"Of course," I said, as I jotted the trigonometric formula down on my notepad and handed it to Bobbie.

SIN<= width (a) 1.5 cm

Length ©3.0 cm

Width (a) 1,5 cm = SIN<

Length ©**3.0 cm**

0.5 = SIN<

< = 30 degrees

Using that formula, a blood drop that's 1.5 centimeters wide and 30 centimeters long, can be determined to have traveled at a 30-degree angle away from the victim to the point of the blood drop's impact.

"Bob, I cannot believe this. I've used that formula for years, but you've memorized the friggin thing."

"I may not be as smart as my brilliant fiancée, but I know what I'm doing, especially with math. You mentioned something about the flies, Bobbie."

She doesn't miss a trick, and flies aren't just annoying insects; they provide clues, leads, and they convey information. Flies consume the blood of a victim. After they chow down, they move to a warm area of a room, such as a lamp, a sunny window sill, or any other heat source. As part of the digestive process, they regurgitate the meal, allowing enzymes to break down the blood into a more easily digestible substance. The flies later return to finish their meal, all the while leaving specks of blood from their feet and from barfing it up. A fly's presence is shown by dark swiping patterns as well as tiny droplets. Houseflies are lappers, unlike horseflies, which bite. The lapping creates small craters in blood spatter, showing proof of fly activity. It takes a lot of experience, besides training, to figure this shit out. If you misidentify the false spatter in dried blood, it can send you in the wrong direction.

Maggots are also important, if somewhat creepy. They like things warm, and a human body's temperature can rise to 120 degrees Fahrenheit during decomposition. In the hands of a skilled lab technician, maggots can help determine the time of death. You don't see this stuff on TV cop dramas.

"I just noticed another thing," Bobbie said. "Look about three feet from that torso image. There seems to be another one. Yes, definitely, look at the knee imprints. I don't need blood analysis to tell me that two people were killed here. And it was a pretty brutal scene. No guns, just knives or some other cutting instrument. From the bone fragments you noticed, Bob, it may have been an ax."

We decided to let the CSU agents do their work without us in the way. I make sure I know a lot about the CSU people working a scene. Just like anybody, these folks come with a variety of skillsets. I knew the people at this house, so I was okay to leave them on their own. We got in our car to go to the house that belongs (or belonged?) to Michael Livingston, the other missing detective. It was also in Brooklyn, on Tillary Street. After the horror scene we just saw, we braced ourselves for another bloody mess.

When we got to the Tillary Street address, the warrant execution team was already there. We hooked on our shields and walked in.

Nothing. The place was neat, and nothing was out of order.

"Bob, something tells me that the two people who were killed at Bradley's place were Bradley and Livingston. We'll know more when the blood analysis is done. Do you have any theory as to what the hell is going on?"

"Well, we know that Bradley and Livingston as well as Simone and Fitzgerald were all detectives working Gracie Mansion duty, Bobbie. Doesn't that tell us that these are connected to the Mayor's kidnapping? Obviously, Simone and Fitzgerald were connected to it because they did the actual kidnapping themselves. My money is on Bradley and Livingston being involved as well."

"Or someone wants us to *think* that's the case," Bobbie said. "Maybe there's no connection at all."

"Are you suggesting that the NYPD is under some sort of organized attack?" I said.

"Yes, that's exactly what I'm saying."

CHAPTER 22

Bobbie

People tell me I think outside the box. That's true, and I think that's why I'm a good detective, not to brag. Bob always tells me he's amazed how my brain goes in a different direction than others, including his. I think that's why Bob and I work so well together. His logic is dead-on, but my intuition takes us to different conclusions. That's why we play so well off each other. And maybe why we love to play *with* each other.

We just got word from the CSU agents that yes, both Bradley and Livingston were the two people killed at Bradley's apartment. But why? And by whom? Logic—normal logic—tells us the murders of the four detectives are connected. That's what Bob thinks, and his logical analysis leads him there. All four detectives worked at Gracie Mansion, and we know that Simone and Fitzgerald were involved in the mayor's kidnapping because they *did* the actual kidnapping. But my gut tells me that we're being manipulated, that we're being sent up the wrong tree. And I think that we'll soon see some major events that will shake the department to its core. I hope I'm wrong, but I think we're walking East when we should be walking West. Does that make sense? I don't know, but that's where my head is aiming.

Puzzles

Bob just walked into the office after a brief meeting with Tim Franken. I'm going to let my thoughts play with themselves for a while. Among other things, we have our wedding to think about, which is next week. I'm going to head home a bit early. We're going to be finalizing our wedding plans tonight, but first I'm planning a little surprise for Bob.

CHAPTER 23

Bob

I needed to pick up a few things at the store, so I got home about a half-hour after Bobbie. As soon as I walked in, I yelled, "Hi baby."

Bobbie answered from the den. I walked in and saw her standing by the bar pouring a couple of glasses of wine. She was barefoot. The only clothing she wore was a tiny thong bikini bottom and a small blouse that didn't extend further than halfway down her cute little ass. Oh, my goodness. I thought we were going to spend the evening finalizing plans for our wedding next week. Looks like Bobbie has better plans, more exciting plans. I walked up behind her, put my hands on her waist and spoke softly into her ear.

"You must be warm with all that clothing on. Mind if I help you out of them?"

She turned around and put her arms around my neck.

"As long as I can help you out of *your* clothes," she said, as she reached down and unbuckled my belt.

"I want to make sure you don't change your mind about our

wedding next week. I don't want your mind wandering."

I took a quick shower to wash away the stress of today, and to welcome the excitement of tonight.

This was much more fun than working on wedding reception logistics. We gradually made our way into the bedroom. After a wild wonderful hour, we both dozed off. I woke and put my arm around her. Her back was against me, and her shoulders were shaking. She was crying.

"Everything okay, honey?"

"I'm fine," she sniffled.

"Am I that bad a lover that it makes you cry?"

"Don't be silly," she said, as she started crying more heavily.

Something was obviously going on, and it wasn't something good. I wrapped both arms around her and kissed the back of her neck. I had the feeling that words weren't needed—or wanted. But the silence, not to mention the crying, began to bother me, so I asked my question again.

"Is everything okay, honey?"

"No, it isn't. Bob, I was so looking forward to our evening together, working on the last-minute details of our wedding. Then what did I do? I greeted you all tarted-up like a whore in heat. I'm sorry, honey, I'm so sorry."

"Bobbie, we have a wonderful relationship, and one of the great parts of that relationship is our love life. You can greet me half naked like that whenever you want. I have no idea what you mean about acting like a whore in heat. You were simply showing me one part of our relationship—strong physical attraction. You were just communicating to me, in a beautiful way, that you wanted to make love."

"But why the hell did I say that stupid goddam thing about not wanting your mind to wander before our wedding, like I was worried you would look elsewhere or stray? Why do I say shit like that?"

"Is it that self-doubt stuff you've mentioned from time to time?"

"I'm afraid it is. I may mention it from time to time, but I feel it—*all* the time."

"Bobbie, let's look at a few things. You have a world-class education and you're objectively brilliant. And yes, I do mean objectively. You're the smartest person I've ever met, and I'm not just saying that. Ever since we started working together, I've felt like I'm your student, your willing student. And let's talk about something else objectively. You're physically beautiful, the most gorgeous woman I've ever laid eyes on. So, what's this self-doubt all about?"

"Beats the hell out of me, Bob. I'm with a great guy who I'm wildly in love with, and I should be laughing with happiness not crying with doubt. Sometimes I'm afraid to grab for the golden ring on the merry-go-round because I'm worried I'll pull my goddam finger off. I think I use self-doubt as a defense mechanism. If something turns out bad that I wanted to turn out right, I can say to myself, well I doubted this and so I shouldn't be surprised. I was really in love with that violent drunk shithead I married a few years ago. I had no doubt about our relationship —at first. But then I realized I should have doubted it from the get-go. So here I am, having turned our lovely evening into a Bobbie head-shrink fest. I'm so sorry, baby."

"Hey, remember when I told you about my Navajo phrase DBT? I told you it means *I love you*, and in a way it's true. But what it really means is 'Don't blow this.' I've screwed up relationships in the past, including my father and my first wife among many others. So now I repeat that phrase to myself constantly, as a sort of mantra. *Don't blow this*. The *this* in that phrase means our relationship, Bobbie.

I'm committed to being your partner for life, in the office and at home. And don't even think about doubting that. Maybe we should come up with a mantra for your self-doubt. How about *DDT—Don't doubt this?*"

She was smiling and breathing softly, no longer upset.

"Have I mentioned how much I love you, Bob? *Don't doubt this.* I kind of like that. I'm feeling better—thanks to you, baby."

We walked into the den in our robes.

"Hey, let's talk about our wedding next week," Bobbie said. "And *I don't doubt this.* We're getting married, honey. So, you forgive me for greeting you as a half-naked floozy tonight?"

"Forgive you? I loved it. I'll even help you pick out a few outfits, maybe one for the office."

"Now *there's* an exciting thought."

We walked to the couch. She stretched out her beautiful legs and perched her pretty little feet on a cushion, laying her head on another cushion on my lap.

"Bob, this will sound like an exaggeration, but I feel like I've been transformed tonight after my talk with you. Thank you for helping me work through that shit, baby."

"Hey, hon, that's what partners are for. That's what lovers are for. That's what I'm for—*for you.*"

"*I don't doubt this*, Bob."

"And *I will not blow it.*"

I have a hard time believing that a short time ago I was prepared to hate this woman. Now I love her more than life itself.

CHAPTER 24

Bobbie

ast night started out great, with some fabulous love-making. Then I disappeared into my head and turned a lovely evening to shit with my mental jujitsu. But the night was resurrected into one of the best nights of my life. I wasn't kidding Bob when I told him that I felt transformed by our talk. He guided me through the weird crap I allowed myself, and even came up with a mantra I intend to live with. *Don't doubt this.* And no way do I doubt Bob, the most amazing man in my life. *Don't doubt this.* I like it.

We walked to the diner for breakfast. This time we didn't hold hands but walked with our arms around each other. *The BBs.* When we got to the diner, Tim Franken joined us along with his assistant Joan Bracken. Last week I had shared with Tim a couple of my thoughts on the recent police murders, but we didn't go near the subject in the diner. Tim, God bless him, is an absolute stickler for keeping sensitive stuff under wraps, as it should be. Tim was scheduled to be out of the office all day for a conference, so Bob and I would get to brainstorm by ourselves, just the way we like it. You would think, with the relationship Bob and I have, that going to work would be a drudge. Far from it. I've always loved my work, but with Bob it isn't just enjoyable—it's fun.

Puzzles

Last night, after we made love and I had my psychotherapeutic breakthrough, we actually did get some of our wedding planning done. We found that we had little to do, having done much of it weeks ago. When you deal with a place like Cipriani, they do most of the work for you. My folks from Miami and Bob's from Boston would arrive tomorrow. The wedding is the day after. Bob and I would be on vacation starting tomorrow, so we planned to take our folks for a tour of New York City. My folks know the city well, but we figured we'd give them a tour so they could get to know Bob's folks, not to mention Bob. I thought we could use one of the NYPD big black SUVs but Tim the stickler wouldn't hear of it, so we didn't even ask him. We would rent a comfortable passenger van from Hertz.

After we left the diner, Bob had to stop by the records office to pick up a file. He walked into our office a few minutes after me. I was standing next to a file cabinet with my back to the door.

"What, no thong?" He said.

"Later, baby."

CHAPTER 25

Bob

I decided to call an old high school friend who had recently started a touring company, Sterling Tours. Tommy Orzo knows the City of New York as if he designed the place, even better than me. What better way to show our folks around than to leave it in the hands of a pro? Bobbie and I hate city driving. Best left to someone who knows what he's doing, like Tommy Orzo. The Lawtons and the Nelsons stayed at the New York Hilton. They got to know each other in the short time they waited for us, and when we picked them up, they were like old pals. They were all in their early 60s. Bobbie's folks ran a real estate brokerage in Miami and my parents owned a small casualty insurance company in Boston. Their income was supplemented by a substantial inheritance from Uncle Neville. It was great being with my folks, whom I hadn't seen in almost six months. My dad and I talked nonstop. I still can't remember what had come between us so many years ago, and I didn't want to recall it, whatever it was. Even assholes like me eventually grow up.

As we drove through the city, listening to Tommy's great narration, I was amazed at how many locations I had worked as crime scenes over the years. Some of the scenes were gruesome as hell and we skipped over telling them about it. When we passed the Manhattan

Mosque, neither Bobbie nor I made mention of the case.

As I looked at Bobbie's parents I could see where she got her good looks from, especially her mom.

As we rounded a corner, the street was blocked by at least 10 patrol cars. Bobbie and I looked at each other. We may be on vacation, and we may be taking our folks on a pleasant tour, but we both had a look of recognition on our faces, a look that said, "We're cops."

"We'll be right back," Bobbie and I said simultaneously as we got out of the van. We walked up to one of the uniforms standing outside a store and flashed our shields.

"What's going on, officer?" Bobbie said.

"Five dead bodies," he said.

"Robbery?" I asked.

"We don't think so, Detective, but we really don't know anything yet. Three of the five bodies are cops."

Bobbie looked at me.

"In all your years on the force, Bob, have you ever gone through a couple of weeks with so many dead cops?"

No, I hadn't, but then I had an unsettling thought—*we're* cops.

"Who's in charge?" I asked.

"Detectives Wright and Swanson."

Bobbie and I knew them both well. We figured it would be piss-poor taste to horn in on their investigation, especially because it wasn't our assignment.

"When we get back from our honeymoon, I want to huddle with Wright and Swanson," Bobbie said. "I have one of my gut feelings that there's a connection to what we're working on."

We got back into the van as a cop began to wave traffic through.

"Do you two ever relax?" Bobbie's dad said.

"Quite a bit, actually," I said, as I recalled our wonderful night of sex just a few hours ago.

We continued our journey through the Queens Midtown Tunnel, heading for Whitestone to see the house the Nelsons once owned, the place where Bobbie grew up. I had seen the place before when we worked the Paxton kidnapping matter a couple of blocks away, but this time I was able to take it in without the distraction of the nearby crime scene.

"I can't believe I grew up two blocks from here, on Ryan Court," Tommy said. "Much prettier name than 147th Street. Hey, wait a minute, I know you folks, even though I was a little kid at the time. You used to own a big red Cadillac, is that right?"

"That's us, Tommy," Bobbie's dad said. "Hey, were you the little kid who always wore a baseball uniform with two hats, one bill facing forward, the other backwards?"

"That's me," Tommy said. "I hope my apparel has improved since then."

"Please pull over, Tommy," Bobbie said as we approached the house where she grew up.

We looked at the place, a typical nondescript Queens house, separated from the neighboring houses by a 15-foot-wide driveway.

"I remember you riding your tricycle up and down that driveway," Maggie Nelson said.

"Was she as pretty as a kid as she is now?" I asked.

Mike Nelson laughed. "She was a scrawny tomboy."

"I remember her too," Tommy said. "She was a few years older than me, but I think I was in love with her. I didn't think she looked scrawny at all."

I was enjoying every minute of this. I looked at my beautiful fiancée and tried to picture her as a skinny little kid on a tricycle. I hope they have some old photos stashed somewhere.

"Hey, remember the big burglary?" Maggie said.

Bobbie laughed and nodded.

"Bob, that's when we knew our little girl would grow up to be a famous detective. There had been a burglary a few houses down from us. Bobbie posted herself outside the police tape and watched everything that went on. She yelled to one of the cops, 'Hey, don't forget *that,*' she said, pointing to a bag lying under a hedge. It turns out that the bag was the most important piece of evidence at the scene. It contained a gun and a wallet belonging to the burglar. So, our Bobbie was solving crimes when she was 10 years old."

"Why does that not surprise me?" I said as I squeezed Bobbie's hand.

We both agreed that our tour was a great idea, and we thanked Tommy, our tour guide, and tipped him heavily.

After our tour we had a quiet dinner at Balthazar, an elegant restaurant on the Spring Street. I spent the time getting to know Bobbie's parents and she got to know mine. Just as I felt about Bobbie shortly after we met, I felt like I've known her folks for years. We enjoyed becoming part of our soon-to-be-expanded families.

In less than 24 hours, Bobbie and I would be husband and wife.

CHAPTER 26

Bobbie

The day of our wedding arrived, and I was so happy I thought I'd pass out.

Bob finally convinced me to keep my maiden name, Nelson. I've been thinking about a book project, and we both thought that the name Bobbie Nelson, having been in the news so often, would help to sell books. Bob, my best-selling partner, would co-author it with me. Maybe we'll put "the BBs" on the author spot on the cover.

Our friend, Father Rick Sampson, greeted us at the door of St. Mark's Episcopal Church, where he was the pastor. Bob and I always attend mass at St. Mark's when we're not on assignment. We love his sermons, which are inspirational and laced with humor. We always get a kick out of one of his favorite sayings as he tries to emphasize Christian reality: "None of us are getting out of here alive." Father Rick is a big burly man with a face that's never without a smile. He also has a booming laugh.

My dad looked totally happy as he walked me down the aisle. I think his happiness was compounded by his memory of that wife-beating sack of shit I once married. Bob stood there with a stunning smile, looking as handsome as I'd ever seen him. Nothing wrong with being wildly infatuated with the man you love.

When Father Rick said, "You may kiss the bride," I thought I'd do a cartwheel. It's not like Bob and I weren't used to kissing, far from it; it's just that we would now kiss as man and wife.

When we walked into Cipriani for the reception, we were amazed by their attention to detail. A line of waiters and waitresses greeted us with champagne glasses and hors d'oeuvres. One hundred people attended the wedding, mainly Bob's friends from the force. My New York contacts had pretty much dissolved over the years. My good friend Janice Patton from Chicago was there with her husband Jason. Frank Jackson, my former partner in the Chicago PD, came with his wife, Millie. Frank's getting up there in years, and I think he's planning on retiring.

A few dignitaries were there, most notably Mayor Paxton and his wife, Nancy, along with Commissioner Ralph Norquist and his wife, Marlene. Our temporary boss, Deputy Commissioner Tim Franken was there with his wife, Karen.

When Bob asked me to dance, we both realized that we had never danced together before. Typical of Bob, he glided me around the floor with total grace. I told him his middle name should be "Astaire." Then, came a fast rock & roll tune. I couldn't get over how Bob did a mean Lindy. Janice Patton and her husband, Jason, danced next to us.

We returned to our apartment — *our* apartment — at 11:30. I headed straight for the shower and then put on my wedding-night best, a see-through negligee. I was diligently working on my born-again flooziness. If Bob likes it, I'll wear it — or take it off. Although we were both exhausted, we made love until the morning light.

The next day we would board the *Queen Mary 2* for a cruise to England.

CHAPTER 27

Bob

B obbie and I boarded the *Queen Mary 2* at 3 p.m. at Pier 90 on 52nd Street. It was a beautiful ship, and big. We had booked a large stateroom with a balcony overlooking the ocean. The room was 20 by 30 feet, and came equipped with a hot tub for two, a detail we both made sure not to overlook when we signed up. The October day was crisp, with temperatures in the mid-60s, the kind of day that filled your lungs with a sweet feeling, hinting ever so gently at the winter to come. We left the balcony door open to let in the fresh breeze. Even though we were in mid-Manhattan, there was no trace of foul city air.

After we unpacked, Bobbie went into the bedroom. What was she going to surprise me with? As I stood on the balcony looking out at the activities on the pier, I felt two arms wrap around my waist.

"Hey, honey, like my new outfit?"

She was naked.

We had intended to watch the departure festivities from the upper deck when the ship left the pier in an hour, but, thanks to my imaginative wife, we had better things to do. We climbed into the hot tub, Bobbie straddling me with her beautiful legs as I caressed her little ass, the water lapping at our bodies. We mutually climaxed as the ship's horn sounded. Is there a better way to start a cruise?

We decided to take a walk on deck to watch the Manhattan scenery as we steamed down the Hudson River. There's something about a walk in the open air after making love. Even for a couple of New Yorkers, the view of Manhattan from the Hudson was breathtaking. The temperature had dropped to 60 degrees, and we wore light sweaters to accommodate the chill. As we rounded Battery Park, Frank Sinatra's *New York, New York* played over ship's the sound system, his voice resonating off the canyons of Manhattan.

We took dinner at one of the sit-down restaurants with table service rather than the buffet. We had both been on cruises before and we knew it's easy to put on pounds on the buffet line. The *maître d* escorted us to a table with a great ocean view as the sun dipped reluctantly toward the horizon. A well-dressed couple sat at the table. They looked like they were in their 50s or early 60s. The man introduced themselves as Tom and Mildred Cunningham.

"And what do you folks do?" Tom asked, engaging in small talk.

"We're detectives with the NYPD," Bobbie said. "Bob and I are partners and we're also on our honeymoon, so we're partners in more ways than one."

"Hey, wait a minute, I know you folks. I've read a lot about you," Tom said, "New York's favorite detective team. I've heard you referred to as the *BBs*. And you, Bobbie, are probably the most famous detective in the country."

"Well, my inspiration is sitting next to me," she said in her typical sweet way.

"I've been meaning to get in touch with you two," Tom said, as he fidgeted with an electronic cigarette.

"I hope you don't want us to fix a parking ticket," I said.

He laughed. "No, I want to talk to you about a book proposal. I'm the editor-in-chief at Random House, and Mildred is senior editor. I can't believe it's such a coincidence that we're dining together. How is this for a great idea? A book about the fine art of being a police detective—written by two of the best detectives in the business. I even have a title in mind—*Detectiving.*"

"*Detectiving?*" Bobbie said, laughing. "Is that a word in the English language?"

"It will be when I make your book a hit."

"Tom, this sounds exciting," I said, "but there are a lot of trade secrets we can't write about. We're the good guys with guns and our job is to chase the bad guys with guns."

"I understand," Tom said. "I envision a book mainly about war stories, and you two sure have a lot of stories to tell. Also, a lot of police-work details are publicly known, so you won't be blowing any secrets. And from Bobbie's articles I've read, there are of lot of exciting things you can write about."

"I've also read your articles in the *Daily News*, Bobbie." Mildred said, as she patted Bobbie's hand. "Just the kind of stuff we're thinking about."

Wow, these two have done their homework. Obviously, they're serious. I think this is a great idea, but I wanted to talk to Bobbie about it alone.

"Hey, folks, I don't want to interrupt your honeymoon talking business, but Mildred and I want to get together with you when we get back to New York. You have the basic idea—a book about what you two do so expertly for a living. There are millions of authors out there who love to write detective novels. Your book can become their bible. I feel a best-seller in my bones."

After dinner, Bobbie and I had a drink at one of the ship's bars. Neither of us likes to perch on barstools, so we sat at a small table next to a window. The sun had been replaced by a full moon.

"So, what do you think, Bobbie?"

"I love this idea, Bob, especially the part about writing a book with you."

"We have a few bucks, God knows, but from what the Cunninghams said, we may be looking at a lot more. And it will be a blast. You're a hell of a writer, Bobbie, and you can teach me some more good stuff."

"Let's go to our room, baby. I've got a few things I want to teach you."

CHAPTER 28

Bobbie

The last thing I expected from a cruise was a pitch for a book proposal from a big-time editor from a big-time publisher. I think I love the idea, and Bob seems to feel that way too. If Bob loves it, I'm in.

What I *did* expect from our honeymoon cruise was a lot of playing around. Since we fell in love, the relationship between Bob and me has been anything but celibate, but there's something about a romantic sea cruise that gets the juices flowing. And *my* juices were definitely flowing and, I noticed, so were Bob's. Thanks to the psychological coaching from my new hubby, my self-doubt is under control, and I want to keep it that way. *Don't doubt this*—Bob's new mantra for me. And what I definitely don't doubt is how I feel all the time on this cruise. All I have to do is think about my handsome new husband and I'm good to go—like now, *right now*.

Bob had gone below to get a new book from the library. Where the hell is he? I used the time to look for my next outfit. I chose the skimpiest thong bikini I could find, one that Bob loves. When I heard him at the door, I bent over the hot tub to turn on the water and give Bob a nice view of my ass.

"Did you find a good book, honey," I said as I walked up to him.

"Yeah, but suddenly I've lost all interest in reading," he said as he removed my top.

Even without a publishing deal, this is a great cruise. My self-doubt is nowhere to be found.

CHAPTER 29

Bob

We haven't talked shop once since we left New York. Most people would think that's a good thing. Why interrupt a honeymoon cruise with talk about work?

But Bobbie and I aren't most people. We're enjoying world-class passion on this cruise, but we both know we want to talk shop—because we love our work, besides each other.

"Hey, honey," I said. "you still haven't told me about your breakthrough idea on the mayor's kidnapping and the cop killings. All you said was that you think the events may not be related."

"I'm convinced they're not related, Bob. I'm convinced somebody wants us to *think* they're all related, and if we think that way, we head in the direction somebody wants us to go. Okay, we know that Detectives Simone and Fitzgerald are involved in the kidnapping because they're the ones who actually pulled it off. Then the other two guys who were on Gracie Mansion duty were murdered. So naturally, we think they were involved as well. I don't think so. I think the deaths of Bradley and Livingston had nothing to do with the kidnapping, even though they were on Gracie Mansion duty. Somebody wants to kill cops, and my gut tells me it's someone or some group on the force—or maybe *not* on the force."

"Bobbie, do you ever think *inside* the box?"

"Sometimes but not often, and this is one of the times I'm definitely thinking *outside the box*."

"Okay, sign me up. Let's proceed on the theory that the cop killings are unrelated to each other, or at least unrelated to the kidnapping, except for Simone and Fitzgerald, of course."

"And I'm not so sure about Simone and Fitzgerald."

"What? Hey, Bobbie, they were on night watch duty when the Paxtons went missing. And they went missing as well. How can you not see the obvious connection with them? Hell, the Paxtons *told* us it was them."

"Yes, the Paxtons were taken from the mansion by those guys. But then both detectives were murdered. Somebody doesn't want us to know who the management team is."

"I really want to write that book with you. I should say, I really want to *help you* write it. You, lady, are just plain brilliant. Is it dumb to say it's an honor working with you?"

"Hey, sweetheart, you're my husband, my partner, and my lover. Don't give me any of that *honor* crap."

"Okay, honey. But it's a nice feeling to totally respect the person I'm in love with. I mean that. Sorry, but I do feel honored."

"Then honor me by taking your clothes off and joining me in the hot tub."

"It will be my honor."

CHAPTER 30

Bobbie

This morning our ship is scheduled to tie up in Southampton, England. Bob and I will then take a bus to London. The cruise was one-way only and we'll return to New York by plane.

It will be my first time in England, and I'm excited. Commissioner Norquist has set us up to meet Nigel Blackwell, the Commissioner of the Metropolitan Police Service (MPS) of London, better known as Scotland Yard.

Bob and I agreed our honeymoon cruise was fabulous, and the vacation isn't over yet.

As we boarded the bus and walked toward the back, I noticed a knapsack on a seat. I've spent my entire adult life *seeing something* and *saying something*, so I walked back to the driver and told him about the unattended knapsack.

"Ah wunna worry about it, mum. Someone will claim it."

Bullshit. I didn't say that of course. I shouted to the few passengers on the bus, "Unattended package." I grabbed Bob by the sleeve. "Come on, honey, we're getting off." A few fellow passengers did likewise.

I dialed the Uber number on my cellphone. As we waited for the car, we listened to a news report on my phone. A bus had just exploded as it entered the road to London. Bob and I hugged. What else was there to do? We just missed being killed. When the car pulled up, I told the driver to take us to the nearest police station so I could report seeing the unattended knapsack on the bus. Hey, I'm a cop. I figured I should save my local counterparts some investigation time and point them in the right direction.

After I reported the incident to the detective-in-charge at the police station, we called another Uber car and continued on our way to London. My phone rang. It was the detective in Southampton I had spoken to about the knapsack on the bus. She called to let us know that the bus that exploded was an empty tour bus, and the explosion was caused by an electrical fire. The driver, the only person on the bus, wasn't injured. She wanted to put our minds at rest, and once again thanked me for my report. Discovering that you didn't narrowly miss being killed is one of life's more pleasant moments.

"Looks like I was being overly cautious, Bob."

"Hey, Wonder Woman, you did precisely the right thing. Precisely."

At 2 p.m. we pulled up to the Scotland Yard Building in Victoria, London. The name on the sign in front said, "New Scotland Yard." Why the hell would they change such an iconic name just because they moved?

A friendly bobby escorted us to the commissioner's office. How cool is that? Two cops named Bob and Bobbie being escorted by a cop called a bobby. I had read that British police are called bobby because a man named Robert Peel organized the first English police department in the nineteenth century. Hence, bobby is short for

Robert. English cops are sometimes called peelers, but bobby is the commonly used name. The Brits are great with language.

We were seated in an anteroom to the Commissioner Blackwell's office. Blackwell himself came out to greet us and apologized that he had just received an urgent phone call and would need a few minutes to handle it. I've noticed over the years that shit doesn't announce itself before it hits the fan. Hey, when you have a big job like his, duty demands attention. He mentioned that he had just read an article about us in the *New York Times Magazine* online. Bob and I had been interviewed extensively for the article, but we didn't expect it to be published until next month. With typical British efficiency he told his assistant to make two paper copies of the article so Bob and I could read it as we waited. Of course, we could have read the article on our phones, but we didn't want to be impolite after his kind gesture.

We cracked up when we read the title of the article: "The BBs – New York City's Dynamic Detective Duo." The article was written by the two reporters who interviewed us. We had gotten along well with them but were surprised that the article read as if it were written by our own PR firm. Looks like the BBs is our official name. Those reporters obviously liked us. It dwelled extensively on a few of the larger cases we worked on, including matters before we became partners. At the beginning of the article was a photo of Bob and me holding hands. On page three was a shot of us kissing. I didn't remember them taking that picture, but I thought it was great. It captured the essence of our partnership. The article went on and on praising us to the hilt. After we finished reading the article, Bob grabbed my hand.

"When we meet with that Cunningham guy from Random House," Bob said, "I think we should hold out for a big advance."

After 20 minutes, Commissioner Blackwell escorted us into his office. It was a large room, about 30 by 35 feet, and decorated in rich wood tones, like something from the nineteenth century. All the furniture was red leather. Nigel Blackwell looked like a British official out of central casting. He wore an expensive wool suit, from Savile Row no doubt. His slightly gray hair was coifed, looking like he had just come from a salon. An aging Irish Setter bounded over to us, his tail wagging in welcome. His name was Winston.

"It's an honor to meet you folks," he said, speaking in perfect Queen's English. I don't think he'd fit in on the *New Yawk* Police Department. "As I'm sure you know, there has been a lot of cooperation between Scotland Yard and the NYPD over the years. I speak to Commissioner Norquist often. After reading that article about you two in *The New York Times*, I think that Norquist may bill me for the time speaking to him. You're a couple of genuine American heroes. I think you two should write a book. It will become required reading in police departments around the world."

His lips to God's ears, I thought, as I remembered we'd be soon meet with a big book publisher. Blackwell was a total gentleman, and we enjoyed hanging around with him. He personally took us on a tour of the building, which Bob and I found fascinating. To our surprise, Winston joined us on the tour, licking my hand constantly. As I looked at the computers and other devices, I could see how there is a lot of cooperation between Scotland Yard and the NYPD. They even use Microsoft Office.

I noticed a package on the floor and was about to open my loud mouth, but it was immediately picked up by a clerk. As we prepared to leave, we asked Blackwell to contact us the next time he's in New York. I hope he takes us up on it. As a detective, I always think of myself as a permanent student, always learning new things. This tour was an important part of my education. Winston appeared to be sad that we were leaving.

That evening, Bob and I caught a performance of the *Phantom of the Opera* at a theater on the West End. Just as good as Broadway, we both agreed, maybe even better. We had great seats in the 10th row. After the play we had dinner at Quo Vadis, a restaurant in Soho. We stayed at the Ham Yard Hotel, a beautiful five-star place right nearby. After our day of traveling and touring we were exhausted. But not too exhausted. Hell, we're never *too* exhausted. Bob reminded me that we were still on our honeymoon as he helped me out of my dress, not that I needed reminding. We would catch our flight to New York from Heathrow Airport in the morning.

It's good we had such an enjoyable evening. It helped prepare us for the shock that awaited us the next day.

CHAPTER 31

Bob

We landed at JFK at 7:05 p.m. It was a Saturday, so we would have the next day to catch our breaths before hitting the office. During the flight, Bobbie and I talked nonstop about our planned book, *Detectiving*. Totally weird name, but what do I know about book marketing. The novel I wrote, *An Army of Blue*, really took off, but I let my publisher worry about the marketing. I *did* come up with the title myself, and the publisher liked it. I began to think about another crime novel I've been toying with. I think I'll pattern the heroine character after Bobbie. But I really need to get working on it. No book has ever written itself.

We planned to meet with the Cunninghams at Random House later in the week.

As we walked out to meet our Uber, I grabbed a copy of *The New York Times* from a newsstand. I stopped dead in my tracks when I read the headline on the first page.

"Three More NYC Police Officers Killed."

I scrolled through the article, reading aloud for Bobbie to hear.

"Holy shit. It says here that four others were killed last week. We were on our cruise and didn't hear about it. My God, we're up to 11 dead cops in the past month alone, seven while we were away. Looks like we've got some work cut out for us."

We got home at 8:45. After what we read in the *Times*, neither of us felt like we were still on our honeymoon.

CHAPTER 32

Bobbie

We just enjoyed the greatest honeymoon either of us could have imagined. But it ended abruptly last night when we read about the latest cop murders. It's Sunday morning, and we're technically still on vacation, but Bob and I knew we just had to do something, Sunday or not. Shit, seven cops killed within two weeks. At nine I called the commissioner's office. I wasn't surprised when Norquist picked up.

"We'll be there in a few minutes," I said.

"Hey, Bobbie, you two are still on your honeymoon. It can wait till tomorrow."

"And what are *you* doing at One PP on a Sunday morning?" I said as I holstered my Glock. "We'll be there shortly."

Although Bob and I like to enjoy a leisurely breakfast on Sundays after church, we just picked up a couple of bagels and headed for the Plaza. This case had our attention, to say the least. Hell, we didn't even make love last night.

When we walked into Norquist's office, he stood, something he seldom does at a meeting in his office. He looked tired.

"This fucking department is under attack. You two took a couple of weeks off for your honeymoon, and what did you come back to? A mountain of shit. Seven cops were murdered in two weeks, a total of eleven in the past month, and we don't have a clue."

Not a clue? That's because Bob and I haven't started working on it yet.

"Commissioner," I said. "from *The New York Times* article yesterday, it seems that all of the murders were done execution-style with a bullet to the back of the head. Is that accurate?"

"Yes, that's accurate. The recent seven murders look like well-planned hits, just like the four before them. I'm glad you're back, Bobbie and Bob. Nobody's better than you two at picking the fly shit out of the pepper. You and Bob are still on your honeymoon and here you are at work on a Sunday. I wish I had more detectives like you guys. By the way, I loved that article about you two in the Times. The title got it right — 'The BBs–New York City's Dynamic Detective Duo.' You two are the best."

"Bob and I are going to hole up in our office and start digging. The first thing we need to look at are the personnel files of the victims."

"There's got to be a pattern. There's got to be."

"Don't worry, Commissioner. Bob and I will figure this out."

"I know you don't come to conclusions until you've gone over the evidence, but do you have any theory you're working on?"

"Terrorism," I said. I thought he'd pee in his pants when I said that. Bob stared at me. I think I caught him by surprise as well.

"Yes, Commissioner, I'm zeroing in on terrorism as a working hypothesis. So where do we go with that hypothesis? We'll know as we work the evidence."

Bob and I were scheduled to be interviewed on TV the next day.

CHAPTER 33

Bob

G ood afternoon, ladies and gentlemen, and welcome to *The Ellen Bellamy Show*. I'm, your host, you guessed it, Ellen Bellamy. My guests are a newly married couple who are not only terrific people to talk to but are amazing at what they do. I'm speaking about two New York City detectives who have become famous for the way they work, Bobbie Nelson and Bob Lawton. The police commissioner has nicknamed them the *BBs*, and a recent article in *The New York Times* made it public. When they married, they agreed that Bobbie would keep her maiden name, Nelson, because she had become nationally famous as a Chicago police detective, and her name would help to sell a book that she and Bob are working on. Bob is already a best-selling author of a crime novel entitled, *An Army of Blue*, which I enjoyed and highly recommend. I can't wait to read their new book. Welcome to my show, Bob and Bobbie."

Ellen Bellamy hosts the most popular show on daytime television. She and her producers have well-earned reputations for booking timely programs. I guess Bobbie and I fit the bill as timely. Ellen is a tall, pretty blond with amazing skills at interviewing people. It's been said of her that she could get a snail to talk. She'd make a good detective.

"So, you two have just recently returned from your honeymoon. Two detective partners who are now marriage partners—a real NYPD romance. Somebody should make a movie about you guys. Bobbie, you were one of the first detectives hired by the New York Police Department from another state after the famous scandals broke out. Please tell us about it."

"Police Commissioner Norquist flattered me by coming to Chicago to have lunch with me and offer me a job with the NYPD. I would have said yes on the spot, but he invited me to fly to New York before making up my mind. I was born and raised in New York City, in Whitestone, Queens, so it didn't take much persuading to get me to join the force. A nice increase in pay helped convince me. The commissioner partnered me with this handsome guy, so Bob and I often refer to Mr. Norquist as Commissioner Yenta. We hadn't worked a month together when we fell in love and Bob proposed."

Bobbie has been on TV so many times she's a natural. Articulate, funny, and camera-hugging beautiful. Ellen seemed to want to direct most of her questions to Bobbie, which I didn't mind at all. I find Bobbie much more interesting than me.

"Bob, tell us about your first encounter with your pretty partner."

"Frankly I was expecting a difficult, overbearing personality, given her fame. But I was happy to be her partner by the end of our first day together on the job. I've never met a more thorough professional. Besides her obvious good looks, I was attracted to her brilliant mind. Bobbie may be a tough cop, but she's also sweet and polite. Safe to say, Bobbie's my partner in every sense of the word."

I was enjoying saying those things about Bobbie on national TV, happy to share my thoughts with the viewing audience.

"People who work together often say that they never seem to stop talking shop," Ellen said. "Care to comment on that?"

"Bob and I often talk about the cases we're working on, and we don't think of it as a negative, even when we're at home. Besides loving each other, we love our work. We love to solve puzzles. So why not talk about it?"

"That's exactly the way I look at it," I said. "The night we came back from our honeymoon cruise we heard about the murders of seven more police officers that happened when we were gone. The next day, a Sunday, we went to our office to begin our investigation, even though we were still on our honeymoon. It didn't bother us, didn't upset us. It was just part of what we do, solve crimes."

"I suppose you can't tell us much detail about the investigation, Bob."

"No, we can't, as I'm sure you understand, Ellen."

"I'm not unfamiliar with law enforcement matters," Ellen said. "As I'm sure you know, my husband Rick is the Secretary of Homeland Security. You won't be surprised when I tell you that Rick is a big fan of the both of you."

Did I hear that right? None other than the Secretary of Homeland Security is a fan of ours? I hoped Ellen wasn't just being polite by saying that.

"Bob and Bobbie, thank you so much for being on my show. I know that I speak for every New Yorker when I say, please keep up the good work and keep our city safe."

As we walked out of the studio Bobbie looked at me and said, "Hey, honey, that was fun. You're a natural on TV. Maybe we should try to get booked more often."

"Something tells me that our appearance on that show is going to impact our investigation, Bobbie—in a big way."

When we got back to our office, we got one of the most important calls we ever received.

CHAPTER 34

Bobbie

When we got back to our office, we watched a replay of our segment of *The Ellen Bellamy Show* on a recording they gave us. I thought Bob looked adorable on TV. But then I always think Bob looks adorable. What else is new?

The phone rang, and I picked it up. I guess I appeared shocked by the way Bob looked at me. "Let me put you on speaker, Mr. Secretary."

"It's Rick Bellamy," I whispered to Bob.

"Good afternoon, Detectives," Bellamy said. "I watched you both on my wife's show. I never miss Ellen's show, and she quizzes me to make sure. It was true what Ellen said this afternoon. I *am* a big fan of you two. The reason for my call is to invite you to meet me at Federal Plaza. I've already cleared this with Commissioner Norquist."

I looked at Bob, who nodded vigorously.

"We'll be there in a few minutes, Mr. Secretary."

Federal Plaza is a short walk from One Police Plaza.

Wow, this is beyond cool. We'll get to meet the famous Rick Bellamy. Maybe I'll ask for his autograph—and maybe he'll ask for mine.

"As we left the studio this afternoon," Bob said, "I mentioned that Ellen's show could have a big impact on our investigation. Do you think this meeting could have something to do with our case?"

"I don't know," I said. "I'm just freaking out that we're going to meet the Secretary of Homeland Security. Did you catch what he said, that he's a big fan of ours just as Ellen said on the show?"

We walked into the Javits building wearing our NYPD shields. Didn't matter, because we still needed to walk through all the beeping, buzzing, clanging sounds of security devices. The Feds are quite cautious.

His assistant escorted us into Bellamy's office, and he stood to greet us.

"Please call me Rick. May I call you Bob and Bobbie or do you prefer BBs?" He said with a laugh.

Looks like BBs is our official name.

"Bob and Bobbie work just fine, Rick," I said.

His office is modest in size, which I expected because his main office is in Washington D.C. He's in New York quite often, I've heard, probably so he can hang around with his pretty wife, Ellen. They own a brownstone in Greenwich Village, not far from our place. They also own a home in Washington. With the millions Ellen makes, they can afford to own houses wherever they want. He motioned for us to sit at a coffee table, where he poured us water. He's quite a gentleman, as I had always heard about him.

"I've followed your careers, I must say, not just out of curiosity, but for tips on how to perform complex investigations. You two impress the hell out of me, as well as a lot of other people in Federal law enforcement, especially here at Homeland Security. Ralph Norquist wanted me to promise not to steal you away from the NYPD. I politely refused to make that promise. But that's a conversation for another time. What I want to see you folks about, and watching Ellen's show triggered it for me, is the rash of police murders we've been experiencing. Let me see if I've got this right."

He then took five minutes recounting each of the murders detail by detail, and he did it all from memory. Easy to be impressed with this guy. I know *I* was. From the look on Bob's face I knew he was too.

His intercom buzzed. "Director Watson is here, sir," his assistant said.

In walked none other than Sarah Watson, Director of the FBI. She was medium height, maybe 5'6", about 60 years old, and wore an expensive business suit. I'd seen her on TV often, and I noticed that she was much more attractive in person. Rick introduced us and motioned Sarah to the coffee table. She insisted that we call her Sarah, not Madam Director. Like Rick Bellamy, she has a reputation for being polite and friendly.

"I was just reviewing the police murders with Bob and Bobbie, Sarah. Did I miss anything?" He said, looking at me.

"No, Rick, you pretty much covered all the bases," I said.

"Without once referring to a note," Bob added.

"Rick has a brain like a file cabinet," Sarah said. "He stores everything in his noggin."

"The FBI, I'm sure you know, is not part of Homeland Security, but Sarah and I work together on a lot of matters. And these police murders have us hitting the alarm button. Are you two aware the NYPD isn't alone in seeing its cops being killed in large numbers?"

"My God," I said. "I read the newspaper every day, and I don't recall seeing anything about police killings in other states, other than normal casualties that are expected."

"That's because most departments are trying to keep it from the press. Let me ask you a question," Sarah said. "In one word, how would you characterize the case you're working on? Bobbi?"

"Terrorism," I said

"Bob?"

"When Bobbie first said that to me, I didn't get it. But I think she's right. We're seeing terrorism, a weird new form of terrorism. What do you think, Sarah?"

"Yes, it's terrorism—terrorism like we've never seen before. Rick agrees."

"I definitely agree," Rick said. "The whole idea about terror is to change people's thinking as well as their behavior. What better way to terrorize a population than to kill the people whose job it is to protect society? I talked to your commissioner about this. In the past month, applications to become a NYPD cop have shrunk to a trickle, and usually the department is swamped with submissions. The same pattern is repeating itself across the nation. People are reading about what appears to be random slayings, and they're rethinking their ideas about a law enforcement career."

"Random is the word, Rick," I said. "When we started to work on these cases—which Bob and I are now treating as one case—we thought we saw a pattern. A number of the murdered cops had been on protective duty at Gracie Mansion, the mayor's residence. We thought we were seeing a clear pattern, not that we could figure it out. But then I realized that somebody *wanted* us to see a pattern. What better way to knock us off the scent?"

"You will find as you get to know her," Bob said, "that when other people are zigging, Bobbie zags."

"I've read that about Bobbie," Sarah said. "How did the *Chicago Tribune* put it? 'Bobbie Nelson has a found a way to solve the unsolvable.' You're one hell of a detective, Bobbie, and Bob here is no slouch either. I'm wondering what are my chances of stealing you away from the NYPD. I know Rick is thinking that too."

"So, here's where we're going with all this," Rick said. "You two are working on 11 cases over which the NYPD has jurisdiction. You've come up with the brilliant idea to treat these separate murders as one case, Bobbie, and you've got me thinking that way too. I'm beginning to think of these cop killings across the *entire country* as one case."

"Maybe we should call them, or it, *The Bobbie Nelson Case*," Bob said. Damn, he's so sweet and flattering.

"Not a bad idea," Sarah said. "Let me now tell you about the plan that Rick and I have come up with. We're going to treat all the cop killings around the country as one central case coordinated by the FBI. We've spoken to Commissioner Norquist about this as well as the police commissioners and chiefs in all major cities. The separate departments will still have legal jurisdiction, of course, for the time being. As you gather evidence and find leads and clues, you will feed it all into the main computer at FBI headquarters in Washington. We have some excellent cyber snoops at the bureau, people who know how to design algorithms to see patterns, and that's exactly what we're looking for, patterns, something that you two come up with regularly."

"But won't this all eventually come under federal jurisdiction with the FBI heading the matter?" I said, as I poured myself another glass of water.

"That just may happen, Bobbie. It just may *have to* happen to keep things coordinated. I've already taken this to the White House. President Fenton, and First Lady Meg, who is also his chief of staff, are on top of this. They get it. Harry Fenton knows a thing or two about fighting terror, and so does Meg. And we're staring at the creepiest form of terror we could ever imagine."

"Don't forget to tell these folks about your plans for them, Sarah."

"Bob and Bobbie, I'm deputizing you two as provisional FBI agents. I've already cleared this with your boss, not to mention the White House. You two will be critical parts of this operation, the *Bobbie Nelson Case*."

"Hey, Sarah," Bob said, "I was being flippant when I suggested that name. I request you don't paint a target on my partner's back."

"Good point, Bob. We won't call it that, although that's how we'll think about it. I know *I* will."

Our amazing meeting came to an end, and Bob and I walked back to One PP. Wow, Bob and I are now FBI Agents. Self-doubt, please be still. Oh, yeah, *don't doubt this*.

CHAPTER 35

Bob

A fter a light dinner, Bobbie and I got back to our apartment at 8:15.

"What a day, Bobbie. First, we were on national TV, then we met Rick Bellamy and Sarah Watson, and then we were sworn in as FBI agents. How do you feel?"

"Like hot stuff. My God, we're federal agents."

"So, it looks like we'll be working the biggest case we could ever imagine, Bobbie. I think Rick Bellamy and Sarah Watson are two sharp people. This isn't just a NYPD matter, but one that involves the entire country, and you're the one who saw it."

"Stop flattering me, baby. You embarrass me. I do admit I think in weird directions, and sometimes it takes us to where we need to be. I can't believe that Watson has gotten the White House involved."

"Bobbie, we're looking at the worst possible terror conspiracy. I mean shit, soon the nation's police departments won't be able to recruit new cops. That's why this has gone all the way to the Oval Office."

"Do you think we'll still be working with Internal Affairs?"

"Yes, for the time being. It still involves cops, bad cops. But this is a hell of a lot bigger than an internal problem. This is terrorism — on a mass scale, Bobbie, and you saw it. You nailed it, honey."

"I'm not sure I feel like I'm a cop or a spy," Bobbie said.

CHAPTER 36

Bobbie

When Bob and I walked into the office after our usual breakfast at the diner, a message was on our desks saying to report to the commissioner's office. Things have changed in the past 24 hours, to say the least. I'm sure Norquist wants to talk to us about our new roles.

When we walked into Norquist's office, we noticed that he was fiddling around with his new Apple watch that his wife, Marlene, bought him for his birthday. He loves messing around with gadgets. Maybe he sees himself as Dick Tracy with his fancy new watch.

"I think you two were great on *The Ellen Bellamy Show* yesterday. If you ever get your own talk show, will you invite me as a guest?"

"I don't think Bob and I are ready to start our own show, Commissioner, but if we do you will be our first guest. We had fun. My mom called and freaked out over our being on national TV. I've been interviewed on TV a lot of times, but yesterday was kind of fun. The country got to meet the BBs. So, let us tell you about our meeting with Rick Bellamy and Sarah Watson."

"I already know most of what went on. Both Bellamy and Watson were polite enough to include me on the details. Shit, the FBI is stealing my two best detectives, so they should at least let me know what's happening."

"Mr. Commissioner, Bob and I still consider ourselves New York City cops, even though we're now provisional FBI Agents."

"Well, it isn't up to you — or me. It's up to the Feds. Last night Sarah Watson told me all about these weird cases and made special note that they're considering them as one case, as you suggested, Bobbie, and not just in New York. I've known Sarah for years, and she's a hell of a fine FBI Director. So, we've gone from thinking about dirty cops to thinking about terrorism. Never in a million years would I have suspected terrorism. But I'm not Bobbie Nelson — Or Bob Lawton. Sarah even brought the issue to the White House. She doesn't miss a trick."

"I didn't think a city detective could become a provisional FBI agent," Bob said.

"It can happen if it's authorized by the White House, which it was. President Fenton listens when Sarah Watson speaks. Speaking of Sarah, she called me this morning to ask me to send you two to FBI headquarters in Washington. Yes, she *asked* me, even though she could have ordered it. Sarah is a polite lady besides being very powerful. My assistant booked you on an 11:30 flight out of JFK. Sarah wants to see you this afternoon. An FBI car will pick you up in the parking lot. At least they aren't hitting *my* budget. You will be staying in Washington for a couple of days at least. I told Tim Franken that you'd be missing from Internal Affairs for a while. It's 8:15. I suggest that you two go home and pack for your trip. Bob, you made a wise choice a few years back to buy a condo so close to One PP. Keep me posted on your schedule."

Our flight landed at Dulles Airport at 12:40. We headed straight for FBI Headquarters and our meeting with Sarah Watson. Neither Bob nor I had any idea what the meeting would be about. Well, of course the big cop-killing case, but we thought we covered most of the bases at our meeting in Rick Bellamy's office.

We were escorted into Sarah Watson's office at 1:30.

Holy shit. Meg Fenton was there, First Lady of the United States. The Feds are definitely taking this case seriously.

"It's a pleasure to meet you two," the First Lady said as she extended her hand. "Sarah has told the President and me all about you. She said that you're the best detectives she's ever encountered, and that's great, because we have a gigantic problem on our hands. Harry, I mean the President, is worried that these police assassinations can get out of control fast, if it's not already out of control. Sarah tells me that you two will be the lead detectives on the matter, even though you're provisional FBI agents. Don't worry about that detail. The President ordered it. By the way, I saw you two on *The Ellen Bellamy Show*. Ellen's a good friend of mine, and I think she did a great job of interviewing you. And you two were terrific. You're definitely partners in every sense of the word. Our country needs you guys, and I know you'll do a great job. I need to run to a meeting. Again, it was a pleasure to meet you, Bob and Bobbie."

Bob and I were enjoying our sudden new status as hot stuff. My God, the First Lady stopped by to see *us*.

A woman FBI agent walked in and Sarah introduced her. Gladys Warren had been with the FBI for 20 years, and from what I would later read about her, she is one sharp agent.

"Gladys is coordinating the cop-killing cases from around the country," Sarah said. "You two will be working closely with her. Besides being an FBI agent, Gladys is also an IT expert. I'm going to ask Gladys to show you around. She'll also fill you in on some recently discovered evidence."

I had once toured the FBI Headquarters years ago when I was on a college trip. But this would be a tour conducted by a seasoned pro, an insider. Come to think of it, I guess Bob and I are now insiders.

"I've heard a lot about you two, to say the least," Gladys said. "Too bad the FBI didn't get to you first before you signed up with the NYPD, but at least we got you as provisional agents. I'm honored to be working with you."

Easy lady to take a liking to. Gladys stood about 5'8," wore her brown hair short, and she had a somewhat stocky build. I noticed a slight scar on her forehead. She always seemed to have a smile on her face, despite the mayhem she deals with every day. Gladys showed us every office in the building. I was impressed by her attention to every little detail.

When we finished the tour, she took us to her office in the IT Department.

"Bobbie, I've heard that you're an expert at designing software algorithms and I think that's great. There's nothing like a well-designed algorithm to sort through tons of complex data. And that's what we have, a tons of complex data."

"Gladys, can you give us an overview of where the case is right now?" Bob said.

"I notice that you call it a case, Bob, singular not plural, and that's exactly how we're looking at it, thanks to Bobbie's analysis—one case consisting of murders in all major cities. Okay, hold onto your hats, because I'm about to lay some heavy stuff on you. In the twenty cities we're looking at, 935 cops have been murdered—in the past month."

I guess Bob and I looked like we were hit by a bus as we sat there wide-eyed. Did I hear right, 935 dead cops in one friggin month? No wonder the White House is involved.

"Gladys, have you come up with anything that can be considered a lead yet?" I asked.

"Yes, one. Yemen."

"Yemen," I almost yelled. "Do you think this may be a foreign terrorist operation?"

"We don't want to make definitive conclusions based on a lead, of course, but that's where we're aiming. I said one lead, but we really have nine, all pointing to Yemen, including hacked emails. So that's what we're thinking."

"Or that's what somebody *wants* you to be thinking," I said.

Bob laughed. "You'll have to get used to Madam Think-Outside-the-Box here, Gladys."

"Bobbie, I've read about your powers of analysis. Feel free to question our assumptions. I mean, *please* feel free to do so. Your theorizing is what put this case on the map. I don't doubt for a minute that you and Bob will find ways to make sense of our leads as we get them."

"Since this case may now involve at least one foreign country, do you expect the CIA to get involved?" I said.

"Yes, I was about to bring that up," Gladys said. "CIA Director Atkins has requested that you two meet with him at the CIA tomorrow. You know him as Charles Atkins, but he's also known by a bunch of other pseudonyms he used when he was a field agent. But everybody calls him Buster. He's a nice guy and smart as hell. He's an old friend of President Fenton and the First Lady. If this case involves Yemen or other foreign countries, the CIA will be heavily involved, maybe more so than the FBI. He and Director Watson work well together. They don't believe in turf protecting; they believe in getting the job done. Although they're not partners, they remind me of you and Bob. Buster loves to solve cases you'll be happy to know. You guys will like him."

CHAPTER 37

Bob

It was a pleasant summer evening, not too hot for August in Washington, which normally sucks. Bobbie and I walked to our hotel, which was only three blocks from FBI Headquarters. It was 6 p.m. so we planned to have dinner at the hotel.

"Yemen," Bobbie said. "Fucking Yemen."

"No, just Yemen," I said, "not fucking Yemen."

"Okay, wise guy. Give me your thoughts."

"I remember the Mayor Paxton saying that one of his three captors spoke with a Middle Eastern accent. *Distinct* was the word he used."

"You're right, Bob, he did say that. Now that we'll be working with data from 20 cities, we'll have a lot to plug into the database. I can't wait to put together an algorithm. One of the first data points I want to populate will be whether anybody heard an accent, especially a Middle Eastern accent."

We went to our room to freshen up before dinner. As soon as we walked in the phone rang. It was Commissioner Norquist.

"Three more assassinations this morning," he said "Two detectives and a uniform. You two have work to do."

He gave us the names but neither of us recognized them, which made me happy. Well, not happy, but not as upset as I would have been if I knew the guys personally. We chatted briefly about our meeting at the FBI.

Bobbie and I looked at each other. For a minute neither of us said a word. Then Bobbie spoke the feeling we both shared. "This body count is getting me nauseous, Bob. We've got to stop it—we may be next."

Yeah, interesting thought. We may be next.

CHAPTER 38

Bobbie

B ob and I were driven to CIA Headquarters in Langley, Virginia, in Fairfax County, not far from Washington D.C. Often, people simply refer to the complex as "Langley," just as the State Department is known as "Foggy Bottom" after the Washington neighborhood where it's located. The place sits on a huge plot of land, a total of 258 acres. The Feds like to do things big.

We were scheduled to meet with the director. Because the FBI people had found evidence involving a foreign country, the CIA would become involved, and maybe even take over the investigation. Then, as our car drove toward the CIA, a chilling thought hit me. I recalled that a Pakistani resident assassinated two CIA employees on the road to headquarters, the same road we were on.

Bob looked particularly great this morning, and I told him so as I stroked his leg. We may be working a huge murder case, but we always do something we enjoy—we love to flirt with each other.

At 9:15 we arrived at CIA Headquarters for our meeting which was set for 9:30. I noticed the famous statue of Nathan Hale, one of our country's early spies during the Revolutionary War. The place is formally known as the George Bush Center for Intelligence, named for the 41st President, who was once Director of the CIA. Two armed guards escorted us to Director Atkins' office. The office was large, as you would expect for a guy in his position. "Buster," as everybody calls him, stood and greeted us. He was a tall guy, about six one, and had a decidedly Middle Eastern appearance. He wore an expensive navy-blue blazer, gray pants, and penny loafers. Yes, penny loafers. For a top spy, the guy looked decidedly preppy. One of the many pseudonyms he used when he was an active field agent was Gamal Akhbar. I had done some research on the man, as I always do. His parents are Coptic Christians from Egypt, hence his Middle Eastern appearance. When he was an active CIA field agent, he acquired the reputation as a "super spook," because of his talents and courage. I read that he has a pleasant, friendly personality, and nothing about him led us to believe otherwise. He graciously gestured us toward chairs around a small conference table.

"Sarah Watson has told me a lot about you two, and I've also done some research. I'm not just being polite when I say, it's an honor to meet you."

An *honor* to meet us? The guy is definitely a gentleman. He insisted that we call him Buster, which blew me away. The Director of the Central Intelligence Agency wants us to call him by his first name. Maybe I should mention this to *Commissioner* Norquist. We told Buster to call us Bobbie and Bob, Of course.

"So, it looked like police departments around the country were having some internal problems with murdered cops," Buster said as he poured us coffee. "That was until we started to connect the dots, or, until Bobbie Nelson started to connect the dots. Don't be surprised If I try to steal you both away from the NYPD."

I recalled Sarah Watson and Rick Bellamy saying the same thing. These top-level Feds sure know how to flatter people. Or maybe they mean it.

"I've spent my professional life fighting terror. I look like I ride a camel, and I speak fluent Arabic, but make no mistake—I'm a jihadi's worst nightmare. I look like them, I occasionally speak like them, but I hunt them down and kill them. What I just said doesn't leave this room, please. I know that the FBI has briefed you two about some leads pointing toward Yemen. When I was a field agent, I spent a lot of time in Yemen. It's a fucking cesspool of terror, pardon my Arabic, and they've taken on the most ambitious terror operation the world has ever seen. If they succeed in what they're after, 9/11 will look like a minor car accident."

"Buster, the word that's rattling around my brain is *why*. Why are they attacking and killing police officers?"

"I think you know the answer to that, Bobbie. I think you know the answer because we're basing our strategy on what you've already theorized, according to Sarah Watson. This is a brand-new form of terror, far different from the bombings and explosions we've grown accustomed to. I call this *structural* terrorism, a type of terrorism that aims at the structure of society, in this case, law enforcement. When you attack and destroy the structure of something, everything that the structure supports comes crumbling down. Sure, after 9/11 people were gripped by fear, but we gradually adjusted and moved on—because the structure of our society was still in place. Remove that structure and we're knocking on the gates of hell."

Structural terrorism? I was impressed with Buster's thoughtfulness and his scholarly analysis. I was also impressed that his words scared the shit out of me. I looked at Bob. He said nothing, just stroked his chin.

Buster's assistant walked in and handed him a piece of paper.

"Pardon me, Buster, but you said you wanted this report as soon as it came in."

I was blown away that his assistant called him by his first name.

145

"This is the new daily report that Sarah Watson just started with all the police departments she's working with, including the NYPD. So, folks, here's the latest number, the most recent report of police assassinations. Fifteen. Yes, you heard me right, fifteen cops murdered in one day, spread across all the departments under study. None were from the NYPD, you'll be pleased to know. This brings the number of cop murders to 950."

"Oh my God," I said. "Is there anything different in the profile?"

Buster became visibly pale.

"Yes, there is something new. All the victims were women."

CHAPTER 39

Bob

I reached over and grabbed Bobbie's hand. I didn't think about it; my hand just reached out as if it was an autonomic movement. When Buster announced that all 15 of the cop murders in the past 24 hours were women, I felt like throwing up. As I squeezed her hand, I looked at Bobbie, suddenly realizing that the love of my life had become a target.

"This report tells us more than the news that the victims were women," I said. "This tells us that there was nothing random about these killings. Yesterday's events were carefully planned murders, well thought-out in advance."

"There's something else in the report that I just noticed," Buster said. "In five of the incidents the shooter was heard to shout 'Alahu Akbar,' meaning 'God is the greatest,' the epithet of choice for a terrorist when pulling off an incident. This report nails it. We're looking at a massive campaign of terror, and as Bob just noted, the events are no longer random, but carefully planned. And what really scares the hell out of me is this. You, Bob and Bobbie, whether you like it or not, are police celebrities. The article about you in *The New York Times* and your appearance on *The Ellen Bellamy Show*, have made you famous, although Bobbie was pretty well-known already. I'm afraid that your fame has also made you ideal targets. I know you're planning to return to New York later today, but I suggest that you consider moving here for the balance of this operation. We can put you up at a decent apartment at the CIA. You can conduct the investigation right from here, and you'll be a hell of a lot safer."

"I think Commissioner Norquist will have concerns about that," I said.

"The commissioner can take his concerns to the White House," Buster said. "Something tells me that the President of the United States will be your new assignment officer."

CHAPTER 40

Bobbie

When Bob and I returned to One Police Plaza, we went right to Norquist's office as he had requested. It was 7:15 p.m. on September 15 and the sun had just gone down a few minutes before. Buster, Sarah Watson, and Norquist had huddled on the phone a few hours earlier.

"Director Buster is hitting the panic button, and I can't say I blame him," Norquist said. "I hate the idea of losing you two, but I think the White House doesn't give a rat's ass about what I want. You guys are pivotal to this operation, but I'm worried about you. I think of you both as friends, not just detectives. Buster is right. You can use your ample brainpower at the CIA where you won't have to worry about a shooter around every corner. I'm assigning two uniforms to accompany you to your apartment tonight. Call here before you leave for the office tomorrow morning and you will have protection. Be careful, BBs, be very careful."

Bob and I met the two cops who would be our bodyguards at the entrance to One PP. Our apartment is only three blocks away, but I think Norquist was smart to assign us protection. This shit is starting to weigh on my emotions, and I know it's gnawing at Bob as well.

I've been a cop for a long time and I'm familiar with danger, but now we've concluded that the police murders are a well-orchestrated series of terrorist hits. Not a pleasant feeling, especially if you're a cop. One of the officers walked 10 feet in front of us, and the other 10 feet behind.

Off to our right we heard a loud bang, and all four of us turned to look. At the same time a car pulled up on our left and just in front of us. A rear door swung open, and a man jumped out with a gun in his hand. He turned toward us and opened fire. I drew my Glock, dropped to a knee, and shot the bastard. I wanted to shoot him in the head, but instead followed my training and fired two rounds mid-torso. I turned to Bob on my left and I thought my heart would stop—and break. Bob was lying on his back on the ground, his face covered in blood. Oh, dear God, Bob, *my* Bob, has been shot. I knelt next to him, still holding my gun and glancing around to see if there may be another shooter. One of our bodyguards ran to the man I had shot to make sure he was out of commission. "He's dead," the cop yelled to us. I had never killed anybody before, never even fired at anyone actually, but I felt satisfaction at having killed the son of a bitch, mingled with my fear and panic for Bob. An ambulance screamed up next to us. The EMTs put Bob on a stretcher and loaded him through the back doors. I sat next to him in the ambulance, my heart pounding like a sledgehammer.

"Relax, honey, this is nothing," EMT Jane Morton said to me after she examined Bob. "Just a lot of blood from a graze wound. Your partner will be coming around any time now, although he'll have quite a headache."

"What happened?" Bob groaned.

"Easy, baby," I said as I put my face next to his bloody face. Jane Morton's happy diagnosis allowed my heart to stop pounding.

We pulled up to the emergency room of New York Presbyterian

Lower Manhattan Hospital. Bob's stretcher was whisked through to a private room, with me next to it. A doctor walked quickly into the room and began to examine Bob, who was now fully awake and alert. I wiped Bob's blood off my face with a towel.

"I can't believe I'm saying this to a man who's just been shot in the head, but you'll be fine, Detective. The bullet grazed the top of your skull and knocked you out. But you probably won't even have a scar, just a headache for a short while."

When the doctor and nurse left the room, I climbed into bed with Bob, not bothering to think about hospital protocol. After what just happened, I couldn't be without him in my arms.

"Bobbie?"

"Yes, honey."

"The ice pack?"

"What about the ice pack?"

Oh shit. I realized he needed more than my arms around him. I was so freaked out I wasn't thinking straight. Bob, *my* Bob, had come within a quarter inch of dying. I'm a cop, and I'm not supposed to let my emotions go, but all I could think about was that son of a bitch who shot Bob, and how I wished I could kill the guy all over again. Revenge is a wasted emotion, and I know that Bob and I will solve this case by calmly putting one foot in front of the other. I picked the icepack off the end table and gently placed it on the bandage on top of Bob's head.

Like Bob, I was exhausted. I dozed off with my face against his, a cozy feeling after the horror that just happened.

After a couple of hours, we woke up. "How do you feel, baby?"

"Not bad, surprisingly. My head doesn't hurt that much. Can you imagine I was shot in the head, and all I need is Tylenol? I spent six months of hellish combat when I was a Marine in Fallujah Province in Iraq. All I got was a slight bullet wound to my left arm. But here I almost got fucking killed in Lower Manhattan. I overheard the EMTs saying you took out the son of a bitch who shot me. Nice shooting, Detective. You killed him before he could get off another round. I think it's safe to say that I married well. How about a kiss, baby?"

"That's the first shot I ever fired at another human being, Bob. I'm glad my aim was good. My years on the shooting range came in handy tonight."

"I'll say it came in handy, Wonder Woman."

"So, it looks like Norquist's hunch was right," I said. "You and I are on the hit list."

"You and me and every other cop in the country. We've got a lot of work ahead of us."

Typical of Bob and me, we already started to work the case—in a hospital room where Bob could have died.

"Did you happen to get the plate number off the car that pulled away, Bobbie?"

"Yes, you know me and my photographic memory. I already called it in. Not much help, though, because the car was stolen. We may know more when they autopsy the shooter."

"Autopsy? I can tell them the cause of death—*my Bobbie*."

The doctor came into the room at 8:30 a.m., wearing a big smile.

"You're good to go, Detective. All tests are positive. You're one tough guy, but I recommend a couple of days of taking it easy."

We arrived at our apartment at 9:45. Four uniforms were stationed outside the building on orders from the commissioner. Norquist told me to stay with Bob so I could keep an eye on him. Like I really needed that advice.

The phone rang. It was Commissioner Norquist calling to tell us he was coming over. I wondered what news he had for us.

CHAPTER 41

Bob

When Bobbie opened the door for Commissioner Norquist, I was lying on the couch with an ice pack on my head. It didn't hurt too badly, but the doctor said I should keep the pack on to prevent any additional swelling. Norquist gave Bobbie a big-brotherly hug and walked over to the couch. Bobbie sat in the chair next to him. He looked upset.

"Last night the city, not to mention the country, almost lost one of its best detectives. And if sharp-shooting Bobbie wasn't on the case, we may have lost her too. This shit has officially gotten out of hand. I've been on the phone with Director Buster from the CIA. We were all expecting this, so it should come as no surprise that Buster wants you to take up residence at the CIA, on direct orders from the White House. Although I hate the thought of losing you two, I must agree with Washington. You're needed there to head up this crazy investigation. I talked to Tim Franken at Internal Affairs and told him I'd be assigning a few officers to help you pack. Although Tim is usually a stickler at keeping departmental and personal matters separate, he knows that this is official business, so you'll have help packing. Buster told me the apartments at the CIA are fully furnished, so all you need to pack are clothes and other personal items. The CIA will assign you new guns."

I couldn't help but notice tears in the corner of both his eyes. He's become a friend, not just a boss. Bobbie and I will miss him. On doctor's orders, we planned our flight to Washington a week from now. Bobbie and I both knew what we'd do during that time. We'll work the case, the Big Case.

That evening, Bobbie sat next to me on the couch. She was crying.

I'd been worried about Bobbie. She's been taking my assassination attempt pretty hard. She says she can't get it out of her mind, and that she's plagued by the sight of me lying unconscious on the ground with blood all over my face. I felt helpless. When Bobbie hurts, I hurt, but there was nothing I could do other than hug her. Even that couldn't seem to shake her emotional turmoil.

The next day we would entertain a special guest, an important guest.

CHAPTER 42

Bobbie

O ur lives have switched into the high-speed lane, especially since Bob was almost assassinated. I keep trying to force that night out of my head, but it isn't working. What the hell do you do when the love of your life almost gets killed as he's walking next to you? The memory of Bob lying there with blood all over his face gnaws at me. We leave for Langley and our new home at the CIA in a few days, but first we need to meet with a visitor, on the recommendation of Commissioner Norquist. He wants us to meet with Dr. Benjamin Weinberg, a psychiatrist who is also a NYPD detective. Bennie is well-known in the department as Bennie-the-Bullshit-Detector, because of his talent for spotting lies on the witness stand. Prosecutors tell people that having Bennie Weinberg in the courtroom is like having a witness hooked up to a polygraph. Besides evaluating witnesses, Bennie also has another talent—counseling cops on the psychological traumas we constantly face. After the shit that Bob and I have been through recently, we both thought it was a good idea to meet the famous Dr. Bennie.

The doorbell rang at 10 a.m. and Bob let him in. Bob insisted that he didn't want to spend a lot of his time lying on the couch with an ice pack on his head. The swelling had gone down to nothing, and his headaches have essentially disappeared.

Dr. Bennie immediately insisted we call him simply Bennie, which I thought was appropriate because the three of us are all detectives. He's a good-looking man, about 5'10" and a bit portly, which he makes up for by wearing expensive designer suits. He's slightly balding but doesn't hide it with a comb-over, which impressed me. I've often thought, if you're going bald, just fucking go bald and don't try to deny it. A good sign for a shrink, I thought.

Bob and Bennie knew each other slightly from courtroom appearances they had shared.

"Good to see you again, Bob, and it's a pleasure to meet you, Bobbie. Wow, I've heard a lot about you. Ralph Norquist was smart to bring you into the NYPD, although you're leaving us for the CIA. I hope it's only a temporary assignment. So, if you don't mind, can you two tell me about the assassination attempt on Bob last week?"

Like a good detective, he gets right to the point.

"Bob, you go first," I said.

"But I was unconscious after the bullet hit my head. Hell, I didn't even see you shoot the guy. So, why don't you tell Bennie your thoughts, hon."

"I won't bullshit you, Bennie," I said. "Since you're known as Bennie-the Bullshit-Detector I figure that should be my best approach."

Bennie cracked up. It's easy to like this guy.

"So, tell me what's been going on in that pretty head of yours after you saw your loving husband almost assassinated."

"It's been seven days since it happened," I said, "but I can't seem to force the images out of my head. The memory of that bastard firing his gun at Bob is with me constantly. I try to force myself to forget it, but I can't. Every time I wake up, the son of a bitch is in front of me, pointing his gun. I just can't get the goddam image out of my mind."

"That's because it's a *green fucking elephant*," Bennie said.

He may be a Harvard Medical School grad, but Bennie has the mouth of a New York City cop.

"A green elephant?" I said.

"Yes, have you ever been in a parlor game where the host tells everybody in the room *NOT* to think about green elephants? So, what do the participants think about? You got it, green elephants, to the exclusion of everything else. They think about it because they try *not* to think about it. Bobbie, when you try to get the image of Bob's shooting out of your mind, you're creating a green elephant, one that won't go away. We human beings love to fuck with our minds. We think we can ignore psychology and simply force unpleasant thoughts from our heads. Doesn't work that way, I'm sorry to tell you. That's a green elephant."

"But Bennie," I said, "the memory of that night tortures me. I don't know how much Commissioner Norquist told you about Bob and me, but we're the closest couple you'll ever meet. I love this man more than life itself. And the image of his being shot gnaws at me like a cancer. I've got to get that night out of my memory."

"So, let me engage in a mind game with you Bobbie, okay? Tell me what the man's face looked like."

"He had a swarthy complexion and eyes that seemed on fire with hatred."

"And how much did his face weigh?"

"What? What do you mean how much did his face weigh? I have

no idea, and I don't get the question."

"Work with me, Bobbie. How much did the man's face weigh? Tell me what shows up in your mind without editing my words."

"Okay, his goddam face weighed 45 pounds."

"And what color is his face?"

"I told you, he had a swarthy complexion."

"Okay, close your eyes and tell me the color of the man's face in your mind *right now*."

"Holy shit," I said, "it's royal blue."

"And what shape is his face?"

"My God, it's square."

Bennie went on for five minutes asking me the weight, shape, and color of the man's face each time I thought about it. I was amazed how the image kept changing in my mind each time Bennie prompted me.

"Great, Bobbie, now let's talk about the gun and the bullet."

"Jesus Christ, Bennie, I don't want to think about it, much less talk about it."

"Hey, Bobbie, you've been doing a great job of fucking with your mind the past week, now give me a crack at it. Tell me about the gun. Hey, Bobbie, look at me. Tell me about the gun."

"It was a Sig Sauer P226. I suppose you want to know the shape of it, what color it was, and how much the goddam thing weighed."

"Exactly, but I want you to close your eyes and speak when I prompt you."

For the next five minutes we went through just that, with the shape, weight, and color of the gun changing every time I spoke.

"Did you see the bullet hit Bob?"

"No, but after I killed the scumbag I looked to my left and saw Bob lying on the ground with blood all over his face. *My* Bob."

This is the worst part of my memory of that night, seeing Bob on the ground bleeding. I broke down crying. Naturally, Bennie then asked me about how much Bob's head weighed, its shape, and the changing color of the blood. As difficult as it was, I did as I was told.

Bennie stood, walked across the room and poured himself a glass of water.

"Tell me how you feel right now, Bobbie."

"I cannot believe this, Bennie. I no longer have that pain in my stomach. I feel relaxed and calm, as if I just came out of a soak in a hot tub. I feel great. Bennie, what the hell just happened?"

"Welcome to the world of reality-based psychology, Bobbie. For the past week you've been trying to force your memories from your mind, as if the memories would say, 'okay, sure, we're out of here.' You've been turning your memories of that night into a herd of green fucking elephants. Won't work. What we just did with this exercise was to give weight, shape, and color to the memories. In our little exercise, you engaged the memories and made them real, not trying to force them from your mind. The next time you feel plagued by that night, do not try to get rid of the memories, make them real. Go through the exercise we just did. Bob can help you. And here's my advice for both of you. You're a couple of seasoned detectives, and as such you see a lot of gruesome shit. Whenever you find something plaguing you, go through the exercise we just went through. It will work wonders for your heads and your lives."

"Will this work with my memories of a drunk wife-beating piece of shit I married a few years ago?"

"Yes," Bennie said. "Give the memories weight, shape, and color—and they'll turn you loose."

"Bennie," I said, "will this work with self-doubt, something that haunts me?"

"And what about guilt?" Bob said. "I have a lot of guilt about past relationships I've blown."

"Bob and Bobbie, what all that shit needs is shape, weight, and color, and the memories will let you be. I must be going my friends. I'm expected in court. Please keep our country safe."

"God bless you, Bennie," I said, "God bless you my friend."

When Bennie left, Bob and I hugged.

"You look wonderful, Bobbie. You look like the weight of the world just left your shoulders. I don't know about you, but I think we're ready to tackle our case."

"Hey, handsome, any more headaches?"

"No, I feel great, and after what Bennie did for you, I feel even better."

"Good, then let's go to bed."

"But Bobbie, it's 11:30 in the morning, a bit early for going to sleep."

"I don't want to sleep."

CHAPTER 43

Bob

Bobbie and I decided to take a rented van with our belongings to Langley. All we needed were clothing and personal effects. So, we were headed to our new home. Home?

We arrived at CIA Headquarters at 3:15 p.m. where a group of people awaited us for our move-in. The apartment wasn't bad, with two bedrooms and two baths, a pleasant living room-den, and a small dining room. The walls were painted a pleasant tannish green. Prints of pastoral scenes adorned the walls. It even came with a view—of the building next door.

The next morning, we would meet with Buster.

———————⊰✦⊱———————

We got up early and went to the gym before our meeting with Buster. It was much bigger than the gym in our apartment, of course, and had a circuit of every exercise machine imaginable. We're both committed to regular exercise, because our work often involves sitting for hours on end. I love to watch Bobbie work out. She's such a jock, it's no wonder she has a fantastic shape. She inspires me to give myself a good workout. When I first worked out in the gym at our apartment in New York after I was shot, my head screamed with pain. That's gone, thank God.

"Congratulations," Buster said when we walked into his office.

"For what?" we both said.

"For passing the FBI background check, which just wrapped up. It will also serve to clear you both as provisional CIA Agents."

"Background check?" I said. "I didn't realize one was being done."

"Welcome to Fedland," Buster said.

His assistant walked into the room. "I suggest you turn on the TV, Buster," she said. I'm constantly amazed how everybody calls him Buster, even his aides.

"Shepard Smith for Fox News, ladies and gentlemen. I have a horrific story to report this morning. At a police academy graduation ceremony in Indianapolis, Indiana, 55 graduate police officers were shot and killed by three individuals using assault rifles. The incident happened just 20 minutes ago. The assailants shouted *Alahu Akbar* and then committed suicide by turning the guns on themselves. This is the latest incidence of attacks on police officers over the past month. No government official has yet to come forward with any ideas about the motives in these attacks. Today's shooting brings the number of police murders to 1,005. The people who protect us now need protection themselves."

Buster clicked off the TV and hit his intercom. "Pete," he said to one of his aides, "call the Indianapolis Police Department and see what you can find out about the three shooters."

Buster moves fast, I was happy to see.

"So, we have over a thousand dead cops in less than a month," he said. "In all my years with the CIA, I've never seen anything like this. Bob, you came damn close to being assassinated yourself. I may be the CIA Director, but I'll be working closely with the two of you, almost as a field agent. We're going to get this shit done. With Bob and Bobbie working the file, I don't doubt that one bit. Whatever you two need from me to get the job handled, just yell."

After our meeting with Buster, Bobbie and I went to the weapons office to get our assigned guns. Bobbie asked for a Colt 45 automatic.

"Hey, hon, why the need for a hand-held cannon? Why not a Glock or a Sig?"

"Bob, if someone else makes a move on you I intend to blow his fucking head off from the neck up."

Bennie Weinberg may have helped Bobbie with her horrible memories, but he did nothing to tamp down her anger over that night.

"Hey, calm down, Wonder Woman."

After we met with Buster we were shown to our new office. It was a good size, about 20 by 30 feet. A large window gave us a pleasant view of a small garden. A six-by-four-foot conference table came with four chairs around it, enabling us to conduct small meetings. The first thing I noticed was that the two desks were on separate walls, not facing each other the way detective desks are normally arranged, well, at One Police Plaza anyway.

"Please help us move those desks so that they face each other," I said to the aide who showed us in.

"We don't do it that way at the CIA," he said.

"You do *now*," I said with considerable volume in my voice. The last thing I need is shit from a subordinate. I arranged for three video monitors, one for each of us that we keep to the side, and an extra large one we use for collaborating on documents or websites. The

CIA has an enormous amount of data for us to work with, which is just what we need. The more data you have, the more you can see datapoints intersecting, especially with Bobbie's ingenious algorithms. And the more data points that intersect, the closer we get to solving the puzzle.

In the afternoon we got a call from none other than our old friend, Father Rick Sampson, the priest who joined us in marriage. He was in D.C. for a church conference and wanted to have dinner with us. Under strict orders from Buster, we could only eat at the CIA, which actually had a couple of decent restaurants. Father Rick joined us at six, and we couldn't have been happier to see him.

"You two are my favorite detectives, not that I'm a connoisseur of detectives. I almost passed out when I heard that Bob had been shot. God bless you, my friend," he said as he made the sign of the cross. "I would have visited you, but I was out of town leading a retreat. Thank God, you're okay, Bob. Our country needs you two, the country that you're trying to save. I don't know much about the case you're working on, and of course you can't tell me, but it seems obvious that it involves all the horrible police assassinations. At least that's what all the pundits are saying."

I was glad we had that dinner with Father Rick. He brought something to our attention that we should have realized. Our case was now known to the public. And if the public knows it, so does the enemy. And if the enemy knows it, our job gets more difficult—a *lot* more difficult.

CHAPTER 44

Bobbie

Our world had become data points. Intersecting data points, conflicting data points, and solo data points. With Bob's help, I was designing an algorithm that I hoped would solve the case, or at least give the field agents some useful knowledge to work with.

If I click on the word "accent," all incidents where the assailant had a non-American accent would appear, including whether it was Middle Eastern. The exciting data points were the ones that crossed or intersected. For example, in a few of the incidents we saw a Middle Eastern accent cross with Yemen and cross with the type of weapon used. The major things we were looking for were the names of people that intersected with the other data points. Hacking computers is a wonderful thing, unless it's you who's being hacked. And, I must admit, nobody is better at hacking computer systems than me. So far, we had come up with 20 names, which Buster thought was great. His people would then see if the names crossed with known terrorists on the CIA "watch list." All 20 of them did. This was tedious shit, but very necessary tedious shit. Thank goodness the database itself handled most of the tedium. Bob regularly gave my shoulders a massage with his big strong hands to relieve the tension, and it was oh so good.

I felt vindicated that Mayor Paxton's kidnapping didn't intersect with any other data points, which had been my theory all along. Whoever was running the show wanted us to *think* that the kidnapping was part of the bigger picture. It wasn't.

Last night there were five more police murders. We were up to 1,010, which sickened me. I ran all the facts we knew about the murders through the algorithm. One name kept popping up, Mustaffa Creezin, a resident of Yemen.

When we told Buster about Mr. Creezin, he said that he would dispatch one of his operatives in Yemen to have a "talk" with him. We never saw Creezin's name again. Buster, we have learned, plays rough, *quite rough*. Bob and I are accustomed to doing things by the book legally. But hell, this is war. We made it a point to not ask questions, especially because we already knew the answers— Buster and his operatives were whacking the bastards my algorithm disclosed. The man who tried to kill Bob didn't read him his rights before he fired, so I didn't feel bad that the targets my algorithm dug out were simply being eliminated.

Another name that appeared regularly was a man named Kevin Cummings. The letters "HG" appeared next to his name in the database, standing for "home grown"—an important data point. All in all, we had 12 homegrowns in the database, radicalized turds who took up arms against their own country. As we expected, Cummings name stopped appearing.

The weeks went by and we came up with more and more names, turned them over to Buster, who would order a "talk." Every time there was a "talk"' the name would not show up again. Did I mention that Buster plays rough? It had been a month, and no new police assassinations occurred.

The work was grueling and eye-straining. If it weren't for my gym sessions, the wonderful back rubs, and regular lovemaking with Bob, I think I would have turned into a gnarly old lady.

"Bob, I think this is working. Not one cop killing in a month. Buster is winning this war one jihadi at a time."

"Well, Buster does his thing very efficiently as we've learned," Bob said, "but your computer brilliance is what's making it happen, Bobbie."

"Hey," I said, "if I didn't have you to bounce data points off, I could have never done this, and I'm not saying that to be polite. Your attention to detail is awesome."

And I *wasn't* just being polite. Bob and I are a team in every sense of the word, and teams win games—and wars. And it's kind of nice to be in love with your teammate.

Another month went by, another month without a cop assassination. Two months without a murder of a cop. With Bob and I doing the brain work, and Buster and the boys doing the dirty work, I was more than happy with our progress.

Buster called us to his office for a meeting.

"History tells us that one of the important things about a war is knowing when you've won. Well, Bob and Bobbie, we've won this war, thanks to you two. There's somebody else who wants to thank you, and he wants to do so today. You're scheduled to appear in the Oval Office this afternoon at two, where President Fenton wants to meet with you."

I thought I'd faint. President Fenton wants to meet with Bob and me?

CHAPTER 45

Bob

A CIA car brought Bobbie and me to the White House. We both tried to act cool, but it wasn't working. We walked under the porte cochere into the West Wing, escorted by two armed Marines.

I had read a lot about President Harry Fenton and his beautiful wife Meg, who, besides being First Lady of the United States, was also the president's chief of staff, a historic first. From everything I knew about them, they remind me of Bobbie and me—two people in love with each other and who get the job done.

President Fenton was a Navy admiral when he ran for office. Of course, he had to resign from the Navy first, along with his wife and chief of staff, Commander Meg. He was the country's first five-star admiral since Chester Nimitz, the World War II hero. Wow, and he's invited us to meet with him. Bobbie and I agreed that we were having yet another one of our hot shit moments.

Another Marine led us into the Oval Office.

The President was seated at his desk, and the First Lady sat on a chair in front of him. They both rose to greet us. The President and

First Lady actually stood. I had always heard that Harry and Meg Fenton are gracious people, and they just proved it. He gestured to the two chairs next to the First Lady.

"It's great to see you two again," Meg Fenton said, referring to the time she met us in Sarah Watson's office. "Harry, meet the famous BBs, America's detective super stars. They like to be called Bobbie and Bob."

"One of the pleasant things about my job is that I often get to meet great Americans, American heroes like you two, Bobbie and Bob," the President said. "CIA Director Atkins had told me all about the great work you two have done. A few months back, our nation faced the greatest terrorist threat we could ever imagine. We were in a seemingly winless war. That was until you two amazing people showed up. My friends, you won the war. I know that you will soon return to your home in New York and continue your fine work for the New York Police Department."

He reached into his desk.

"I will now give you a token of thanks for the service you did for your country, the Presidential Medal of Freedom." He draped the medals around our necks as a camera man clicked away. Meg stood next to him, smiling ear to ear. Then he looked down and read, "This award is for *especially meritorious contributions to the security or national interests of the United States, to world peace, or to cultural or other significant public or private endeavors.* Well-earned my friends, well-earned. God bless you and please continue your great work."

As Bobbie and I got into the car for our ride back to the CIA, we didn't speak. Bobbie was crying, tears of happiness — and pride, I hoped. I leaned over and kissed her.

When we walked into Director Buster's office, we were cheered by about 30 people, a five-minute standing ovation. Buster walked up to us and said, "There's something you two should be wearing. Please hand the medals to me." Meg Fenton had alerted him about the Medals of Freedom. He draped the medals over our necks, stepped back and applauded us more.

"I wish I could convince you folks to stay with us, but I know you want to get back to your home in New York, not to mention the fortunate NYPD. You two won the God-forsaken war, and President Fenton's honoring you with these medals is his personal thanks, and the thanks of a grateful nation. You will always be in our hearts, my friends."

Bobbie started to cry again. I began to fill up myself. Besides cracking tough cases, Bobbie and I seem to have a knack for collecting good friends, especially Buster.

We returned to our apartment, where Bobbie immediately called her parents, after which I called mine. Our folks totally freaked out over the news about our Medals of Freedom. Then I called Commissioner Norquist.

"Buster just called me with this great news," Norquist said. "I'm so proud of you two I could fucking pass out. Please tell me you're returning to the NYPD."

"Of course, Commissioner," Bobbie said. "Hey, we're cops."

CHAPTER 46

Bobbie

On Monday, the day after Bob and I returned to New York, we were scheduled to meet with Tom and Mildred Cunningham, the editors from Random House whom we met on the cruise. We had decided to take another week off so that, in the event Random House was ready to move forward, we would begin our book.

"Since you folks were away," Tom Cunningham said, "I've been following you carefully in the papers, as well as doing some additional background research. That article about you in *The New York Times Magazine*, not to mention your appearance on *The Ellen Bellamy Show*, have made you two celebrities. And your being awarded the Presidential Medal of Freedom has more than put you on the map. It also got the attention of senior management at Random House. You two are poised to write a book on detective work that will become an instant classic. I've been authorized to offer you an advance of $10 million."

"Fifteen," I said without batting an eye. After what Bob and I have been through I've developed a few extra pounds of mojo.

"How about 12?" He said.

"Fifteen is better, much better," I said.

He reached his hand across the desk. "Deal."

He then handed us a contract, with the understanding that we would pass it by our lawyer.

So, Bob and I are on our way to becoming big-time authors. *Detectiving*, the weirdest-named book ever, would soon be launched. I felt confident we'd get the job done. I love to write and so does Bob, a best-selling author himself. Our lives are never dull. I think our banker will be happy too.

I wondered what would await us at One PP when we return to our office next week.

But first, it's time to write the book.

CHAPTER 47

Bob

O ur meeting at Random house lasted three hours, although the contract negotiation took only 10 minutes, thanks to my wife's well-honed chutzpah. As sweet and gentle as she is, Bobbie sure knows how to drive a hard bargain. Wow, $15 million. And that's only the advance.

Bobbie and I don't like to waste time, and when we latch onto something new, we like to get it done. Hey, we fell in love with each other in a month. We wanted to get a solid jump on our latest project, the forthcoming book, *Detectiving*, by Bobbie Nelson and Bob Lawton. So, we took another week off and got to work. We treated the book project as a case.

I love writing fiction, and I managed to get it right with my best-selling novel, *An Army of Blue*. When I write fiction, I don't do a detailed outline, because I find it impossible to envision an entire story from beginning to end. When I began my novel, I tried to do a formal detailed outline after reading a book on that subject. I tried and tried, but it just didn't work. Stories have a way of unfolding in front of you, which is why it's so much fun writing fiction. You surprise yourself, or rather the story surprises you. My novel kept taking off in interesting new directions, and each time it did I would need to revise the goddam outline. I finally packed it in and decided to heed the advice of the great Stephen King—Come up with a general idea of the story, then populate the pages with interesting characters, and let the characters show you how the story unfolds. So, I did just that and I had a blast. And I also managed to sell a piss-load of books.

Non-fiction is different, as both Bobbie and I agreed, and so did Mildred Cunningham, our editor at Random House. We needed a detailed outline first and would then write the book. Not to brag, but Bobbie and I know a hell of a lot about the business of being detectives. That's what landed us the book deal in the first place. So, we began our careful outline.

Bobbie came up with the idea that parts of the book should read like a novel, although we would keep to the facts strictly as if it were a newspaper article. So, I began to come up with chapters about cases we both had worked on, either together or before we met. The only factual difference would be fictional names, except for names of those who were convicted, which was public knowledge anyway.

Our outline poured out smoothly. Here is the first outline draft.

Chapter 1 – Overview of Law Enforcement in the United States

Chapter 2 – The Differences Between Uniformed Police Officers and Detectives

Chapter 3 – The Education of Law Enforcement Officers

Chapter 4 – The Equipment Used, Including Firearms

Chapter 5 – Arrest Procedures

Chapter 6 – Search Procedures

Chapter 7 – Crime Scene Investigations

Chapter 8 – Blood Analysis, Including Different Types of Stains

Subchapter – Everything you Ever Need to Know About Flies and Other Insects

Subchapter – Scientific and Mathematical issues

Chapter 9 – Fingerprints

Chapter 10 – DNA Analysis

Chapter 11 – The Fine Art of Interrogating a Witness

Chapter 12 – The Legal Process and the Courts

Chapter 13 – Punishment—Jails, Prisons, and the Death Penalty

Interspersed within and between these chapters would be our "war stories," written in fiction-style by me.

By the end of the day, Bobbie and I realized we had our basic outline. It only took us a day and a half. We know our stuff.

As we worked, we would brainstorm on what we call "beats," ideas and scenes we want to include. After that, we would fit the beats into the appropriate chapters.

At 6 p.m. on Wednesday, Bobbie suggested we relax and that I mix us some martinis while she took a quick shower. She walked back into the room wearing a gorgeous short negligee that wrapped around her stunning body like a caress. We were about to write a very exciting chapter.

CHAPTER 48

Bobbie

After a week of working on our book, we felt that we were off to a great start, and estimated we'd have a first draft ready for our editor in two more weeks of part-time work.

We returned to One PP, where we were scheduled to meet with Commissioner Norquist. It was 5:30 p.m.

As we opened the door to Norquist's office, about 25 people broke out into cheers. He had planned a welcome-home party for us, along with streamers, confetti, champagne, the works.

"Ladies and gentlemen, it's my honor to welcome back to the NYPD two of the finest detectives in New York City history. While they were borrowed away from us by the CIA, they put their time to good use and won a horrible war, a war that was declared on the police of the country. Let's hear another round of applause for NYPD royalty, Bobbie Nelson and Bob Lawton."

NYPD *royalty*? The commissioner knows how to flatter people. Bob and I were elated. To be among good friends is a feeling that's hard to beat. When I spoke to him earlier, Commissioner Norquist said to make sure we had our Medals of Freedom with us. He reached out and we handed him the medals, which he draped around our necks. Another round of applause, this one louder. Bob gestured to me to say a few words.

"The people at the CIA are pleasant and smart as hell," I said, "but nothing like you, our family at the NYPD. I can't tell you how happy Bob and I are to be back. Hey, we're cops, NYPD cops."

The corks popped and the champagne flowed. Bob and I agreed that we enjoyed being cops much more than we liked being spies.

As we were leaving, Norquist told us to be in his office first thing in the morning.

It wouldn't be a party.

CHAPTER 49

Bobbie

B ob and I walked into Norquist's office at 8:30 a.m.

He stood and smiled. It was more like a grimace.

"Good morning, Commissioner," we both said.

"The name's Ralph, guys. If you folks can address the Director of the CIA by his first name, the least I can do is bow to NYPD royalty and adopt the same policy." I had told him that Buster insisted we call him by his first name, and obviously Norquist took it to heart. *NYPD royalty*? He was being really sweet and flattering.

"So, what exciting things do you have planned for us, Commissh...I mean Ralph?" I said.

"I wish I could welcome you two back with an easy case to sink your teeth into, but unfortunately I cannot. What I'm about to put on your talented shoulders is like something out of a horror movie, a really scary and creepy horror movie."

He paused to let his words sink in. Ralph is great at inserting drama into a conversation.

"You've heard, I'm sure, about the market for body parts and organs."

I was suddenly glad that Bob and I had a light breakfast.

"Sure," Bob said, "that's been going on for years as disgusting as it is. Has something new shown up?"

"Yes, it has been going on for years," Ralph said, "but it's now taken on a new dimension, a horrifying dimension. In the past, organ stealing for money has been a typical mob hit. They would kill someone they intended to murder anyway, and then give the organs to an organ-gathering network for a profit. It was always a small-time operation, even though the mob was involved. That has changed. Organ theft, preceded by murder, has now grown to Amazon-sized dimensions. From what we know so far, it's a conglomeration of scumbags, and they're organized like an army."

"Is there one group that heads up the enterprise?" I asked.

"Yes," Ralph said. "Hold onto your hats, and maybe be prepared to throw up. None other than the MS-13 gang, the cruelest pack of motherfuckers on the planet, is heading up the operation. And cruelty is the keyword. When they find an organ 'donor' target, they combine the organ harvesting with a hunting exercise. That's right, in typical MS-13 fashion, they've turned it into a goddam sport. Before they kill the victim, they take him to a forest, give him a head start, and hunt him down. Sometimes we think civilization has come a long way, until we see something like this."

"How do they cash in on the harvest?" Bob asked.

"They use layers of middlemen, who simply turn around and fence the organs to willing buyers. Bobbie, Bob, I want to shut down these sons of bitches. I just wish New York had the death penalty. These people are animals, fucking animals."

"Ralph," I said, pleased that I could call him by his first name, "do we have any inside information about these creeps?"

"Yes, we do, Bobbie. Two MS-13 lovelies realized that the barbarity was too much even for them, so they came forward. They're in lock-down at Rikers Island in a form of witness protection program. In the view of the rest of the gang, their lives aren't worth a nickel, so that's why we need to protect them."

"What are the victim profiles?" Bob asked.

"Young healthy people between 15 and 22, people with their lives ahead of them."

"Can you tell us more detail on what goes on?" I asked.

"I'd rather let you two pros speak to them yourselves. If I tell you what I know, I think I'll puke. The corrections officers at Rikers are expecting your call. Eat light before you interrogate them. I'm serious."

The next day, Bob and I would engage in an interrogation we'd never forget.

CHAPTER 50

Bob

Bobbie and I were happy about our new case assignment. Well, we weren't happy about talking to sub-human slime, but we were happy we'd have a shot at bringing this horrible shit to an end. We couldn't believe our ears yesterday when Norquist us told about this savage enterprise. Harvesting organs is bad enough, but turning it into a sport by hunting the victims down and killing them is beyond belief.

A patrol car took us to Rikers Island, New York City's main jail complex. Rikers Island is a 413 -acre island in the East River between Queens and the Bronx. Many people think of Rikers as a human cesspool, harboring some of the most vicious criminals in the city while they awaited trial. A corrections officer (CO) was waiting for us at the entrance. Norquist had called ahead to arrange for our visit. I had been to Rikers quite a few times over the years, and I always hated it. Besides the noise of criminals screaming and cursing at you, the stench of the place is almost overwhelming. One of the inmates' favorite pastimes is to hurl feces into the hallway. Bobbie took a disinfectant spray bottle from her purse, squirted some on her wrist, held it up to her nostrils and took a deep breath. Then she handed the bottle to me. The CO led us down a series of hallways. I noticed that the farther we got, the fewer the prisoners, and the less it stunk. The unit we headed to was reserved for, as Norquist put it, witness protection. We were led to an interrogation room, where our first interrogee sat, shackled to the table by his ankles and wrists. I asked the corrections officer to wait outside the room. He objected, but I explained to him that this was on the commissioner's orders, which was a lie, but fuck it. MS-13 is known for bribery, among other lovely activities, and I wanted to be sure that the CO wasn't in on any deals.

Our two interrogees were being protected as witnesses but were also imprisoned on charges of first-degree murder. I had already discussed this with the DA, who had told their attorneys that he is willing to consider a plea bargain, on the condition that the former MS-13 boys cooperate.

Our first interrogee was Sancho Almeda, a pleasant-looking guy about age 25. About as pleasant looking as you can get with all the tattoos. What do these gangs find so fascinating about tattoos? Beats me. It *does* establish the bearer of the tattoo as a member of the gang. He spoke perfect English, with only a slight Spanish accent. Even if he didn't speak English, that would be fine with us, as both Bobbie and I are fluent in Spanish.

MS-13 always amazed me as a gang phenomenon. MS stands for *Mara Salvatrucha*. Some people think the gang is named for *La Mara*, a street gang in San Salvador, and the Salvatrucha guerrillas who fought in the Salvadoran Civil War. Also, the word *mara* means gang in Central American slang and is derived from *marabunta*, an aggressive type of ant. "Salvatrucha" may be a combination of the words *Salvadoran* and *trucha*, a Central American dialect word for being alert. The number 13, most agree, is for the letter "m" being the 13th letter in the alphabet. So, the marketing department of the gang likes the brand, MS-13.

Estimates vary, but most agree that the number of gang members ranges somewhere between 8,000 and 10,000 in the US, and 30,000 to 50,000 worldwide. To say that it's complicated is an understatement. It's first of all a social organization and secondly a criminal enterprise. We middle-class Americans have our country clubs, and service organizations like Kiwanis, Lions, and Rotary from which we satisfy our desire for community. The poor kids who get sucked up into the tentacles of MS-13 find their community in a world of stark violence.

And make no doubt about it, violence is at the heart of the MS-13 and is what makes it a target of law enforcement in the United States, Central America, and beyond. Violence is central to the MS-13 philosophy, if you can honor their shit with the word philosophy. Violence is its *modus operandi*, and is also used for evaluation and discipline of its own members. One of their more sickening practices is a tradition called a "beat-in," where a prospective member is viciously thrashed before he can join the ranks. It also builds a sense of cohesion and camaraderie within the gang's various cliques. Unlike soldiers, who engage in violence by necessity, these creeps perform the acts because they enjoy it. This ferocity has enhanced the brand of MS-13, allowing it to grow in size and geographic reach. But it has undermined its ability to enter more sophisticated, money-making criminal activities. Potential partners see the gang as an unreliable, highly visible target, and the gang's vicious outbursts reinforce that reputation.

That was until recently, as Bobbie and I are learning. MS-13 has learned to be secretive about its activities. The sickening new program of organ harvesting is right up the gang's creepy alley. They use violence to generate revenue, as well as a way to enhance their social status among themselves. Lovely people.

Bobbie and I discussed whether it was a good idea for her to be involved in the interrogation. We were worried that the code of *machismo* would get in the way, and that our interrogees would not feel comfortable talking to a woman. Bullshit. Bobbie is the finest interrogator I've ever seen, and I insisted she be part of the questioning with no restrictions. Hell, these guys are after plea bargains, so they're not going to flex their macho muscles around us.

"My name is Detective Bob Lawton, and this is my partner Detective Nelson. Do you mind if we call you Sancho?"

He nodded, almost politely, after giving Bobbie a thorough going-over with his leering eyes. I briefly thought of pummeling him, but realized that wouldn't fit in with today's mission. After I went through the preliminary questions, I began the interrogation.

"Sancho, do you recognize the name Hector Allesandro?

He started to cry. No fake tears here, but loud sobs accompanied by heaving shoulders. This went on for almost five minutes. Bobbie and I looked at each other and shrugged.

I let him gain his composure. Any detective knows that if you try to butt in on a crying jag to get information, you may as well cancel the interrogation.

"Hector Allesandro is the little dude I killed last March. He was 15 years old and really short."

"Can you explain how you did that, Sancho?" Bobbie asked.

He started crying again. If remorse affects a plea bargain, which it does, he's already shaved a few years off a possible sentence. This interrogation, including the crying outbursts, were taped and would be included in our report to the district attorney.

"It happened in Prospect Park in Brooklyn on April 20, 2018 at 11:30 at night. My bros turned Allesandro loose and counted 10 minutes on a timer. Then they sent me after him."

"How were you able to see him at 11:30 at night?" I asked.

"One of my bros gave me these things I think they call night-vision goggles. It was almost like daylight."

"And what, if anything, did you do then?" Bobbie asked, as she shredded a napkin.

"I took off after the little dude. I could see him stumbling around and tripping over bushes and shit."

"Did you carry a weapon?"

"Yes." Sancho started to cry again. I wondered if he'd been coached on the fine art of plea bargaining.

I glanced over at Bobbie. She gave me a look that said, "Keep going." Bobbie and I have acquired a skill for communication without speaking. A glance, a wink, a nod is all we need. If you're as close as Bobbie and me, words often aren't necessary.

When he came around, I asked him to describe the weapon and its ammunition.

"It was a 22-caliber rifle with rubber bullets."

Rubber bullets? Rubber fucking-bullets? Of course, I didn't say that, but I think the surprise on my face resonated with my interrogee. I noticed Bobbie put her face in her hands.

I took a deep breath, suppressing my urge to throw up. I then asked a question to which the answer was obvious, but I needed to ask it anyway.

"And why did you use rubber bullets?"

"Because the idea wasn't to kill him, but to slow him down—and hurt him."

I took another deep breath. Bobbie went pale as a sheet.

"Did he scream as you shot him with the rubber bullets?" Bobbie asked.

"No, the bros taped his mouth shut."

"It must have been difficult for him to run through the night being shot by rubber bullets, and only being able to breathe through his nostrils." This wasn't really a question, just my attempt to rub this bastard's face in it and remind him what he'd done to that poor innocent kid.

"Sancho, did there come a time when you stopped chasing Hector Allesandro?" Bobbie asked. Although Bobbie is a calm, cool interrogator, I had the feeling that she wanted to smash a chair over this creep's head.

"Yes, when he fell and stopped moving."

"How long did it take for that to happen?" She asked.

"One hour after I started to chase him."

I wanted to rip this scumbag's face off, but I took a breath and reminded myself that interrogations are best kept unemotional, as my partner often reminds me.

"And after he stopped moving, what did you do?" Bobbie asked, her face showing pure disgust.

"I wrapped a cord around his neck and choked him until his heart stopped beating. We're not supposed to spill blood because blood helps preserve the organs we sell."

"Okay, we're going to take a short break." I went into the hallway and told the CO to take the prisoner to the bathroom and then return him to the interrogation room.

Bobbie and I huddled after we visited the restrooms. She grabbed my hand.

"It's going fine, honey. This is the most disgusting interrogation I've ever been involved in. Let's not forget to get as many names as possible."

We continued our questioning when the prisoner was brought back in.

"Sancho, can you give me the names of other gang members involved in this organ harvesting operation?"

"If I tell you that, Mr. Bob, my life isn't worth shit. They'll find me here and kill me."

"Well, first let me say that you're in a witness protection unit, and nobody can get near you. Also, I should point out, I have the ability to get your case transferred to Oklahoma, where they not only have the death penalty, but death by firing squad." That, of course, was complete bullshit, the part about my ability to get the case transferred. I have no such authority. But I felt no hesitancy about lying to this slime ball to get him to open up.

Apparently, I got through to him. He gave us 10 names, much more than I had hoped for. Some of the names were lies, I was sure, people he wanted revenge on for one thing or another. But at least it was a start, 10 more animals to interrogate and squeeze for information.

At 1 p.m. we broke for lunch before we would meet with the next interrogee. Bobbie and I had a light lunch—a *very* light lunch—in a small dining room reserved for cops and other friendlies.

"I think we can use a shower, honey," she said. I didn't think she was flirting with me, as she often does when mentioning a shower. *I* sure as hell needed a shower. Maybe I'll use Brillo to wash the scum off me.

<hr />

Our next interrogee was Eduardo Sanchez, another MS-13 retiree. He was also 25 and, like Almeda, covered in standard MS-13 tattoos.

His story wasn't much different from Almeda's. Another tale of a young man, this one age 16, who was turned loose in a forest, hunted down and killed so his internal organs could be fenced. The major difference in his story and Almeda's was that the young prey that Sanchez hunted was pursued in the month of February, and he wore only shorts and a tee shirt. It's hard to believe that some people who call themselves human can be so cruel. The good news is that he gave us 20 more names.

So, our day at Rikers was a wrap, and we were driven back to our apartment. We both showered, separately, neither of us feeling very amorous after our disgusting day of interrogations.

We then called an Uber and went to the beautiful French Restaurant, La Grenouille, on 52nd Street. After our lovely day at Rikers, Bobbie and I both agreed that we wanted as much pleasant civilization as we could get. After dinner we went to the Metropolitan Opera House and saw *L'Italiana in Algeri*, a hysterically funny opera by Rossini. We both agreed that we didn't want to see anything heavy and tragic. We had enough of that at Rikers.

CHAPTER 51

Bobbie

The next morning Bob and I met with Commissioner Norquist (Ralph) after our revolting day at Rikers Island. At least we enjoyed a funny opera and a pleasant dinner at La Grenouille last night, although I didn't have much of an appetite. I think we did a good job of interrogating the two MS-13 turncoats. We got 30 names, many of whom we were sure comprised MS-13 organ-harvesting management. It may not be all of them, for sure, but it was a great start.

"How I could possibly do without you two is a mystery to me," Norquist said. "As I've said countless times before, job well done."

"The two guys we interrogated were deep in the program," I said, "and I'm sure most of the names they gave us are good. In my opinion, Ralph, I think we should arrest these creeps now. If they aren't the whole management team, they're a big part of it, and they'll lead us to the others. Do you agree, Bob?"

"Yes, I completely agree with Bobbie, Ralph. We should round up these animals."

"Okay," Commissioner Ralph said, "I'm going to pull the

trigger—today. I've started already, as I waited for the information you just gave me. I'm ordering these 30 savages rounded up in an ESU (Emergency Service Unit) operation."

In the NYPD, the Emergency Service Unit is essentially a SWAT team, as it's known in other departments. The main difference is that the ESU at the NYPD is a regularly manned component of the department, as opposed to SWAT teams which are typically a collateral function and are convened as needed. Beyond that, the ESU and a SWAT team are basically the same. SWAT stands for *Special Weapons and Tactics*. All major police departments as well as the 56 FBI field offices around the country have SWAT teams at their disposal. SWAT teams are used for high risk situations, such as hostage incidents or rounding up dangerous criminals. A SWAT team mission is more of a military type action than a typical law enforcement operation. An *Enhanced* SWAT team is a force of 40 officers and heavy-duty weapons, including MP5/10mm machine guns and M4 carbines. Given the barbarity of the MS-13 organ harvesting, I think the commissioner is on target to use the ESU. Norquist doesn't want to blow this one.

"Bob and Bobbie, we're going to war with these fucking animals. I've already contacted FBI Director Watson for her to assign three FBI SWAT teams in addition to the ESU we have on call at the NYPD. This organ harvesting shit stops *now*."

Bob and I don't think of ourselves as part of the muscle end of the NYPD, except in rare cases, such as when I killed the man who shot Bob. Our part of the organ harvesting battle is on hold for now. We'll be involved again soon as interrogators when they round up the creeps.

Within 24 hours, all 30 of the MS-13 suspects were arrested and are in custody at the Metropolitan Correctional Center, a short walk from One Police Plaza. Wow. Those ESU and SWAT people don't kid around. Commissioner Ralph assigned six other detectives to work on the interrogations, all of whom have worked on MS-13 matters over the years.

All the interrogating detectives speak fluent Spanish, including Bob and me. Our fellow detectives all look up to us, I'm proud to say.

Within 48 hours, the MS-13 organ harvesting operation was brought to a total standstill, except for the criminal prosecutions. One of the shocking and sickening things that came out of the interrogations was the number of people who had been abducted and turned into hunted prey before being killed for their body organs. No fewer than 78 young people, who had been reported missing, were the victims. So, the operation was a success and, I'm proud to say, Bob and I made it all happen.

We felt more relaxed and calmer than we had in a long time. So, what do we do when we feel relaxed and calm? We went home to our apartment, undressed each other, showered, and climbed into bed. Bob and I love it when we're eye to eye, cheek to cheek, and well, you know.

CHAPTER 52

Bob

Commissioner Norquist, or Ralph as we call him now, called Bobbie and me into his office.

"You two have been working your asses off and I want you to take a few days off." He reached over and handed us a set of keys. "These are for my beach house in East Hampton, and please be my guests for a week. While you're there you may want to check out some houses for sale, a place where you can invest some of your new book-deal money. I've said it so many times, I'm almost tired of listening to myself, but you two are the best detectives in the NYPD. So, my friends, head east and chill for a few days."

"Ralph," Bobbie said, "I can't believe this. The only reason for this meeting is to give us keys to a beach house?"

"Of course not," he said laughing as he handed Bobbie a file. "Here's a triple homicide I want you to work on. You BBs love to keep busy. It will give you something to do when you're not smelling the ocean air and walking along the beach. See you guys next week."

After we walked into Ralph's sparkling beach house in East Hampton and unpacked, Bobbie and I decided to go antique store browsing in the village. The weather was perfect, and we enjoyed our walk. We even left our guns back at the house. We bought a couple of antiques we thought would look great in our apartment. We were, to use a word strange to us, relaxing.

That afternoon, we planned on completing the final draft of our book, *Detectiving*, before it would go to Mildred Cunningham, our editor. Every book needs an editor, but Bobbie and I felt confident that we were about to deliver an excellent piece of work. Bobbie and I know our stuff.

After we completed our writing chores in the den, Bobbie sat down at the kitchen counter while I made us a shaker of martinis. We looked at each other and both had the same thought. We've gotten to know each other's thinking just from a glance. So, I picked up our new multiple murder file, set it on the counter, and opened it. I read aloud from the summary on the first page.

We then went page by page, making careful notes as we always do. The case was about a triple homicide of a family from the Riverdale section of the Bronx. A 35-year-old mother, her 13-year-old daughter, and 15-year-old son had been killed, each shot in the head.

A Department of Justice study disclosed that 62% of violent crimes were committed by offenders known to the victims. As any detective will tell you, the perpetrator is often a close family member, including the father.

But in this case, the father had died of a heart attack two years before. The two detectives assigned to the case before us, (who knew that the case would eventually be assigned to Bobbie and me) had done some excellent preliminary investigation, including pouring over emails from the mother and the two kids. Nothing disclosed any ill will between the victims and anyone with whom they corresponded. The detectives fanned out and interrogated neighbor after neighbor, as they should. Nothing. There was no evidence of loud screaming or that the family had troubles with anybody. Every neighbor they spoke to expressed shock that such nice people were murdered. The CSU unit gathered all the necessary blood evidence and fingerprints. None of the prints matched any criminal or suspect in the NYPD files. It could have been a random killing.

Although I would never say it to anyone but Bobbie, it soon became apparent why Commissioner Ralph wanted us to handle the case. It was a puzzle, and nobody figures out puzzles better than Bobbie and me. This would be a tough case, just the kind we like to work on.

I poured our martinis and sat next to Bobbie. We clinked glasses and kissed.

"So, partner, how do you think we should proceed?"

She smiled and stroked my face.

"Like we always do—*together*."

PART TWO

CHAPTER 53

Bobbie

"W" ow, you look pretty this morning," Bob said.

"Don't tell me I look pretty when I'm pissed off."

"Okay, you look pretty pissed off."

I cracked up. Leave it to Bob derail my self-centered anger with his humor.

"What's the matter, baby?" Bob said.

"I'm a friggin First Grade detective and I shouldn't have to put up with shit from a clerk in the records office."

I had inadvertently placed my working file folder under a folder that contained evidence I took from a crime scene. Simple mistake, which should have been simply corrected by the clerk. But no, she wanted a written order from Commissioner Norquist, who happened to be out of town for five days. And now I'm without my file folder, which includes my notebook. I can do without my notebook as easily as I can do without my eyes.

Bob volunteered to handle the problem, of course. My partner is insanely handsome, and all the clerks in the records office are women. Bob returned five minutes later. He didn't just convince the clerk to surrender the folder, she actually handed it to Bob.

"Thanks, honey," I said. "You sure have a way of communicating with women, don't you?"

"Well, I convinced you to marry me, didn't I?"

Bob and I had just returned from our relaxing week at Ralph Norquist's beach House in East Hampton. As usual, we used some of our vacation time to work a file, a difficult file — *The Morton Case,* a triple murder of a young woman and her two teenagers.

Loretta Morton, age 35, was found in the kitchen, dead of a gunshot wound to her head. Her daughter, Janice Morton, age 13, along with her 15-year-old brother Jason, were found in the living room, also dead from gunshots to the head. The detectives who did the initial case workup while Bob and I were away did a good job, but their thorough work didn't come up with a clue — not one goddam clue. This was shaping up to be the kind of case that Bob and I love to work — a difficult one, even though a sad one.

Although the Bronx isn't known for beauty, the Riverdale area is a pretty, almost suburban neighborhood of expensive homes and condos. The Morton house was large and was situated on a half-acre overlooking the Hudson River. When Bob and I visited the place, I immediately noticed that the property was surrounded by tall hedges. That may provide privacy, but it's lousy for security because it gives cover to prowlers — or assassins. The late Thomas Morton was a wealthy art dealer and left his family well-provided for. One fortunate thing for our investigation was that Thomas Morton was quite well-known and showed up in the newspapers and magazines often. Loretta Morton was also somewhat famous as a talented ceramic artist. Our first task was to find what may be hiding in plain sight—on the Internet.

So as not to duplicate our efforts, Bob and I agreed that I would concentrate on researching Thomas Morton, and Bob would research the murder victims, Loretta Morton and the two kids, Janice and Franklin.

Bob and I love to work together, but sometimes our work is tedious, such as pouring through the Internet looking for data points that intersect, especially data points involving names. Whenever we came across a name in the same article as one of our target names, we would tell each other, and then we'd make a note of that name in our separate files.

I was glad we faced each other across the desk. Whenever I felt angst coming on, I would take a moment to stare into Bob's hazel eyes, which always calmed me. You would think I'd get used those gorgeous eyes. Never happened, and I don't think it ever will, not that I want it to.

After hammering away for three hours, we noticed a name that appeared often, and in articles about each of our targets, Thomas, Loretta, Janice, and Franklin Morton. The name was Angelo DiCrispino. Nothing dramatic, nothing that could be called a clue— except the constant appearance of his name was a clue in itself.

Bob said he'd temporarily stop searching for the three family members and would concentrate on Angelo DiCrispino. I readily agreed. Who is this guy, and why does his name keep appearing near our target names?

CHAPTER 54

Bob

Angelo DiCrispino isn't a unique name, but it's not a common one, like John Smith. I found a lot of Angelo DiCrispinos in my Internet search, most of whom showed nothing remarkable, except for one. An Angelo DiCrispino is a mob enforcer from New York City, a Mafia hit man in other words. A number of newspaper articles, as well as NYPD records, made his mob involvement apparent. Hold on, slow down. Just because I found a guy with the name of a known criminal doesn't mean it has anything to do with our case, as my outside-the-box-thinking partner reminded me. But it *is* a piece of information I need to chase down. Could these murders have been mob hits? Something worth speculating about.

I bounced my ideas off Bobbie, as she does with me. Bobbie agreed that Angelo DiCrispino deserves attention, a lot of attention.

CHAPTER 55

Bobbie

B ob and I found numerous mentions of a guy named Angelo DiCrispino in the same articles as our murder victims as well as the late father who died of a heart attack. But *did* he die of a heart attack? My ever-diligent Bob went to the hospital and looked up the autopsy report. Yes, it was a heart attack, but there was more. The report read, "Cardiac arrest secondary to a choking incident." Could the father, Thomas Morton, have been murdered as well as the mother and two kids?

Bob tracked down everything he could find on the mysterious Angelo DiCrispino, and discovered that a man by that name is a mob enforcer, a hit man.

Further research showed that he once lived in Chicago and worked with the local Mafia, which had been almost obliterated in 1943 when they nailed Al Capone. The man now lives in New York, in Riverdale. Interesting—he lives in Riverdale, where the Mortons once lived and were murdered. Because of DiCrispino's numerous scrapes with law enforcement, his fingerprints and DNA were on file. So, it's simply a matter of comparing the prints and DNA, which the detectives found when they inspected the crime scene. Simple, no? But no print or DNA sample matched that of DiCrispino, not one. We were disappointed, but not surprised. Hit men, who kill for a living, are experts in hiding their tracks.

Bob and I would soon learn that DiCrispino's employer has been on the rise. The mob was no longer defeated.

CHAPTER 56

Bob

Bobbie and I walked to our favorite diner for our usual breakfast. I got it right a few years ago when I bought a condo, a whole building actually, such a short walk from where I work. I now share it with Bobbie, my wife, my partner, the love of my life.

As we walked into the diner, hand in hand, we were greeted by a few of our fellow cops. Everybody seems to know that Bobbie and I are crazy about each other. They also respect our professionalism. I must admit that we're damn good detectives, especially Bobbie. I've always been proud of my work, but there was something refreshing about being a student of my partner, yes, a student. Bobbie knows her stuff.

After breakfast we walked to One PP, arriving at 8:15 a.m. We like to get to work early. After we walked into our office and closed the door, we hugged and kissed. It may seem crazy for two married people, who made passionate love the night before, to begin their day at the office with a hug and a kiss. But that's the way it is with Bobbie and me. It's what we do. It's who we are. And I intend to keep it that way. Bobbie always keeps a small bottle of hand wash in her purse to wipe the lipstick off my face.

Margie Nathan, Commissioner Ralph's assistant, knocked and entered our office with a huge file under her arm.

"Here's more stuff on the *Palermo Incident Case,*" Margie said. "The commissioner called me this morning, even though he's on vacation, and told me to give this new material to you. He asks that you give this case your undivided attention, not that I need to tell that to you guys. Enjoy, BBs, you have some big work cut out for you."

Everybody seems to call us the BBs, and I'm getting to like it. Bobbie and Bob—the BBs.

Before he left for vacation, Norquist dropped a bomb on us, a matter we call *The Palermo Incident* case. It seems that the mob, aka the Mafia, aka La Cosa Nostra, is in resurgence, a huge resurgence. Ever since the Giuliani administration, everybody thought the Mafia was old history. Not so.

In the Mafia Commission Trial, which ran from February 1985 through November 1986, then U.S. Attorney Giuliani indicted 11 organized crime figures, including the heads of New York›s infamous "Five Families," under the Racketeer Influenced and Corrupt Organizations Act (RICO). The charges included extortion, labor racketeering, and murder for hire. *Time* magazine called this the "Case of Cases," possibly "the most significant assault on the infrastructure of organized crime since the high command of the Chicago Mafia was swept away in 1943." The *Times* quoted Giuliani's stated intention: "Our approach is to wipe out the five families."

Gambino crime family boss Paul Castellano evaded conviction when he and his underboss, Thomas Bilotti, were murdered on the streets of Midtown Manhattan in December, 1985.

Three other heads of the Five Families were sentenced to 100 years in prison in January 1987. The Genovese and Colombo family leaders, Tony Salerno and Carmine Persico received additional sentences in separate trials, with 70-year and 39-year sentences to run consecutively.

Most observers believed that Giuliani ridded the country of some of the worst criminals at large. Or so it seemed. But it didn't last, as recent events have been telling us.

The Five Families still exist, although with new names. They are now the Marquessa, Gandolfo, Rubino, Lombardo, and Critello families. And they've expanded their portfolio of activities from extortion, labor racketeering, and murder for hire. Although they're still involved with those lovely enterprises, they now include massive drug smuggling, prostitution, and online gambling. As Ralph's assistant said, Bobbie and I have our work cut out for us. And, because Bobbie and I are now on the case, so does the mob.

Because the two of us have strong suspicions about the mob hit man, Angelo DiCrispino, we included the Morton murders with our Mafia cases, especially the *Palermo Incident* case.

The Mafia Commission Trial in the 1980s was an FBI show. But now, on specific orders from the attorney general, Bobbie and I would lead the new investigation. We've become kind of famous recently, having busted a couple of large cases. We were enjoying our day in the sun. Commissioner Norquist, or Ralph as we now call him, is a friend as well as a boss. He kindly, if somewhat embarrassingly, refers to us as "NYPD royalty."

Well, royalty or not, we have work to do. TV cop shows often portray detectives as swashbuckling gunslingers, who violently defeat the bad guys each week between commercials. The reality is that detective work means interrogating witnesses, examining blood stains, analyzing fingerprints, and hours of looking at evidence. Yes, we carry guns, but unlike the cops on TV, we seldom use them. The only times I've fired my gun, not counting my time as a Marine captain in Iraq, was on the practice shooting range. Bobbie only fired her weapon once in the line of duty, when she saved my life by killing that would-be assassin.

"Honey, this is a big one," Bobbie said.

"Big one? I'd say so. Two American senators and a congressman have been assassinated in Sicily. The commissioner is calling this the *Palermo Incident* case. The CIA will have jurisdiction over there, but we can at least start digging. Let's review what we know already. Your thoughts?"

"Well, we know that both senators and the congressman were investigating the Mafia, and were very public about it," Bobbie said. "I recall when Rudy Giuliani headed up that mob trial in the 80s when he was U.S. Attorney, the Sicilian Mafia offered $800,000 for his hide. These bastards play for keeps. The FBI investigations, as well as our own, tell us that the mob is playing a new role, a *big* new role. They've squeezed out the low-level loan sharks and other turds, and are now bringing it all in under the Mafia brand. We need to be careful, Bob. I don't think we should go anywhere without protection, and I don't mean just our own guns. Shit, if they're willing to whack elected government officials, you and I are small fry. Thank God Ralph has assigned us bodyguards."

Bobbie and I were concerned that we may be on the hit list.

We'd soon find out that our concerns were well-founded.

CHAPTER 57

Bob

At 6:30 we walked to our apartment. As we walked in the door, Bobbie screamed, "Bob, stop!" She lowered her shoulder and pushed me back into the hallway, like a running back throwing a block. The force of the explosion blew the door open. It hung there, cockeyed, on its hinges. We hugged, wrapped in the sickening feeling that we had just missed being killed. Bobbie would later tell me that, as soon as we walked into the apartment, she saw a package on the floor next to the kitchen counter. If you see something, say something, or in Bobbie's case, *do something*. Once again, she saved my life—and hers. I have a great partner.

Our bodyguards weren't injured because they walked behind us.

Our apartment was a crime scene for the next 24 hours. The kitchen and den were totally destroyed, and the rest of the place smelled of bomb smoke. The clothing in our drawers and closets was covered in the smoke, so we told our driver to take us to a nearby store where we would pick up new duds. Our bodyguards accompanied us. For the near future our new home would be the nearby Marriott Residence Inn.

How the hell do we get any investigating done from a hotel room?

But then the thought occurred to me that we couldn't get anything done if we were dead.

CHAPTER 58

Bobbie

B
ob and I sat in the den of our Marriott Residence unit. We were under strict orders not to move, orders straight from Commissioner Ralph, even though he was on vacation.

At 8:30 a.m. the phone rang. It was the commissioner. "I'll be there in 10 minutes," he said.

"But you're supposed to be taking a well-earned vacation," I said, but he had already hung up.

The doorbell rang and Ralph Norquist walked in, accompanied by one of our bodyguards.

"Vacation or not," Ralph said, "when my two best detectives, not to mention my good friends, almost got fucking killed, I knew I had to come here. You two are going to hate what I'm about to say, but I'm putting you into the Witness Protection Program, and I've already cleared it with the FBI. The place where you'll be staying isn't far from here, and you'll be closely guarded. The Mafia plays rough, as you saw last night when you were almost killed by bomb. No fucking way will I give them another chance."

"But Ralph," I said, "how can Bob and I interrogate people from behind closed doors?"

"For the time being, and I have no idea how long that may be, you will be out of the interrogation business, even though you and Bob are the best on the block when it comes to questioning witnesses. But you can't question people if you're dead. As you will see shortly, the place where you'll be taken is large and comfortable. You two will spend your time reviewing files and coming up with theories. I'm sorry, but this isn't negotiable. I want you two alive, my friends."

An hour later we were taken to a beautiful brownstone on East 65th Street, after we underwent a do-over by a police makeup artist. Bob was given blond wig and a beard and wore a pillow under his shirt to make him look heavy. My blond hair was covered in a black wig, and I was also plumped up with stuffing under my clothes. We both wore dark-rimmed eyeglasses.

"Hey, chubby lady, you look alluring," Bob said.

"You too, fatso. C'mon let's get undisguised."

After we changed into normal clothes, we took a tour of our new surroundings. Just as Ralph Norquist said, the place was beautiful. Two floors of our own, and an apartment downstairs for our bodyguards. It had a huge den, with a plexiglass-surrounded terrace that had a great view of Central Park. It sported three bedrooms, two and a half bathrooms, a well-equipped gym, an eat-in kitchen, and a small dining room. Bob and I agreed that it was the prettiest prison we could imagine. But it was a prison.

Above us was a lovely outdoor garden with a running track surrounding it. A small table created an outdoor eating area for taking meals outside in good weather. The walls, of course, were all bullet-proof plexiglass. Witness Protection means witness protection.

As Bob was inspecting the gym, I decided to rummage through

a large steamer trunk in the corner of the den. I couldn't believe my eyes. "Oh, my God," I yelled. "Look, Bob, our favorite boardgame, *Clue*. There was also a chess set, checkers, multiple decks of cards, *Monopoly,* and *Risk*.

We both knew we'd be busy analyzing evidence, but it can only go so far without people to interrogate, and we had none. We'd have plenty of time for games, working on our book, as well as the usual playing around that Bob and I love. We may be prisoners against our will, but it was beginning to look like fun. We had a light dinner—the fridge was amply stocked with food—and played a game of *Clue*. It was almost a draw, but I won.

We still had some work to do on the project for which we had been paid a $15 million advance—*Detectiving*, our soon-to-be-launched book.

When we spent a week at Ralph Norquist's beach house, we got a ton of work done on the book. Bob and I submitted the first draft to our editor, Mildred Cunningham from Random House. After we worked on Mildred's edits for a couple of hours, we were both tired, but I wanted to put some positive thoughts in our heads before we went to bed, something to give us perspective on being in the Witness Protection Program.

"Hey, Bob," I said. "Let's think about some things we should be happy about. You go first."

"We're alive," Bob said.

"We're uninjured," I said.

"We're in love," we both said.

CHAPTER 59

Bob

obbie and I were beginning to hate the Witness Protection Program. We'd been locked up in this apartment for two months. We're both accustomed to getting things done, to making things happen. Hey, we're cops, we're detectives. We both love our work, because of what we do — we solve puzzles. But being locked up doesn't make it easy to solve anything, even though the surroundings are beautiful. Yes, we play games a lot. Bobbie, with her devilish imagination, even came up with the idea to play strip poker. But we're not cut out to play games, although I must admit the strip poker is exciting, especially because I'm a good poker player. I love baring her gorgeous body, one article of clothing at a time.

Our editor was happy with the draft we sent her, but of course, as a good editor, she had excellent suggestions and demands. So far, we'd hit all the deadlines she set for us, and we expected to finish the rewrite in three weeks. But we both felt restless.

The mob investigation team, of which Bobbie and I are supposedly in charge, has been busy gathering information, but information gathering can only go so far without hitting the streets and asking questions. Commissioner Ralph wants to keep us safe, and I can't disagree with him. Hell, after our apartment was bombed, we realized that we're targets. But Bobbie and I have always taken our work seriously, and it's hard to be serious when locked up in an apartment.

Bobbie's going stir crazy too.

CHAPTER 60

Bobbie

B eing a prisoner is no fun, even when you're in beautiful surroundings. It does have certain benefits. Our sex life has always been best described as "frisky," but here, we make love at least once a day, sometimes twice. Hell, yesterday we did it three times. Nothing like an exciting game of strip poker to get your juices flowing. Bob's just plain sweet, and never stops surprising me. I don't just love him, I like him. We're spouses, we're partners, and we're also best friends.

But we both agreed that the Witness Protection Program was getting on our nerves. Bob and I have handled some huge cases, solving puzzles like we always do. We wrapped up that big terrorist plot where cops around the country were getting assassinated. Then we cracked the case involving the horrible gang, MS-13, where they were harvesting body organs from innocent young people.

But we're anxious to get back to our work. Some have called us the two best detectives in the country, and we want to resume doing what we do so well. Working with Bob is great. Good partners know how to bounce ideas off each other, and we do just that. Bob has a finely-honed sense of logic. He would put together pieces of evidence that took us toward a solution. I'm more intuitive, on the other hand. Bob tells me that I think outside the box, and that's true. As he loves to say, I walk East when others walk West. So, we complement each other perfectly. Being in love with your partner is a bonus, a nice bonus.

But Bob and I need to get back to doing what we're good at, and it isn't screwing our brains out, although we love to do just that. We need to solve puzzles.

What we didn't know is that tomorrow we'd have an answer to our restlessness in the Witness Protection Program.

CHAPTER 61

Bob

A t 2 p.m. one of our bodyguards buzzed us and said we had a visitor, and that it had been cleared with headquarters. When I asked him who it was, he said we'd find out soon enough. Why the cloak and dagger?

Our doorbell rang and when I opened it, there was none other than Sarah Watson, Director of the FBI.

Bobbie and I had met her many times before. She's one of our favorite people; soft-spoken, polite, and talented as hell at what she does, which is running the most important law enforcement agency in the country.

"Bobbie and Bob, it's great to see you two again. You've done great work for the NYPD, the FBI, the CIA, and not to mention the nation. As I've said many times before, you two are the best detectives there are."

Uh, oh. Could there be an agenda behind all this flattery?

"So how do you like it in the Witness Protection Program?" She asked.

"Well, to be honest, Sarah, Bobbie and I don't feel like we're getting anything done."

"I think I may have a solution for that," she said. "As you're well aware, the country's problem with organized crime has recently hit crisis proportions. Hell, that's why you folks are here, because of a mob assassination attempt on you. It's gotten bad and is getting worse as we speak. *The Palermo Incident*, as it's called, where two senators and a congressman were killed, has law enforcement in crisis mode, especially the FBI. I have agents fanned out across the country trying to get a handle on all this. We're working closely with the CIA, which has a small army of agents in Palermo."

"So, is this a Sicilian problem?" Bobbie asked.

"That would make it a bit easier, at least from an intelligence gathering point of view. Yes, it is a Sicilian problem, but it's also an American problem. The Sicilian Mafia has morphed into hundreds of smaller units, and the foot soldiers aren't just Sicilian. History tells us that the Mafia in Chicago was wiped out during World War II in 1943. After that came the successful efforts by Rudy Giuliani in taking down the infamous Five Families in New York. What was once the Bonanno, Colombo, Gambino, Genovese, and Lucchese families have been replaced by the Marquessa, Gandolfo, Rubino, Lombardo, and Critello families. I'm sure you two are aware of this because I know you like to keep on top of things. But these aren't just name changes. The mob units have strengthened, grown, and are heavily financed. To put it bluntly, the Five Families are back. And here's something that may shock you. The old Chicago Mafia that died in 1943 when Al Capone went to prison, has also made a resurgence, a huge resurgence. The City of Chicago has always had a serious problem with corruption, as you well know Bobbie, having lived and worked there for many years."

Bobbie raised her eyebrows as if to say, "Tell me about it."

"Let me guess," Bobbie said, "the government of Chicago is in bed with the mob."

"You got that right, Bobbie. Just like in the days of Al Capone, it's often difficult to see where the mob stops and the government starts."

"Is there a lot of cooperation among the Mafia families?" I asked.

"More than cooperation, Bob. The American Mafia, if I can use such a term, has become corporate and sophisticated. It's no longer the days of a guy jumping out of a car with a machine gun, although that still happens. The mob has been studying the way big successful corporations run, and they're patterning themselves that way. The big difference, of course, is the end product of its activities. We're seeing a gigantic enterprise of loan sharking, murder for hire, drugs, and prostitution, just to name a few of its product lines. Where good companies fear to tread, the mob happily fills the shelves."

Somehow all this involves Bobbie and me, otherwise she wouldn't be here. I figured I'd get right to the point.

"How does all this involve Bobbie and me, Sarah?"

"I'm dusting off your status as provisional FBI agents and I'm reappointing you. You won't go through an update of your background check because we want to keep this secret, and having a bunch of people asking questions about you could also raise some questions with the mob, which listens closely. You folks haven't been involved in any illicit activities I should know about, I assume," she said with a laugh.

"Bob cheats at strip poker," Bobbie said.

Sarah cracked up. "I'll make careful note of that for the record."

"All of which brings me to the reason for our meeting. Bobbie and Bob, I'm requesting that you two go undercover—deep undercover—and that you move temporarily to Chicago, the new center of the Mafia's activities. You will be in Evanston, a suburb on the northern border of Chicago. I say that I'm requesting it because I refuse to order you to do this because it may be dangerous. A good makeup artist can work wonders, as you found when you moved here to the WPP. Bob, I recommend that you immediately start to grow a real beard. Bobbie, you're probably the prettiest detective on the street, but we can change that."

"Oh, great, Detective Skank reporting for duty," Bobbie said.

"Don't worry, Bobbie, you'll still be pretty as Bob will be happy to know, but you'll be different, quite different. Pads under clothing can make a big difference. And you can remove them at night—when Bob cheats at strip poker," she said with a laugh.

"Can Bobbie and I talk this over and let you know tomorrow?"

"Of, course; take longer if you wish. If you accept, you will live in a lovely, secure place and will have four bodyguards with you at all times. We'll talk again soon."

When Sarah left, Bobbie and I sat on the couch.

"So, what do you think, honey?" Bobbie said. "Do you want to go back into the spy business?"

"First I have a question. Who said I cheat at strip poker?"

"I was only kidding. I *let* you win. Let's grab a deck of cards and talk about the FBI stuff later."

CHAPTER 62

Bobbie

We woke up to a beautiful late April morning and decided to have a light breakfast on our rooftop garden. We have a big decision to make after our visit from Sarah Watson.

"So, what do you think, Bob, should we take up Sarah on her clandestine operation and move to Chicago?"

"I like the idea, but only if you do, honey. You lived in Chicago for a long time so it's not as if we'll feel lost. You sure as hell know your way around the city, so we should be able to get the job done."

"Like we always do?" I said.

"Yeah, like we always do, partner. I'm not too crazy about getting padded up like a freak every day, but it will be a nice break after being cooped up here. And we'll still be in the most important place — together."

"I say let's do it, honey," I said. "Hell, we'll have four bodyguards and disguises so I think the danger will be minimal. Sarah said she'd tell Ralph Norquist if we agree. I think this will be exciting."

CHAPTER 63

Bob

I n two weeks, we were ready to move to Chicago. Our flight was scheduled for later in the afternoon.

At 8 a.m. our makeup artists appeared. My beard was starting to grow in after two weeks, so I didn't need to worry about glue all over my face. We insisted that we each be made up separately in other rooms because we wanted to see how we looked at first glance. I was now a blond, with a blond beard to match. An FBI makeup artist would visit us every two weeks in Chicago to keep our new hair color in shape. Our padding wasn't designed to make us look fat, just overweight.

The time had come, and we both walked into the den.

Bobbie, my gorgeous shapely blond Bobbie, was a plump woman with frizzy black hair, crazy big eyeglasses, and buck teeth, Yes, buck-friggin teeth. She didn't have the advantage of growing a beard like me, so the teeth were necessary to change the appearance of her pretty face. We both requested that we didn't wear heavy face makeup, which can be a bitch when the temperature soars. As intimately as I knew her, I could pass her by in the street and not realize she was my Bobbie. Like her, I also had dark rimmed glasses.

These makeup people know what they're doing.

Bobbie looked at me and didn't even laugh.

"You thtill look gorgeouth, baby," she lisped through her new false teeth. I honestly couldn't say the same about her. I briefly thought about how pleasant it would be when we returned home at night and could remove our padding—and Bobbie's buck teeth. We looked forward to our new adventure. If I wrote an autobiography about Bobbie and me, the word dull would never appear.

CHAPTER 64

Bobbie

Bob and I boarded our flight at JFK, due to arrive at O'Hare Airport at 2:50. Bob stared at me, but I don't think he was admiring my normally pretty puss. I couldn't believe they gave me buck teeth. Not only were they ugly, they interfered with eating, not to mention talking. I now thpeak with a lithp. I guess I'll lose weight, but you will never know it because of my body padding. I kept reminding myself that we need to look at this as an adventure, not just a detective assignment. Bob and I love to help each other out of our clothing at night. With all this padding crap, it will be a special pleasure.

Our FBI car picked us up outside the terminal at O'Hare. I insisted that it *not* be a big black SUV. Nothing says "Hi, I'm from the government," louder that a big black SUV. It was a burgundy Nissan sedan. We drove up to a beautiful large house in Evanston, a suburb on the northern border of Chicago. Chicago and its surrounding suburbs are often known as "Chicagoland."

Our cover story, as it was leaked to our neighbors, was that we were professors of criminology at Northwestern University, Mr. George Fleming and Mrs. Nancy Fleming. Sarah Watson's people did a perfect job of forging our credentials and lining us up with the part-time teaching jobs. What didn't need forging was our knowledge. Bob and I are more than intellectually equipped to teach criminology at a university, as we both have done from time to time over the years, me at the University of Chicago and Bob at Columbia. Classes would start in two weeks, so we had time to familiarize ourselves with the textbooks.

Our huge temporary home came with seven bedrooms, including four separate full suites. Bob and I would inhabit a suite on the second floor, with our four bodyguards scattered over the others. Our suite covered the entire floor, we were happy to see. It included two bedrooms, three bathrooms, a small kitchen, a den, a dining room and, thank goodness, a small gym.

Tom Blackburn, the guy in charge of our security detail, invited us to have supper with him and the rest of the group. He politely emphasized that it was only an invitation, and that we were more than welcome to dine alone upstairs if we wished. He and the other guys get it. Privacy is important, especially if you're undercover. But Bob and I took him up on his offer to dine with them. We wanted to get to know the men in charge of keeping us alive and safe. Also, these guys were highly trained FBI agents, so bouncing ideas off them seemed like a good idea.

None of our bodyguards were from New York or Chicago, better to keep their identities hidden. Sarah Watson knows what she's doing.

But first we wanted to go upstairs and get out of our friggin padding, not to mention my buck teeth.

Tom Blackburn didn't' miss a trick. He gave us all name badges and reminded everybody that Bob and I were George and Nancy Fleming, and that we should be addressed that way at all times. He's right. When you're undercover, your job is to *stay* undercover.

We had a great supper. Agent Tim Holloway loves to cook and he's great at it. All the guys were dying to know about the adventures of Bob and Bobbie (George and Nancy?), the famous BBs. We had fun sharing our war stories with our bodyguards.

The next day, Bob and I planned to visit Santoro's, a restaurant in Chicago's Loop district, known to be a mob hangout. It would not be a pleasant lunch.

CHAPTER 65

Bob

obbie and I (that is, Nancy and George Fleming) taught our morning criminology classes at Northwestern University, not far from our house in Evanston. Bobbie told me she had a difficult job teaching with her false buck teeth. After our classes, we got into the car for our trip to Santoro's, the mob restaurant. Agent Tim Holloway would be our driver and Pete Johnston would ride shotgun. Tim punched the address into the GPS, although Bobbie could have given directions, having known Chicago like a bee knows a hive.

On the way to the restaurant, Bobbie removed her false teeth and reviewed for us the basic rules of "how not to look like a cop." Don't walk with your arms spread from your sides, because cops do that to avoid scraping against their sidearms. Don't sit with you back to the wall, because cops like to see what's going on. Don't stare into people's faces, because that's what cops do. Criminals know these things, and I'm sure mobsters are experts at it. Have I mentioned that Bobbie knows her stuff?

The four of us walked into Santoro's at 12:15. It was dark, and nicely appointed with photos on the walls. I was shocked that one of the photos was of none other than Al Capone.

We were seated at a table in the middle of the restaurant. A nearby table was occupied by six guys who spoke loudly.

"Heyy, Patsie the Peach. Heyy, Rocco the Rock. Heyy, Billy the Butch, etc. etc."

These clowns could get jobs as extras in a remake of *The Godfather*. Bobbie unobtrusively switched on her recording device and set it next to the bread dish. Bobbie affected a smile over her buck teeth, but I could tell she was seething. She's one-quarter Italian, and I knew it gnawed at her for these creeps to darken her heritage. The goombahs behind us switched to Italian. Of course, they didn't know it, but Bobbie speaks and understands Italian fluently, as she does five other languages. Bobbie is no slouch.

As we sat there, Joey the Jelly, Micky the Mooch, and Louie the Lou, joined the group behind us, and immediately began to speak Italian. They spoke in muffled tones, not knowing that Bobbie's recording device could pick up a fly fart. Suddenly one man's voice got loud. It was Micky the Mooch. He was the apparent leader of the group, if voice volume can be used to evaluate leadership.

Suddenly Bobbie's eyes got as wide as saucers. She immediately put her hand over them and pretended to wipe her forehead, as she didn't want the boys at the next table to detect that she'd heard something important.

Knowing Bobbie as I do, I knew it *was* something important. I was dying to hear what she had to say later after she removed her false teeth.

I enjoyed my meal of perfectly cooked Chicken Parmigiana. "How did you like your lunch, hon," I asked Bobbie.

"It thucked," she said. "I normally love eating mutthels, but thucking them out of the thells wath impothible."

CHAPTER 66

Bobbie

When we got back to Evanston after our lunch at Santoro's, Bob and I couldn't wait to get out of our disguises.

"Gimme a kith, handthome," I said.

"Bobbie, your teeth?"

"Holy thit. Thorry, thweety."

I went into the bathroom, removed my lovely buck teeth, brushed my real teeth, and gargled for two minutes.

I walked out of the room and flashed Bob my best smile—with my *real* teeth.

"I think I'll call you Bucky," Bob said, laughing.

"Bobbie works fine, wiseass. Now give me that kiss, and no, not a *kith*, a kiss."

It was after five, so we all decided to have an early dinner, a light one after our luncheon feast at Santoro's. Again, Bob and I ate with our bodyguards. We realized that meeting regularly with four experienced FBI agents would only help us get the job done. Our guys aren't just the muscle end of the bureau; they're all bright as hell.

I turned on my voice recorder and put the volume on high. Because the recording was all in Italian, I played it slowly and translated. I put it on hold when we got to the part where Micky the Mooch spoke loudly.

"Hang onto your hats, guys," I said. I then resumed the recording and translated.

"Okay, boys," the Mooch said, "here's the word right from the top. This operation will now be run from Chicago. I wish old Scarface could be here (referring to one of Al Capone's nicknames). Our next item of business is to whack that motherfucker Commissioner Norquist in New York."

"Dear God," Agent Holloway yelled, "we've got to warn him."

"Relax, Tim," I said, "I already called the commissioner on the secure line when I went to the ladies' room at the restaurant. Thank God I heard that Mooch guy."

"Sorry, Bobbie—I mean Nancy—I should have realized that one of the BBs got it handled."

Micky the Mooch continued. "After we take care of Norquist, we're gonna work on the rest of the cops in the country, one by one, and sometimes 10 by 10," he said, laughing. I put the player on hold.

"Bob and I and the rest of the country thought we put an end to this shit when we stopped that huge cop-killing terror plot," I said. "Looks like it's about to start all over again. Law enforcement is beginning to look like a dangerous way to make a living." I hit the play button, and Micky the Mooch resumed talking.

"Our job is simple, guys, but it's going to take a lot of manpower and a lot of time. Cops want to stop us. The fewer the cops, the less we need to worry about. Soon, only assholes will want to become cops. I'm running the show here in Chicago and Angie Dee is in charge in New York."

I put the device on hold. "Bob, do you think Angie Dee could be Angelo DiCrispino, our suspect in the *Morton Case*?"

Bob jotted down a note. I hit play.

"Who's in charge of this operation?" Patsie the Peach asked.

"I can't tell you that, Patsie. I can't tell anybody that. As we've learned over the years from the FBI and the cops, secrecy is the name of the fucking game."

The rest of the Mafia conversation concerned their loan-sharking operation in Chicago. I turned off the machine.

"What do you need from us, Bobbie, I mean Nancy?" Lead Agent Tom Blackburn asked.

"We want you guys to keep your eyes and ears open," I said. "If you think of something that may be important, Bob and I want to hear about it. You're all experienced agents, and that's why we're bringing you inside this mess. I've discussed this with Director Watson, and she has no problem with it. She handpicked you guys, so she has no concern about your knowing what's going on. But she wants to communicate directly with only Bob and me in what she calls 'executive sessions.' I'm going to call her right after this meeting. Thanks for your attention, guys. I recommend you always keep an extra magazine in your pockets. Bob and I are doing just that."

CHAPTER 67

Bob

After we met with our bodyguards, Bobbie and I huddled in our room to prepare for our call with Sarah Watson. We're beginning to think of our FBI agents as our *team*, not just our bodyguards.

Bobbie and I went over our notes and what we'd emphasize to Sarah. I told Bobbie that she should conduct most of the conversation, because she was the one who translated the shocking words we heard. I texted Sarah to make sure we wouldn't be interrupting her dinner. She called us immediately. I put her on speaker, knowing we were secure.

Bobbie reviewed our eavesdropping lunch and gave Sarah a blow-by-blow account of what we heard. Sarah shocked the living shit out us by saying that there had, indeed, been an assassination attempt on Commissioner Norquist that afternoon. Thanks to Bobbie's warning call, the would-be-assassin was killed before he could get off a round. How the hell can a guy with a loaded gun enter One Police Plaza? Looks like we're up against a tough enemy, an extremely tough enemy.

The thought crossed my mind that if it weren't for Bobbie's

fluency in Italian, our day would have consisted of nothing more than a tasty meal. And thank God Micky the Mooch spoke loudly about assassinating Norquist. If we needed to wait to hear Bobbie translate it from the recorder, Ralph would be dead.

"Bob and Bobbie," Sarah said, "Do you have any idea how high-up in the organization these men were?"

"Only that the guy who they call Micky the Mooch was in charge of the meeting," Bobbie said. "We didn't get any of their last names, only the stupid mob nicknames they give themselves. Have you ever heard of Micky the Mooch?"

"Yes, Bobbie, I'm quite familiar with Micky the Mooch. His name is Michael Muchado, and he's been a lynchpin in the Chicago mob for years. He's a very dangerous man. Any time you're near him, make sure the safety's off on your guns."

"Sarah, does the name 'Angie Dee' ring a bell with you?" I asked.

"Yes, he's Angelo DiCrispino, a mob enforcer in New York. Was he there?"

"No, but we heard his name. He's a suspect in a murder case that Bobbie and I were working on." We went over all the names of the mobsters with Sarah and then reviewed our plan for our next action, the next restaurant for lunch. These mobsters like to eat well.

CHAPTER 68

Bobbie

A fter we heard the chilling words of Micky the Mooch yesterday, we were all on heightened security. Our FBI guys all sported M16s strapped to their shoulders as well as their regular sidearms in their holsters. Our house—the safe house—was decked out like a military base. The entire perimeter was covered by wireless motion alarms, and one of the agents would man a security camera on a rotating basis. By touching different buttons, the agent could see every square foot of the property surrounding the house. Every window and door in the house was protected by motion detectors.

Sarah had secured three vehicles for us, realizing that one car for six people would raise eyebrows. At my urging again, none of the vehicles was a big black SUV, as sure a sign of government as a tattoo on a gang member. We had a red Ford Expedition, a beige Chevy Suburban, and a green Toyota Land Cruiser. All the vehicles were large in the event that all six of us needed to go somewhere together.

Today's destination was Venicia, an Italian restaurant in the Rogers Park section of Chicago, right near Evanston, another place that intelligence indicated was populated by mobsters. To avoid people seeing us move as a group, only two agents accompanied Bob and me for lunch. We took the Toyota Land Cruiser.

As soon as we walked in, we saw a group of men seated at a table in back. They looked like goombahs. Being part Italian myself, that's probably an inappropriate thing to say, but sorry, they looked like *goombahs*.

The *maître d* led us to a table about 20 feet from the group of men. No way would we ask to be seated closer to them, as that may arouse suspicions. No problem. My listening device is so sensitive it can pick up voices from across a large room. I nicknamed the device, Big Ears. I set it next to a water pitcher and pointed the recording end toward the goombah table.

Bob looked at me, smiled and winked. I flashed him my best buck-toothy smile.

Unlike our lunch yesterday at Santoro's, we weren't close enough to hear the conversation, but would need to rely on my device to record the words and do our listening later.

We all spent a long few minutes perusing the menu to buy us some time. If the boys in the back are anything like yesterday, they weren't just there for lunch but for a meeting. We asked the waiter detailed questions about the menu. When Bob asked the waiter what the chicken parmigiana was made from, the guy looked confused and said, "chicken." We all cracked up, which was the purpose of Bob's question. The more we laugh the less we look like cops. It takes a lot of thinking to be a good detective.

We ate as slowly as we could, noticing that the goombahs were taking their sweet time, sipping Sambuca. To take up more time, we all ordered dessert, fruit plates only. The tables around us emptied, making us begin to look conspicuous. Well, this is a scouting operation, so we can skip a few things the boys were talking about,

I figured. I scribbled a note to Bob, suggesting that we hit the road. He nodded in agreement. As we got up, Pete Johnston cracked a really funny joke. We laughed hysterically, trying to look as un-cop as possible.

We got back to Evanston at 4 p.m., having spent a long time at lunch. How do these mobsters find anything else to do besides endless lunch meetings? We couldn't wait to listen to Big Ears.

We were in for a shock.

CHAPTER 69

Bob

L ike all people, detectives need to brace themselves for occasional disappointment. When we got back from Venicia, we listened with excitement as Bobbie prepared to translate the conversation her device had recorded.

The "goombahs" were little league soccer coaches and met to discuss the upcoming playoffs. They spoke English, not a word of Italian, so Bobbie didn't even need to translate. Our eavesdropping lunch was nothing but a waste of time. We laughed. There was nothing else to do. Just as with a surveillance operation, you need to brace yourself for frustration, which was definitely what today was all about—frustration. Bobbie and I flipped a coin to see who would use the gym in our apartment first. We didn't want our luncheon routines to hit our waistlines. Bobbie won the toss, and we went to our apartment.

After we removed our pads, and Bobbie's false teeth, she put on her sweat suit and hit the gym. I love to watch Bobbie work out. It's no wonder she has such a gorgeous figure.

As Bobbie took a shower, I began my workout, feeling good that I'd at least accomplish something today.

Puzzles

After I showered, I walked into the den, wearing my robe. Bobbie was lying on the couch, reading a magazine. She stood, smiled, and dropped her robe to the floor. The frustrations of today suddenly disappeared. We began our second workout of the day. I love to see my chubby buck-toothed partner transform into a gorgeous, sexy woman after hours.

CHAPTER 70

Bobbie

If somebody asks me what I do for a living, I could honestly say, "I have lunch." I recognize that, as a detective, I need to do things that are productive and can lead to solving a case. Eating lunch at a known hangout of Mafia types only makes sense. Yes, it can sometimes be frustrating, as yesterday when we discovered that we recorded a bunch of little league soccer coaches talking shop. So what. Frustration is part of the job, something you need to live with. The day before yesterday we hit pay dirt, so sometimes it works.

Today we plan to have lunch at Pietro's an Italian restaurant in the Bridgeport area of Chicago where the late Mayor Daly used to live. Agents Pete Johnston and Tom Blackburn would accompany us today, with Tom driving the Ford Expedition. According to the intelligence reports we read, Pietro's festers with mobsters. It was raining slightly, doing wonders for my already frizzy black-dyed hair. At least it wouldn't bother my beautiful buck teeth.

"My, you look lovely today," Bob the wiseass said.

"Thame to you, thweety," my teeth said.

The hostess seated us next to a table of eight men. Because

intelligence tells us this is a goombah hangout, maybe we'll get lucky. I placed Big Ears, my recording device, next to the bread dish. Bread, just what I need. I aimed the mic of Big Ears toward the next table.

Bob looked down at a sheet of paper and recited a funny joke, cracking us all up, and announcing to anyone listening that we're not police.

They spoke Italian. Although my device would record their every word, I strained to hear if they were saying anything interesting. They spoke softly, so I couldn't pick up much. That's what Big Ears is for. But I did hear one name mentioned over and over—Micky the Mooch. The Mooch was not at this meeting. A guy named Billy the Butch was doing most of the talking. If I heard the Italian word for "whacked" once, I heard it a dozen times. I think our listening session tonight will be interesting.

They kept talking about some guy named Bobbo the Bob. Cute name. Maybe I'll nickname my partner that. It seems that Bobbo the Bob had just arrived from New York, and he announced some big plans, which I didn't catch, but would later. According to Billy the Butch, Bobbo the Bob would join them later. Looks like we're going to need to eat quite slowly.

As we ate our lunch, we cracked jokes to make us laugh. A tall overweight man walked up to the table next to us, whom we would soon learn was Bobbo the Bob. "Heyy, Bobbo the Bob; Heyy, Billy the Butch; Heyy, Tony the Tank," etc., etc. Maybe I'll change my name to Bobbie the Cop. One man took up almost the entire end of the table. Tony the Tank was built just like that, an army tank, a fat army tank.

After their charming hellos, they all resumed speaking Italian. I could give them lessons on proper Italian, but I don't think they'd be interested. I noticed they spoke in hushed tones, but not too hushed for my Big Ears device. I did hear Micky the Mooch repeated constantly. Apparently, Micky the Mooch is a popular topic of conversation.

As we slowly finished our fruit cup deserts, the goombahs arose and started to walk out. We waited for five minutes after they left and then we walked to our car. From the snippets of conversation I caught, I knew our meeting this evening would be exciting.

As we pulled up to the house in Evanston, Tim pressed a button on the dashboard, causing the gate to swing open.

Bob and I went to our apartment to get undisguised, especially my goddam buck teeth.

We all gathered in the kitchen for my translation. Tom Blackburn stood by a window holding his M16. Tim Holloway, our resident FBI chef, prepared a chicken dish.

I played the recording and began to translate. I recited aloud anything that sounded interesting, leaving out stuff like, "Hey, try the lasagna, it's fucking great."

The guys seemed to hang on every word of my translation, and so did I because this was the first time I heard the conversation clearly.

Holy shit, what did I just hear? I backed up and hit play again.

"Micky the Mooch says the Big Guy isn't happy with the speed of things," Bobbo the Bob said. "We whacked five cops in New York this morning, but the boss says that's not enough." I put it on hold. "Did you guys catch what I just translated? Five dead cops in New York just this morning."

The secure phone rang, and Tim picked up.

"It's Director Watson."

"Hi, Sarah, can I put you on speaker?"

"Yes, please do," Sarah said, "I want everyone to hear this. I just got off the phone with Commissioner Norquist in New York. Five policemen were assassinated this morning. He just found out about it."

"He just found out about it? I was just translating our eavesdropping session today, and one of the men said that had happened. I recommend, Sarah, that you stay on the line and listen to my translation. It will take a while."

"I have absolutely nothing more important to do, Bobbie, please continue."

I repeated my translation of Bobbo the Bob saying that Micky the Mooch announced that somebody he referred to as "The Big Guy" wanted the cop killings to speed up, and mentioned that five cops were whacked in New York this morning.

I hit play and continued to translate. Almost everything we heard was important, with no more analysis of the taste of the lasagna.

"The Big Guy says he likes the number 10," Bobbo the Bob said. "He wants to see 10 cops whacked in one day in one city, this time in Chicago. Once that's done, the Big Guy wants every hit to be 10 at the minimum, with a bonus offered for anything over that number."

"Please put it on hold Bobbie, I'll be right back." Sarah said.

We all knew what she was about to do. She wanted to warn the Chicago police about what she heard. She came back on the line.

"I just had my deputy contact the Chicago Police Superintendent about the threat. I hope it's not too late. Please continue, Bobbie."

"As you guys know," Bobbo the Bob said, "Micky the Mooch runs the show in Chicago. When the Big Guy wants something handled, get out of Micky's way because he'll get it fucking done."

Bob motioned to me and I put Big Ears on hold.

"Sarah, do you have any idea who this Big Guy is?" Bob asked.

"We're not certain, but we think it's Alphonse Gandolfo, head of the Gandolfo family in New York. He's a vicious son of a bitch. We'll know more as the days go by. Since you BBs have been on this case, I've signed more wiretap warrant applications than I have in the past year. Please continue, Bobbie."

Tony the Tank spoke, his mouth half-full of pasta.

"When Micky the Mooch says jump, I say how high. I'm going to turn my people loose on this today. Ten cops? Shit, that's nothing. And I like the idea of a bonus for more than 10. The Big Guy knows what he's doing, and so does Micky the Mooch. We'll get this fucking thing done. I know *I* will."

"When is this supposed to happen?" Billy the Butch asked.

"Both the Big Guy and Micky the Mooch want it to happen tomorrow, beginning in the morning," Bobbo the Bob said.

"Please hold, Bobbie. I'll be right back," Sarah said.

When she came back on the line, we all knew what she did. She had her deputy warn the Chicago Police Superintendent about the newly-announced timing of the attacks. But even though Sarah was able to sound the warning to the Chicago police chief, what could he do? The Chicago Police Department employs 12,000 cops. Should they all walk around with their guns drawn?

I went through the remainder of the recording, with nothing much more than what we already heard. And we heard plenty. Just as in the terrorist incidents, the police departments of the country are under attack.

Sarah Watson signed off and told us to call her immediately about anything new we learned.

This crap was starting to get scary, really scary.

CHAPTER 71

Y ou wanted to see me, Don Gandolfo?"

"Look at these photos, Vincenzo. Tony Pasquarelli took them. The two chubby people you're looking at are detectives with the NYPD. They've been deputized as FBI agents, and are in Chicago to spy on us. Every day they have lunch at one of the restaurants where our people hang out. The two are married. Ever hear the names Bobbie Nelson and Bob Lawton?"

"Yeah, aren't those two the famous detectives who have been in magazines and on the news?"

"Yes, they are, Vincenzo. That buck-toothed fat lady you're looking at is none other than Detective Bobbie Nelson, one of the hottest pieces of ass I've ever seen. When she worked in Chicago, the *Chicago Tribune* carried an article about her, calling her a real-life Sherlock Holmes. She may be a hot fox, but she's one tough cop. And the fat guy with her is her husband, Detective Bob Lawton, a slim muscular guy with dark brown hair, not the chubby blond you're looking at. And he doesn't wear a beard. So, they've disguised some high-powered people and sent them to spy on us."

"Do we know where they're staying, Don Gandolfo?"

"Yeah, a place in Evanston, which the idiots think is a safe house. Here's the address."

"Do you want me to take care of them?"

"No, I don't want them whacked—not just yet. I want them followed so we can find out what they're up to. I had one of my people rent an apartment across the street from where they're staying. I want you to stay there and watch the house carefully. When they leave the house, I want you to follow them. You're good at tailing cars."

"I'll go there today, Don Gandolfo."

"This is an important job, Vincenzo. Do it right and I'll take good care of you."

CHAPTER 72

Bob

B obbie and I went up to our apartment after the big listening session with Sarah Watson. We sat in the den, sipping a couple of martinis I had mixed for us.

"Bob, this shit is even worse than the terror attacks on police. The goddam Mafia has become more organized than they've ever been, and they have every reason to kill cops, which they're probably doing as we speak."

Not only does the mob have a reason to kill cops — they have every reason in the world to kill Bobbie and me. Sarah Watson convinced us to come out of the Witness Protection Program, but I'm beginning to question the wisdom of that move. Every day, Bobbie and I have lunch at another gangster hangout, and every day I wonder how long we can continue without being spotted.

I really need to stop this crap. We're getting results, big results as Bobbie and I always do, and soon the results will start to show in the statistics. The important thing is that we're uncovering names and giving them to the FBI, along with our recordings. I can easily see that in the near future, our recording sessions will be put into evidence when these bastards are prosecuted. The one name we haven't gotten is the real name for The Big Guy, although Sarah Watson thinks it's Alphonse Gandolfo, head of the Gandolfo family in New York. Unlike the old days of mob activity, this new reality sees a lot of cooperation not only among the families, but also between different states and cities. As Sarah Watson has observed, the Mafia is becoming modern and corporate in its structure.

"Hey, Bobbie," I said. "you're looking pensive tonight."

"Yeah, I'm pensive because I'm worried. Bob, I think we're making a stupid assumption. Want to guess what it is?"

"Yeah, our stupid assumption is that the mob leadership is stupid. We spy on them and assume they don't know they're being spied upon."

"Exactly. Our disguise costumes are good, but maybe *too* good. We're easy to pick out of a crowd, me with my friggin buck teeth and you with your blond hair and beard. The first time some of the mob people scc us, no problem, but what about the next time? Sarah has given us 27 restaurants where mob bosses hang out. Can we believe that they never have lunch at a different place? If so, what happens if they remember seeing us at another restaurant? I think we need to train a lot of agents to eavesdrop, which isn't rocket science. All they need to do is what we do— Sit and try not to look or act like cops and point a recording device like Big Ears toward a group of suspects. That's it. I can still do the translating if the targets speak Italian, but I don't need to be on-site at a lunch place, and neither do you. And the agents should be rotated regularly so that they never visit the same restaurant twice."

"I think you're right, honey. If we spend all our time visiting mob hangouts, it's only a matter of time for somebody to recognize us. Those creeps may sound stupid, but they're not."

The phone rang. It was Sarah Watson. The time was 8:30 p.m.

"Don't leave the house," Sarah said loudly. "We've intercepted some emails accompanied by photos of you two in your disguises, along with photos of you without the disguises. Two shots were taken at two different restaurants. Bottom line—the mob is on to you. Your cover is blown, completely blown. The restaurants you've visited have given us valuable names and leads, but those sources have just dried up."

"Bobbie and I have been worried about exactly that, Sarah. I'm putting you on speaker. My amazing partner sitting next to me has come up with a new idea."

Bobbie explained her plan, which is to use a large number of agents and rotate them so they never show up more than once at a mob restaurant. Because, as Sarah put it, our cover is blown, Bobbie's plan is not just a good idea, it's essential—unless we want to get killed.

Sarah told us she'd call again in the morning.

CHAPTER 73

Bobbie

Bob and I didn't get much sleep last night, and it wasn't because we were feeling frisky. We couldn't sleep because of what Sarah Watson told us yesterday. Not only is our cover blown, but the mob has photos of us in our disguises, and also *without* our disguises. I felt like I was walking along the edge of a tall building with no railing to hold. Tom Blackburn, our lead bodyguard, ordered the other three agents to carry an M16 at all times, and reminded us to always wear our service revolvers except while sleeping. He continuously monitored the yard on the surveillance camera.

At 8:45 a.m. Sarah Watson called. I put her on speaker.

"I'm about to tell you two what you already know. We've got to get you back into the Witness Protection Program. You'll fly to New York tomorrow and we'll meet you at JFK. I'm sending one of our makeup artists to you this afternoon so you will have different disguises. Don't worry, you won't need to wear heavy padding, and Bobbie won't wear false teeth. Sorry, folks, but your covers are so blown that I refuse to leave you there in danger of your lives.

Our makeup artist arrived an hour later. She shaved off Bob's beard, gave him a short haircut and died it black. She did mine into a pixie cut. No false teeth, thank God. She then handed us two naval officer's uniforms. Interesting disguises, but the uniforms didn't change our faces.

Bob's stripes were those of a lieutenant commander, and mine were those of a lieutenant. I hope he doesn't order me to salute him. We weren't excited about the idea of returning to friendly prisoner status in the Witness Protection Program, but we sure as hell were happy to be leaving Illinois and our shortened life expectancy. Bob and I drafted a set of instructions for our replacement spies. It was simple, really, because there wasn't much to do except sit at a table with a recording device and try not to look like law enforcement.

Bob and I love our work as detectives, but we hated to be on the run and hunted.

This shit is getting old.

CHAPTER 74

Bob

Bobbie and I, along with all four of our FBI bodyguards, arrived at O'Hare Airport at 1 p.m. for our flight to JFK at 3:05. We sported our naval officer uniforms, which I thought was a smart move on Sarah's part, even though as a former Marine officer I felt out of place. But it beats my blond hair and beard. But I was worried, as was Bobbie, that it didn't change the appearance of our faces, and, as Sarah told us, the mob knows what we looked like before the disguises. But soon we'll be out of here and on our way to New York.

After we checked in, all six of us went to our boarding area. The agents' FBI identification enabled them to accompany us to the departure gate. Bobbie and I agreed that we'd miss these guys, who had become friends, not just bodyguards.

Bobbie announced that she needed to use the ladies' room. Tom Blackburn and Pete Johnston stationed themselves on either side of the ladies' room door.

Ten minutes went by, then twenty.

I was worried that Bobbie may be sick. I walked over to Tom

Blackburn and said, "I think we need to check on Bobbie." I felt my stomach twist.

He flagged down a woman wearing the uniform of a TSA agent, flashed his FBI badge, and said, "Please check on a woman in a naval officer's uniform. She's been in there a long time and we're worried she may be ill."

One minute later the woman came back out.

"There is no woman in a naval officer's uniform in there," she said.

"We're going in," I said.

The TSA woman said, "I'll go with you." When we walked in she shouted, "Police business, everybody stand where you are." Sharp lady.

But the room was empty. The TSA lady told us she had to knock down a makeshift barricade to enter the first time.

I pointed toward a hatch about two feet above floor level.

"Where does that lead?" I asked. By that time a couple of airport cops had entered.

"That leads to a conveyor belt that goes to a storage room," One of the cops said.

I unholstered my Glock.

"Hey, what the hell is that about?"

I flashed my NYPD shield and said, "Long story." He looked at my Navy stripes, then at my shield, then at my gun.

"Pete and I will go," Tom said, "then you can follow us, Bob."

We climbed through the hatch and positioned ourselves on the conveyor belt for our journey to the storage room. As my mind was freaking out, I tried to flip into detective mode, and scoured the walls of the tunnel for anything that could provide a clue to Bobbie's whereabouts. Nothing.

I called Sarah Watson to let her know what happened. Within minutes, the airport was covered with FBI agents.

Where the hell could Bobbie be?

CHAPTER 75

Bobbie

G reat, simply fucking great. I was washing my hands in the ladies' room when two women, best described as Amazons, grabbed me by my arms. Each of them was just shy of six feet and had the shoulders of a linebacker. I noticed a third woman, wearing a cleaning uniform, barricade the entrance to the ladies' room from the inside. Amazon Number One crawled through a hatch in the wall and Amazon Number Two pushed me in behind her. I was followed by Amazon Number Two and the cleaning lady.

We sat on a conveyor belt which took us through a tunnel. After a couple of minutes, we were deposited in what looked like a storage room. I immediately noticed that the room was empty. By this time, they had removed my pistol, handcuffed me, and put tape over my mouth. They pushed me toward a door, which opened next to a SUV. I was told to lie on the floor and keep my mouth shut. Keeping my mouth shut was easy because it was taped.

After what I estimated was a half-hour, the vehicle stopped. Amazon Number One yanked me off the floor and shoved a fabric bag over my head while Amazon Number Two dragged me out of the SUV. We went into what I assumed was a house because we had to climb four steps to enter. I was pushed into a seat as Amazon Number One pulled the bag off my head. We were in a suburban kitchen.

My hands were cuffed in front of me, not behind my back. *BIG MISTAKE.*

"Micky will be here in a half-hour," Amazon Number One said to Amazon Number Two in Italian, obviously not knowing that I speak the language. I wondered if she was referring to Micky the Mooch. I had one simple set of objectives—to remain calm, observe what was going on, and wait for an opening. Although I had fired a gun only once in the line of duty, when I killed the guy who shot Bob, I had a ton of training over the years, including training for a situation just like this—being held prisoner.

I noticed that Amazon Number One had placed her gun on a side table, about ten feet from where I sat. I couldn't believe she did that, and I struggled to keep an expression of shock from my face. I'm quite an athlete, as Bob always reminds me, and I can move fast. I noticed that Amazon Number Two stood there with her arms folded in front of her. The cleaning lady, meanwhile, had driven off.

In two quick strides I reached the side table, grabbed the gun, flipped off the safety, and fired two rounds into the torso of Amazon Number One. I then did the same for Amazon Number Two as she reached for her gun. They both lay dead on the kitchen floor. I ripped the tape off my mouth, which was tricky because my hands were cuffed together. It hurt like hell. I looked at my cell phone, which the bitches had neglected to take from me, and got the location of the house from Google Maps. Then I called Bob. He didn't say hello, he just screamed my name. I didn't have a moment to waste because Micky (the Mooch?) would be arriving shortly. I gave Bob the location from my phone. That's all I needed to do. Bob's one hell of a cop, and he'd take it from there. Within four minutes, I heard two police sirens. I stood on the front stoop with my cuffed hands in the air. Crime scenes can be fluid and scary, and I didn't want to risk getting shot—again. As two of the cops ran crime scene tape around the place, the other two questioned me in the front parlor, away from the bloody kitchen. One of the cops found the handcuff keys on a chain around the neck of Amazon Number One, and uncuffed me.

I answered their questions slowly and deliberately, being careful not to provide too much information. I'm sure Sarah Watson wants to treat this whole matter with the utmost secrecy. Ten minutes later, Bob and the FBI agents walked up to the door, hooking their badges onto their jackets. I'm sure the cops who questioned me must have freaked out. Here they were questioning a woman naval officer who had just showed them her NYPD shield, hugging another naval officer who had just shown them his. Bob and I hugged for the longest time I could remember, and we hug a lot. I asked him not to kiss me because my lower lip was bleeding from my ripping the fucking tape off.

Micky (the Mooch?) never showed up.

Bob had already spoken to Sarah, who arranged for an FBI Gulfstream to meet us at the airport.

"A Gulfstream?" I said to Bob. "Maybe we can draw the curtain and play around." I figured a dumb little wisecrack was called for. I was keeping it all together. Later I would break down into hysterical tears on the plane as Bob held me in his arms. I pride myself on being a tough cop, but I had come closer than I ever had to being killed. Not a pleasant feeling, even for a "tough cop."

CHAPTER 76

Bob

My stiff upper lip was beginning to quiver. Bobbie, *my* Bobbie, was almost fucking killed. If she wasn't such a well-toned jock, that's exactly what would have happened. The mob would have pumped her for information and then knocked her off, as Micky the Mooch and the Big Guy are fond of doing.

When we got to the Witness Protection Program location, Sarah Watson was there waiting for us. It was a beautiful house in Tenafly, New Jersey, an upscale suburb not far from Manhattan. It was surrounded by trees, a security fence, and a large defensible lawn. When we walked in, Sarah broke down in tears and hugged Bobbie. Then she hugged me. Yes, tough-as-nails FBI Director Watson cried.

"Bobbie's brief kidnapping has the entire bureau on crisis alert. My God, it's hard to believe what happened. To abduct someone from a ladies' room at a crowded airport shows a new level of brazenness. Chutzpah should be a Sicilian word. It was my idea to put you two into disguises so you could spy up-close. We, including myself, didn't realize the sophistication of this newborn mob. Never did we imagine that they'd station people at their favorite restaurants to see if they're being observed. This isn't the old mob, not by any stretch."

"Sarah, just tell me one thing. I won't need to wear buck teeth here, will I?" Bobbie said.

Sarah cracked up.

"No, you won't be wearing disguises here. I know that you two got restless the last time you were in WPP, but this time it will be different. You will be working the intellectual side of law enforcement, helping us design systems and new methods of surveillance."

Bobbie and I aren't emotionally constituted for inactivity. Sarah's idea that we would work the "intellectual side of law enforcement" wasn't doing it for us. Bobbie's translating, of course, worked wonders, but she isn't the only law enforcement agent who speaks and understands Italian. Dozens of FBI agents know the language, we're sure, not to mention people in the NYPD, so translating shouldn't be a problem. We needed to be outside the Witness Protection Program, and we politely requested that Sarah make it happen. We reminded Sarah of her excellent idea of disguising us as naval officers. But then Sarah reminded *us* that Bobbie was kidnapped and almost killed — in her Navy uniform. We realized that if we left the safety of the WPP, we would need disguises again, but not pads and buck teeth. Bobbie was a particular problem. Without buck teeth, her gorgeous face would stand out in a crowd, especially a crowd that knows our identities. I can always grow a beard and change its color from time to time. Sarah also reminded us that nobody, including Bobbie and me, had any idea how the mob figured out we'd be at O'Hare Airport that day. Sarah suspected, as did we, that the information had to come from only one place — inside. Not a comforting thought, but a realistic one.

Then Bobbie came up with a new idea. We would dress as clergy, Catholic clergy. I'm going to be a priest, and Bobbie a nun. Even the goombahs, who see religion as some sort of mystical cult, would be hesitant to whack a person of the cloth. Would it work? We still can't be seen together all the time at the same restaurants, looking like a couple of religious people dating. We figured the only way to make it work would be for us to split up, and not dine at a mob restaurant together. But for our first excursion we would go together. Bobbie would be partnered with a woman FBI undercover agent, also dressed as a nun. I would wear a gray wig. Just as we learned in Chicago, we couldn't go to the same restaurant more than once but would switch off with other agents. In New York, the FBI identified 15 restaurants as mob-friendly places. For our first outing we would go as three, two priests, including me and an FBI agent, and Bobbie the nun. It took some doing to find the right religious habit for Bobbie so as not to accentuate her generous boobs. She wore the severe old-fashioned habit of the Dominican order. I couldn't help cracking up, having just recalled that I made passionate love to this nun a few hours ago.

The first restaurant we chose was Francesco's on the lower East Side. We were fortunate to be seated at a table next to one with eight men, a possible mob meeting. We bowed our heads in prayer to say grace before meals. Bobbie then carefully placed Big Ears with the mic toward the table next to us. As always, we told a lot of jokes so we could assume a non-cop appearance with our laughter. The meeting next to us was conducted in hushed tones, leading us to hope that some serious stuff was being discussed. Then we recalled our lunch in Chicago where we sat next to the little league soccer coaches, who spoke softly. As always, the evening translation would tell us whether we had a productive outing or not.

Later we would learn, just as with the soccer coaches in Chicago, our eavesdropping that day was a waste of time. The group we spied on was a Kiwanis Club.

CHAPTER 77

Bob

B obbie and I sat in the den of our safe house in Tenafly, New Jersey, reading the Sunday *New York Times* as we sipped coffee. Bobbie had just opened the *Book Review* section.

"Holy shit," she screamed. "Bob, we hit the non-fiction *Best Seller List* at number two. *Detectiving* is a best seller, a best-friggin-seller! Gimme a hug, baby."

Bobbie the jock then did three cartwheels and a handstand.

The secure phone rang. It was Ralph Norquist. I put him on speaker.

"I am so fucking proud of you two, I can't stand it," he said. "My two best detectives are best-selling authors. Well I wish you *were* my detectives, which you will once again be after you get out of that goddam Witness Protection Program. I read your book cover to cover. It's the best damn book on detective work ever written, and the BBs got it done, which is no surprise."

If we weren't in the WPP, I'm sure we would have a day full of congratulatory phone calls, but, because our phone number is secret, they were mainly emails. Buster called from the CIA, and, of course, Sarah Watson from the FBI. What floored us was a call from President Fenton and First Lady Meg.

We enjoyed our day in the sun, even though we couldn't venture forth without disguises. I can't believe we're best-selling authors. What can be better news than this?

The next day we'd find out.

CHAPTER 78

Bobbie

S arah Watson's in town, Bob. She says she wants to see us, and get this—for the first time that I can recall, she sounded happy as hell about something. She had already called yesterday to congratulate us on our book hitting the best-seller list, so it must be something else."

We weren't planning any religious-garbed stakeouts that day, and therefore we weren't dressed as a priest and a nun, just blue jeans and sweatshirts. Bob and I agreed that we were getting fed up with this stakeout crap in disguises. It got me kidnapped in Chicago, and we figured it was just a matter of time until the mob figures us out and blows our cover again. We wished to hell that we could go back to doing what we we're good at—being detectives. But, because Mafia management was on to us, we needed to live in a safe house and venture forth only when disguised. This sucks.

At 11 a.m. Sarah Watson was escorted into our den by one of our bodyguards. She wore the biggest smile I had ever seen on her.

"I'll get right to the point," she said as she plopped down onto a chair, still smiling. "We've decapitated the Mafia. Welcome back to a normal life. You two have earned it. The following gentlemen are safely in custody of the Justice Department: Micky the Mooch, Bobbo the Bob, Tony the Tank, Angie Dee, and a few dozen others, the most significant of whom is none other than Alphonse Gandolfo, better known as the Big Guy. In a plea bargain, they even coughed up the name of the cop who ratted you out. Thanks to your efforts, we have a mountain, and I do mean a mountain, of evidence against them, including solid facts pointing toward first degree murder convictions. You no longer need to worry about your covers being blown. Rick Bellamy told me his wife wants to have you on *The Ellen Bellamy Show* again. Yes, you can once again be on national TV. You guys can stop wearing disguises. Welcome back to freedom."

We each took turns hugging Sarah, and then hugged each other. This news was right up there with our book becoming a best seller.

So, we're free. No more Witness Protection Program. No more disguises. No more Bobbie in buck teeth. Our safe house in Tenafly was lovely, but we both knew it was a lovely prison. I felt like I was breathing in fresh ocean air. We're free.

CHAPTER 79

Bobbie

Bob and I didn't even question whether we'd return to the NYPD after being freed from the Witness Protection Program and wearing disguises. Hey, we're cops, we're detectives, we solve puzzles. It's what we do.

Commissioner Ralph assigned a crew to help us move our stuff back to our apartment. It's not as pretty as the house in Tenafly, but it's ours, it's home—and we're free to leave it whenever we want. With our new book royalty wealth, we've discussed getting a bigger place, but we still want to be close to One Police Plaza. Maybe we'll check out Greenwich Village, where Rick and Ellen Bellamy live, about 20 minutes from One PP. We definitely plan to buy a beach house, maybe near Ralph's place in East Hampton.

It felt great to be home, free and undisguised. Bob and I can now lead a normal life, whatever the hell normal is.

"So, honey, now that we're free and living back home, what should we do?" Bob asked.

"We should head to Police Plaza first thing in the morning and see what new case Ralph has for us."

"Somehow, I knew you'd say that, Bobbie. Gimme a kiss, Wonder Woman."

PART THREE

CHAPTER 80

The man awoke suddenly — at 2 a.m. He rolled over to attempt to fall back asleep. Then he realized why he had awakened. A woman screamed, loudly at first, then a steady sound, almost growling, followed by a series of screams that sounded almost like barks. It continued almost non-stop for minutes.

He tried to fall back to sleep again, but then recalled a big news story from the mid-1960s, the story of Kitty Genovese, a 28-year-old woman who was murdered as she repeatedly screamed. Nobody in the surrounding apartment building called the police, as the story went, and the woman finally died a horrible death.

His conscience kicked in.

Get your sorry-ass hung-over body out of bed and do something, he thought to himself. He grabbed his cellphone as he walked over to the second story window and peered outside. He could see nothing, but he heard it again. The loud, horribly anguished screams — screams of pain and fear, but worse than that; they were guttural, almost animal-like.

"Dear God, what are they doing to that poor woman?"

He called 911.

CHAPTER 81

Bob

After breakfast at the diner, Bobbie and I walked to One PP. It felt great to be free to walk around, not even accompanied by bodyguards. It's a wonderful side-benefit to Mafia management being locked up.

A note on our desk said to report to Ralph's office as soon as we got in. The way the note was scribbled, we knew Ralph was excited about something. When he wants to convey emotion, email doesn't do it for him.

We walked into his office and I noticed he didn't look happy. He stood and greeted us as he always does, but he didn't smile.

"I hope you two had a pleasant evening last night, because things are about to get unpleasant. Have you heard about that 911 call that came in about 2 a.m.? It's the talk of the department."

"Yeah, Bob and I heard some cops talking about it in the diner this morning. It sounded pretty horrible," Bobbie said.

"I'll say it's horrible. We've got a fucking serial killer on our hands. Like all serial killings, it didn't become obvious until we'd seen a few victims. So far we have an even dozen murders."

"What makes you think it's a serial killer?" Bobbie asked. Her question may have been obvious, but Bobbie knows how to control the often-loquacious Ralph Norquist.

He reached into a drawer and retrieved a six-inch Phillips screwdriver and tossed it on his desk.

"Oh shit," Bobbie and I said simultaneously.

"Yeah, oh shit, indeed," He said. "This isn't the actual weapon, of course, but it's an exact replica of the other 12. The method of delivery is a downstroke to the forehead, plunging it right into the brain of the victim. Last night the bastard's aim was off. According to the 911 caller, the victim, a 30-year-old woman, took 10 to 15 minutes to die, judging from her terrifying screams. The CSU people who responded to the scene reported that the screwdriver didn't penetrate deep into her brain, but deep enough to cause horrible suffering, and finally death. I'm furious that the intake detective didn't spot this right away. Twelve murders, all done with a fucking screwdriver. I mean, shit, two similar incidents within a short period of time should have raised an eyebrow, and any more after that should have been seen as an obvious pattern. I could kick my own ass for not assigning this case to you guys immediately, but the asshole who took the intake notes didn't bring it to my attention. I told him to make sure his old uniform fits, because I'm putting him back on foot patrol duty as of this morning."

"Any pattern among the victims?" I asked.

"No, and that's why I'm giving this case to you BBs. No fucking pattern at all, which, as you know, makes it a tough case to crack, the kind of file that's tailor-made for you two. Anybody can buy a screwdriver in any hardware or convenience store, and they don't come with serial numbers. Just walk in, pay cash, and walk out with a murder weapon."

"What are some of the victim profiles, Ralph?" Bobbie asked. I would have thought he'd answer that when I asked my question about patterns, but Bobbie is good at *Ralph Management.*

He looked at a piece of paper. "35 year old female librarian; male truck driver age 32; seamstress, age 52; female nurse, age 49; female bus driver, age 36; male bartender, age 53; male chef, age 39; female dentist, age 45; male doctor, age 60; female lawyer, age 55; waiter, age 42; male carpenter, age 28; male plumber, age 37.

"So, six males, six females, with occupations and ages all over the place."

"What about timing of the events?" I asked.

"Here's where we see a pattern, besides the murder weapon. Each of the killings occurred exactly one week apart, and all on Tuesday night or early Wednesday morning, between 11 p.m. and 2 a.m. That cuts down on the possible witnesses we can interrogate, and we've yet to find even one. Another pattern we see is the locations, but it's a pretty wide pattern. Each murder occurred in one of the five boroughs of New York City. The first was in Manhattan, and then Queens, Brooklyn, etc. And then the pattern repeats itself. It seems as if the creep keeps a geographic schedule as well as time and date. I think it's safe to assume that the next one will be this coming Tuesday night or early Wednesday in the Bronx. That's tomorrow. We're dealing with one sick fuck, which is the usual profile for a serial killer. Any thoughts, guys?"

"Well, we know that New York City is high up on the list of cities that have seen serial killers," Bobbie said. "Some criminologists say it's number one. But, of course, that doesn't give us any useful information. The time of day doesn't help either, because obviously the killer wants to remain unseen in the darkness. The geographic and date information is interesting, but at this point I don't see how interesting it is. We know that some serial killers like to stick to tight patterns, such as always on Tuesdays, and always in a different borough, and always in order of the next borough." Watching Bobbie as her brain starts to work a case is an experience I never tire of.

"I assume that friends and family members of the victims have been interviewed," I said.

"Well, because that shithead intake detective didn't see the patterns, we're behind on comparing any victim backgrounds. But I know you two will take care of that. I don't envy you. It's always stressful to interview friends and family of victims, but when it's a senseless killing that makes it even worse."

This is one bitch of a case as Ralph indicated. As of now, we have no fingerprints. We hope we'll find some DNA evidence, which is becoming increasingly critical in crime investigating. When scouring a scene of a killing, we collect any piece of clothing as well as cigarette butts and other litter. It's amazing that many criminals aren't aware that saliva on a cigarette butt can link them to a crime. Criminals aren't notoriously smart. Same goes for serial killers. Although there's a popular misconception that serial killers are evil geniuses, studies show otherwise. They may be evil, but they are seldom geniuses. Bobbie once told me that the average IQ of a convicted serial killer is 93, which is below average intelligence. Evil geniuses may make for good movie or TV drama, but it doesn't often happen in reality. Devious maybe, but seldom smart.

"Okay, Bob and Bobbie, I'm turning you loose. This one's a bitch, as you may have already surmised. Keep me posted whenever you find something. I have a feeling the mayor's office is going to be all over my ass on this case."

Bobbie and I smiled at each other as we left Ralph's office. Although the case is sad, with all the innocent dead bodies, the case itself is just what we love—difficult. Or as Ralph put it, "a bitch." And now it's "*our* bitch."

CHAPTER 82

Bobbie

I t's Wednesday morning at 7:45 and Bob and I just got to our office after breakfast at the diner. Ralph predicted, and we agree with him, the next screwdriver killing should have been last night in the Bronx. It's a disgusting feeling to know that some innocent victim has been murdered in the past few hours. At eight we got a call from Ralph. What he said didn't surprise us.

"Sometimes I hate to be right, and this is one of those times," Ralph said. "Another screwdriver whacking, this one in the Bronx as we expected, near a bus stop by Crotona Park. According to the ID on the victim, she was a 23-year-old waitress who had just gotten off work at the Wayside Restaurant about four blocks away. We don't yet have an exact time, but we know she got off work at 11 p.m. and the restaurant is no more than a five-minute walk."

"Bob and I are going there right now," I said. "When was the body discovered?"

"Just a half hour ago in a clump of bushes by the bus stop. A cop on routine foot patrol came upon the body. The crime scene is all yours, my friends."

Bob and I went to the parking lot where our driver awaited us. We know the driver well, Tim Blanco. We like and trust him, but we didn't speak openly about the case. Even though we trust Tim, it's always a bad idea to speak openly about a matter in front of people not assigned to the case. "Need to know," as the feds like to say. Also, "loose lips sink ships," and all that. I'm getting pretty good at cop clichés.

We pulled up to the bus stop near Crotona Park in the Bronx at 9:35 a.m. Crime scene tape surrounded the area. The detective in charge at the scene escorted us to the body. We were happy to see that the CSU people had already bored holes in a three-foot radius around the body to collect insect evidence. Creepy little bugs often put you on the road to solving a crime. The young victim is a pretty woman, or at least she *was*. I don't think I'll ever get used to viewing the body of an innocent victim, a person who was alive and breathing a short while ago. You didn't need to be a coroner to determine the cause of death—a screwdriver stuck in her forehead. Her clothing was not in disarray, leading us to believe that there was no sexual molestation. But we'd await lab work before we make that final conclusion. Never make a final conclusion until you have the evidence—*all* the evidence. Yes, we would come up with a working hypothesis, but we always remind ourselves to be open to new ideas. The head of the CSU gave us a plastic bag filled with items they retrieved from the scene. No cigarette butts, which I pointed out to Bob. From what we know to date, only in six of the 13 murders were cigarette butts found at the scene. So, it's possible the killer doesn't smoke, or is trying to give it up, or is *very careful*. Or possibly there's more than one killer, although we doubt that.

Commissioner Ralph was dead-on accurate when he called this case a bitch. Another dead body and no witnesses. I hope I'm wrong, but it seems the killer knows how to conceal evidence. At this point, the only thing we can predict is that the next screwdriver murder will occur next Tuesday night or early Wednesday in the Borough

277

of Richmond, aka Staten Island, which is huge. If this was a TV cop show we could put out word for all cops on Staten Island to be on the lookout for a guy with a screwdriver. I think of myself as an excellent detective, and I'm also partnered with a pro. But, shit, sometimes you just say to yourself that you need to wait for clues to show up. Not a pleasant thing to say to yourself. That bastard is wasting the lives of innocent people, and as of right now we don't know squat. Bob and I take our cases personally. We *really* want to stop this shit.

I told the detective at the scene to make sure to tell the medical examiner to preserve the screwdriver, which was a pretty dumb-ass thing to say, as if the medical examiner doesn't know what he's doing. I tend to babble on when I'm feeling frustration, and I was definitely feeling frustrated. The "evidence bag" the CSU lady gave me only contained some scraps of paper, which could have been simply litter, so I didn't think we'd get much info when the lab did its work.

Just as Ralph said, this case is a bitch of a puzzle. That's okay. The BBs are good at puzzles.

CHAPTER 83

Bob

L ast night Bobbie and I had dinner with Rick and Ellen Bellamy, who live nearby in Greenwich Village. We've become good friends with them ever since Bobbie and I were on *The Ellen Bellamy Show* a few months ago. Normally, Bobbie and I would never discuss an active case with people not assigned to it, but the Bellamys are different. Rick is the Secretary of Homeland Security, and Ellen was deputized as a provisional FBI Agent by Director Sarah Watson herself. That was at Rick's request. He recognized his wife's keen mind when she helped the FBI with a couple of important cases. Before she became a TV star, Ellen was a well-known architect. She noticed a lot of strange facts about a huge shopping center project she was working on, and she brought it to the attention of the FBI, where Rick was once head of the Joint Counterterrorism Task Force. She uncovered a terrorist plot to bomb the shopping centers. Ellen and Rick co-authored a book about the case, entitled *The Shadows of Terror*. She'd make a good detective. But I don't think she'd like to give up her $45 million a year TV gig. CBS management had a fit when Ellen was deputized, but as the star of the most popular show on daytime television, they wouldn't dare fire her. She brings in a fortune in advertising dollars.

We not only felt comfortable talking about the screwdriver murders with the Bellamys, we welcomed it. The more brains that are focused on this weird case the better, and the Bellamys certainly have brains. We explained to them the only pattern we could see, the day of the week, the time, and the rotating locations around the five boroughs of New York City.

As Homeland Security Secretary, Rick has seen his share of confounding fact patterns, and he shared his encyclopedic knowledge with us. But we all recognized that the only factor we were missing is the profile of the killer, a profile that may lead us to find him. Rick pointed out that there may be more than one murderer, but we thought that was unlikely.

"I think I know the perfect guy to work this case with you, a colleague of yours in the detective ranks of the NYPD," Rick said. "Do you know Bennie Weinberg, better known as Bennie-the-Bullshit-Detector?"

I felt stupid that we hadn't thought of that before. Of course, our old friend Bennie, not only a detective but a psychiatrist.

I just placed a call to Bennie. Can he be the key to solving the screwdriver murders?

CHAPTER 84

Bobbie

Bob and I are scheduled to meet with Bennie Weinberg tomorrow. He'll be in court all day today. We decided to pour over the evidence once more to see if we could give Bennie something solid to look at, something to plug into an algorithm, something to tickle that brilliant mind of his. We were looking for some similarities, any similarities, among the profiles of the 12 murder victims. Their ages and occupations were all over the place, as Ralph Norquist pointed out when he assigned us the case. I hate the word random, but that's what this series of murders was beginning to look like.

We knew that all the victims were married. Bob came up with the idea to see how long they were married. Neither of us could figure out why we would do that, but working data takes a lot of ideas, whether the ideas seem to make sense or not. Once again, we plowed through the data. Holy shit! There, right in front of us, a pattern emerged. All the victims had been married within three months of being killed. Bob nailed it!

Newlyweds!

But that in itself didn't tell us anything, although it did send us in an interesting direction. The killer was singling out newlyweds. Does that mean he has a problem with that fact? Could it be that he's envious of people who recently married, maybe even jealous of them? Bob and I agreed that we had come up with a profile similarity, which can be a breakthrough. But does a newlywed-hater get his name into a database somewhere? Does a newlywed-hater act in any particular way? Could he be divorced? Could he be a widower? Could he be a long-time bachelor and hates to see people betrothed? Could he have been jilted and went over the edge emotionally? We didn't know where we were going with our discovery, but at least we had a big question. Why would anybody hate newlyweds? And why would someone hate them enough to plunge a screwdriver into their heads? Is the man a psychopath? It seems to me that if you brutally murder newlyweds, you're fucking crazy.

We knew Bennie Weinberg would have some great ideas for us. We hoped.

———✦———

Bennie Weinberg walked into our office at 10:30 the next morning, looking his usual dapper self.

I love Bennie's comical nickname, Bennie-the Bullshit Detector, for his talent at spotting lies on the witness stand. Bennie came up with a list of traits he looks at when evaluating credibility, including perspiring, hand fidgeting, eye movements, voice strain, and even complexion. Bennie knows his shit.

Bennie is a psychiatrist as well as a NYPD detective. Besides his expertise at evaluating the credibility of witnesses, he's also well-known for helping cops work through the traumatic crap we so often face. A while back I thought I was losing my mind trying to erase the memory of Bob being shot. Bennie, God bless him, helped me get my mind back on track by coming to grips with my horrible memories of that night, the night I almost lost Bob, the love of my life. Stop trying to force the memories out of my mind, Bennie advised. Instead, focus on what happened, and don't try to squeeze them from your mind. I followed his advice and came to grips with that night. Bennie screwed my head back on. Bob and I think of Bennie as a good friend, not just a colleague.

Multi-talented Bennie is also an expert on serial killers and once wrote a book on the subject, *The Serial Killer Mind*, hence our call for help. His book is a standard police manual for working serial-killer cases. Bob and I just finished re-reading it.

"Bennie, as you know, Bob and I have been assigned to what we've named the *Screwdriver Case*, one of the most sadistic serial-killing cases the department has ever seen. We both know a bit about mentally ill killers, having worked as detectives as long as we have. Bob and I have also read your excellent book. What we need your help with is trying to isolate just what kind of human being the killer is, if I may use the term 'human being' broadly. Bob and I assume, as I guess most people do, that the killer is insane, a psychopath. Are we working with a level-headed assumption? Give us your professional opinion as a psychiatrist and as a detective."

Bennie put his hands together in front of him and cracked his knuckles. I think he does that to get his thoughts flowing.

"Well, let's start with a working hypothesis that the screwdriver killer is a psychopath or a sociopath," Bennie said. "The big question is what is his motive. A psycho's motive can be broken down into four types: visionary, mission-driven, hedonistic, and power-seeking.

"A visionary psycho believes he's being spoken to by demons, or maybe even God. He often suffers from hallucinations, and the demons are part of the hallucinations. Son of Sam is a case in point—sort of. Berkowitz originally told investigators that he was responding to the voice of a demon in his head, a dog named Harvey, which belonged to his neighbor, Sam. Most shrinks, myself included, upon hearing that information, diagnosed him as a psychopath. But it subsequently came out that his story was a hoax, and he admitted as much. He was found competent to stand trial. When I first read about the case, I assumed he was a psychopath, but I was wrong. Serial killers can be full of shit.

"A mission-orientated psycho believes he's serving a function to society by removing a perceived evil, such as prostitution or even immigrants. There was one famous case where the killer went after priests. Yes, a mission-driven psycho thinks he's doing good deeds. But in our case, the victim profiles don't get us anywhere. The *Screwdriver* victims are all across the board as to age and occupation.

"A hedonistic psycho kills for sexual pleasure. Often the only way they can achieve an orgasm is by killing somebody. They're notorious for being sloppy because they're so eager to commit the next murder so they can have the next climax. Can you imagine getting sexual gratification from plunging a screwdriver into somebody's head? But as I said before, I don't think this creep is a hedonistic killer, because those types are often sloppy. This guy is very methodical. Also, there is no evidence of sexual molestation in any of the murders."

"A power or control-seeking nut can also be seen as *thrill killers*. The classic example is the nurse or doctor who kills patients by overdosing them with medications or withholding medication. These are commonly called 'Angel of Death' cases."

"Bennie, just yesterday Bob came up with a similarity in profiles. All of Mr. Screwdriver's victims were married—and get this, they were all married within three months of the murder. Five were married within two weeks of being killed. This creep is murdering newlyweds. We don't know where we're going with this, but it does establish a pattern."

"That's fantastic, Bobbie, a pattern. You just changed my mind from what I said before. I now think he's *mission-driven*. But, as you just said, you don't know where you're going with this. But it does narrow down the type of psycho this character is. For some reason he wants to kill newlyweds. My gut tells me the guy was jilted sometime during his life and wants revenge on people he wished he could be, so he's on a mission to kill them."

"Bennie, could you please explain what exactly a psychopath is and how it differs from a sociopath? Bob and I have been researching both terms and there seems to be a lot of disagreement among mental health people as to what the words mean."

"Yeah, there's a lot of overlap between those two diagnoses, but there are major distinctions between the two, and those distinctions aren't too subtle. Start with the word, 'conscience.' Sociopaths and psychopaths both suffer from a lack of conscience, or I should say it's their victims who do the suffering. If you or I did something bad to another person, our conscience would suffer. The reason our conscience kicks in is because we're normal people — and we *have* a conscience. If somebody falls in front of us, we try to help him up. If somebody spills her groceries, we offer assistance. If we hear a person scream, we want to know what the problem is. Society couldn't exist without this thing called conscience. It's sort of like a deal we all make with one another. If I hurt you, my conscience will bother me and I'll feel bad, which means I probably wouldn't have hurt you in the first place."

"What are the major differences between a sociopath and a psychopath, Bennie?" Bob asked.

"Let me start with psychopaths," Bennie said. "Some of the most dangerous motherfuckers on the planet are psychopaths." Bennie's New York cop mouth was on full display. "They're dangerous because they tend to be highly intelligent, are fond of planning their evil work, and couldn't give a rat's ass how much they hurt their victims. Not only don't they care, but they *enjoy* hurting their victims.

They can be articulate, loquacious, and charming, even holding leadership positions. Most researchers think that psychopathy is a genetic malformation of the mind. Yeah, they're born that way, or at least with a tendency to be that way. They may even be happy, if you define the word 'happy' broadly.

"Sociopaths, on the other hand, also exhibit a lack of conscience, but not in all cases. They tend to be unhappy losers. Most mental health researchers think that a sociopath gets fucked up because of nurture, not nature. For example, an unhappy childhood from being constantly bullied, a pattern the sociopath imagines is constantly repeating as he goes through life. If you or I get treated badly by a surly waitress, we shrug it off and maybe leave a smaller tip. But the sociopath would see it as a personal attack on him."

"Do you have a hypothesis that you're working on, Bennie?" I asked.

"Yes, my money is on the word psychopath. I see a hell of a lot of planning going on in these killings. These murders aren't spontaneous acts of anger or any other emotion. They seem to be carefully planned out. I mean shit, he commits all the murders on a Tuesday night or early in the morning on Wednesday. He even carefully plans in what borough of New York City his next hit will be. And, from the evidence you're uncovered, he takes the time to research newlyweds. That marital research is easy for him. All he has to do is look at the wedding announcements in the newspapers. This doesn't mean he's intelligent. Anybody can make a list of newlyweds in New York City and work down the list every week. It almost seems like he's taunting us, which isn't rare behavior for a psychopath. Yeah, this scumbag is a psychopath on a mission, one of the worst I've ever seen, and I've seen a lot of them."

I got up and walked across to the kitchen to get us a pitcher of ice water. My mouth was dry and I think it's from fear, my fear that we won't be stopping this bastard anytime soon.

"Bennie, please summarize for Bob and me where your thinking is so far. From what you said, the killer appears to be a mission-driven nut who's out to murder newlyweds."

"Yeah, but where does that get us as far as trying to figure out his next move?" Bennie said.

"Good question, Bennie," Bob said, "how do we figure out his next move? You know Bobbie and me—we like to get the job done, and we always *do* get it done. But after our talk, I don't see a way to proceed. Any suggestions, my friend?"

"Yes, Bob, I do have a suggestion, and you're not going to like it. You two are going to need to wait until the killer makes a mistake, and they always do. You two are the best fucking detectives on the block, and yes, you like to get the job done. I know you hate the idea of waiting for something over which you have no control, but that's what you will need to do—wait."

"And as Bob and I wait, the bodies will continue to mount up."

"Yes, the bodies will mount, and I know that two pros like you hate that idea because you see it as your jobs to save lives, God bless you. I just read your best-selling book, *Detectiving,* and I loved it. I gave it a five-star review on Amazon. I suggest you reread your brilliant writing. In the book you even touched on the need to wait to solve a case, and this is one of those times you will need to wait. I promise you; the killer will fuck up—he'll make a mistake. When? We just don't know. Hey, I'm needed in court. Commissioner Ralph told me he's assigning me to this case, so we'll be seeing a lot of each other. Please be patient, guys. I know it isn't easy, but it's your only option at this point."

Today is Friday, four days to next Tuesday. It's a sickening feeling knowing that someone else will be killed in a short time. But Bob and I agree that Bennie's right. We need to wait. This sucks.

CHAPTER 85

Bob

B obbie and I aren't cut out for waiting, but that's what we need to do. Today is Monday, and we worked through the weekend tweaking Bobbie's computer algorithms. We found nothing, diddly squat. The victim profiles are no longer totally random because we've narrowed it down to the killing of newlyweds. That said, how the hell do we find a killer who hates newlyweds? Tomorrow night another victim will have a screwdriver driven through his or her head.

Some detectives say that solving a case does not involve luck. Those who say that are full of shit—luck has a lot to do with it. Hell, Berkowitz in the Son of Sam case was picked up after a routine traffic stop.

Tuesday night came and went, and yes there was another screwdriver murder, on Staten Island as we predicted. The following two Tuesdays saw the same result, in the predicted boroughs of the city. But suddenly, we caught a break, or hoped we did. At the last three murder scenes there were cigarette butts. Forensics told us that the DNA matched *at all three sites*. Bennie had told us that cigarette-smoking killers often enjoy a smoke after doing their deed. The DNA was compared to all known criminals and suspects in our records and there was no match with the database. But, hallelujah, next to one of the stubs was a small cardboard coaster from a bar in Queens. Could be nothing, but it could be something. It could be *THE BIG MISTAKE.*

Bobbie and I went to Sammie's Suds, a bar in Forest Hills, Queen, the name of which was that was on the coaster at the crime scene. From the name, we expected it to be a dive, but it's a pleasant spot. Decked out with expensive lighting, it didn't have the feel of a typical bar. Behind the bar itself was a full mirror, which also cast light back into the room. The furniture was expensive and tastefully arranged. The crowd didn't appear to be typical "bar-hounds," and consisted mostly of couples. We had little to go on, so we decided we'd quietly collect some cigarette butts from the ashtrays on the outdoor sitting area before we would question anybody.

The next day we brought the cigarette butts to the forensics lab. Oh, my God, pay dirt—or so we thought. The DNA tests showed no fewer than ten cigarette butts matched the samples from the sites of the recent killings. We went back to Sammie's and asked to see the owner, Sam Vitarelli. The bartender pointed us toward an outside table, and said that was Mr. Vitarelli sitting there. He was smoking a cigarette. We introduced ourselves and he asked us to sit at the table with him. First impressions often take you in a wrong direction, but we noticed that Sam Vitarelli was a really nice guy. We made up a bullshit story that we were investigating a nearby burglary and asked if he could answer a few questions. We didn't really want *words* from him at this point—we wanted cigarette butts from the ashtray in front of him. We had collected butts from our last visit, but now we hoped we could match a face to the cigarette butts. Bobbie, with her years of training, surreptitiously picked up six butts from the ashtray using a tweezers, including one that he had just ground out. She engaged him in conversation as she plucked the butts, taking his attention away from what she was doing. Bobbie's a pro. We thanked him for his time and took off, heading straight for the evidence lab at One Police Plaza.

"This could be nothing, Bobbie. Just because we got matching DNA from butts in a large ash tray doesn't mean they belong to Mr. Vitarelli."

But, we both agreed, if the DNA wasn't a match, we would dispatch some other plain clothes to visit the bar, quietly photograph a smoker, and carefully collect the butts from the ash tray. The next day we got a shock, a pleasant surprise. The DNA tests matched the butts that we had collected from Mr. Vitarelli's ash tray. Well, it wasn't really a pleasant surprise, because we had both started to like friendly Sam Vitarelli. But suddenly, he was no longer a "person of interest"—he was a suspect.

We went back to Sammie's and told Mr. Vitarelli we'd like him to come in for questioning. In case he refused, diligent Bobbie had already obtained an arrest warrant based on the DNA analysis. All he said was, "Sure," as he told his assistant manager to take over. As we drove to One PP, Bobbie and I explained to him our suspicions and read him his Miranda rights.

"I hope I'm not being arrested for smoking," he said with a chuckle, "It's legal to smoke at the outdoor bar. Maybe it's bad for your health, but it's legal."

I had the sinking feeling that he was being straight with us. He refused to ask for a lawyer, which I thought was stupid, but I was happy that he passed up on his right to counsel so we could move ahead quickly. Bobbie explained exactly what we were thinking, and pointedly asked him how his cigarette butts could have wound up at the scenes of the "nearby burglaries." He seemed befuddled, having no idea how his butts were found somewhere else. We asked him his whereabouts on the past three Tuesdays.

He had rock-solid alibis. On the first two Tuesdays he was in Florida visiting his parents, and showed us photos with times and dates. Last Tuesday he hosted a big party at the bar for one of the regulars. If needed, he could produce over 50 witnesses.

But there was a positive aspect to the Sammie's Suds cigarette butts. Sam Vitarelli had installed surveillance video cameras after a robbery two years before. Sam is a cautious guy. Anybody who walked into Sammie's would be recorded. Because serial killers are usually loners, we doubted that the killer arranged for someone else to pick up the butts — it had to be Mr. Screwdriver Man himself. The other positive aspect of the Sammie's investigation is that it showed us the killer was careful. Why else would he arrange an elaborate plot to frame Sam Vitarelli? And maybe he lives near Sammie's Suds in Forest Hills. We questioned Vitarelli for an hour, asking him if anybody may have it in for him. Nothing.

But we had something — a month of videos from the surveillance cameras. Sam Vitarelli voluntarily gave the videos to us. Bobbie and I then began a mind-numbing task of watching the videos that captured the outside ashtray where Sam would take his cigarette breaks. We could have assigned this task to a new detective or even a uniformed cop, but Bobbie and I had decided to keep our theory secret to avoid the possibility of word getting to our target. We like to be careful. Therefore, we posted ourselves in front of the boring videos.

After five hours of staring at an ash tray, *there it was*. Sam had just finished a smoke, ground it out in the ash tray and went inside. A tall Caucasian man with short black hair walked over to the ash tray with studied casualness, slipped on a latex glove, withdrew the still-smoldering cigarette butt, stamped out the remaining ash, and put it in his jacket pocket. The video couldn't have been clearer. We went to visit Sam at Sammie's, bringing with us the video clip of the ash tray scene on my iPad. We also had still photos that the lab technicians made for us. As detectives who have been around the block a few times, Bobbie and I know how to brace ourselves for disappointment. Hope is an emotion that often doesn't get you far, but we both hoped Sam would recognize the guy from the video or the photos. But whether he recognized the guy or not, we had the photos. Before we left for Sammie's we brought the photos to the evidence office where technicians would run them through facial recognition software.

A half-hour later Sam walked in. We showed him the video and he watched it five times, all the while shifting his eyes between the video and the still shots.

"Holy shit, yeah, I recognize this guy," Sam said. "He comes in once or twice a week, always alone. He seldom talks to anybody, just sits at the bar nursing beers. His name is John Reynolds."

"How do you know his name?" Bobbie asked. "I thought you said he seldom talks to anybody."

"Gin Mill Marketing 101," Sam said. "Whenever a new face shows up, I always introduce myself and ask the person's name, in hopes that he'll become a regular. I also asked him if he lived nearby, and he said, 'a couple of blocks from here."

Neither Bobbie nor I believed the guy's name was John Reynolds. If he is who we hope he is, he wouldn't be so stupid as to give his real name. But he did make another *Big Mistake,* as Bennie Weinberg had predicted—he stole DNA evidence that he would use to frame somebody from a place he frequented, not knowing there were surveillance cameras.

Because we had both taken a liking to friendly Sam Vitarelli, we were happy as hell that we now had a solid suspect other than Sam.

CHAPTER 86

Bobbie

B
ob and I knew it was *stakeout time*. Sam Vitarelli had told us that the cigarette butt burglar was a regular at Sammie's and would show up once or twice a week, sometimes more often. We had the guy's face imprinted on our minds from the video and the photos. All we needed to do was be there to collar the guy when he walked in. We already had one charge against him— Obstruction of Governmental Administration for placing fraudulent evidence at a crime scene.

So, we planned to spend maybe a week or more at Sammie's Suds in Forest Hills. Sam is a stickler for safety, and even had a metal detector at the door to check for guns. We would alert him that we were on our way and he would turn off the detector so we could enter with our service revolvers. Because we didn't plan on getting sloshed every night, we would have a light meal of bar snacks and pitchers of iced tea. Last night, Tuesday night, there was another screwdriver murder, this one in Manhattan as predicted. The body count was up to 20.

At 7:15, the front door opened.

There he was.

We waited for him to ensconce himself at the bar. I hit the code on my phone to alert a nearby patrol car. We then approached him, me on one side, Bob on the other. We agreed that Bob would do the introductions.

"My name is Detective Robert Lawton with the New York Police Department. You're under arrest for suspicion of murder. You have the right to remain silent. Anything you say can and will be used against you in a court of law. You have the right to an attorney. If you cannot afford an attorney, one will be provided for you. State your name and address for the record."

"Please put your hands behind your back," I said as I grabbed the handcuffs from my pocket.

The guy jumped off the stool like a toad. Bob, big strong former Marine Captain Bob, planted a pile-driver of a punch to the guy's stomach. The guy bent over, gasping for air. I cuffed one hand and then dragged his arm around for the other one. We heard the siren of the patrol car and slamming doors. We escorted Mr. Screwdriver to the back seat.

When we arrived at One PP we went straight to the interrogation room, surrounded by six uniforms. I told one of the cops to turn on the video recorder and make sure it was working. The creep said he didn't want an attorney, which shocked us. I made sure the video recorder was working and loudly repeated his Miranda rights. No fucking way did I want this bastard to say that a confession was coerced.

His name was Simon Barton from Forest Hills.

Bennie Weinberg walked in as planned, introducing himself as Detective Weinberg.

"Well, if it isn't the famous Dr. Benjamin Weinberg himself, Bennie-the-Bullshit Detector," Mr. Screwdriver said. "I suppose I should feel flattered."

I was glad I wasn't near a screwdriver because I had a sudden fantasy of plunging one into this creep's head.

"So, let me tell you what I've been busy with for the past couple of months."

Holy shit, this isn't going to be simply a confession, but more like a campaign speech. This bastard is *proud* of what he does. He then calmly and by memory, recounted the name, age, and occupation of each one of his victims, going in the order of their murders. He also recited how long each of the victims had been married. During the interrogation, we also learned that he had, indeed, been jilted— twice within the past year.

After he was done, and before we sent him to the lockup, I had to ask a question, if only to put my mind at ease.

"Can you tell us why you murdered those people?"

"Didn't you know?" He said calmly as he smiled, "A dog named Sam told me to do it."

"Take this animal to the lockup," Bob said to the nearby sergeant. "I want two uniformed officers outside his cell at all times."

Bob, Bennie, and I walked to the cafeteria at One PP. We would have preferred the diner or a nearby restaurant, but we know we'd be talking about sensitive stuff concerning the prosecution of Simon (*The Screwdriver Man*) Barton.

"So, Bennie," I said, "have you added to your knowledge of serial killers with the slime we caught?"

"The difference with this guy is that he went to great lengths to avoid us coming up with an accurate identification. But, as I predicted, he made a mistake. The tavern coaster, which he apparently dropped by accident near the planted cigarette butts, was the first mistake. His second mistake was gathering the cigarette butts at the bar, not realizing that he was being videotaped. You guys then took it brilliantly from there and nailed the bastard. And no way in hell will his confession be disallowed, thanks to your caution Bobbie. Great police work my friends."

So, the case was basically closed. What's next?

CHAPTER 87

Bob

That afternoon we saw Barton the Screwdriver Man to the lockup. Bobbie and I then walked into Commissioner Norquist's office.

"I know you've heard me say this before, but you two are unbelievable, just fucking unbelievable. We have our hands on a guy who wanted to be the one of the worst serial killers this city has ever seen, and you two stopped the son of a bitch by your excellent police work. When I call you NYPD royalty I mean it."

Bobbie and I have long ago started to think of Ralph Norquist as a friend, not just a boss. He sure isn't afraid to throw around flattery. Come to think of it, I believe his flattery is justified.

"We got a major assist from Bennie Weinberg," I said. "That is one shrink who knows his stuff."

"Yes, Bennie's a great guy and perceptive as hell, but you two nailed it by good old-fashioned detective work. For the next edition of your book you should add this as a chapter."

"So, Ralph, can Bob and I take a few days off, or do you have another big case for us to handle?"

"Of course, you can take a few days off, and please accept my invitation to stay at my beach house in East Hampton. And, in answer to your alternate question, yes, of course I have another huge case for you two to handle."

He handed me a file, a thick file.

"*The Screwdriver Case* was a walk in the park compared to this shit," Ralph said.

"Tell me it's another serial killer," I said.

"Well, it's more than that, if there *can* be more than that. Yes, it involves a serial killer, but there's more than one; it's a group of serial killers, and they seem to coordinate with each other."

"Dear God," Bobbie said, "Is there one *modus operandi* of the killers?"

"Yes, in all states where the murders occurred, the killing was done by a poison dart from a dart gun," Ralph said. "And it gets worse. The poison used doesn't kill immediately. The victim takes as long as an hour to die, and the suffering is horrible."

"Are the victims men or women?"

"They're both, and they're all *schoolteachers*, 75 across the country. So far 45 women and 30 men have been killed. Some group of psychos has declared war on the American educational system."

"This is like the police terrorism case that Bob and I worked last year," Bobbie said. "How many states are involved so far?"

"Twenty states have seen teachers killed by dart guns, but the number will obviously go up."

"But how can Bob and I work cases from other states?"

"I already spoke to FBI Director Watson. Sarah will once again deputize you two as FBI agents. I just keep worrying that she'll try to steal you guys away from me permanently."

"Don't sweat it, Ralph. Bob and I are cops, NYPD cops."

The next day Bob and I hired a rental car for our trip to Ralph's beach house in East Hampton. Having a friendly boss who owns a beach house is a nice employment benefit.

CHAPTER 88

Bob

There's nothing like working a serial killing case that makes you want to take a few vacation days. Problem is, we had another serial killer file with us, but that's okay, Bobbie and I love to work cases. We also love to play around. And fresh ocean air makes for great playing around.

After we had a light lunch, Bobbie walked up to me and gave me a hug.

"Hey, handsome, we've been neglecting something important recently."

"What?"

"Us."

She squeezed me as if she thought I was going somewhere. I wasn't going anywhere. I was exactly where I wanted to be.

"Hey, Bob, what's that I feel below my waist?"

"It rhymes with election," I said.

"Election? Sounds exciting. Let's go to bed and vote."

"Think I'll win?"

"I think we'll *both* win," she said.

We spent a wonderful couple of hours in the big bed in the guest room overlooking the ocean. I didn't even think once about our big new serial killer case.

"You know what we should do now, Bobbie?"

"Go skinny dipping in the pool?"

"My partner always reads my mind. I'd help you out of your clothes, but you're already naked."

"So, let's go!" she said.

The swimming pool was perfectly blocked off from prying eyes on three sides with Leyland cypress trees and had a great view of the ocean on the other. We still had complete privacy because the ocean-facing side was on a bluff. After we made love — again — this time in the swimming pool, we figured we should take some time to talk about Hamptons real estate. We both agreed that we need to take more time off from our gruesome tasks of working criminal cases, even though we love our work.

"Hey, Bob, we talked about it the last time we stayed here, so let's put some real planning behind this. Yes, we both love working cases, but isn't it great to get away for a few days? Tomorrow we should meet with that real estate lady who Ralph told us about. I never had this ocean air in Chicago. Lake Michigan may be pretty, but it doesn't have the wonderful salt-air smell. And the smell of the ocean makes me horny as hell, as you may have noticed."

That night we went to the Palm East Hampton, a terrific steakhouse. It was quite expensive, but, with our combined salaries, not to mention my inheritance of $10 million and our book royalty advance of $15 million, we can afford an expensive restaurant, not to mention Hamptons real estate.

The next day we met Lorie Fitzgerald, the real estate broker that Ralph recommended, at Bostwick's Chowder House. Lorie was a well-dressed woman, about age 45 I figured, with short brown hair and a pretty face. Lorie insisted that she buy lunch and we didn't argue. I don't doubt that she wanted to make us feel beholden to her. What the hell, I figured. Ralph wouldn't steer us wrong.

I thought that Lorie looked sad. At one point during lunch, I saw a tear roll down her face. No way could I not say something to her.

"Hey, Lorie, is everything okay?"

"I'm sorry, really sorry," she said. "You two are enjoying some time off and were kind enough to meet with me and here I am showing you a pickle puss."

"Care to talk about it?" I said.

"I know you two are detectives, so I'm sure you'll know what I'm talking about. That fucking serial killer, or I should say killers, plural. My younger sister, a real sweetheart of a person, was murdered three weeks ago. Yes, by a goddam poison dart. It took the poor kid 45 minutes to die from the poison. The scumbags who are doing this should be buried alive."

"Was you sister a schoolteacher?" I asked.

"Yes, like all the others. Are you two familiar with the case?"

"Yes," I said, "Bobbie and I are the lead detectives in New York, and we expect to manage the case nationally as provisional FBI agents."

Lorie's sad face suddenly showed a big smile.

"Oh my God, that's great news. Ralph Norquist tells me that you two are the best detectives in the NYPD. Bob, Bobbie, you guys need to find the fucking animals who are doing this."

I'm sure she doesn't have the mouth of a New York City cop as a matter of habit. But she was obviously sad about her poor sister, and who can blame her? Bobbie and I would later agree that we both felt guilty about taking off a few days when we should be working the big case. But that's nonsense, of course. We need time off every now and then if only to keep our minds sharp. But here we were seeing exactly the kind of witness we need to interview; a family member of a victim who can give us some characteristics to add the victim profile. We were sitting toward the back of the restaurant and spoke in hushed tones. We both took out our notebooks.

"Lorie, Bobbie and I would like to ask you a few questions if that's okay with you. It may be painful, so we can schedule it for another time if you wish. It wasn't our plan to discuss anything but real estate with you, but after what you just told us about your poor sister, this suddenly takes precedence."

"Please fire away. Ralph told me I would be questioned by detectives, and here I am sitting with the best. I'm here for whatever questions you want to ask. I'm just glad to see it's you two, the BBs. I just feel shitty that I'm not showing you what may become your dream house."

"No problem, Lorie," I said. "We can reschedule your showings for another time."

"What was your sister's name, how old was she, and what grade did she teach?" Bobbie asked.

"Amy Jones was 29 years old and taught middle school. She was recently divorced. Amy was killed in Brooklyn, about two blocks from her school."

Lorie started to fill up again. I felt bad, but Bobbie and I were doing what we needed to do.

"Besides teaching, is there anything else you can tell us about Amy?" I said.

"Yes, she wrote extensively on teaching methods. As young as she was, she was a real scholar and was often invited to give lectures at university education programs."

Bobbie and I both jotted down that information. This was a special characteristic, and special characteristics often point toward clues. I've never seen a clue that said, "Hi, I'm your clue." No, you need to tickle them out of the woodwork. As the novelist Jack London once said, "You can't wait for inspiration. You have to go after it with a club." The same holds true for clues.

She gave us a website that Amy diligently kept up to date with her teaching blogs, which are all found on a website called *amyjones. com*. An important data point, I just realized, was the extracurricular activities a schoolteacher engaged in. Could this pattern repeat itself among more victims? That's what police work is all about. Victim profiles are critical pieces of information when hunting down serial killers.

The next day Bobbie's algorithm would develop some mojo.

CHAPTER 89

Bobbie

The following morning, Bob and I made ample use of the excellent gym in Ralph Norquist's beach house. Working up a sweat does wonders for your brain. Last night Bob and I really worked up some sweat, but not in the gym. Nothing gets my mental faculties flowing better than an evening of sex with Bob. Or an afternoon. Or a morning. Whenever.

We knew we had to start working the big case. Yeah, we're on vacation, but when a case calls to us we always answer. We *need* to answer; hey, it's what we do; we solve puzzles. Vacation or not, our case demanded attention. We realized that walking along the beach or sitting around reading would take more effort than digging into the Poison Dart Case. With Bob's help, I started the Poison Dart Algorithm, beginning with the information we were given about Amy Jones, Lorie Fitzgerald's murdered sister. Using my laptop, I began to put the datapoints into my software, while Bob poured over Amy Jones' writings on her website. She wrote a lot of heavy academic treatises about teaching theory. Mixed in with the academic writing were practical articles on teaching methods.

Problem is, there is no simple word or phrase that would appear on Amy Jones' resume, or on any teacher's resume for that matter. Okay, she's a scholar who writes a lot about her subject, but as we looked at the other victims. I could assign a data point only after reading about the person. The name I chose for my data point was "scholarly," even though that word may not appear in a person's profile. And we had 75 profiles to study to see if the word scholarly was a fit. Another case best described as "a bitch."

CHAPTER 90

Bob

obbie and I enjoyed our few days off in East Hampton, even though we spent a lot of time working on the Poison Dart Case. We have a theory that Bobbie will use to create one of her brilliant algorithms, the theory that the schoolteachers who were murdered had scholarly backgrounds. But we've both learned over the years not to fall in love with a theory, because it can occasionally send you in the wrong direction.

And that's exactly where our "scholar" theory sent us—in the wrong direction. We laboriously poured over the profiles of the 75 murder victims, and only a small handful of them could be described as scholarly.

"Bobbie, what else about Amy Jones stands out besides her scholarly work?"

"Well, we looked at age, which gives us nothing. Amy Jones was 35, and the other victims ranged all over the place with age. Amy was divorced, which gives us something else to look at, although I have no idea how a divorce can have anything to do with this crap."

"Hey, Bobbie, we first thought that the length of marriage could have nothing to do with the Screwdriver Case, but we were wrong. Maybe divorce is something we should look at."

Although we didn't expect it to lead anywhere, Bobbie and I began to research divorce statistics among various occupations. We always follow a lead, whether it seems to make sense or not.

"Holy shit," Bobbie yelled. "Bob, check this out. The average divorce rate in the United States is between 40 and 50 percent. Among schoolteachers the rate is just shy of 27 percent, which is well below average. Now let's look at the stats on our victims — 100 percent, yes, 100 fucking percent were divorced. And 100 percent is a hell of a lot higher than 27 percent, which is the average for schoolteachers. I know that correlation doesn't mean causation, but 100 is 100. I hate to use the word obvious when researching a case, but I think it's obvious that someone or some group disapproves of schoolteachers getting divorced and disapproves of it enough to viciously kill them."

My phone rang and I picked it up.

"Hi, Bob, Sarah Watson here."

When Sarah calls, I know it's something big.

"I'm in New York at Federal Plaza today. May I ask you and Bobbie to meet with me. Homeland Security Secretary Bellamy would like to see you too."

I had put Sarah on speaker, and Bobbie nodded her head to me.

"We'll be there in less than 10 minutes, Sarah." Federal Plaza is a short walk from One Police Plaza.

We walked into the Federal Building, going through the usual routine of beeping, buzzing, and clanging security devices. Federal security isn't impressed by the NYPD shields that Bobbie and I wear.

Rick motioned us to a small conference table after greeting us warmly. Besides his considerable power, Rick is a gracious gentleman. Our friend Sarah Watson is a perfect lady, polite and unaffecting.

"It's always a pleasure to see the BBs again," Sarah said. "You two have had a hell of an influence on law enforcement, including federal law enforcement."

"Ditto that, Sarah," Rick Bellamy said. "You two are the best detectives in the whole country in my opinion."

"Something tells me that you've already figured out why Rick and I wanted to see you."

"The Poison Dart Cases?" Bobbie and I both said simultaneously.

"Yes, The Poison Dart Cases, the most vicious serial killings we've ever seen. I already spoke to your boss, Commissioner Norquist, and I wasn't surprised that he assigned the New York cases to the BBs. My God, 75 schoolteachers have been horribly murdered with a slow acting poison from a dart. Do you guys have any theories that you've working on?"

"Yes," I said. "Just before you called my brilliant partner came up with a theory that's hard to avoid. Bobbie, why don't you tell these folks what you've come up with."

"Well, *we* came up with it, Bob. You'll have to pardon my humble partner; he loves to flatter me. So, here's what we've got. Bob and I poured over the victim profiles, all 75 of them, and we came up with a shocker. While statistics show that only 27 percent of schoolteachers get divorced, a number well below the national average, all 75 of the Poison Dart victims were divorced. That's *100 friggin percent*. By any statistical analysis, that number leads us to conclude that the killer or killers are targeting divorced teachers. We've come up with a working hypothesis, and I stress that it's only a hypothesis at this point. The killers are what Bennie Weinberg would call mission-driven psychopaths. We think that they see divorced teachers as giving a bad example to kids. We're going to meet with Bennie shortly to further explore this theory and see if he can help us with these cases."

"Bobbie, a while back, when you and Bob worked on those cop killing cases, you came up with the idea that the cases all across the country were one big case, singular not plural. Because these killings occur in all states, I think we should view them the same way you did the cop killings — as one big case. I'm dusting off your provisional FBI Agent badges and I'm reappointing you. Yes, I've cleared this with Commissioner Norquist. Whoever these creeps are will soon find out what it's like to come up against the BBs. You won't need to move to Washington again as you did the last time, but can work this case right from One Police Plaza. Hell, you've got a ton of FBI agents right nearby in this building, so if you need help, you'll get it."

Ralph had predicted what Sarah just said.

"I know I speak for Sarah and myself when I say that you just blew our minds with your divorced schoolteacher analysis. It's the kind of thinking we expect of you two. Your idea of working with Bennie Weinberg is excellent. Nobody bullshits Bennie-the-Bullshit-Detector."

"So welcome back aboard, BBs," Sarah said. "The nation's educational system is in your hands."

CHAPTER 91

Bobbie

S o, Bob and I are once again federal agents, not just cops, although we prefer to be just cops, detectives, puzzle solvers.

"So, Bob, we've got our *Big Theory*, that the killers are targeting divorced teachers. You know how that makes me feel?"

"Yes, I do, Bobbie. You feel like hell because the outside-the-box brain of yours hates to be locked into a theory, no matter how logical the theory looks."

"Yeah, the reason I hate to be locked into a theory is because somebody could be enticing us into the theory. Remember those cop-killing cases. When the mayor was kidnapped and two of his police bodyguards went missing, we assumed the two things were connected. But, as we later learned, the kidnapping and the cop-killings had nothing to do with each other. But somebody wanted us to *think* they did and sent us in the wrong direction. Is it possible that the Poison Dart Killers want us to think the murders have something to do with the schoolteachers being divorced? Hell, whoever is doing this knew it was just a matter of time before we saw the statistical link that all the victims were divorced. Are we being manipulated?"

"I think you're right, Bobbie. We need to be on guard that somebody is trying to send us up the wrong tree. But I suggest that we work with the data we have right now, and then be ready to swerve."

"I agree, honey, we should start with what we know. Any ideas on how we can find people who are upset about teachers being divorced?"

"Bennie is scheduled to meet with us tomorrow. He's in Brooklyn today working with a prosecutor on a series of depositions. In the meantime, we should try to focus on the divorced-teacher theory."

"How do you suggest we start, Bob?"

"As usual, with our old friend, Google. We should start with the variations of the search string, 'divorced teachers or schoolteachers.' Maybe we'll find some people who have gone public with their upset over that. This will be tedious as hell, but we're used to that."

"Bob, let me ask you a question. How do you personally feel about teachers getting divorced?"

"I think it's terrible. They should try to work out their differences and not create a bad example for the kids. You?"

"Yes, I feel the same way. But I wouldn't kill somebody over it."

<hr/>

Bob and I have a lot of basic detective work to do. First, we agreed we'd try to find something through Google, maybe an article or a blog post decrying teacher divorces. After three hours, we both came up with a few blog posts, all complaining about teachers getting divorced. But they were nothing more than reasonable complaints. One of the authors was a school superintendent from the Midwest. He suggested that school districts should consider terminating a teacher who gets divorced, much like they do when a teacher is arrested for, say, drunk driving. Another was from a parent who was the head of a parent-teacher committee, suggesting pretty much the same thing, that a divorce should result in a disciplinary action. Neither of these blog posts, Bob and I agreed, indicated that a serial killer was behind them. All they showed was a reasonable disapproval of a teacher getting divorced. Either Bob or I could have authored the posts.

The next thing we need to address is the physical evidence — the poison darts themselves. It's a good thing Sarah Watson has given Bob and me overall command of the investigation, because we would have everything sent to One PP for safekeeping. We researched every company that manufactures darts that could be fashioned into poison darts. We found 12 companies that manufactured darts that could be fired from a small caliber rifle or a gun specifically designed for shooting darts. Not much of a lead. Of the 75 killings, only 10 darts were made from the same company. Because there were only 12 companies, that was no lead at all.

Research on the retailing of the darts was not helpful. Any purchase could be made with cash, and there are no statutes requiring an application to buy a dart. I thought I found an interesting lead in a few posts on the web. More than one person used the term, "Flying Betsies," when referring to the darts. The term is also used when referring to a certain type of firework. But I did put those two words into my algorithm that will search the Internet every day, looking for any mention of poison darts or Flying Betsies.

We also researched the evidence from the autopsies of the victims. All the poisonings were from cyanide, small amounts of it, enough to kill, but not enough to kill quickly. A bunch of sick fucking people are behind this. I say "a bunch," because we had concluded that there was more than one serial killer. Similar homicides around the same time in various states led to that inevitable conclusion. Could any of these be "copycat" killings, always a possibility with multiple murders. But that seems unlikely because all of the victims were schoolteachers and all of them were divorced. But we didn't dismiss the copycat possibility. We *never* dismiss possibilities.

Commissioner Ralph, bless him, assigned a junior detective to work with Bob and me. Her name is Joyce Randolph, and she's terrific at plowing through data. Joyce's main assignment is to wade through the Internet hits for poison darts that my algorithm disclosed.

So, we were involved in a lot of tedious work, but that's what solving puzzles requires. And once the puzzle is solved, it's time to cheer. But that time had not yet come, not even close.

The next day we would meet with Bennie Weinberg, and it couldn't have been soon enough for me. We looked forward to turning our favorite serial killer expert loose on the Poison Dart Case.

CHAPTER 92

Bob

This is Shepard Smith for *Fox News*, ladies and gentlemen. The bizarre story of the poison dart serial killings has just gotten stranger. In the past 24 hours, no fewer than eight lawyers have been killed by poison darts. All of them were divorce lawyers. This comes on the heels of the 75 similar murders over the past month. All those victims were schoolteachers. The murders were accomplished by a dart soaked in cyanide fired from a small caliber rifle or a dart gun. We'll keep you updated on this horrific story as we learn more. In other news…"

Bennie Weinberg walked into our office at 8:30 a.m. Like us, he prefers to start the day early.

"So, how's my favorite cop shrink?" I said.

"You heard the news, I guess," Bennie said. "Our poison dart killers have just expanded their selection of victims to divorce lawyers."

"Bobbie, tell Bennie about your research this morning."

"Every one of the eight lawyers has represented a schoolteacher in a divorce case at one time or another," Bobbie said. "All eight murders occurred within an hour of each other—and here's the worst part—the killings happened in five different states. So, yes, as we suspected, we're dealing with a group of serial killers, all focused on the same victim profile, divorced schoolteachers, and after last night, anyone who has represented a schoolteacher in a divorce."

"Bennie, let's review the types of psychopaths that you told us about when we worked that screwdriver murder case," I said. "The knowledge you gave us in that case helped Bobbie and me nail the killer."

"I won't kid you guys; this case freaks me out. We're not only dealing with a psychopath, but a gang of psychopaths. In answer to your question, Bob, the profiles of psychopaths can be broken down to four different types, and sometimes they overlap, as we've discussed before. The categories are visionary, mission-driven, hedonistic, and power-seeking. I think you two know the type we're dealing with."

"Mission-driven," both Bobbie and I said at the same time.

"Yes," Bennie said, "these creeps are on a mission to kill schoolteachers who got divorced. And now the mission includes the lawyers who represent them. The lawyer murders convince me that we're dealing with a group of psychos on a mission. If you were a lawyer, would you be willing to represent a schoolteacher in a divorce after last night? If you're a schoolteacher and want a divorce, it looks like you'll need to represent yourself because no divorce lawyer will touch your case with a 10-foot pole. Based on last night's numbers, we know that the killer gang consists of at least five people. The only positive thing about the numbers is that it increases the likelihood of somebody making a mistake. Can you guys tell me about any crime scene clues?"

"There are no clues," Bobbie said. "The crime scene consists of a dead body with a poison dart. No prints, no DNA, no forensic evidence at all, except we know the poison is cyanide."

There was a loud knock on the door of our office, and in walked Joyce Randolph, our diligent junior detective sleuth.

"I'm sorry I'm late but I found some interesting stuff that Bobbie's algorithm kicked up. I'm glad Doctor Weinberg is here because I think this requires the eyes of a shrink. Check this out from a posting this morning." She then read to us from a page she was holding:

"The selfish, self-centered scum who call themselves teachers don't have the common decency to show their students some simple moral leadership by conducting their lives according to the word of God. But no, they trash the solemn vows they made and divorce their spouses. The nation's children are subjected to vermin who don't care, who don't show an example, who are willing to throw away their sacred vows. Their despicable lives aren't worth living. vengeance@thewordofgod.com."

"Holy shit," all three of us said.

"Type in the website on your computer, Bobbie, and I think you'll shout a few more holy shits," Joyce said.

Bobbie swung her large monitor toward us so we could all see. In large typeface across the top of the home page were the words:

"The Word of God Does not Tolerate the Breaking of Vows." Under it were the words: "Those who put asunder what God has joined together are evil. Those who call themselves educators and who get divorced can look forward to a journey to hell. The Word of God shall save the children from the scourge of vow breakers."

The site went on, page after page, denouncing divorce in general, but with special vitriol for divorced schoolteachers.

"Joyce," Bobbie said. "Have you figured a way to narrow down the websites you're looking at?"

"Yes," Joyce said. "I've come up with two indicators, two ways to characterize each website and I suggest that Bobbie plug these into her algorithm. The indicators are '*disapprove*' and '*hatred.*' Some of the posts simply show disapproval of teachers getting divorced. But others, a few significant others, bristle with hatred."

"Did you get the IP address of the computer that hosts this site, Joyce?" Bobbie asked.

"Yes, the idiot who runs this site didn't even try to mask the IP address. It's in Drexel Hill, Pennsylvania, an upscale suburb of Philadelphia. We can't get an exact street address, but we can subpoena it from GoDaddy, the Internet service provider for the site."

"I think the subpoena should come from the FBI" I said. "I'll call Sarah Watson herself."

"Did I mention that serial killers eventually make a mistake?" Bennie said.

CHAPTER 93

Bobbie

A sk any detective and she'll tell you it's a thrill when you get a break on a case. Joyce, our diligent assistant, gave us the break. Well, I'll take a little credit for my algorithm. Breaking the websites down into 'disapprove' and 'hatred' was a brilliant idea. GoDaddy, the Internet service provider for that hateful website, thewordofgod.com, was hit with a subpoena from the FBI. We got the physical address as well as the contact names of the people who own the website. Sarah Watson's deputizing Bob and me as provisional FBI agents was a great move, enabling us to work closely with the FBI.

The physical address of the computer's IP address was 234 Highland Street, Drexel Hill, Pa. Bob and I planned a road trip to Drexel Hill, a toney suburb of Philadelphia. We need to move with a lot of caution, however. The Poison Dart killers are located across the country, so we don't want to blow it by charging in with our guns drawn. But we do need to gather intelligence, including photos of anyone seen entering 234 Highland Street. We checked out the house using Google Earth. It was surrounded by condos and rental units. With any luck, we'll be able to rent a place with a view of the house in question. Joyce called the rental agent for a building across the street. Success! We will rent a unit right across the street with an unobstructed view of 234 Highland Street. Fortunately for the FBI budget, we were able to rent it on a month-to-month basis. Bob and I planned to stay at the rental apartment on Highland Street for a few days.

I picked out a burgundy Nissan from our vehicle lineup.

Two hours later we pulled up to our rental unit. It provided a perfect view of the subject house.

I asked Commissioner Ralph to assign another junior detective to work with Joyce on reviewing my algorithm every day, as well as monitoring the websites they found. In just one day, Joyce and her colleague found three more websites devoted to spreading hatred of divorced schoolteachers. They were www.teacherdivorce.com, www.asunder.com, and www.noteacherdivorce.com. All three sites were hosted by GoDaddy.com. We took that fact as an indication that the killers coordinate with each other. Subpoenas disclosed that they were hosted on computers in Salt Lake City, Utah; Billings, Montana; and South Bend, Indiana. I called Sarah Watson and asked her to assign agents to stake out those places, just as Bob and I were doing in Drexel Hill.

We photographed three men who regularly went in and out of the target house. I emailed the photos to Joyce, who would bring them to the facial recognition department. Sarah Watson would follow up with the same procedure at the other three locations.

Bob and I decided we would wait two weeks before taking any action, in order to give Joyce the opportunity to find any additional teacher-hating websites.

Common sense, not to mention legal ethics, required us to contact school administrators nationwide about our finding that the poison dart killings were focused on divorced teachers. Under the circumstances, we figured it's impossible to keep what we found secret. That, of course, would eventually filter down to the killers themselves, but we just need to live with that fact. The American Bar Association took care of warning divorce lawyers.

Stakeout duty can be miserably boring. At least our furnished unit was pleasant. Bob and I know how to fight boredom, and we did so each night. Nothing like making love to stave off monotony. Playing around with Bob makes a stakeout tolerable.

After one week, we figured we had enough photos and headed back to One Police Plaza. We were dying to see what the facial recognition technicians came up with.

Joyce met us in our office and the three of us headed to Commissioner Ralph's office to update him. Joyce did have a surprise for us. One of the inhabitants of the suspect house in Drexel Hill had a long record of arrests, mostly for violent crimes. We would learn more as the photos from the three other locations were put through the tests.

"Your analysis of the victim data has put this case forward by miles, Bobbie," Ralph said, "but we have a problem as you know. Every friggin school district in the country has been alerted, and I don't doubt for an instant that the poison dart killers have gotten the word. Obviously, we had to talk to the school districts. We had no other ethical choice. I just got a memo saying that five more poison dart murders occurred last night. I know you two want to wrap this up, and so do I, but I'm afraid we'll need to exercise a bit more patience. We have four locations under surveillance, thanks to the subpoenas served on GoDaddy. We can't go any further now because we need to wait until the facial recognition people are finished. Joyce told me that one of the men from the place you staked out has a long criminal record. As soon as we have enough evidence, I'm going to ask Sarah Watson to pull the plug and order an FBI SWAT team operation on all four of the locations."

CHAPTER 94

Bob

B obbie and I returned to One PP at 2 p.m. Joyce had told us over the phone that the facial recognition technicians had finished checking out the eight men from the four server locations in Pennsylvania, Montana, Utah, and Indiana.

Facial recognition software is good, but not foolproof. It's controversial in many jurisdictions, and some have outlawed its use. But we weren't looking to convict anyone based on facial recognition, but only to check the backgrounds of the people in question. We did find that one of the guys from Drexel Hill, where Bobbie and I were staked out, was a known criminal with a rap sheet like a phone book. Of the seven remaining suspects, all of them had backgrounds in web design. Further digging showed us that they hung around weird websites. By weird, I mean they seemed to focus on conspiracy theories. The strange unifying conspiracy theory they all subscribed to was what we suspected — a hatred of divorced schoolteachers.

So, what did we have? So far, nothing more than strong hunches. We didn't even have enough evidence to make an arrest, just evidence that the servers at the four locations hosted the hateful websites. We poured over the websites, aided by our talented junior detective Joyce Randolph. But still we had a lot more of nothing. All the websites spewed hatred of teachers who got divorced, but none of them called for any violence or recriminations, other than to urge school administrators to terminate a divorced teacher's employment. Hardly a crime. We didn't have anything that could enable us to make an arrest or get an arrest warrant. We sure as hell didn't have any forensic evidence. A dart doesn't have much of a surface to pick up a fingerprint, and besides, it's simply a matter of using latex gloves when handling the darts.

Six of the "hatred" websites were managed by people best described as religious nuts.

We concluded that we *did* have enough information on the addresses to call for interrogations. We advised the FBI agents working the case to properly Mirandize the suspects, in case the interrogations resulted in enough evidence to make an arrest. Bobbie and I would return to Drexel Hill to question our suspects. We brought four uniformed officers with us, on loan from the Philadelphia Police Department.

The big question we would ask of each interrogee was whether he had purchased a dart, a dart gun, or cyanide in the past year—under oath. They were all smart enough, we assumed, to know that a dart purchase can't be traced, especially if the transaction was cash. But it would lead us analyze the suspect's reaction to the question. Liars, really good liars, are rare, except on TV cop shows. Our years of experience as detectives, supplemented by coaching from Bennie-the-Bullshit-Detector, have given Bobbie and me a talent for spotting lies. The interrogee's reaction would at least tell us if we had a hot lead. The search warrants also covered computers and computer equipment. Often, the truth lurks hidden on a hard drive.

Thanks to Sarah Watson, we also obtained search warrants of each of the other locations. We all agreed that if we found a dart, a dart gun, or cyanide, we would have sufficient probable cause to make an arrest.

Bobbie and I had four people to interrogate. We didn't doubt that one or more of them wouldn't know what the hell we were talking about. Maybe. But possibly we would find a ring of divorced teacher haters.

Our first interrogee was Richard Rangel, who said that he was an Internet webmaster. Rangel was a 45-year-old with a master's degree in computer science from the University of Pennsylvania. He was 5'10" with black hair and glasses. His physical appearance is best described as nondescript.

"Are you married, Mr. Rangel?" Bobbie asked.

"Yes, happily married," He almost yelled. He didn't so much speak the words as spit them at us.

"Have you ever been divorced?"

"Never!" This time he *did* yell. I wondered if this asshole realized he was painting a picture of himself for us.

Bobbie and I took turns asking questions, which always included a form of the word "divorce." Every time he was asked such a question, his anger was on full display.

He asked if he could use the bathroom. One of the cops accompanied him. Another one of the officers walked up to us with an evidence bag in his hand.

"Anything interesting, officer?" I asked.

"I'd say so," the cop said. "How about six darts, a dart gun, and a small bottle of cyanide?"

"Holy shit!" both Bobbie and I yelled.

Rangel returned from the men's room.

"Mr. Rangel, you're under arrest on suspicion of murder. You have the right to remain silent. Anything you say can and will be used against you in a court of law. You have the right to an attorney. If you cannot afford an attorney, one will be provided for you."

Bobbie made a quick phone call. Within five minutes, four FBI agents walked into the house. I looked out at the street. There was one car and medium sized van, which I was happy to see, because that vehicle would transport the folks at this house to the federal Metropolitan Correctional Center in Manhattan. The place is secure as a vault and is run by the Federal Bureau of Prisons. I was exercising my authority as the provisional FBI agent in charge of the case.

The agents read each of the other three their rights, put them in handcuffs, and escorted them out to the van for the two-hour ride to Manhattan.

As Bobbie and I walked out through the hallway, we were temporarily out of sight of anyone. We couldn't resist a hug. Hey, we nailed it—so far.

CHAPTER 95

Bobbie

Bob and I arrived at the Metropolitan Correctional Center with our Drexel Hill poison dart prisoners. When they were read their rights, all four of them demanded an attorney. Hey, fair enough. It's the law. I looked forward to seeing how their attorneys would handle the darts, the dart gun, and the cyanide.

Six federal marshals showed the dart boys to their new temporary home.

Bob and I walked to One Police Plaza, not far from the Correctional Center. We wanted to hole up in our office and conduct conference calls with the FBI agents at the other suspected poison dart locations in Utah, Montana, and Indiana.

We discovered three more "dart" locations. Bob ordered FBI agents to those locations after Joyce got us the IP addresses and subpoenaed the physical addresses from the website hosting companies.

So, we had no fewer than 16 suspects in the Poison Dart Case, not counting the new suspects we'd get from the latest addresses. Bob and I didn't doubt that round-the-clock interrogations, accompanied by some judicious plea bargains, would cough up any stragglers.

When we finished our last conference call, Bob stood and walked to my side of the desk. It was 6:30 p.m.

"Bobbie, please stand up."

"Sure, honey, why?"

"I want to hug you. Actually, I don't want to stop hugging you. We nailed this, baby, we fucking nailed this. Let's go out for dinner and a couple of drinks. We should raise our glasses and toast the teachers of the country, people whose lives are no longer in danger."

"Thanks to us?"

"Yeah, thanks to us, and especially your brilliant algorithms. Gimme a kiss, baby."

The intercom sounded. It was Ralph Norquist's assistant asking us to go to his office.

Ralph stood, with the widest smile on his face I had ever seen.

"A month ago, I felt bad. I felt bad because I knew I had assigned an impossible case to you two. Yes, fucking impossible. But, as I learn all the time, nothing is impossible for the BBs. There's a thing called basic police work, and then there's a thing called basic *Bob and Bobbie police work*. I'm so fucking proud of you two I could faint. Because of you guys, the teachers of the country no longer need to fear for their lives. The BBs got the impossible job done—as usual."

The phone rang. "It's the President, Mr. Commissioner."

"What president?"

"The President of the friggin United States."

"Good evening, Mr. President, Ralph Norquist here. I'm with Bob Lawton and Bobbie Nelson, may I put you on speaker, sir?"

"Stand by for President Fenton and First Lady, Meg," his chief of staff said.

"The last time I spoke to you two I awarded you the Presidential Medal of Freedom for your outstanding work. I just got off the phone with the Speaker of the House. This Friday, two days from now, Congress will award you the Congressional Gold Medal. You guys are two great Americans."

"Hi, Bob and Bobbie, it's Meg," the First Lady said. "My sister is a schoolteacher—a *divorced* schoolteacher. Thanks to you two she no longer needs to constantly look over her shoulder for fear of being murdered. God bless you."

"I repeat what the First Lady said. God bless you," President Fenton said.

I broke down in tears. I like to think of myself as a tough cop, but fuck it. Sometimes you need to let your emotions go where they want to go. I noticed Bob wiping a tear from his eye. Commissioner Ralph gave each of us a bear hug. I noticed that his eyes were wet too. Ralph is definitely a good friend, not just a boss.

"Commissioner, I suggest you turn on the TV," Ralph's assistant said.

———❖———

"Wolf Blitzer for *CNN*, ladies and gentlemen. Tonight, our nation is a safer place, certainly safer for our schoolteachers. The most horrible serial killings we have ever seen are over. The detectives who solved this case are none other than Bob Lawton and Bobbie Nelson, the famous BBs, as they're called, from the New York Police Department. They were deputized as provisional FBI agents and given command of this case. That was only a month ago. As you will recall, this amazing couple were awarded the Presidential Medal of Freedom for cracking that horrific case of police assassinations. Besides being detective partners, the BBs are also married to each other, partners in every way. Once again, our nation owes its gratitude to two amazing detectives. In other news…"

Ralph just smiled and reached over to hand me a set of keys.

"When you finish up in Washington Friday, don't report here, report to my beach house in East Hampton."

"Yesss," I yelled as I gave him a hug.

"The last time you were there, your vacation was interrupted by the Poison Dart Case. I know you had intended to look at some real estate to invest your substantial book deal money. Well, this time you won't have a file to work on, because I'm not assigning one to you. I'll save that little surprise for when you return. Bob, you've been talking about writing another novel. Why not use your time at my place to work on it. I know Bobbie will love to work on it with you. Relax and enjoy, BBs. You sure as hell deserve it."

CHAPTER 96

Bob

At 7:30 a.m., Bobbie and I headed for Ralph's beach house in East Hampton. We wanted to get an early start because we love that place. We had already had breakfast at the diner. Hey, some traditions never change. We rented a car from the nearby Hertz outlet. I hate to drive in the city, although I need to in order to get to a crime scene if we can't catch a ride in a patrol car. But this was Saturday morning, so the traffic wasn't bad at all. There will be plenty of traffic as we approach East Hampton, but when we get to the beach house, it will be worth it.

Yesterday, Bobbie and I enjoyed another one of our hot shit moments. When we were awarded our Congressional Gold Medals, Congress was in session. An important budget resolution was up for vote, and the attendance was almost 100 percent. So, we got to bask in applause from the entire House of Representatives. Our medals were draped over our shoulders by Congressman Bob Metcalf, Speaker of the House. I remember his words.

"Bobbie Nelson and Bob Lawton, it's my honor to award you the Congressional Gold Medal, which is bestowed upon those *who have performed an achievement that has an impact on American history and culture that is likely to be recognized as a major achievement in the recipient's field long after the achievement.*"

Bobbie and I know our shit.

On Monday, we're scheduled to meet Lorie Fitzgerald, the real estate broker we met at the beginning of the Poison Dart Case. As someone who lost a sister to one of the killers, Lorie has developed a real fondness for us after we cracked the case. She said she had some beautiful waterfront properties to show us. After our huge advance from our book, *Detectiving*, we had a few bucks to throw around.

We began our short vacation by walking around the charming village of East Hampton. Bobbie and I are both city people, but we love East Hampton and its calm beauty. At one in the afternoon, we stopped for a light lunch at Bostwick's Chowder House, one of our favorite local eateries. We both had New England clam chowder, which was fabulous.

When we got back to the house, we talked about my upcoming novel. I insisted that it wouldn't be *my* novel, but *ours*. Hell, the last book we collaborated on became a huge best seller, so why go solo now? We envisioned a detective thriller. I want the major protagonist, the hero if you will, to be a beautiful blond lady named Betty Neilson (Like Bobbie Nelson, get it?). Bobbie insisted that we should have two heroes, Betty Neilson and a handsome guy detective named Rob Layton.

"Will there be sex scenes?" I asked.

"Of course, lots of them."

"Will we write them together?"

"Definitely," she said. "How can I write a sex scene without my honey?"

"Okay, I'm in. Rob Layton will be Betty's partner—and lover."

"I think we should have a live rehearsal to get our ideas flowing, baby, sort of like a dry run."

"How dry?"

"Not *too* dry. A shower would be nice. Let's help each other out of our clothes and get on with the rehearsal."

Bobbie kicked off her shoes and unbuckled my belt, all the while staring at me with those gorgeous eyes.

"I think Betty and Rob are in for some excitement, honey. Let's write a few scenes tonight."

"How many scenes?" I asked.

"As many as you can handle, handsome. Now help me out of my panties."

I can feel a best seller in my bones. Well, not just my bones.

CHAPTER 97

Bobbie

B ob and I had a wonderful time last night doing dress rehearsals for our new novel. Well, they were really *undress* rehearsals. Maybe we'll get around to putting something down on paper. Maybe. No rush.

We're due to have lunch with our real estate broker friend, Lorie Fitzgerald.

We walked into John Papas Café, where Lorie was waiting for us. It isn't an elegant place, but bright and cheery, and the food is terrific. Lorie ran across the room and threw her arms around us. Fortunately, it was early and there weren't a lot of people in the restaurant. The few who were seemed to get a kick out of Lorie's enthusiastic greeting.

"I love you guys. I just wish to God you were on the case before my sister got murdered by one of those poison dart animals. You two are beyond doubt the best detectives in the country."

We were seated at a table in the rear, which was good, because the effusive Lorie tends to talk loudly. She reached into her bag and withdrew two books, *Detectiving* and *An Army of*

Blue. "Here, please autograph these for me. I read them both and loved them. I left a five-star review for both on Amazon. Please tell me you're working on another book."

"As a matter of fact, Bob and I are working intensively on our next book, which will be a novel about a couple of detectives."

"Very intensively," Bob said. I nudged his leg under the table, giving him a wink as I did.

"Wow, what's going to be the book's title?"

"We're thinking of calling it *Rough Draft Rehearsal,*" I said. Bob cracked up and winked at me. Lorie looked confused.

"So, have you found a nice house for us?" Bob asked, changing the subject from our private joke inuendoes.

"I think I've found the perfect house, not just a nice house. It's a 8,000 square foot beauty situated on an acre of land on Georgica Pond."

Wow, Georgica Pond is beautiful, I recalled. It's a 290-acre coastal lagoon on the border of Wainscott. When he was president, Bill Clinton used Steven Spielberg's house on the pond as the summer White House.

Lorie continued after she saw the looks on our faces when she mentioned Georgica Pond.

"It has gorgeous sunsets over the pond. The place was built five years ago, so it's relatively new. The owners are the co-CEOs of a software company that just moved to California, so it's unoccupied now. We can take a look at it after lunch. It's a bit pricey, but within the range that Bob gave me, well slightly within the range, which is seven million. But you two are best-selling authors besides detectives, so I know you can swing it. I even came up with the idea of a name for the place—*BBs on the Pond.*"

"If we buy the place, Lorie, that will be our little secret," I said. "Bob and I like to keep our whereabouts unknown." I didn't bother to tell Lorie about our time in the Witness Protection Program.

The waiter came to take our drink orders. Bob and I ordered iced tea. We didn't want anything alcoholic because we wanted to focus on the house Lorie found. Lorie also ordered an iced tea. She's a real pro, and never drinks on the job. We sipped our drinks as Lorie went on non-stop about the house she hopes we'll buy. We trust Lorie and like her. Even though she'll make a large commission if we buy it, we didn't think she was in any way pressuring us. Hell, in East Hampton, there are plenty of buyers in the multi-million-dollar range. Lorie wouldn't just be the selling agent; she's also the listing agent for the property, so she'll make money whether or not we buy it. She started to tell us about some of the amenities but stopped herself because she wanted us to see them, not just hear about them. As we say in the novel-writing business, show don't tell.

The waiter came to take our lunch orders. Lorie recommended the prawn salad, which she says is fabulous. Hey, if we're trusting her to find us an expensive house, I figured why not take her menu recommendation. I love prawns, and so does Bob.

After lunch we piled into Lorie's Mercedes and headed for the house on Georgica Pond, which was only two miles away. The neighborhood was simply beautiful, with one exquisite house after another. I always think of myself as a kid from Queens, and never gave opulence much thought. But we had just received our first royalty check from *Detectiving*. It was $20,000, even though we had already received a $15 million advance. Bob's average royalty check from his first novel is $5,000 per month. And, God knows, with the huge amount of overtime Bob and I put in, our combined salaries are over $300,000. Hey, life's too short—why not live it up a little?

Lorie didn't point the house out to us, but drove by it a couple of times, faking that she was lost. She definitely has a flair for the dramatic. When she finally pulled into the driveway, Bob and I both gasped. It was the house we kept nudging each other about as we drove around. It was two stories high and had a long, elegant, sloping roof. The shingling was classic New England, but it was obvious that the house was almost new. Next to the swimming pool was a tastefully designed pool house that matched the design of the home. We walked through the front door into a huge hallway with a vaulted ceiling over which was a large roof skylight. I couldn't recall ever seeing such a spectacular entrance hallway. We walked around the first floor.

"Knowing you guys, you will love this," she said as she opened a door to a gymnasium—it was too large to be called a gym. It looked like a commercial exercise club, with every type of equipment you can imagine. Four large TV screens adorned the walls. Bob and I like to watch TV as we work out, and with this place we'd have a view from every piece of equipment. About 50 feet from the gym was what can best be described as a playroom. It boasted a huge pool table, a ping pong table, and three card tables. The wall panels were made of sumptuous cherry wood.

We then walked into the kitchen/dining area. If we were so inclined, we could host a party of 75 without ever leaving the room. From the glass doors by the dining area we could see Georgica Pond, a lovely view to dine in front of. Naturally, it had every type of appliance imaginable, including some things I had no idea what they were for. Maybe I'll learn to cook. Let's not get carried away. God gave us restaurants for a reason. Bob tells me I make great reservations.

Each of the eight bedrooms was *en suite,* with an elegant modern full bath included. There was also a master bedroom suite on the first floor, which will probably come in handy if Bob and I grow old in this place. The master suite upstairs took our breaths away, with its lovely view of Georgica Pond beyond the second-floor deck. It was almost all glass, with windows and sliding doors leading onto the deck. In the bathroom was a hot tub. Bob and I *love* hot tubs. A small kitchenette was the perfect spot to make coffee to sip on the deck and look at the water. In the hallway outside the master suite was a large closet. Lorie opened the door and we saw that the closet was a sauna.

The furniture was beautiful. Obviously, the owners have exquisite taste.

"Hey, Lorie, we don't have enough furniture to fill up one room in this place," I said, laughing.

"Oh, I forgot to tell you, Bobbie, the house comes fully furnished, including the gym."

Wow, seven million was starting to look like a bargain.

Lorie took us to another room on the first floor near the gym.

"Hey, Bob, I think this should be our office. There's the perfect spot for facing desks."

"Oh, I read about that in your detective book," Lorie said. "So, detectives like to face each other so they can communicate about their cases. Do you also write books together that way?"

"Well, we work on books in a variety of places (*like the bedroom*)."

We took one more trip through the house to see if we missed anything.

"So why don't I let you two chat while I go outside." Lorie seemed to know that sometimes the best pressure is *no* pressure.

Bob and I looked at each other and had one of our non-verbal conversations.

"Do you think there is any wiggle room in the price?" I asked. She gave me the answer I expected.

"I'll be honest with you guys; this house is priced to sell. It hasn't formally gone on the market yet. When it does, I expect a bidding war and a sale on the first day."

"We'll take it," Bob and I both said.

Case closed.

CHAPTER 98

Bob

S o, Bobbie and I finally got around to buying our vacation house. Arguably it's a lot bigger than we need, but we figured we would invite our parents regularly. The place is so huge the four of them could stay with us for a week and we'd hardly see them. Bobbie was beyond happy. I don't think she's stopped smiling since we made the offer. That alone is enough to make *me* happy.

We arrived home to our apartment Sunday night at 6 p.m. Good grief. After touring what will soon be our new house in East Hampton, our apartment felt like a broom closet. Looks like we'll be heading east quite often.

My phone beeped, alerting me that I just got a text. It was from Commissioner Norquist asking us to be in his office first thing in the morning. He said he has a huge case for us. Ralph never exaggerates. If he says it's huge, it's *huge*.

On Monday morning, Bobbie and I had breakfast at the diner, as usual. We talked nonstop about our new house, and about our plans to entertain a lot. Bobbie suggested that we should invite Tom and Mildred Cunningham from Random House to stay with us for a weekend. Always a good idea to keep in touch with your publisher, especially because Bobbie and I are working on a new book. Working? We really need to get something down on paper, although our rehearsals are wonderful.

At 8:30 we walked into One PP and headed straight for Ralph's office. We were both dying to tell him about our house in East Hampton, but something about the look on his face told me he had more urgent stuff to talk about. And who was sitting there in front of Ralph? Our old friend Buster from the CIA. I think my idea that Ralph had something urgent to talk about was accurate. Buster stood and gave us both bear hugs. In the time we spent working at the CIA we had become good friends.

"I hope you two had a nice time at my place in East Hampton," Ralph said, and immediately changed the subject. "I guess you're wondering why Director Buster is here. We're going to talk about a cluster fuck of Olympian proportions. Over to you, Buster."

"I guess you two have heard about violence on college and university campuses getting out of control," Buster said.

"You're not kidding it's getting out of control," Bobbie said. "You can't turn on the TV without seeing another news report about campus violence."

"I guess you're wondering how this involves me and the CIA," Buster said. "Here's the story in a nutshell. Our people on the ground have found that this shit isn't the normal flareups by some crazy ideologues who are upset about one thing or another. No, it isn't that at all. It's a carefully orchestrated plan and it's coming from the Middle East, which is why the CIA is involved. Our cyber spies at headquarters have found stuff that will make your heads spin. When you worked with us at the CIA. Bobbie, we learned a truckload from you about designing software algorithms to track fluid data. And what we've found has scared the shit out of us. Here's the bottom line. Some group has set up as its goal to cripple the American higher education system, which is a backbone of our culture and a large part of our economy. The riots we're seeing aren't spontaneous groups of nuts who want to bitch about their latest set of grievances."

"Buster, can you give us some numbers so we can appreciate how bad it is," I said.

"As of today, there are 5,300 colleges and universities in the United States, including some small colleges that specialize in one thing or another, up to places like Harvard. Not counting the specialty schools, there has been a full-blown riot at 100 colleges and universities in the past month. That's right, 100 of them. Not a lot of education is going on. And just like back in the 1960s, a favorite game we see being played is the occupation of a school's administrative offices. The dean's office at Stamford has been occupied for going on three weeks. They, whoever the hell *they* are, also take over the offices of faculty departments. Some parents are yanking their kids out of schools altogether, so as not to waste tuition money on scenes of violence with classes called off. Student loan applications are way off because nobody want to be burdened with a ton of debt and no degree to show for it. At the University of Pennsylvania, not a single class has been conducted in two weeks. Some dedicated professors are inviting students to their homes to conduct classes, but that won't work for large courses. Guys, we're looking at a gigantic economic and cultural war."

"My son is a junior at the University of Michigan," Ralph said. "He hasn't been to one class in a month. Marlene and I are about to pull him out, as Buster just noted that many people are doing. Bob and Bobbie, this is one fucking crisis."

"And how does this involve Bobbie and me?" I figured it was time to ask the obvious question.

"On orders straight from the White House, I'm authorized to deputize you two once again as provisional CIA agents," Buster said. "We need the best detectives in the country on top of this shit, and that, of course, would be you BBs."

"Would that involve Bob and I moving to the CIA again?" Bobbie asked. From the look on her face I could see that she just remembered that we're buying a beautiful house in East Hampton, not an easy commute from Langley, Virginia.

"No, Bobbie, it won't. You will continue to work out of the NYPD, as Commissioner Ralph will be pleased to know. Your assignment, quite simply, is to quietly infiltrate colleges and universities and gather intelligence. You won't need makeup, but should try to dress like professors, whatever professors dress like these days. Bobbie, you're a friend, and I'm not saying anything out of school when I say that you're a beautiful woman, as your husband Bob knows only too well. Your first job will be to look, how can I say this, 'frumpy.'"

"I hope you don't want me to wear buck teeth like the time when Bob and I were assigned to Chicago to spy on the mob."

Buster and Ralph cracked up. "No, Bobbie, you will still have your lovely smile," Buster said, "But we want you both to look inconspicuous. Nobody is better than you two at getting people to open up and talk. Your jobs are simple: to gather intelligence and find out who the leadership is behind these riots. We've got to find out who or what group is leading this riotous movement. Please try to avoid sounding like cops."

"Buster, my friend," Ralph said, "you're talking to the two best detectives on the street. You don't need to tell them how to question people."

"Where do you recommend that we start?" I asked

"You can pick any college or university, but I recommend NYU. A new president was appointed last week, and he's a great a guy. I've invited him to this meeting, and he'll be here in a few minutes.

He isn't your typical university president. He's not afraid to give orders and he expects them to be obeyed. He's a former Marine Corps general."

"What's his name?" I asked.

"Michael Bennett. Most people address him as 'General Mike.' From the look on your face, Bob, it seems like you know him."

"Know him? I served under him as a staff officer in Iraq. As you put it, Ralph, he's a great guy. I can't picture him in an academic setting, but General Mike is a flexible leader."

CHAPTER 99

Bobbie

I can't believe we're about to meet Bob's former commanding officer from the Marine Corps. Bob introduced me to him once when the general was in town. Buster said that General Bennett is a big fan of Bob, and I had gotten that same impression when I met the guy.

"General Bennett is here for the meeting, Mr. Commissioner," Ralph's assistant announced.

Although he wore a civilian suit, Bennett looked like a Marine general out of central casting. He's a tall man, at 6'5" and carries himself like the disciplined warrior he was. He's 58 years old but looks much younger. His short-cropped brown hair was streaked with gray. When he looks at you with his steel blue eyes, you feel compelled to salute.

"Great to see you again, Captain Lawton," Bennett said as he strode over to shake Bob's hand.

"When Commissioner Norquist invited me to this meeting, I was going to call you, Bob, but I figured I'd leave it as a surprise. Hi, Bobbie, good to see you again. I don't know if you folks are aware of this, but Bob Lawton was one of the finest officers in the Marine Corps. One of my proudest moments was when I awarded him the Bronze Star for valor. Thanks to his quick thinking and heroism, he prevented his rifle company from being overrun. Captain Bob here was one hard-charging grunt."

"Holy shit," I blurted, embarrassing myself.

Bennett resumed speaking, but I couldn't help staring at Bob, *my* Bob, a genuine war hero. What else has he been keeping from me?

"I stand before you folks in a capacity that amazes me, General Mike said. "Never in a million years would I have expected the NYU board of trustees to pick me as president. Military people aren't too popular with university trustees. But with the insanity we've been seeing on campuses across the country, I guess they figured it would be a good idea to pick a president who knows how to give orders. I've spent a lot of time with Director Buster over here, and I've learned that the campus riots we've been seeing are not spontaneous bursts of ideological nonsense, but a concerted effort to undo American higher education. Some group wants to destroy our colleges and universities, and that will be the beginning of an effort to destroy our country. Buster explained what your roles will be, Bob and Bobbie, and I'm here to tell you to consider me part of your team, not just at NYU, but wherever you need me. You served me well in the Marine Corps, Bob, and I'm here to serve you."

"Mr. Commissioner, I suggest you turn on the TV," Ralph's assistant said.

"Good afternoon, ladies and gentlemen, Robin Roberts here for *ABC News*. It seems that every day I bring you yet another report about the violence on American college and university campuses. Today is no different. We are receiving reports that a major riot has broken out at Columbia University, where hundreds of rioters are attacking the school. A large bomb exploded a few minutes ago, destroying the office of Seymour Jenkins, the university president. Fortunately, he was not there at the time, but many of his staff have been killed or injured. As I speak, the fire is raging out of control, and it looks that the entire building may be destroyed. As with so many of the other incidents, we don't know the pretext for the rioters' actions, other than to maim, kill, and destroy property. The few placards that were caught on videotape read, '*Freedom Now*,' whatever that means. Ladies and gentlemen, America's campuses are being demolished. I will bring you updates on this disturbing story as we get more reports. These aren't just demonstrations, they're riots, they're crimes. In other news…"

General Bennett continued. "Well, it seems that ABC just gave us a backdrop for this meeting. I'm going to turn this over to Director Buster to fill us in on more information."

"General, if I may…" Buster said.

"Please call me Mike, everybody. As I said, I'm on Bob and Bobbie's team, and we're going to work closely."

"Thanks, General, I mean Mike," Buster said. "Our main job, and Bob and Bobbie will lead the effort, is to gather intelligence. As you've heard, Bob and Bobbie are two sharp-as-hell detectives, and we'll be relying on them heavily. I've spoken often to President Fenton, and although he didn't say it, I think we can assume that we'll declare war on whatever nation is involved in these incidents. Recall the *Bush Doctrine*: Any state that harbors enemy terrorists is itself the enemy. Although it hasn't been formally declared yet, we're at war, a war I intend to win. Mike, would you please review for us your suggested plan?"

"I'm going to hire Bob and Bobbie as associate professors of criminology. I know that Bob once taught that subject at Columbia, so it won't take him much to handle the job. I understand that Bobbie taught criminology at the University of Chicago, so she'll be able to fit right in. I don't suggest they change their names or identities, because they're obviously likely candidates for the jobs. They won't be terribly busy with their teaching schedules, because we haven't held a goddam class in any subject for almost a month because of the disturbances. As you know, my main job as a university president is to promote the school and raise money. Well, that's a joke. Since the campus riots began, donations to colleges and universities have slowed to a trickle, which is an obvious aim of whoever is behind this. I'll have plenty of time to help Bob and Bobbie in their intelligence gathering. I must run along. I just got a text from my assistant that a large mob is forming at NYU. We have some interesting times ahead of us."

We'd soon find out just how interesting those times will be.

CHAPTER 100

Bob

After we met in the commissioner's office, Bobbie and I went to our office.

"Hey, handsome, I need to tell you how proud I am of you. Oh my God, the Bronze Star. I had read about it when I researched you, but I didn't delve into detail because I'm not really up on military stuff and I had no idea what the Bronze Star was. From what General Mike said, you saved the lives of your whole rifle company. My honey is a real war hero."

"Forget about being proud. Just tell me you love me—that's my highest award."

"Yes, I love you, sweetheart, and I'm also proud of you. I knew I married a great guy, but now I'm finding out that I married a great man. I think it's fabulous that we'll be working with General Mike, your old boss."

"I agree. I could see that Mike is treating this operation as a mission, and having served under him in Iraq, I can tell you that General Mike likes successful missions. So, what do you think, Bobbie, how do you see us working this program?"

"Basic detective work, hon. I see us quietly working the crowds and asking questions without looking like cops. That's something you and I know how to do better than anybody. I think we should use voice recorders. If we're seen jotting things down into our notebooks it would look suspicious, although I hate the idea of not using my notebook. I think we should drop hints and say things like, 'I've heard that this riot was planned by the American Nazi Party, or the Communist Party, or the liberals, or the conservatives.' Something tells me that the average demonstrator is not part of the management behind this crap, and they'll give a spontaneous reaction to whatever we say."

"Hey, we should go shopping and buy some professorial-looking clothes."

"What do you think of Buster's idea that I should look *frumpy*, Bob?"

"You can't do the impossible, Bobbie, and for you to look frumpy is just that, impossible. But you should get some baggy clothes, so the bastards don't get distracted by your gorgeous figure."

"So where should we start, honey?"

"Where we always start—*together.*"

CHAPTER 101

Bobbie

Bob and I reported to the pre-law department on a Wednesday morning at the Greenwich Village campus of NYU. The old uptown campus at University Heights in the Bronx is a thing of the past, having closed in 1973 because of financial problems. The old uptown campus now houses Bronx Community College. The pre-law department includes the subject of criminology, the course that Bob and I will teach.

The campus was somewhat quiet that day, except for about 50 students gathered in Washington Square Park with placards saying, "Fuck You NYU." The phrase, "get a life" seemed appropriate.

We each carried a bag loaded with books, trying to look as faculty-like as possible. I wore a pair of baggy jeans and a light denim jacket. I don't know if I looked like a *frump* as Buster suggested, but I sure as hell felt like one.

Bob and I had started to take Arabic lessons with an online Rosetta Stone course. It wasn't easy, even though I'm pretty good at languages, I must admit, but I was having a hard time with Arabic. It bears little similarity to any of the tongues I speak. Our main objective was to catch snippets of conversations. Then we'd try to make sense of those snippets.

Bob and I casually walked by a few of the placard carriers. We're good at appearing "casual." We've worked undercover so many times, it just comes naturally. I overheard a guy saying in Arabic, "Stern at 1 p.m.," apparently referring to the Stern School of Business. I *think* that's what he said, but he could have said, "What's for lunch?" My Arabic definitely needs work.

On the hunch that I got it right, Bob and I walked in front of the Stern School of Business at 1 p.m. I *did* get it right, I was pleased to see. All 50 of the placard people marched up to the entrance, this time chanting the words on their placards, "Fuck You NYU," a five-syllable phrase perfect for a chant. I wonder if they're good at poetry.

As Bob and I strolled through the entrance, one of the placard boys ran after us. The son of a bitch grabbed my jacket from behind. Bob hauled back and delivered a right hook to the creep's jaw. From the cracking sound I was sure he broke it. It's a bad idea to mess with Marine Captain Bob. We continued on our way to the auditorium, where we assumed a demonstration would be held. I glanced over my shoulder and saw Mr. Broken Jaw try to communicate with one of his colleagues. He was hardly able to speak. Bob throws a wicked punch.

We sat at the rear of the auditorium. One of the placard folks sat next to me. "Are you guys from the ACLU?" I asked. The guy answered me in pigeon Arabic. It was obvious he couldn't speak a word of English. Curious, because all the classes are taught in English. Obviously, this guy was off-campus talent. I softly made a note into my recording device.

Another placard guy sat in front of us. "Do you think we should leave?" Bob said, a simple non-suspicion arousing question, one aimed at starting a conversation. Bob is cool. The guy turned his head and said, in perfect English, "Why miss the fun?"

Within a minute, four of the placard boys ran to the head of the auditorium with some sort of tanks strapped to their backs. They hosed down the auditorium platform with whatever was in the tanks. One of the guys slipped and fell on his ass. Obviously, the tanks contained some sort of oily substance. Another one of the placard people threw a lit cigarette lighter to the stage, which quickly became engulfed in flames. Holy shit, they're burning the building down.

"Let's go," Bob said.

We walked quickly out of the soon-to-be-burning building, surrounded by placard bearers. I turned into an alcove and dialed 911 to report the fire.

When we got outside, Bob and I typed into our cellphones, or made it appear that was what we were doing. We were taking photos of the placard folks as they emerged from the building. I also listened carefully with my newfound, although slight, understanding of Arabic. I repeatedly heard the word "brotherhood,' sometimes in English. Phrases like "The Brotherhood strikes again" were repeated over and over, along with the familiar, "Alahu Akbar" (God is the greatest).

I heard one guy, an apparent leader judging from his position in the crowd, say to another man named Mustaffa, "I just reported our glory to Sana'a." He said it in English. Oh, my God. Could this be pay dirt? Sana'a is the capital of Yemen, although there is some dispute about that. According to Buster, Yemen is a "cesspool of terrorism." I whispered what I had just heard to Bob. He stared at me wide-eyed and dictated a note into his device.

The placard folks appeared excited as they watched the Stern School of Business go up in flames. Excitement is good, both Bob and I know, because excitement often results in loose lips. We both realized that taking photos was important, because many of the faces will eventually be hooked up with names by our facial recognition software. I heard constant references to Sana'a and the brotherhood as we clicked photos of the speakers. It was as if they were all writing lyrics to the same song.

We stopped by the office of General Mike to report what we saw. He was distracted, to say the least, as one of his major buildings—the Stern School of Business—burned to the ground. Obviously, Mike didn't have the time for a meeting. I guess General Mike figured his new role as a university president would be much more peaceful than commanding a Marine regiment. Doesn't seem to be working out that way.

"I'll call you as soon as I can get a couple of minutes," General Mike said. "I want to hear what you've heard."

We realized that we had gathered enough evidence for one day and wanted to get back to the office to compare notes and make phone calls. One of the calls would be to our friend Rick Bellamy, Secretary of Homeland Security, who owns a brownstone near the NYU campus. An unmarked car picked us up near the entrance to Washington Square Park. I noticed that the chant began again, "Fuck You NYU." I also noticed that the chanters chanted with Middle Eastern accents. As I watched the smoke billowing from the remains of the Stern School of Business, I realized that this was not the typical detective assignment for Bob and me. We told the driver to take us to the back of One Police Plaza, not the main entrance.

CHAPTER 102

Bob

We went straight to Ralph Norquist's office to report the day's findings. Buster had already returned to Langley. We told Ralph what we found, but especially what Bobbie heard with her improving Arabic ear.

"So, you heard Sana'a, the capital of Yemen, repeated as well as the word 'brotherhood.' Did you hear anything about ISIS or al Qaeda?"

"No, not one mention of those words," Bobbie said, "but this was only our first day. Bob and I took dozens of photos, which we'll give to the facial recognition people right now."

"I suggest you call Phil Cummings in California, a CIA agent staking out Stanford University. Phil is fluent in Arabic and you can compare notes with him."

"My Arabic definitely needs work, Ralph. Yes, I picked up a few things, but not nearly as many as I missed."

We then went to the office where the facial recognition technicians do their stuff and gave them all the photos we took that day.

Bobbie then placed a call to CIA Agent Phil Cummings on Ralph's suggestion. If our observations align, we thought, we may be close to zeroing in on the case.

It didn't happen that way.

Cummings, who had been staking out Stanford University, had a shock for us. He told us he didn't hear the word 'Sana'a' nor the word 'brotherhood' once, not even once. And he had been on his stakeout for five days. He did hear a lot of references to Riyadh, the capital of Saudi Arabia, and one reference to ISIS. He also heard a lot of references to Tehran. Tehran? Shit, our stakeouts aren't showing any similarities. "Back to the drawing board" is a phrase that all detectives hate, but that's exactly where we found ourselves. But then it occurred to me that the dissimilarities between what Cummings heard and what I heard may be clues in themselves. Detective work means keeping open to possibilities.

With the burning down of the Stern School of Business, we figured the NYU campus would be relatively free of protesters and rioters, at least for a few days. So, tomorrow we would visit Fordham University in the Bronx. According to our data, Fordham has seen its share of radical activity in the past few weeks.

We called General Mike to update him on our activities.

"Captain Bob," General Mike said, "I wish to hell I had a rifle company under my command, with you leading it. I cannot fucking believe that the Stern School of Business has burned to the ground. It looks like my new job is burning out from under me. We've got a goddam war on our hands. I can't believe I'm saying this, but NYU reminds me of Iraq. I'll see you guys in a few days."

Because we weren't listed on the faculty at Fordham, we would need to wear disguises, something to which Bobbie and I had grown accustomed. No padding, no buck teeth, but disguises nonetheless. We would both wear the uniforms of United Maintenance Company.

Commissioner Ralph ordered them delivered to our apartment, where we tried them on.

"My, you look charmingly frumpy in your maintenance uniform, Bobbie."

"At least I'm not wearing buck teeth, wiseass. Hey, let's have a drink, honey. Something tells me that Fordham will be quite interesting tomorrow."

CHAPTER 103

Bobbie

I hate disguises, but sometimes they're necessary. Bob and I couldn't risk being recognized by one of the placard people at Fordham who may have seen us at NYU. Buster had told us that the demonstrators often move from one campus to another.

Also, we didn't have the cover of being faculty members as we did at NYU, so our Fordham persona would need to be different. I must say I looked lovely in my baggy United Maintenance Company overalls. My baseball cap also looked charming.

We walked into the student union building and tried to look busy as maintenance workers. We moved light folding chairs from one wall to another, hoping nobody would realize that what we were doing made no sense at all. Our strategy today would be walk around and start conversations, something Bob and I are good at.

Holding one of the chairs, I walked over to a young woman who was reading a magazine. In my years as a detective I've developed a sixth sense for talking to people who seem communicative. Bob has the same talent. "Wow, these campus riots are sure getting out of hand, aren't they?" I said. "Did you hear about that building being burned down at NYU yesterday?"

"Yes, I did, but it hasn't happened here at Fordham — yet."

I introduced myself, and she told me her name was Dolores. I told her my name was Roberta.

Well, it is.

She seemed to want to talk. "The semester ends next week and I'm out of here. My parents refuse to pay any more tuition to a place where classes are regularly cancelled because some pack of assholes are protesting something. I don't blame them. I can't afford to pay my own tuition, so it looks like I won't be getting a university degree anytime soon."

"Do you have any idea who is behind this crap?" I asked, walking into the opening she just created.

"You haven't heard?" Dolores said. "It's an outfit called EOA. I'm told it means '*End of America*.' At first, I thought it was bullshit, because it sounded so dramatic, but I've been told that by so many people I'm beginning to believe it."

Holy shit, this may be an important lead. My recording device in the pocket of my United Maintenance Company overalls was doing its thing.

"Do you have any idea where that organization is located, Dolores?"

"Somewhere in the Middle East, from what I've heard."

"You don't speak Arabic by any chance, do you, Dolores?" Hey, sometimes grabbing for a straw in the wind pays off.

"No, I don't but my roommate does." Dolores then told me the Arabic words for *End of America* or EOA.

Oh my God. I recalled that I heard that phrase countless times yesterday at NYU, although I didn't understand it at the time.

Dolores excused herself and got up to leave.

"Running to class?" I asked.

"I wish. I have a dentist appointment. Nice talking to you, Roberta."

Bob and I decided to have lunch at the cafeteria in the student union building. Just a couple of maintenance workers taking a break.

"I noticed you talking to that guy wearing a hat, Bob. Did he have anything interesting to say?"

"Yeah, I'll say it was interesting. Ever hear the phrase '*End of America*?' "

"I just heard it from that girl I was talking to. She even gave me the Arabic translation of the phrase. I realized I heard it constantly yesterday at NYU. After lunch, let's do a little more furniture moving and then head back to One PP to work the phones."

CHAPTER 104

S o how was your day, honey?" Nancy Drummond said, laughing, to her husband. Carl Drummond was the Dean of Academic Affairs at the University of Iowa.

"I'm glad to see you laughing when you asked me that question. To answer you, my day sucked, as does every day on my job. Once again, the executive committee of the board told me to cancel all classes. This has been going on for three weeks. What am I running, a chat room?"

"Hey, honey when I asked you how your day was, I was making a joke. But I notice you aren't laughing."

"How can I laugh? The demonstrators are once again taking over the goddam university. And now I'm worried about something else — my job. Why the hell do they need an academic dean if there's no academics going on? All I do is sit in my office answering emails and reading books."

"Is there anything new, or is it just more of the same?" Nancy said.

"Yes, there is something new. The demonstrations, to use a ridiculous term, are becoming increasingly violent. That shocked me — at first. Everybody knows that the school is covered by surveillance cameras, and you know that if cameras are trained on you, you will eventually be arrested if you're caught engaging in violence. But no arrests have been made. I spoke to the local police chief, and he had some interesting observations. He told me that they tried everything they could to track down the violent demonstrators, but they weren't able to find anybody. You heard me; the bastards who were caught on camera can't be found. There seems to be steady waves of new demonstrators every week, replacing the ones our surveillance cameras picked up. You know me well, Nancy, and you know that I've been a supporter of academic freedom all my life, and yes, sometimes that freedom includes demonstrations. But these aren't demonstrations, they're fucking riots. We've been trying to get a handle on just what the demonstrations are aimed at. That got us nowhere. The demonstrations seem to have one simple objective—to shut down the university. I just hope the government is going to do something about this."

CHAPTER 105

Bob

Yesterday, Bobbie and I had a few more chats with students as we moved folding chairs from one wall to another. I wonder if anybody noticed our pointless furniture moving. We again heard the words *End of America* and the acronym, EOA, and also heard that the people we spoke to think that the organization, if you can call it that, is from the Middle East. Outside the student union building we heard a chant beginning. *End of America* seemed to be the words of choice among the chanters. Guess it beats, *Fuck You NYU,* especially because we were at Fordham.

When we walked into Ralph Norquist's office, none other than Buster was there. As long as I've known him, I've noticed that Buster has a knack for showing up unannounced out of nowhere. We were happy to see him and looked forward to one of his detailed updates.

"Agent Phil Cummings reported to me from Stanford," Buster said. "He's heard the words *End of America* and EOA constantly. He thinks the words are new, because he just began hearing them. But now he hears them non-stop. My IT guys have inserted the words into their search algorithm. I wish Bobbie Nelson was there to help us."

Bobbie just smiled. She's grown accustomed to Buster's flattery of her skills.

"We don't know if it's the name of an organization or just a phrase some group likes to use, such as the Iranian epithet of choice, *Death to America,*" Buster said, "but it does give us something to focus on. And we sure as hell need something to focus on. Phil Cummings confirmed that he's also heard that the people saying the words come from somewhere in the Middle East. Let me tell you about some news I got from the Department of Education. College and university applications have slowed to a trickle, and dropouts are sprouting like bamboo. People are looking at American institutions of higher learning as the equivalent of walking into a riot, which isn't far from accurate."

Ralph's assistant walked in—she didn't even knock as she grabbed the remote and turned on the TV.

"Wolf Blitzer for *CNN* ladies and gentlemen. The unrest on American college campuses can no longer just be called unrest, but full-blown criminal violence. Yesterday at the University of Wisconsin, a building was bombed and burned to the ground before emergency vehicles got there. This same thing happened a week ago at Columbia and two days ago at NYU. At the University of Delaware just this morning, there was a full-scale riot, accompanied by gunfire. You heard me—gunfire. Here in New York City, the president's office at Hunter College has been occupied by 30 armed protesters. *CNN* management has assigned a full-time producer and five reporters to cover the campus violence. If you wish to avoid danger, one way to accomplish that is by avoiding college campuses. Of course, that begs the question: Where do the students go? Needless to say, *CNN* will be following this story closely and constantly. In other news…"

"I imagine you're flooding the Middle East with operatives, Buster," Bobbie said.

"I can't confirm that."

"You just did," she said, laughing. Bobbie is turning into a pretty good spook.

Buster cracked up.

"One thing that amazes me," I said, "is the number of demonstrators and rioters across the country. How the hell do they recruit all these people?"

"From the accents we're hearing," Buster said, "we think most come from Middle Eastern countries. Besides that, there are people in our country who just love to protest—anything, whether they understand it or not. But they have *leadership* and that's what we need to learn about. There's nothing spontaneous about this violence. They make the 1960s look like nothing more than Beatles music. So, it's the management we're after, the group that is organizing this violence and making it happen. Soon, our moles on the ground will tell us more." He looked at Bobbie and winked when he said that. Although he wouldn't admit to flooding the Middle East with operatives because Bobbie and I don't have the sacred "need to know," it was obvious that the CIA is doing just that. Having worked with Buster before, we know that he plays rough—*very rough*.

"We're inviting some suspected terrorists to come to Langley to be interrogated."

"Inviting them?" Bobbie said.

"Yes, at the CIA we're very polite. Which brings me to a request I want to make of Commissioner Ralph here. When we have a few 'guests' in place I want the two best interrogators in the land to help us. That, of course, would be the BBs."

Bobbie and I are scheduled to close on our new waterfront home the day after tomorrow. I wonder if we'll ever get to visit the place.

"Consider it done, Buster," Commissioner Ralph said. "Bob and Bobbie will join you at the CIA. I'll repeat what you've heard me say often—please don't steal my best detectives away from me. Just let us know when you have enough 'guests' for them to interrogate."

CHAPTER 106

Bobbie

B ob and I closed on our beautiful East Hampton waterfront home this morning. The closing was in Manhattan at our request. That was fine with the seller's attorneys because their office was in Manhattan. Bob and I couldn't have been happier — sort of. Our new assignment, especially now that we'll be headed to Langley, won't allow for much time off. We mailed keys to both our parents and asked them, more like it begged them, to go to East Hampton and stay at our new vacation home. We recommended taking our cousins too. At least our families will get to enjoy the place.

Bob and I are scheduled to fly to Langley tomorrow to interrogate Buster's "guests."

———————⊹∘⊹———————

Our plane touched down at Dulles Airport at 10:30 a.m. A CIA car awaited us to bring us to Langley. We met with Buster in his office, where he introduced us to Marcia Barrett, an agent who was fluent in Arabic and Farsi. My studies have been coming along, and so have Bob's, but with something as important as an interrogation we knew we'd need a translator. The three of us walked to the interrogation room, which was equipped with the usual one-way mirror. The room was pleasantly cool at 71 degrees, which was good, because Bob and I would soon be turning up the heat.

Mustaffa Antar was a skinny guy, about age 30, with a long beard and a shock of black hair. I immediately disliked the guy, especially because he and his colleagues were keeping Bob and me from our new vacation home in East Hampton. But we have an important interrogation in front of us, so I tamped down my negative emotions as I always do. To be a good interrogator it's essential to keep your emotions under tight control. His English was pretty good, so Marcia would be needed only for the occasional word or phrase.

Bob and I agreed that he'd begin the questioning, in case Mustaffa had an issue with being questioned by a woman. If he does, fuck him. I'll be all over his head in a few minutes.

After some preliminary chitchat, Bob got down to business.

"Mr. Antar, are you familiar with the words *End of America*, also stated as EOA?"

"I am not knowings what you be speaking about."

Marcia, a tall pretty brunette, is well known in the agency as a "tough broad," one who doesn't put up with shit from an interrogee.

She spoke to him in English, well more like yelled at him. "Mr. Antar, you are aware that the CIA has guaranteed you leniency in exchange for your full cooperation. Unless you want your sorry ass in prison for the rest of your life, I suggest being straightforward with us. And I know that you can speak perfect English, so stop playing games and answer Detective Lawton's question."

I was happy that Marcia was there. She'd make a good cop.

"I repeat my question," Bob said, "are you familiar with the words *End of America*, also stated as EOA?"

"Yes," Mustaffa said, staring at the floor.

"Is it an organization?" Bob asked. "Hey, answer my question, please."

"It's sort of an organization."

"Like you're *sort of* an asshole?" Marcia inquired. I really like this lady.

"It's more like a movement," Mustaffa said.

"So, *End of America* is a movement?" I said. "Please tell us the names of the people who run this movement." Bob had nodded to me, indicating that I should join in the questioning.

"There is only one person. His name is Randolfo Martin."

Bob, Marcia, and I just stared. We couldn't believe what we had just heard.

"Oh, dear God," I said. "Oh, dear God Almighty."

Randolfo Martin is the son of the late Bartholomew Martin, the former President of the United States, America's first and only dictator. Bartholomew Martin defeated Matt Blake after he waged a campaign of lies and slander, portraying Blake as being soft on terrorism. The day before the election saw horrible scenes of explosions at children's amusement parks around the country. The Bartholomew Martin people, with their billions in bribe money, convinced journalists that the explosions were the result of Matt Blake's actions or inactions. A subsequent investigation found that the bombings were caused by Martin's people, although it couldn't be proven. Martin won in a landslide, and he brought with him a bulletproof majority in both houses of Congress. Overnight, we Americans saw our basic rights evaporate in a storm of executive orders. Within a few months we barely recognized our country. Blake defeated him in the next election, thank God. Three years later Martin was accused of bombing the Republican National Convention where Harry Fenton had just won the nomination for the next presidential election. Martin was arrested, tried, and convicted of 412 counts of first-degree murder. A lot of Americans, myself included, felt relieved when he was assassinated in prison. His older son, Antonio Martin is serving a life sentence in prison. When Antonio Martin was the president of the rogue nation, Concordia, he aimed his sights on the world's shipping industry, and almost brought it to a halt. Dozens of ships were sent to the bottom of the sea, along with passengers and crews. Lovely family.

Buster has told me that he thinks Randolfo, age 41, may be the worst of the Martins. Buster calls him a "ruthless scumbag." He has been hiding in the shadows, typical of a Martin, quietly planning the latest surprise for the United States. And now our interrogee tells us that Randolfo is behind the campus riots and heads up the "movement" called the *End of America*. We suddenly had a new ballgame.

"And where is Randolfo Martin located?" I asked, when I recovered my voice.

"I can't say."

"Horseshit," Marcia yelled, "where is the man located?" I'm definitely going to try to recruit Marcia into the NYPD.

"Tehran," Mustaffa said.

"Bob, we need to take a short break," I said. "Buster needs to hear this."

Marcia speed-dialed Buster on her phone. He walked into the interrogation room in less than three minutes, while an agent escorted our interrogee to the hallway.

"We have two words for you, Buster," I said. "Randolfo Martin."

Like the seasoned spy he is, Buster is talented at putting on a poker face. He disciplines himself to hide his feelings from the person he was speaking to, so he could keep his thoughts to himself. But he didn't even try to mask his feelings. He stared at us wide-eyed and took a deep breath, exhaling audibly.

"Oh, my God, Randolfo Martin," Buster said. "We've been trying to keep track of him, but he just disappeared. Did you find out where he is?"

"Tehran," Bob said. "Our interrogee didn't want to disclose that, but your colleague Marcia here is quite a persuasive woman."

"I've told anyone who would listen, including President Fenton, that Randolfo is the worst of the evil Martin family," Buster said. "The son of a bitch will stop at nothing to amass power, and now he wants to destroy America's higher education system. He may be holed up in Tehran, but we can be sure he has thousands of his followers across the United States."

Marcia's phone sounded with a chime.

"I think we should turn on the TV, Buster." He insists that everybody, including subordinates, simply call him Buster.

"Nora O'Donnell for *CBS News*, ladies and gentlemen. We have yet another sickening story of campus violence to report. An estimated 200 protesters have invaded the administration building at Brown University in Providence, Rhode Island. I call them protesters, but, as usual, it's unclear just what they're protesting. Besides screaming, shouting, and chanting profanities, this event involved hundreds of rocks thrown at every window. This comes on the heels of another riot three hours ago at the University of New Mexico, where hundreds of rioters also threw stones. Besides millions of dollars in property damage, these events hit right at the core of what these schools are all about—teaching students. In campus after campus, these riots are resulting in regular classes being cancelled. It's no exaggeration to say that our nation's higher educational system is under a massive attack. We will be following these stories closely, so stay tuned to *CBS News* for the latest."

"I've got to take this to the White House," Buster said. "Something tells me that President Fenton will want to take the gloves off."

CHAPTER 107

Randolfo Martin met with his aide William Tomlinson at his palatial mansion in Tehran, overlooking two acres of manicured gardens. At the far end of one of the gardens was a koi pond. They sat on chairs on the mahogany deck with a view of the gardens. Tall grasses swayed in the gentle breeze.

"Tell me, William, what do you have to report on our latest attacks?"

"I have excellent news, sir…"

"Sir? How many times do I have to tell you William, my name is Randolfo, not sir or any other name you choose for me? And don't tell me you have *excellent* news. Just give me the facts and I'll do the evaluating."

Like his father and brother before him, Randolfo insists on a strict set of communication rules. He always referred to a subordinate by his full first name. William was William, never Bill or Will. He also insists that subordinates call him by his full first name. And he also demands that an aide never give him adjectives or adverbs when describing something. He wants to do his own analyzing, not as handed to him by a bootlicking subordinate looking to impress his boss.

"Our 'demonstrations' are having their desired effect, Randolfo. In the past week alone, we have seen riots at no fewer than 50 American colleges and universities. As you planned, the riots are resulting in massive cancellation of classes. As soon as a class is announced, we launch another demonstration. As you know, sir, I mean Randolfo, we have been concentrating on large colleges and universities. Soon we will train our sites on smaller institutions and junior colleges as you have commanded. According to a report by the American Treasury Secretary, property damage alone has passed the $500 million mark. You picked the appropriate name for this movement, *End of America*, because that is what we are seeing."

"What, if anything, is being done to combat us, William?"

"On-campus security guards as well as local police forces have tried to stop our efforts, but they are overwhelmed by the number of people we throw into the demonstrations. As you know, our people are well disciplined. They move from campus to campus to avoid their photos being taken by surveillance cameras."

"That is all, William. I expect another full report in two days."

Randolfo lit a cigar as he looked out over the gardens and laughed. "Yes, the *End of America* is coming."

CHAPTER 108

Bob

S addle up, honey, we're going to the Oval Office," I said.

"Are you serious?"

"I just got off the phone with Buster. President Fenton wants to meet with us as well as Buster and General Mike Bennett from NYU. Mike is in Washington today, and he'll meet us there."

"Why would the president want to meet with General Mike?" Bobbie asked.

"I have no idea, but I'm sure it's important."

A CIA car picked up Bobbie, Buster, and me at Reagan Airport for the 30-minute drive to the White House. We had just heard about another campus riot, this one at the University of Vermont. The office of the school's president is occupied by at least 25 people. All classes, of course, have been cancelled.

Two Marine guards met us under the porte cochere leading into the West Wing. The Marines, I noticed, weren't just wearing side arms but had M16s slung over their shoulders.

When we entered the Oval Office, General Mike was already there as well as First Lady, Meg. President Fenton, always the gentleman, stood to greet us. A former five-star admiral, the President always carries himself with a military bearing. He didn't look happy. First Lady, Meg, who I always think is almost as beautiful as Bobbie (almost), looked tired, not her usual effusive self.

"I'm about to do something I hate, but I have little choice," President Fenton said. "I'm suspending the Posse Comitatus Act of 1878, and I'm declaring a national emergency under the National Emergencies Act. The Posse Comitatus Act, as you know, precludes members of the armed forces from acting in a civilian setting. But the police departments across the country simply don't have enough personnel to combat these goddam campus riots. I've asked my old friend General Mike Bennett here to join us today. Mike, when you were hired as president of NYU, I figure you thought you'd have a nice quiet job after your courageous service in the Marines. Looks like you're back in combat, except without a uniform and a weapon."

"I'm honored to be here, Mr. President. As you know I was once the commanding officer of Bob Lawton here. Captain Bob was the finest officer in my command. He's a great guy."

"He's the best," Bobbie said, smiling. Damn, she can be embarrassing at times.

"The reason I invited Bob and Bobbie to be with us today is because they're two of the sharpest detectives in any police department, if not *the* sharpest. It should come as no surprise that Bob and Bobbie, with their amazing skills at interrogation, have discovered that none other than Randolfo Martin is our enemy."

"The most miserable scumbag on earth," the First Lady said.

"I think Meg characterizes him accurately, if somewhat bluntly. Like his father Bartholomew and his brother Antonio, before him, Randolfo Martin is one of the most dedicated enemies our country has ever faced. With his hordes of adoring minions, he is attacking the heart of America, our higher education system. According to the Secretary of Education, there hasn't been a regularly scheduled class at most colleges or universities in seven days, and at some institutions it's been over a month. The University of Vermont cancelled its classes this morning after the president's office was forcibly occupied. That bastard is holding the nation's youth hostage to his insane delusions. And he's picked the safest place he could find to hide, Iran, a country that means us nothing but harm, a country only too happy to host our enemy. I just might have to ask Congress to declare war on Iran. I believe in what's been called the Bush Doctrine, after President George W. Bush—a country that harbors our enemy *is* our enemy. War is a bad thing, but that's what is going on, a war. As I found out in my many years at sea, sometimes the pathway to peace is covered with explosions. Director Buster, do you have any comments?"

Buster got visibly pale, because he knew he needed to be careful with his words.

"Intelligence gathering is the most important thing, sir, and that's why I'm happy to have a couple of New York City cops working with us. Bob and Bobbie have taught us a few things at Langley about computer algorithms, not to mention the fine art of interrogating suspects."

"Buster, I know that you're fanatical, to use a word, about the 'need to know.' Do you think you can share with these folks the intelligence you've gathered about the identities of the rioters?"

"Yes, sir, I can share that, because it's not something we're keeping secret. Thanks to intelligence from Bob and Bobbie here, as well as our agents on stakeout at other colleges and universities across the country, it almost seems like a foreign army is occupying our campuses. From the photographs they've given us, we see a lot of people on the CIA and FBI watch lists—a *lot*. We know that these 'protesters' as they call themselves, aren't your typical fanatics looking to raise hell about perceived injustices. The world of journalism seems to have gotten the message too. From what we've learned from just Bob and Bobbie alone, a large number of the campus radicals don't even speak English, not a word of it."

"General Mike, do you want to say something?" the President said.

"Yes, sir, to amplify what Buster just said, we've been seeing these events play out at NYU as well. And if I may comment on your intention to use the armed forces, I must agree, although it isn't my place to agree or not. I hate the idea as much as you, sir, but the only alternative is to simply cede our country's campuses to the foreign radicals. We find ourselves in a defensive posture, and that's what we need to do—to defend our institutions of higher learning."

"Which brings me to another announcement I want to make," the President said. "Mike, as a university president and former Marine general, you have some unique qualifications. I want to appoint you to a new position in our government, Director of Campus Security. Besides your reputation as a warrior, I also know that you're an impeccable administrator. Our defensive forces on campuses will be coordinated through your office. It will be part of the Department of Homeland Security, and you will work closely with Secretary Rick Bellamy, a terrific guy. You'll work out of the New York office at Federal Plaza, with plenty of support from the FBI, not to mention Bob and Bobbie and the NYPD as needed. But you'll need to resign your position as president of New York University. Does that work for you, Mike?"

"I'll be honored to take the position, Mr. President, and I have no problem resigning from NYU. As a university president my major job is public relations and fundraising. Raising money in this environment is almost impossible. My chief of staff told me that she finds it difficult to even book me for a speaking engagement. I also look forward to working with Detectives Bob and Bobbie. Nobody is better than them, I've been told, at working tough cases. We'll get this done, Mr. President."

As we drove back to the CIA, Buster said, "No sense you guys sticking around indefinitely at the CIA. You can fly down here if need be to supervise some interrogations, but you're free to head back home to the NYPD. I know Commissioner Norquist will be delighted to hear that."

So, Bobbie and I headed back to the NYPD. Our lives have taken a weird turn of late.

CHAPTER 109

Bobbie

O ur flight from Washington landed at JFK at 9:30 a.m. on a Friday.

"Hey, Bob, you know what this is?" I said, as we climbed into our Uber.

"Well, it appears to be a laptop computer."

"It certainly is, and it works as well in East Hampton as it does here. Let's take off for a few days and head for our beautiful new waterfront home."

Bob didn't say anything. He wrapped his arms around me and kissed me on the lips. I think he liked my idea.

I called the commissioner's office to let him know we'd be taking off for a few days.

"Great," Ralph said. "Marlene and I are headed to our place in about an hour. We're dying to see your new house. Let's plan on dinner tonight."

Bob and I pulled up to our beautiful East Hampton house at 1:15 p.m. It was mid-June, and the weather was perfect, with low humidity and temperatures in the mid-70s. This would be our first time in the house as owners, and it looked even better than the first time we saw it. My parents and Bob's spent a few days there last week. They're becoming real pals, I was happy to hear, and I was also happy we could share our great new house with them. We carried some luggage with us so we could outfit the house for our brief stays. I hoped the stays wouldn't be too infrequent. Our lives recently had been nonstop stress, and we agreed that buying this place was one of our better ideas. Bob and I would never be completely off the job, but with our beautiful office overlooking Georgica Pond, we could get work done and relax at the same time. A laptop, a cellphone, and an Internet hookup and we're ready to boogie. We walked around the gigantic house and reacquainted ourselves with it. When we walked into the game room, Bob challenged me to a game of pool. I always loved to play pool and would do so often in Chicago with my pal, Janice Patton. I must admit that I'm pretty good at billiards, although I hadn't played it in a while.

"You like to shoot pool?" Bob said, with a look of happy shock on his face.

"I don't like it, I *love* it. Rack'em up, baby."

Bob's a very good pool player—and so am I. We flipped a coin to see who would go first, and I won. We agreed that we'd play three games. Bob cracked up when I ran the table on my first round, winning the game. Then he did the same. No surprise; we are always discovering new things about each other. Bob won the three-game match by two points, and I took my clothes off. Yes, I took my clothes off—that was our wager. I know, I know, we're crazy. Strip billiards? Don't knock it if you haven't tried it. We headed for the bedroom and some afternoon fun.

As we got out of the shower after making love, the phone rang. It was Ralph Norquist. I invited him and Marlene to come see our new house, and then we'd have dinner at The Palm East Hampton.

We've always enjoyed staying at the Norquists' house in East Hampton, but our place was, well, huge. We took them on a tour of the entire house. Ralph and Marlene freaked out over it, especially the views.

"Our place is like a little cabin compared to this. I think I'll write a book," Ralph said. "What did you tell me your advance was? $15 million if I recall."

"Go for it, Ralph. Bob and I will beta read it for you. With your name, you'll have a ready-made market."

We walked into the Palm East Hampton shortly after six. Because it early and not quite at the height of the season, the place wasn't crowded.

We were shown to a table in the back, as I had requested.

Anytime we meet with Ralph, the subject always gets around to business, so I figured a little privacy was a good idea, and the table in the back worked. Rather than avoid talking business, Bob and I brought them up to date on what had been happening at the CIA. We knew we could speak openly around Marlene. She's discrete and she gets it. Also, the campus riots were anything but secret, so we spoke freely.

Marlene is a professor of English at the City College of New York. She's a tall, pretty woman with light green eyes and graying brunette hair. She's thin as a rail, which I found surprising from the way she chowed down.

"So, how's everything at City College, Marlene?" I asked, afraid of what I was about to hear.

"I haven't been to class in two weeks, because there haven't *been* any classes. Ralph tells me you're his best detectives. I hope you guys can do something about this shit. I've been teaching college for 30 years, and I never could have imagined what's going on. These creeps aren't protesting anything; they just want to shut us down. Kids are dropping out in droves and getting menial jobs rather than sit around in the student union building playing board games or reading novels. Student loan applications are way down, because nobody wants to risk being saddled with gigantic debt, not knowing if they'll get a degree to justify it. Ralph tells me this crap is orchestrated, like a war of some sort. Do you folks agree with Ralph? Don't worry, you can disagree with the boss if you are so inclined."

I laughed at Marlene's comment about disagreeing with the boss. Bob and I always feel free to disagree with Ralph, one of the reasons we enjoy working for him. But we didn't disagree, especially after what we've found out recently.

"No, Marlene," I said, "We don't disagree with Ralph one bit. This lunacy we're seeing is orchestrated, carefully orchestrated. And the goal is to shut the country down by first shutting down higher education."

"I haven't seen you two in a few days," Ralph said. "Are you at liberty to disclose what you've learned or is there a 'need to know' issue? Knowing you two, I'm sure you've learned a lot."

"Actually, Ralph, and this may surprise you, the CIA's position is to make as much of this as public as possible. Director Buster wants the country to know what's going on and who's causing it. That's President Fenton's position as well."

"So, don't keep us in the dark, Bobbie," Marlene said. "Who the hell are these people?"

"Does the name Randolfo Martin ring a bell?"

"Holy shit," Ralph announced loudly, turning a few heads in the restaurant. "None other than the son of the former President of the United States, that evil bastard Bartholomew Martin. I thought we were done with the delightful Martin family when Bartholomew was assassinated in prison and his other son Antonio was sentenced to life. Where is the son of a bitch working from? Let me guess— Iran?"

Bob and I cracked up. Ralph is one sharp guy and he has a way of nailing conclusions accurately.

"Yes, Iran," I said, "Tehran specifically. Randolfo knows how to pick bodyguards."

"How did you find out it's him?" Ralph asked. "From what the CIA and FBI tell me, he's the most secretive bastard on the planet."

"We got it from a prisoner who Bob and I interrogated at the CIA."

"Why does that not surprise me?" Ralph said, laughing. "When the BBs interrogate somebody, information flows like a river. Is it some sort of organization?"

"A few of our interrogees characterized it as a 'movement.' It's called EOA or *End of America*. The very name of the organization tells us what their aim is. Yes, it's accurate to say that we're at war."

"And my students and I are on the field of battle," Marlene said.

CHAPTER 110

The *MV World Odyssey* cast off its lines from the Broadway Pier in San Diego. Built in Germany in 1998, the ship was originally named the *Deutschland*. The ship now serves as the seagoing "campus" of the "Semester at Sea," an educational program run by Colorado State University. It isn't a huge vessel by cruise ship standards. She's 575 in length, with a 76-foot beam, and can accommodate 600 students. The ship has 10 decks and nine classrooms.

This voyage would last 106 days, and the ship would visit 11 countries, 12 cities, and 4 continents.

Sergeant Jerome Patterson commanded a platoon of six US Army soldiers, stationed on the ship on orders from the new Director of Campus Security, General Mike Bennett. One of Bennett's main administrative tasks was to assign military units to college and university campuses, including floating ones.

The first classes were scheduled for Monday morning.

Nineteen-year-old Melanie Tompkins, a sophomore at Cornell University, sipped coffee with her friend and fellow Cornell student, Clair Bixby.

"I cannot friggin believe this, Claire. I feel like I'm in heaven. My parents are the two greatest people in my life, and they gave me this Semester at Sea as a reward for making dean's list last semester at Cornell. I love sea travel."

"Did their decision have anything to do with all the goddam campus riots, Melanie? I know it had a lot to do with my folks signing me up for this cruise."

"Yeah, they're both so fed up with all the violent bullshit, I think they would have yanked me out of school if this Semester at Sea wasn't an option. Cornell has seen its share of riots recently. I doubt we'll see any of those so-called 'demonstrations' out here on the ocean. My God, just think, Mel, we'll actually attend classes. How refreshing."

"Hey, to change the subject, Claire, have you noticed that a lot of our fellow students speak with heavy Arab accents? One guy I tried to start a conversation with didn't speak a word of English, not one goddam word."

"Maybe he was just trying an imaginative way to flirt with you."

"Wise guy. The little shrimp barely came up to my shoulders. Hey, what's that noise?"

They heard a chant coming from the deck below. *Colorado State, a place of hate, Colorado State, a place of hate, Colorado State, a place of hate...*

"Holy shit, Claire, you don't think we're hearing a fucking demonstration? Class starts in 20 minutes. Do you think it will happen?"

"Mel, this sounds awfully familiar. Let's go to class. It's below on deck three in classroom 301. Let's see if we can find a seat."

They took the escalator down to deck three. They passed room 303, another classroom. The hallway outside of room 303 was occupied by about 25 people with placards, all chanting "Colorado State, a place of hate." They continued down the passageway to classroom 301 where their English literature class was about to begin. Another group of placard-waving chanters occupied the space outside the room. Claire and Melanie carefully made their way to the classroom. They walked in and took their seats. Professor Barbara Dimitri stood at the front of the room behind a lectern and addressed the class. Nobody could hear a word she said because of the throaty chanting in the hallway. *Colorado State, a place of hate,* etc. etc.

Professor Dimitri is a short woman at 5'3." Her pretty face left no doubt that she was furious. She walked to the door and stepped into the hallway. "Hey, do you mind?" she screamed, "I'm trying to teach a class."

Melanie couldn't believe what she saw next. The little professor almost flew backwards into the classroom, fell flat on her back, her nose bleeding badly, obviously from having been punched. Instinctively, Melanie ran to the door, slammed it shut and locked it. The screaming and chanting continued unabated, now accompanied by the sound of objects slamming against the bulkheads. Melanie had some medical background when she worked as an EMT at her father's ambulance company. She ran to Professor Dimitri, who was now sitting up, stanching the blood from her nose with a handkerchief. Her dress was covered in blood. Melanie stared at the woman's face and realized that her nose was broken. Dimitri had also cracked her head against the floor when she fell backwards. Melanie advised her to remain seated, for fear that she may have suffered a concussion as well as a broken nose.

Sergeant Patterson ran to deck three along with two other soldiers from his six-man platoon. They carried M16 assault rifles, armed with rubber bullets. His orders were to use force to prevent violence, but to avoid lethal force. He shouted, "Stand down, backs against the wall."

Melanie heard him and opened the door a crack. "In here please, soldier." His two corporals kept their guns trained on the crowd as he walked into the classroom. He introduced himself.

"Look at this, Sergeant," Melanie said. "Those bastards broke this poor woman's nose."

Although his orders were to avoid lethal force, he did have the option to do so if a civilian is injured or attacked. He removed the rubber bullet magazine from his M16 and slammed in a new magazine of live ammunition.

"Everyone stay right here until further notice," he shouted to the students and the bloody Professor Dimitri. The chanting in the hallway had resumed. *Colorado State, a place of hate, Colorado State, a place of hate,* and so on.

As he walked into the hallway with his M16 at the ready, one of the demonstrators lunged at him with a bat. Patterson opened fire, and the man's lifeless body fell to the deck. He told the two soldiers to remain with their guns trained on the crowd. He also told them to replace their rubber bullet magazines with live ammunition. Patterson then went to the ship's bridge and sent out a radio signal with a code sign to three American warships that steamed nearby. Part of his job was to remain aware of any US Navy ships in the vicinity and to call them in the event of violence.

Within 20 minutes, the American destroyer, *USS Vincennes* approached the *World Odyssey*. A helicopter launched from the *Vincennes* and landed on the afterdeck of the ship. Six heavily armed Marines jumped to the deck, reinforcements for Sergeant Patterson's beleaguered soldiers. Assisted by the Marines, the ship's master at arms placed all the demonstrators under custody because some of them had engaged in violence, clear grounds for arrest. They would be held at the movie theater in the aft end of the ship under guard of the heavily armed Marines. Part of the curriculum of the Semester at Sea program called for movies in the ship's theater every night.

It wouldn't happen as scheduled, because the theater was now a makeshift jail.

The Semester at Sea program would conduct no classes that day.

CHAPTER 111

Judge Sheila McCrary was the Chief Bankruptcy Judge for the Southern District of New York. John Roberts, Chief Justice of the United States Supreme Court, had appointed Judge McCrary to take on a new role in addition to her regular judicial duties. It was now her job to monitor and oversee bankruptcy filings by any American colleges or universities. She was in a meeting with David Abrams, her chief clerk.

"David, I'm concerned. To be more accurate, I'm scared shitless." Judge McCrary is known for her salty tongue. "I just reviewed the total bankruptcy filings of colleges and universities this morning. Dear Lord, no fewer than 1,275 institutions have filed for bankruptcy. We know what that means for some small towns and cities where those colleges are located. It will have the same effect as if a major manufacturing plant closed. Lights out. These goddam demonstrations are taking a toll, a heavy toll."

"I don't think of them as demonstrations, your honor, I think of them as riots. My sister is a sophomore at Yale. She hasn't attended class in three weeks—because there were no classes to attend. As we read from the filing papers, the financial picture is bleak. Parents across the country are pulling their kids out of school, because they see no purpose in attending. Judge, I think it's obvious that somebody is trying to shut down our entire system of higher education. My God, I just heard about that Semester at Sea program run by Colorado State. There was a riot on their ship just last week. A riot on a ship, of all places."

"All we can do is monitor this shit, David, which is my job. This is the most depressing judicial assignment I've ever had. And it doesn't look like the picture is going to improve anytime soon. Just yesterday there were 25 more demonstrations, or as you put it more accurately, riots. You and I have our degrees, David, but a lot of these poor kids will never see a college diploma. People are beginning to see college enrollment as the equivalent of shooting craps. I just hope to hell the government is getting a handle on this situation."

CHAPTER 112

Good evening, ladies and gentlemen, I'm Leslie Stahl for *60 Minutes*. Tonight, we're going to take another look at the shocking and compelling drama that is unfolding at our nation's college and university campuses. Last week my colleague, Bill Whitaker, interviewed five college presidents about the situations on their campuses, and we were shocked to hear their stories, tales of class cancellations and wanton violence.

"In this edition of *60 Minutes*, we're going to look at how law enforcement is handling the problem. The right to protest is so fundamental to our way of life that it almost doesn't bear repeating. But what we've been seeing over the past few months goes beyond simple protest demonstrations. In far too many instances, the protests have turned to violence, horrible violence. Demonstrations are turning into full-blown riots.

"So how do we balance our sacred right to protest with our equally important right to personal safety? That is the subject of this segment of *60 Minutes*. Joining us this evening are two well-known police detectives, Bobbie Nelson and her husband and detective partner, Bob Lawton. In an article in *The New York Times* entitled, "The BBs – New York City's Dynamic Detective Duo," their famous nickname, the BBs, made its public introduction. Bobbie and Bob were partnered as detectives less than two years ago. Within a couple of months after they began their partnership, they married, becoming partners in more ways than one. Having spent some time with them before the show, I can tell you they are probably the closest couple I've ever met. They finish each other's sentences and even communicate with just a glance or a gesture. They're famous for solving difficult cases, both before and after they were partnered. It was no surprise that NYPD Commissioner Ralph Norquist assigned them one of the toughest cases imaginable, the campus riots. To handle this assignment, Bobbie and Bob have also been sworn in as provisional CIA and FBI agents, giving them jurisdiction in other states.

"Welcome to *60 Minutes*, Bob and Bobbie. Please give us your opinions on these campus demonstrations, which some people have simply branded riots. Bobbie?"

"Law enforcement is involved in these matters for two reasons," Bobbie said. "First is because of the violence, which has begun to spin out of control. The other reason cops are involved is that we suspect that these incidents are not spontaneous protests but are meticulously coordinated criminal activities."

"And who is at the top of this pyramid?" Leslie asked. "Is one person or group organizing these activities?"

"It's a group, often referred to as a *movement*, and yes, one person is at the top," Bob said.

"Are you at liberty to tell us who this person is?"

"We have conclusive evidence that the man heading this up is none other than Randolfo Martin, the son of the infamous Bartholomew Martin, the former President of the United States, also known as America's first dictator. His brother Antonio, you may recall, is serving a life sentence. The group even has a shocking name—*End of America*."

"I must say I'm surprised that you were able to disclose his name to us."

"That came filtered to us right from the White House," Bob said. "President Fenton made it known to our superiors that he wants that information out in the open. He wants our country to know who we're up against, a ruthless tyrant. Unfortunately, he's hiding in a place over which we have no jurisdiction."

"A colleague of mine teaches a course at the Columbia School of Journalism," Leslie Stahl said. "Or I should say *taught* a course, past tense. Classes haven't been held for three weeks because of the disturbances. I understand that's the case across the country. That group has taken it upon itself to force class cancellations. Can you tell what your investigations have disclosed about the *End of America*, which I understand is also referred to by its acronym, EOA?"

"We've discovered a lot, Leslie, from documentary evidence as well as countless interrogations, conducted by Bob and me as well as detectives and federal agents across the country. Simply put, *End of America*, and its leader Randolfo Martin, wants to put an end to our system of higher educations, a key part of our culture as well as a major component of our economy. I believe President Fenton was accurate when he said that a war has been declared on the United States."

"And President Fenton has taken the shocking step of suspending the Posse Comitatus Act, thereby allowing our armed forces to act in civilian settings," Stahl said. "Any thoughts on that, Bob?"

"It may have been a radical step, but I don't think he had much choice," Bob said. "The NYPD, along with police departments across the country, simply doesn't have enough officers to respond to riots and carry on normal police functions. This campus violence has turned the country on its head."

"That ends our show for tonight, Ladies and gentlemen. I think

I speak for us all when I say that I feel safer knowing that Bobbie Nelson and Bob Lawton are *on the case*. Tune in next week for another edition of *60 Minutes*."

CHAPTER 113

Bob

I think our appearance on *60 Minutes* may help move the case forward. I was surprised when President Fenton let it be known that he wanted us to disclose the name of Randolfo Martin. At least it lets the country know who we're up against, a ruthless tyrant, or an "evil scumbag" as the First Lady puts it.

Bobbie and I enjoyed our brief stay at our great new home in East Hampton. We both agreed that having a place to get away, even if only for a couple of days, was a wonderful way to relieve stress. And we sure as hell had enough stress to relieve. We're in a war against a brutal enemy, but we agreed that we shouldn't let the bastards control our lives. Bobbie and I have decided that we're going to live our lives, despite the shit we have to deal with.

Detectiving, our best-selling book, has been taking off like a rocket. It's been number one on *The New York Times* Nonfiction Best Seller list for 11 weeks. Our advance of $15 million has long since been paid back, and now we were enjoying royalties of almost $100,000 a month. The sales have also helped bring my novel *Army of Blue* back into the sunlight, and it's raking in royalties of $25,000 a month. Our book royalty bucks happily coincided with an email message I received this morning. I'm dying to tell Bobbie about it.

Bobbie just walked in, having gone to the records office to retrieve a file.

"Hey, Bobbie, you and I have been complaining about the size of our apartment lately. Any more thoughts on that?"

"Yeah, I'm conflicted as hell, honey. I love that we're so close to the office, and the place really is pretty, but when we return from East Hampton, I feel like we're living in a shoebox."

"Well, baby, I got a wonderful email this morning. Our next-door tenant, Tom Ralston, told me that he and his wife won't be renewing their lease when it expires next month. They have an option to extend it for a year, but they're waiving that option."

"Oh, my God!"

"Yeah, oh my God. If we break down the wall, we'll have a huge 3,000 square foot apartment. We can put in a hot tub and a pool table—yes, a pool table. With the extra rooftop space, we'll be able to construct a running track, a rooftop garden, and an outdoor dining area just like that beautiful place we stayed in when we were in the Witness Protection Program."

"Holy shit, honey, this is a fabulous idea! Thank God for our book royalties."

"Speaking of book royalties, you and I need to get cooking on our next novel."

"I thought we were cooking just great, especially with our *dress rehearsals*," Bobbie said.

"Yeah, but we really need to put some stuff down on paper. We can still do our rehearsals."

"Maybe we should just publish it as an audiobook," she said with a wink, "groans, moans and all."

She walked over to me and stroked my face. Then she picked up the phone.

"Who are you calling.?"

"Tim Brady, that architect guy we've become friends with. We need to meet with him so he can start drawing up plans. I just read in the *Times* that he got an award from *Architectural Digest* for apartment designs."

When Bobbie gets on a roll, she likes to keep rolling.

"Bob and Bobbie," our assistant said, "click on the TV." Bobbie put down the phone.

———————✧———————

"George Stephanopoulos for *ABC News*, ladies and gentlemen. Our national crisis of campus violence continues unabated. Last week President Fenton, in a controversial move, suspended the Posse Comitatus Act of 1878, which was intended to keep American armed forces from intervening in civilian matters. But, in my opinion, he really had no choice. Our nation's police forces simply don't have the manpower to deal with the constant riots. And, as we reported yesterday, no place seems safe from armed protesters.

"The cruise ship *World Odyssey* serves as the ocean-going campus for the Colorado State University program, Semester at Sea. True to form, what is referred to as a 'demonstration' broke out on the ship just before the first planned morning classes. The demonstration soon turned violent as one of the protesters punched a woman professor in the face, breaking her nose. The embarked Army platoon responded to the scene, and the sergeant in command shot and killed a man who charged him with a bat. Marine reinforcements from a nearby destroyer stormed aboard, and the protesters are now being held under armed guard in the ship's theater. The soldiers were aboard on orders from retired Marine General Michael Bennett, whom President Fenton recently appointed to a new position known as Director of Campus Security. The office is part of the Department of Homeland Security. General Bennett briefly served as president of New York University. *The World Odyssey* is headed for its homeport in San Diego, California, where its cargo of violent demonstrators will be taken into FBI custody.

"We have received reports that the organization behind these violent demonstrations is known as *End of America*, or its acronym, EOA. And, as we learned recently, the man who heads up that EOA program is none other than Randolfo Martin, the son of the former President of the United States, and America's first and only dictator, Bartholomew Martin.

"Ladies and gentlemen, as President Fenton said when he declared the national state of emergency, 'America is at war,' a war not of our choosing, but a war that is being brutally waged by some strange force. *ABC* will keep you up to date on these bizarre developments. In other news…"

"So, what do you think, baby?" I said.

"I think I'm going to do what I was about to do before that TV announcement. I'm going to call our architect friend to start plans for our apartment. Bob, you and I know how to handle tough cases and we'll handle this one. But I'll be dipped in shit before I put our lives on hold because of Randolfo Martin's creeps."

"You're even more beautiful when you're angry."

"Well I'm so fucking angry maybe I should run for Miss America."

CHAPTER 114

Bobbie

Wartime Bobbie Nelson here. Yeah, wartime, all because of an evil bastard named

Randolfo Martin. I've only fired my weapon once in the line of duty, when I shot the man who tried to assassinate Bob. But I would love to empty an entire magazine into the skull of that slimy animal, Randolfo Martin. He's trying to destroy the American higher education system, and he seems well on his way. But he's going to have to come through the BBs to do it. Maybe Bob and I should start our own movement, EOR, or *End of Randolfo*. Fuck him.

But, as I often remind Bob—and myself—anger is an emotion that gets you nowhere, even though Bob tells me I look pretty when I'm angry. But anger does help to focus you on your mission, and our mission is to stop that ruthless piece of shit. I think President Fenton got it right to declare a national emergency and appoint General Mike as Director of Campus Security. I really like General Mike, and, God knows, he's a big fan of Bob.

Bob looks especially cute this morning, but I always think he does.

His lightly starched white shirt highlighted his gorgeous physique. Maybe we can play a game of strip billiards later. Oh, right, we don't have a pool table—yet. Maybe strip poker? Hey, time to get to work.

"Bob and Bobbie," our assistant said, "CIA Director Buster is here."

Buster never tires of surprising people.

Buster walked in and gave each of us a bear hug. We're becoming really good friends with this guy. He looked tired as hell, and I told him he's been working too hard. Maybe he should buy a house in East Hampton, but he probably can't afford it. Hey, write a book! Okay, time to pay attention.

The three of us walked over to the small conference table.

"Coffee? You have a choice of decaf or regular."

"Decaf, please. My nerves are jangled enough. To get right to the point, I need you guys at CIA for a couple of days; how about starting tomorrow?"

I remembered that Bob and I are scheduled to meet with the architect tomorrow to start working on plans for our new apartment—the one that will have a hot tub—and a pool table.

"How about the day after tomorrow, Buster?"

"Fine. We have a new group of guests we've captured—don't ask me how we capture people, okay? There are eight of them and I want you guys to pump them for information. You two amaze me the way you climb inside an interrogee's head. We have some great spooks at the CIA, but nobody can hold a candle to the BBs when it comes to interrogation."

He was being really sweet and flattering, but he's also right. *Nobody* interrogates people like Bob and me.

"Are we looking for anything specific," Bob asked, "or just to see whatever information we can get?"

"Good question, Bob. We have what we think is the most important intelligence. We know that the top dog is Randolfo Martin..."

"You mean the top *scumbag*," I interrupted, embarrassing myself.

Buster just laughed. He knows me by now.

"We also know that he's in Tehran, and we know what EOA means. We also have a pretty good handle on how these demonstrations play out—and that they're becoming increasingly violent. So, here's my point. Suppose, just suppose, we removed the man at the top..."

"You mean whack the son of a bitch?" I politely inquired.

"Well, something like that," Buster said with a wink. "What we really want to know is how deep the philosophy, if you can call it that, goes. In other words, is this just a Randolfo Martin show, or will the participants carry on without him? If we find it's a Randolfo command performance, that makes things easier, because the rioters will eventually disperse without his leadership."

"But that would be speculation," Bob said.

"Well, it bothers me also, Bob," Buster said, "but not too much. Hell, President Fenton has taken the gloves off, and General Mike, his newly appointed Director of Campus Security, knows how to kick ass. And you two have seen me in action. You know that I play rough—*very rough*. If these 'demonstrators' try to carry on without their charismatic leader, we'll have them on the run in no time."

"Bob and I have discussed this a lot, Buster. Do you see much sympathy for these creeps, even though they don't seem to protest anything specific at all?"

"Besides you folks, me, President Fenton, and the rest of the government, do you know who else is really pissed off? The

American people. They've had it up to their ears with this shit. I think a lot of people will be ready to hold our jackets for this fight. The last thing I'd ever want to see is martial law, but that's where these bastards are pointing us. Okay, I gotta run. See you folks in Langley the day after tomorrow."

After Buster left, we sat there with our thoughts.

"You know what we should do, honey?" I said.

"We should have a nice dinner and then go to a musical comedy."

"Perfect idea. I love you, Bob."

CHAPTER 115

Bob

obbie and I walked to our apartment where we'd have lunch with Tim Brady, our architect friend. We didn't want to meet in a restaurant because, knowing Tim as we do, he would already have some preliminary drawings for us and would want spread them out on the dining room table. Bobbie had already given him the bare bones of our idea—knock down a wall and double the size of our apartment. We've had Tim and his wife over to our place a few times before, so he knew the layout in his head. Bobbie ordered lunch from a gourmet deli around the corner. She may not know how to cook, but she sure knows how to order.

When I opened the door to let Tim in, he looked like he just won the lottery.

"Oh, my God, this is going to be fun!" he yelled.

"Does that mean you're not going to charge us?" Bobbie said, laughing.

"Of course, it doesn't mean that. Hey, fun and money go together."

He spread his drawing out on the dining room table.

"I have a good memory for physical spaces," Tim said, "so these plans are based in my recollections, without precise measurements, of course."

Bobbie and I were shocked at what he had come up with in just two days, without measuring anything. Bobbie had told him that the apartment next door was almost a cookie cutter image of our place, except with an opposite layout. He didn't so much redesign the apartment—he reinvented it. He removed one kitchen and doubled the size of the other one. He expanded the master bath and included a huge hot tub. Next to the den, he set aside space for a pool table. He even designed a small theater on a sloping platform to mimic the experience of a real playhouse. He also put in a modest sized gym. Although he had no measurements at all, he did a rough sketch of our rooftop running track, garden, and outside dining area.

So, fuck Randolfo Martin, as Bobbie loves to say. The BBs are getting on with our lives. We'll worry about Tehran later.

CHAPTER 116

Deputy Foreign Minister Hamid Rashadi met with his colleague, Minister Ramin Abbasi, at his office in Tehran. The two had been close friends for years, ever since they served together in the Iranian Army. They are both high level officials in the Iranian government. Many, especially those best described as "moderates," hope to see Rashadi as the next prime minister after Ali Khamenei. The subject of their meeting was the new "guest" of the Iranian government, Randolfo Martin.

Rashadi's office was large at 25 by 30 feet. All of the furniture was plush leather, Rashadi's favorite type of decorating. The sun streamed in from the window overlooking a courtyard, casting the room in a pleasant glow. The walls were decorated with pastoral scenes by Hudson River School artists, his favorite school of art. Rashadi reached under his desk and grabbed a bottle of Kentucky bourbon. He poured them both a healthy splash.

"Ramin, we have known each other a long time, and we both know that Iran has a sudden problem on its hands, a huge problem. Prime Minister Khamenei insists on spouting his crazy slogan about America as *The Great Satan*. Although we'd never discuss it with anyone other than ourselves, Ramin, we both know that *The Great Satan* should really be seen as our *Great Friend*. Our *guest*, as Khamenei refers to Randolfo Martin, is every bit as insane as his late father, Bartholomew. And he's using that group *End of America* as a play tool to destroy the American educational system. What say you, my friend?"

"Hamid, I share your concern about this matter. As you know, I have met President Fenton and his lovely and brilliant wife, Meg. President Fenton is a steady leader and a thoughtful man, but not one to be trifled with. When he served in the American Navy, he was known as a fighting admiral, never one to shy away from combat. And Randolfo Martin is doing the last thing you would ever want to risk with a brave man like Fenton. He's pushing him into a corner, giving him no other option than to come out fighting. And our prime minister is coddling Randolfo Martin, that evil bastard. Khamenei sees anyone who opposes America as our ally. As we both know, nothing could be further from the truth. What will happen if the United States declares war on Iran?"

Rashadi poured them both another splash of bourbon.

"We both know the answer to that question, Hamid. It will mean the destruction of our country. And all because our supreme leader allows Randolfo Martin to do as he pleases. If President Fenton chooses the military option, I expect to see the overwhelming majority of the American people supporting his actions. The Americans are sick and tired of seeing colleges and universities turned into scenes of riots. They spend their hard-earned money on tuition, and their sons and daughters don't even have the opportunity to attend class. Have you been in touch with our friend...?"

"Please, Ramin, don't mention his name, even in this room. But, to answer your question, yes, I have been in touch with him."

"That's good. Buster will figure out a solution to this problem, my friend."

CHAPTER 117

Bobbie

I mildly freaked out over Tim Brady's plans for our expanded apartment. Well no, not mildly freaked out—totally freaked out. That guy really knows his stuff. Wait till he takes measurements! So, our place may not be like our house in East Hampton, but 3,000 square feet plus a rooftop track, garden, and outdoor dining area is not bad. And we'll still be right near One PP. God bless book royalties.

Buster sent a CIA Gulfstream to pick up Bob and me for our trip to Langley. Wow, do these government types know how to spend taxpayer money. A Gulfstream? Why not economy seats on a regular flight? Bob and I felt like we were in an episode of *Criminal Minds,* where a group of FBI agents shuttle around in a Gulfstream. We landed at the old Langley Air Force Base, now charmingly known as Joint Base Langley-Eustis, a short drive from CIA headquarters.

Our assignment was to interrogate eight people who were "invited" by the CIA. We figured it would take the better part of two days to do our questioning. We were happy to see our old friend Marcia Barrett, CIA agent, Arabic/Farsi interpreter, and ass-kicker-on-call.

We met Marcia for breakfast at one of the agency cafeterias, where the food was quite good, as Bob and I had learned from our previous visits. All three of us had breakfasts low on carbs, as it's important to be alert when interrogating prisoners. We decided that we would get right into our interrogees' heads, as Buster would say. We would ask questions, all of which were a variation of—"What are you demonstrating against and who do you take orders from?"

Our first guest was Muhammed Alkaldi, who had been arrested at the University of Illinois-Urbana for throwing a punch at a cop during a "demonstration." He was advised, as were all the others, that his cooperation would result in leniency. How Buster would provide leniency I didn't know, nor did I care.

"Mr. Alkaldi, I understand that you were arrested on June 2nd at the University of Illinois during what is best described as a demonstration; is that correct?" He spoke perfect English, leaving Marcia to observe, which is fine by me. She's a damn good observer.

"Yes, but the police officer tried to punch me, I was only protecting myself."

I didn't doubt he was telling the truth, but it was irrelevant to our interrogation.

"Mr. Alkaldi, what were you demonstrating against?"

"Injustice."

"Can you be a bit more specific, sir?"

"The criminal American university system, as Sheik Randolfo advised us."

Sheik Randolfo? They even gave that piece of shit a title? Of course, I didn't show any emotion, and just continued my questioning.

"And can you tell us to what specific injustices this Sheik

Randolfo fellow was referring?"

"Injustice against students."

"Such as?"

"Forcing them to attend class."

Don't argue, I reminded myself, even when hit by something that is patently absurd and made no sense whatsoever.

"Mr. Alkaldi, do you think that class attendance may be necessary for the students' education?" Sometimes I like to ask obvious questions.

"It is not necessary to advance the propaganda of the infidel."

I had a sudden desire to review our architect's plans for our new apartment, but I realized it was necessary to continue with this dipshit. I figured it was time to drive to the heart of the issue.

"Mr. Alkaldi, suppose, just suppose for the sake of speculation, that Sheik Randolfo decided to abandon his leadership of your group. Would you continue on without him?"

"The sheik would never abandon us."

"That was a hypothetical question, asshole," Marcia advised. "Answer Detective Nelson's question."

Marcia is definitely my favorite spook. I think I'm going to recommend that Commissioner Ralph fly down here and try to recruit her into the NYPD.

"So, to clarify my question, I am not saying Randolfo Martin *would* abandon you, but if he changed his mind what would you do?"

"I would await further orders."

"In other words, you wouldn't continue with your demonstrations until you got an order from Randolfo Martin, is that correct?"

"As I said, I would await further orders."

"But what if he gave you no further orders?"

"I would do nothing. Sheik Randolfo Martin is our leader."

"So, just to make sure I heard this correctly, without orders you would not demonstrate or participate in demonstrations?"

"That is correct. I would wait for orders."

"And just so I understand how this works; you receive specific orders from Sheik Randolfo, such as the one that got you arrested at the University of Illinois. Did he specifically order that demonstration?"

"He always gives us orders through one of the brothers who assists him,"

"Did he ever *personally* order a demonstration?"

"No, he does it through the brothers."

"Do you have a list of these brothers? In other words, how do you know the orders came from Randolfo Martin?"

"A brother would never lie to us."

"So, you don't even know who these brothers are, is that correct?"

"That is correct, I don't know their names."

"Mr. Alkaldi, did you ever hear the phrase 'blind obedience?'"

"Yes, blind obedience in the name of Allah."

"Thank you, Mr. Alkaldi. I don't have any further questions now, but we may need a follow-up meeting. An agent will return you to your cell."

Before our next interrogation, which Bob would conduct, I wanted to have a debriefing with Bob and Marcia.

"So, what do you guys think about this fucking robot?"

"Well, I have two observations," Bob said. "First, the guy insisted he doesn't demonstrate unless ordered to by Randolfo or someone on Randolfo's staff."

"Or who *says* he's from Randolfo's staff," Marcia said. Good point.

"Secondly," Bob said, 'this whole thing appears to be a Muslim show, a radical Muslim show, as we've suspected. But there's a problem with that. Randolfo Martin is not a Muslim, and he's said that publicly many times. He's using these people, and they don't seem to have a problem with that. I mean shit, the guy even referred to Randolfo as *Sheik*. Great job, Bobbie. I think we know where we're headed."

CHAPTER 118

Bob

My job was to interrogate the next prisoner, Ali Multafi. Bobbie, as usual, did a professional job questioning Mr. Alkaldi. The biggest piece of information she gathered is that the disciples will not continue with their demonstrations without the okay from Randolfo or one of his lieutenants. But those were the words of one man, one robot. If it's true that the lackeys only act on word from Tehran, that would certainly focus our options. And Buster is good selecting the right option.

The CIA agents who "invited" Mr. Multafi to come in for questioning believe that he's a leader in the ranks of the *End of America* people. They told Buster that they heard the man's name constantly in chatter.

"Good morning, Mr. Multafi. My name is Detective Bob Lawton, and I'm here to ask you a few questions."

"I have nothing to say to you."

"Listen to me, dickbrain," Marcia Barrett said with considerable volume, "unless you want to spend the rest of your wretched life in solitary confinement, I suggest that you answer Detective Lawton's questions."

Bobbie and I agree that Marcia is our favorite spook.

"Mr. Multafi, do you take orders from a man named Randolfo Martin?"

"Yes."

I questioned Multafi for two hours. His responses mimicked those of our first interrogee. Yes, Randolfo Martin is running the show, yes, they call him Sheik, and yes, he gives orders through his lieutenants.

And he's holed up safely in Tehran.

Bobbie, Marcia, and I continued our interrogation of the remaining six men. This interrogation wouldn't have moved so smoothly were it not for Marcia-the-ass-kicker. I got the impression that she scared the hell out of these guys. I agree with Bobbie that we should try to steal Marcia away from the CIA and recruit her into the NYPD. Our remaining interrogees told us pretty much the same as our first two: that the orders come from Randolfo, and the orders come through intermediaries, and the interrogee would not act without orders. But the last guy, Muhammed bin Hashim, had something to add, and he shocked the living shit out of us. He said that the *End of America* people would soon focus their demonstrations on high schools.

CHAPTER 119

President Harry Fenton sat in his private dining room at the White House, along with First Lady Meg. He loves to begin his day by having breakfast with Meg. He thinks of her as his one-woman cabinet. The subject of their meeting would be a familiar one, one that has begun their day for weeks — the *End of America* movement.

"Those two cops from New York who call themselves the BBs are simply unbelievable, Meg. Seeing them work is like watching a detective movie."

"I agree, honey. According to Sarah Watson, they're the best detectives she's ever seen, including her people at the FBI. And they sure as hell know how to dig up information. Have they given us anything new lately?"

"Yes, new. New and big. I just got word from Buster at the CIA that they've recently interrogated eight denizens of that weird EOA movement. I guess it should be no surprise, but that turd Randolfo Martin is not only pulling the strings; he completely controls all of the demonstrations that are tearing apart our country's campuses. And get this — one of the interrogees said that Martin is setting his sights on our high schools. You heard me, *high schools*."

"Holy shit, honey, this is getting out of control, if it hasn't already gotten out of control."

"And nothing happens unless the word comes from Randolfo Martin through one of his lieutenants."

"What do you think will happen next?"

"Take a deep breath, Meg. I wouldn't be surprised if Buster orders his people to have a 'talk' with Randolfo. You know what that means."

CHAPTER 120

Bobbie

B ob and I were happy with our interrogations at the CIA over the past few days. Buster was beyond happy. We're all convinced that the *End of America* movement will not take any actions without explicit word from Randolfo Martin, issued through one of his henchmen. So, we know who holds the levers of power, but equally important, we know how the levers move. We began to feel confident that the *End of America* will soon end, largely because of the information we coaxed out of the prisoners.

We BBs know our shit.

We moved a few boxes of essentials from our apartment to a nearby Marriott Courtyard Hotel. Construction on our new 3,000 square foot apartment will begin today, and we couldn't be happier. The Marriott is just a couple of blocks from our apartment, so we'll be able to visit regularly to check on the construction progress. Tim Brady's final plans for the apartment were perfect. We'll still be right near One PP, but we'll have some newfound luxury. Hey, if you can't enjoy money, why have it in the first place? Our room at the Marriott was fine by us, not luxurious, but neat, clean, and functional. And, it was still near Police Plaza, just two blocks farther than our apartment. It wasn't just a room but a small suite, with two bedrooms, two full baths, a den, and an eat-in kitchen. Our contractor estimates that the apartment will be finished in six weeks, so the Marriott will be our home for a while.

We met Ralph and Marlene Norquist at the diner for breakfast. They told us that they were going to their house in East Hampton for a few days, and suggested we take some time off to enjoy our new place. Wonderful suggestion, especially because it came from the boss.

Bob and I decided we would throw a party, our first get-together at our new waterfront home. But we wanted it to be a "working party." I think that sometimes we plan to work while we take a few days off, so we won't feel guilty about relaxing. Stupid, I know, but that's Bob and me. The BBs get antsy if we're not solving something.

We arrived at our house at 4:30 on Friday afternoon, looking forward to our party. We had recently hired a house cleaning service, and the place was spotless. The mid-September weather was perfect, in the high 60s, and the salty fragrance off Georgica Pond was wonderful.

We invited Buster, who blew us away when he said he'd bring his wife, Peggy. We didn't even know Buster was married. He likes to keep his mouth shut about personal matters. He and Peggy arrived at 5:15. Peggy is a tall, strikingly pretty brunette. She's a CIA agent, not to our surprise. I couldn't help but notice that she had once suffered a broken nose, and it was still somewhat askew, although attractive in an odd way. Without prompting, she told us her nose was broken as she tried to arrest a suspect. She was unable to get medical attention for quite a few hours, hence her slightly crooked nose. Peggy Atkins jokingly refers to herself as Peggy Buster. Peggy and Buster will be staying over for the weekend. We also invited our new friend, agent Marcia Barrett and her husband of three months, Bill Barrett, who is also a CIA agent. Marcia's first husband had been killed two years ago by a self-proclaimed jihadi. No wonder Marcia seemed to harbor some angry shit about the gentlemen of the sand. Marcia and Bill will be staying over as well. Commissioner Ralph and his wife Marlene would arrive shortly.

So, we all had a "need to know," which was good because we figured Buster would have some interesting things to tell us about *End of America*. Although she's not in law enforcement or espionage, we had no problem talking openly in front of Ralph's wife, Marlene. She's cool and discrete. We arranged for the dinner to be catered by the Palm East Hampton. We also hired a serving crew. I really should learn how to cook someday. Screw it—that's what telephones are for.

Bob served drinks from our sumptuous bar in the den.

Buster stood. "Folks, I wish to propose a toast to two of the most talented law enforcement people on the planet, the famous BBs. They're also fabulously talented authors, hence this lovely home, bought with book royalties." Buster is so sweet, it's difficult to think of him as a hard-nosed spook. And he *is* hard-nosed, as we'd find out shortly.

I was dying to get down to the status of our war, the war on America, the *End of America*.

"Buster, why don't you tell us your thoughts about the interrogations that Bob, Marcia, and I conducted the other day," I suggested.

"Yeah," Bill Barrett joined in, "From what Marcia tells me it seems we have made some big headway on those *End of America* animals."

"Well, I'd like to hear Bob and Bobbie's thoughts on the subject," Buster said. "Their amazing interrogations, aided by Marcia here, have put us forward by light years. We now know that all marching orders for the demonstrations come straight from Randolfo Martin through his closest aides. Nothing happens unless it comes through Randolfo. He closely controls the strings, which didn't surprise me. So, Bob and Bobbie, your thoughts?"

"Bob and I think it's time your people had a 'talk' with Randolfo Martin, Buster. Your 'talks' always bring results."

Bob and I knew, and I'm sure the others did as well, that a "talk" means somebody gets assassinated.

Bob walked to the bar and poured us another round of cocktails. He walked around the room serving the drinks from a tray. Bob is the perfect host. I think I'll send him to cooking school as a birthday present.

Buster stood and smiled. He raised his glass. "I propose another toast," he said, "to the end of the *End of America*. Yes, my people had a *talk* with Randolfo — five days ago."

Holy shit! Did Buster just tell us that he whacked that evil bastard?

The room erupted into happy mayhem. Did I hear correctly? Could it be that we now live in a Randolfo-free world?

"Is the war over, Buster?" Bob asked, his eyes like saucers.

"We'll know more as time goes by, but there hasn't been a campus demonstration in four days. Not just a lack of riots, but no demonstrations at all. There's nobody at the top to pull the trigger."

The next morning, I was afraid to turn on the TV. But I also looked forward to it. My God, Randolfo Martin now resides underground, way underground.

CHAPTER 121

Wolfe Blitzer for *CNN* ladies and gentlemen. My job as a reporter is to do just that, to report the news. But sometimes the lack of news is a story in itself. Well, hang onto your hats, folks, because I'm pleased to say, for the first time in months, that there are no campus demonstrations to report. There hasn't been a violent demonstration in four days. Actually, there haven't been any college or university demonstrations of any kind in four days, violent or not. It's as if the people involved have decided to stop their criminal activities. For weeks we've been speculating whether the riots were planned from a central authority of some sort. If that's so, management of the *End of America* movement seems to have retired or taken a vacation. I give you this report with no small amount of trepidation on my part, because I hope I won't again start to report campus riots. But let's take good news when we can get it. In other news…"

CHAPTER 122

Bob

It's been two months since Buster told us about his operatives having a "talk" with Randolfo Martin. His moles on the ground have confirmed that Randolfo Martin is where he should be — in a grave. It's also been two months without a single incident of a demonstration or riot on any campus. Bobbie and I have returned to what we love, being cops, being detectives, solving puzzles. We were proud of our work as CIA spies, but now we return to the profession we're cut out for.

And we're delighted with our new 3,000 square foot apartment, into which we moved last month. Tim Brady's plans were exciting, but nothing like the finished product. It certainly isn't as big as our house in East Hampton, but 3,000 square feet is a huge apartment.

We just walked into Commissioner Ralph's office. He was smiling. He told us that he was delighted that his son had resumed attending classes at the University of Michigan.

He then handed us a file, a big file, another case. No surprise that it involved a serial killer. Fifteen bodies so far, and not one lead. This killer uses a gun. Or guns, I should say. He's careful to use a different gun for each killing in order to throw off our forensics. But we know it's a serial killer, because he always leaves a note on his victims—in ancient Greek. Looks like Bobbie will need to learn yet another language. The murders occur all over New York City, and, we were shocked to learn—at all times of the day.

I think Ralph likes to assign Bobbie and me tough cases. We love it when he does. The harder the puzzle, the more fun it is to solve.

And Bobbie and I will handle this puzzle like we do all our cases—*together*.

Characters – *Puzzles Book 1*

Almeda, Sancho – MS-13 Gang member

Atkins, Peggy – Buster's wife

Barrett, Marcia – CIA agent and interpreter

Bellamy, Ellen – Talk show host

Bellamy, Rick – Secretary of Homeland Security

Bennett, Michael – Retired Marine General and University President

Blackburn, Tom – FBI Bodyguard

Brady, Tim – Architect

Buster – CIA director, aka Charles Atkins

Cunningham, Mildred – Book editor

Cunningham, Tom – Book editor

Fenton, Harry – President of the United States

Fenton, Meg – First Lady of the United States

Franken, Tim – Deputy Commissioner for Internal Affairs, NYPD

Gandolfo, Alphonse – Mobster. Head of the Gandolfo Family, aka, the Big Guy

Holloway, Tim – FBI Bodyguard

Johnston, Pete – FBI Bodyguard

Jones, Bradley – Missing Detective

Lawton, Bob – Detective, NYPD

Livingston, Michael – Missing Detective

Martin, Randolfo – Terrorist leader.

Muchado, Michael – Mobster. Mickey the Mooch.

Nelson, Bobbie – Detective, NYPD

Norquist, Marlene – Professor and Commissioner Ralph's wife

Norquist, Ralph – NYPD Commissioner

Patton, Janice – Math Professor and friend of Bobbie

Paxton, Arnold – NYC Mayor

Paxton, Nancy – Mayor Paxton's Wife

Randolph, Joyce – Junior Detective, NYPD

Sanchez, Eduardo – MS-13 gang member

Shackleford, Tim – IT Department head, NYPD

Warren, Gladys – FBI agent

Watson, Sarah – FBI Director

Weinberg, Bennie – NYPD detective and psychiatrist

The Books of Russ Moran

All books are available on Amazon.com, and also as ebooks on The Kindle or a Kindle app on your smartphone or iPad.

The Gray Ship **– Book One of** *The Time Magnet Series*
http://amzn.to/16GPumH

"This provocative, intensely powerful novel is a must-read for sci-fi fans and Civil War aficionados, though mainstream fiction readers will find it heart-rending and inspiring as well. A rare read that's not only wildly entertaining, but also profoundly moving." — Kirkus Reviews

The Thanksgiving Gang **– Book Two of** *The Time Magnet Series*
http://amzn.to/1NzBs7N

"I had never read a book before written in an efficient, minimalistic prose. Instead of writing what most readers want to read, he gives voice to life-like characters, with their flaws and prejudices. They are not infallible superheroes. It's always nice to find a new voice in fiction and to enjoy creativity at its best." — C. Ludewig. "Breakneck pacing and virtually nonstop action" – Kirkus Reviews

A Time of Fear **– Book Three of** *The Time Magnet Series*
http://amzn.to/1zdjaG9

"His story is fascinating, and adds even more depth to this already cavernously deep novel. Amazingly unique, chilling and well written, Moran weaves a future that is both desperate and hopeful. Blending modern fears with science fiction results in a tale that will keep you reading long into the night." Five stars!" —Heather

The Skies of Time – **Book Four of** *The Time Magnet Series*
http://amzn.to/1CCC3jg

In *The Skies of Time*, you will recognize the two main characters, Ashley Patterson, now an admiral, and her husband, Jack Thurber. They met and fell in love in *The Gray Ship*, and now they're in for the adventure of their lives in *The Skies of Time*. Ashley and Jack have been such prominent characters in all four books of The Time Magnet Series that I feel like they're old friends. You will also recognize some of the other characters. But if I told you who they are, it would ruin the fun.

"I'm big fan of this series and this one may be the best. I hope there is another book to this series since it keeps getting better. There are a few questions I have about certain events that makes the next one even more suspenseful. These are great books to binge read one after the other." — Time Travel Fan

The Shadows of Terror – **Book One of the** *Patterns Series*
http://amzn.to/1IDQzJS

A novel that explodes off the front page of your newspaper.

Terrorism has a new face, a face that's obscured in the shadows. The radical forces of destruction have learned to make themselves invisible to the West, and preventing a terrorist attack has become almost impossible.

A new war has begun, World War III.

Rick Bellamy, an FBI agent who specializes in counterterrorism, is engaged in his own war, a war with no end.

Bellamy's wife, Ellen, a prominent architect, discovers that she's in the middle of the greatest terror plot to date.

To defeat the enemy, Bellamy first has to uncover the clues, to shine a light on the shadows. He has to find patterns – before it's too late.

"Move over James Patterson and Mary Higgins Clark. There's a new guy in town. Russ Moran's new book – *The Shadows of Terror*."
— Frank O.

The Scent of Revenge - **Book Two in the *Patterns Series*.**
http://amzn.to/1UvDRmw

The world is at war with the forces of terror. FBI Agent Rick Bellamy and his wife, Ellen, find themselves in the middle of a sinister terrorist plot.

Someone is attacking young prominent women, inflicting a horrible disease.

Nobody knows its origin, nobody knows how to stop it, nobody knows how to cure it.

Rick Bellamy and a team of scientists want to go on the offense. But how?

Will the lives of the women be changed forever? When will the attacks stop?

"Heart pounding, can't put down thriller that will force you to look at terrorism in different light. Life in America will never be the same." —Cold Coffee Cafe

Sideswiped - **Book One in the Matt Blake series of legal thrillers.**
http://amzn.to/1MkxX35

Trial lawyer Matt Blake took on a perfect case.

It involved a sideswipe collision in which his client's husband, an investigative reporter, was killed. The evidence of negligence was overwhelming. Eyewitnesses testified that defendant was talking on his cell phone when he hit the other car.

But was it negligence? Was it an accident?

Or was it murder?

Matt uncovers evidence that the act may have been intentional. Somebody wanted the man silenced. Somebody wanted the man dead.

Somebody had a lot to hide.

The signs started to point to the highest levels of government.

An open-and-shut personal injury case suddenly became a vast conspiracy of terror.

"This book hooks you in from the first line. *Sideswiped* draws you into the world of Matt Blake and you become emotionally attached to him and his journey. The story itself is so well-written and moves quickly there is never a dull moment." —Sarah Elle

"Moran demonstrates the depth of his writing talent by developing a new genre with *Sideswiped*, a legal thriller. Branching out from his previous novels dealing with time travel, Moran goes in a whole new direction with Book One in the Matt Blake series. He creates a wild but totally believable story of modern day intrigue and suspense. Moran also deftly weaves into this book some of my favorite characters from his prior novels. I am looking forward to starting Book #2 - *The Reformers* — Frank from Lynbrook on August 16, 2016

***The Reformers* - Book Two of the Matt Blake series of legal thrillers, is the sequel to *Sideswiped*.**
http://amzn.to/2m8uMdu

The forces of radical Islam are on the run.

Their leadership has been decimated, their ranks thinned, their power disappearing by the week.

Their recruiting efforts have been cut off, the radical websites shut down, and the attraction of jihad is losing its appeal among the young.

With targeted assassinations, military strikes, as well as the loss of oil fields and gold mines, radical Islam is fast losing power.

But who is responsible?

It isn't the United States Government. It's a new force the world has never seen before.

Lawyer Matt Blake and his wife Diana find themselves in the middle of the most gigantic plot the world has ever seen, a conspiracy that's only begun to grow.

"I've been a fan of the author, Russell Moran, since reading *Sideswiped* a few months ago, so I admittedly went into this book with quite high expectations. That being said, I had no idea that "*The Reformers*" was going to play out in the way that it does and I can see myself giving this book a re-read in the future. In fact, I am even more impressed by the storyline of this read than the last and it has left me excited to see more." Lucidity.

The Keepers of Time – **Book Five of the Time Magnet Series**
http://amzn.to/2wjVSTt

Admiral Ashley Patterson and her husband Jack have done it again. They've traveled through time, 200 years into the future—aboard a nuclear aircraft carrier, Ashley's flagship.

They discover a new world, a strange new world—a post-nuclear war world—one that is both a beacon of hope, and a cry of despair.

They meet a group of people who call themselves *The Keepers of*

Time, an organization dedicated to preserving history and culture amid the horrors of a dystopian future.

The world around them has harkened back to a primitive and savage past, one that includes human sacrifice.

Ashley knows they must have to get back to the present to warn the government of the unspeakable horrors that await.

But finding the way back to the present is their greatest challenge, an almost insurmountable one.

"A wild time travel yarn that starts fast and doesn't slow down until the end."

A Reunion in Time
http://amzn.to/2tneIsg

What if a 37-year-old adult travels back 20 years in time and finds himself in high school, followed by his 36-year-old wife? They're now teenagers, 17 and 16.

Adults in teenage bodies, they struggle to convince the people from their past that they are real, not apparitions. With the benefit of hindsight, they know the history of the past 20 years, and it isn't pretty.

Rick and Ellen are married, and now have to adjust to married life as teenagers in 2001. Rick is a senior FBI official and Ellen is a famous architect.

But everybody sees them as kids. Nobody believes that they're married, and nobody believes their stories—until Rick and Ellen predict 9/11.

How do they find their way back to the year they came from? How do they warn the authorities of the cataclysm that will occur in the future? The answer is to find the time portal—the wormhole—

that brought them to 2001. But the site has changed. It's no longer the place where they crossed the wormhole. Will they live out the balance of their lives beginning as teenagers? "We've all wish we could go back to earlier times with the mind we have now. This Russell Moran book takes you there and it is a fun creative romp well worth reading. *A Reunion in Time* is highly recommend!" Kindle Customer.

The President is Missing – **Book Three of the Matt Blake series.**
http://amzn.to/2t9v7wu

While he was addressing the nation from a submerged nuclear submarine, President Blake's message is suddenly cut off. Anyone listening heard an explosion. The explosion was followed by floating debris five minutes later.

First Lady Dee Blake has doubts, which she shares with naval high command and the new president. She thinks the explosion and the debris were a ruse to make people think the sub was destroyed, and her husband with it.

Could the sub have been hijacked and the president kidnapped?

But who would commit such an act? What is its purpose?

Was it Russia, China, Iran, or a shadowy group of freelance terrorists?

The new president appoints Dee as his Chief of Staff, with explicit instructions to find the missing submarine—and President Matt Blake.

Her life, and the life of the nation, suddenly take a horrifying turn.

Robot Depot
http://amzn.to/2zXW7C2

Mike Bateman is a visionary businessman, the creator and CEO of the fabulously successful chain of stores, Robot Depot, a company dedicated to selling robots and Artificial Intelligence machines for a variety of uses.

The company is a darling of Wall Street and is the most popular destination for consumers and businesses looking for labor saving devices.

But the company caught the eye of ISIS, the terrorist Islamic State. They discover a great way to deliver bombs – using the products of Robot Depot to kill people.

Robot Depot changed from being a popular company to an object of fear because of the tampered products it sells. The terrorists use the company for "terror spectaculars," including the destruction of a skyscraper, a drone attack on Yankee Stadium, and the bombing of a children's sailing regatta.

Mike Bateman and the FBI are in a race to stop his products from becoming weapons, a race to stop the wanton killings. His wife and partner, Jenny, discovers the true meaning of terror one horrible summer day.

A Climate of Doubt
https://amzn.to/2OSwcHR

Forget what you ever heard about climate change.

Forget your preconceived notions about reality itself.

Instantly, you are in a new world, a horrifying world, a world you don't understand.

On a hot summer day, Homeland Security Secretary, Rick Bellamy, and his wife Ellen, a famous TV talk show host, walked along the ocean front trying to escape the heat. Suddenly the temperature dropped from the high 90s to below freezing in a matter of minutes. It began to snow—*on July 16.*

The temperatures across the country and the world plummeted, creating winter in summer.

Bellamy and the rest of the government struggled to cope with the suddenly new climate, but to cope, they first had to find out what happened.

Scientists from academia blamed the weather on a sudden acceleration of climate change, but they were unable to explain a 60-degree temperature drop in a matter of minutes.

Two astronauts in an American space station realized that the sudden weather calamity coincided with a test of the 20 satellites that the space station controlled.

Attention focused on a huge American corporation that owned the space station and the satellites. Could there be a connection between the satellite tests and the radical drop in temperature?

As the deaths piled up and the world economy tilted toward disaster because of gigantic summer blizzards, Rick Bellamy and his team struggled to find answers before it was too late. Was it a sudden shift in climate change or did it have something to do with the satellites? The biggest question remained—was the catastrophe an accident, or was somebody controlling the weather? Was it terror?

Bundle up and get this page-turning thriller. You're in for a wild ride. The book was published in May of 2018. It's Book Four of the Matt Blake Series. Matt and Dee Blake take on their biggest challenge to date, along with our old friends, Rick and Ellen Bellamy.

The Maltese Incident – A Story of Time Travel **(Book One of the Harry and Meg Series), the prequel to** *The Violent Sea.*
https://amzn.to/2RclZCT

You're on a beautiful cruise ship.

The April sky is full of stars.

Suddenly, the ship rumbles, and instantly the stars disappear.

"What the hell was that?" Captain Fenton yelled.

"Beats me, captain. I've never seen anything like it," the first officer said.

They would soon discover that the ship, *The Maltese*, had just traveled through time—millions of years to the past.

The captain, Harry Fenton, a highly decorated naval war hero, realizes the greatest battle of his life lay ahead of him.

Captain Harry, a widow, falls in love with a beautiful passenger, Meg Johnson, an executive with the company that owns the ship.

After a whirlwind romance, they marry—in the ship's ballroom—100 million years in the past.

Captain Harry convinces the passengers and crew that they must move ashore to a tropical island because the ship is running out of fuel and supplies. He organizes a group to go ashore and inspect the island.

An ancient forest inhabited by dinosaurs awaits them.

Meg wants to go with them. Harry, fearing for her safety, tries to convince her to stay on the ship.

Meg demonstrates that she is proficient with a gun by taking apart a rifle and reassembling it—in 15 seconds. Harry marvels that he's never seen such an expert gun handler—or accurate shooter. So, AR-15 in hand, Meg joins the inspection party. Charging dinosaurs are no match for Meg Fenton's firepower.

Will the 1,000 souls ever make it back to the time they came from, or will they remain stranded in the distant past?

A scientist aboard theorizes that, to return to their present time, they need to go back to the time portal, or wormhole, that brought them to the past.

But the ship doesn't have enough fuel for the journey.

Realizing that their lives have hit the reset button, the crew and passengers construct a community in the forest—Malta Town.

Under Harry and Meg's leadership, they create a court system, a legislature, and all the elements of a small budding democracy. Meg figures out a way to harness hydroelectric power from a nearby waterfall. Everybody thinks of Harry and Meg as the heart and soul of Malta Town. They begin their new lives—among the dinosaurs.

The Maltese Incident is a riveting tale of time travel, love, courage, and horror.

Get this page turner now and prepare for the ride of your life.

Published in June 2018.

The Violent Sea – A Story of Time TravelBook Two of the Harry and Meg Series, the sequel to *The Maltese Incident.*
https://amzn.to/2AT5ypI

The Violent Sea is a novel of war, time travel, military history, the second in the Harry and Meg Series. It's also a sweet romance between Harry and his wife, Meg.

Rear Admiral Harry Fenton has done it again. He's traveled through time to a different era. He finds himself, with a serious head injury from a fall, at Pearl Harbor Base Hospital on May 16, 1942, three weeks before the Battle of Midway. His wife and aide, Lieutenant Meg Fenton, is worried sick, and waits for him—in 2018.

Admiral Harry is the commanding officer of Carrier Strike Group 14 in 2018, but the people in 1942 think he's a busted-up hallucinating sailor who imagines himself an admiral.

Admiral Raymond Spruance is commanding officer of Carrier Task Force 16. After hearing about Harry's time travel stories, Spruance orders him brought to his flagship, the *USS Enterprise*. After Harry tells him about his time travel experiences, Spruance is convinced the man is insane.

But after speaking to him at length, Spruance is amazed at Harry's knowledge of naval tactics and strategy. He calls Harry's bluff and orders him to stay aboard the *Enterprise* for her upcoming engagement at the Battle of Midway.

By the end of the battle, Spruance is convinced Harry is an admiral, and thinks of him as a friend.

Now Harry needs to figure out how to travel back to 2018, to his carrier command, but most importantly, to the love of his life, Lieutenant Meg.

After Harry returns to the present, the Fentons are deployed on Harry's flagship, the *USS Gerald R. Ford*. The ship encounters another wormhole, this one in the ocean. They are transported to 1944 and participate in the Battle of Leyte Gulf.

The book took me 10 months to write. It went through 20 drafts and three rounds with my editors. I did copious research for the book to ensure its historical accuracy. If you enjoy the genre of time travel, I think you will love this book. I got to know my two main characters in the prequel, *The Maltese Incident*. Harry and Meg are deeply in love but enjoy constant banter and wisecracks. One of my favorite characters, Admiral Ashley Patterson of *The Gray Ship,* makes an important cameo appearance in *The Violent Sea.*

I'm a fan of surprise endings and I believe *The Violent Sea* delivers. It's available on both Kindle and paperback.

A Sea of Fear – A Novel of Time Travel - Book 3 of The Harry and Meg Series.
https://amzn.to/2GERuSx

You're Five-Star Admiral Harry Fenton, whom President Blake calls the greatest fighting admiral in American history.

Along with your Navy Commander wife, Meg, you lead your carrier strike group against the worst enemy the country has faced since World War II, a small nation that is intent on destroying the world's shipping industry. The seas of the world have become scenes of plunder, pillage, and mass murder.

The president has convinced you to come out of retirement and put an end to the looming crisis. He promotes you to Fleet Admiral, the highest-ranking officer since Admiral Chester Nimitz.

You and Meg were having a pleasant retirement, running a world-class resort that you bought in Rhode Island. But when the president pleads you to "Give 'em Hell, Harry," you know that you can't ignore his call to duty.

As people who have time traveled in the past, you come up with an idea to travel three years into the future. With President Blake's blessing, you and Meg lead a group of officers into the future. What you find is horrifying, an America taken over by a totalitarian dictator.

You return to the past and report your findings. President Blake, hearing your terrifying story, convinces you that you have an even bigger call to duty, the greatest challenge of your life. You take on the challenge for one reason—Meg will be at your side.

As in the first two books of the Harry and Meg Series, *The Maltese Incident* and *The Violent Sea*, *A Sea of Fear* is a sweet romance between two of literature's most exciting and likable characters, Harry and Meg Fenton.

A Sea of Fear is a story of war, politics, time travel, and love.

About the Author

In addition to the 18 novels discussed above, I also published five nonfiction books: *Justice in America: How it Works—How it Fails; The APT Principle: The Business Plan That You Carry in Your Head; Boating Basics: The Boattalk Book of Boating Tips; If You're Injured: A Consumer Guide to Personal Injury Law; How to Create More Time.* My latest nonfiction book is *The Novel - A Writer's Guide - Discover the Joy of Writing Fiction* published in November 2018.

I'm a lawyer and a veteran of the United States Navy I live on Long Island, New York, with my wife and editor, Lynda, a Shih-Tzu named Sammie, and a Golden Retriever named Maggie.

A Personal Request

I hope you enjoyed reading *Puzzles, Book 1* as much as I enjoyed writing it. Bob and Bobbie are now two of my favorite characters. You will be seeing more of them in future books.

Please consider leaving a brief review on amazon.com. Book reviews are the lifeblood of an author.